Don't Kiss and Sell

Jillian Rose

www.JillianRoseBooks.com

YOUR BEST SELLER
BOOK

Don't Kiss and Sell

Copyright © 2018 by Jillian Rose.

Published by Your Best Seller Book

FIRST EDITION

ALL RIGHTS RESERVED. No part of this book may be used or reproduced in any form or by any means whatsoever, including but not limited to, being stored in a retrieval system, or transmitted in any form or by any means, electronic, mechanical, photocopying, translation into any language, recording, or otherwise, without written permission of the author.

For information regarding permission, contact the author at
Jillian@JillianRoseBooks.com

Printed in the United States of America

ISBN-13: 978-0-692-09729-8

DEDICATION

To my mother, Iris: Without your unrelenting support, I would have never had the courage to put my writing into the universe. Your love is what pushes me to persevere even on the toughest of days. Thank you.

To my father, Steven: You are the wind beneath my wings. I love you.

To my Gram, Pearl: I know you're reading this from heaven, my Guardian Angel.

To my friends: You have faithfully been there through the highs and lows. While some of these characters are based on you, in real life, you are shoulders on which I stand. Thank you all for being you.

For all my former colleagues: This novel is loosely based around the events from a professional experience in the financial services industry. While I won't name you directly, the impact you had on my life both professionally and personally is profound. I am forever grateful for the everlasting friendships we formed, and for all the lessons you taught me about business, life, and myself.

To anyone who reads this novel: Thank you. Enjoy.

CHAPTER 1

It started when my Dad fired me. "Close the door," he said, as I stepped into his early 1990s era floral wallpapered and emerald green carpeted office. I followed his instructions, which of course made the thin walls shake as the door shut. With my shoulders slumped, I sat down in the yellow leather chair designated for guests and customers. My dad was squinting at his e-mail, with his Harry Potter spectacles on his face just below his eyes. There was a hodge-podge of printed material strewn across his desk including inventory summaries, uncompleted to-do lists, and fundraising requests from various non-profit organizations. If the FBI came in with a search warrant, they would be shit out of luck. You couldn't find anything piled on a desk where it looked like ten briefcases had exploded in a fit of corporate fury.

As my dad typed one finger at a time in response to whatever was in his inbox, I looked above him at a version of myself from thirteen years ago in a picture frame. The 1999 version of Jayden had very frizzy hair and un-tweezed eyebrows - poor girl. I made a mental note to get rid of that picture and replace it with a straight-haired, plucked eyebrow photo.

I gazed out the window and couldn't help but chuckle at the parallel of how the outside world was as dated as the office I was sitting in. The cars along the street were all turn of the millennium Hondas and Subarus. Welcome to blue-collar Pennsyltucky.

Yup, you left your little Mediterranean paradise to return to this crap hole, I thought as a rather sad Toyota Camry rolled along down the street, probably on the way to the Turkey Hill gas station for the driver's dire need for a pack of Marlboro's. Sad Camrys didn't roll their way down pot-holed filled streets in Tel Aviv. My life was more along the lines of being picked up by some tech start-up hotshot in a Mercedes with a price tag four times what it would in the States. For a millisecond I could almost taste the seemingly endless glasses of champagne at the nightclubs along the boardwalk. *Stop, that's in the past. You're now in this ugly chair. Deal with it.*

But somehow here I was, sitting here in Grayton, staring out the window, waiting for my father's explanation as to why he summoned me.

Finally, he looked away from the computer screen and faced me. "I think it would be best if you looked for employment elsewhere," he said flatly. He wasn't one to waste getting to the point and this was no exception.

I looked down at the sea of papers in front of me. "That's fine," I answered. Don't cry. Don't argue with him. Just let him show who's boss. It's not like I didn't know this was coming anyway. But of course, hearing the message out loud always stings more than the inklings. Instead of reacting, I decided to just sit there. If you don't have anything nice to say, don't say anything at all, right? But just because I wasn't going to verbalize my opinions didn't mean he wasn't. After all, he was the boss.

"Jayden, you come in at any damn hour you please, yap away on the phone, and then take your two hour lunch, and leave early.

Come on. It's obvious you don't like working here. You are just wasting your time. Find something that will put some cash in your pocket, sock your money away, and then move out of here. There's nothing for you here in Grayton. And you hate it anyway." As usual, he was right. I wasn't entirely financial free after gallivanting around Israel. Not to mention I was living under his roof and therefore had nowhere to bring home any random hookups. Not that the selection of men in this town was anything worth shaving your legs for, never mind getting naked.

Hearing the things I knew were true but hated listening to sent me into my default setting: defense. "Well, excuse me for not having a love affair with Xerox and Ricoh," I said, my eyes barely making contact with my father's as I rolled them in a fat circle.

I grew up in a sea of JAPs whose Daddies were tax attorneys or cardiac surgeons driving Mercedes Benzes while their wives carted the kids to soccer practice in a Porsche Cayenne. So, being the daughter of a wholesale exporter for office equipment did not give me a lot of street cred. People also assumed we were broke because, who on earth buys crap like used office equipment? Then I got to a certain age where I realized people with hidden heavy pockets are much better off than the ones with dollar signs on their foreheads. When your net worth isn't public knowledge, there is no walking around with a target on your head for favors. There are no expectations of donations for the local Blah Blah Society of Ridiculousness. There are no rich people analyzing and passing judgment on you because of which store you buy your socks or which salon you get your highlights and Brazilian waxes.

"No, but Jayden, it wouldn't have killed you to get off your butt and put in more of an effort." He was not going to tolerate my twenty-five year old self who was armed with nothing but an International Business degree, which, of course, he paid for. I was too ignorant and selfish to take anything seriously. Just because he had only been a business owner for almost twenty years didn't mean he knew anything. I could figure it out on my own, anyway.

I really did try to learn the ropes. But the amount of manufacturers, models, pricing, distribution conditions, and profit margins floated in my head like sea garbage. So was I sprinting into the office at 7:30am every day with a tray of coffees for everyone and a fat smile on my face? Negative.

Clearly, I had no big dreams of being an heiress to Ira's empire. There was a list a mile long of what I did *not* want to do, but my "aha" moment with a vision for my life's calling had not struck. For the twenty-two year olds out there who have had that moment, lucky you as the rest of twenty-somethings swim in a sea of doubt and uncertainty. When I graduated college, it was also the height of the recession, so everyone was scrambling for anything that provided a paycheck, regardless of the pedigree their hard-earned degrees provided.

I did what any other young woman would do. Instead of persevering through a job market that had shriveled to a prune, I ran from it. I ran to Tel Aviv to, you know, get back to those Jewish roots by slugging shots of Arak at the nightclubs which ran the strip of the city's boardwalk, the Namal. As in, to help foreign students learn English.

So, when my dad suggested I move home and work for him until I figured my shit out when I couldn't find a full time job, it seemed like the only answer. The thought of daily free lunches (salads) were a huge perk. Maybe I could get Friday happy hour instituted as well?

I sat silently and stupidly, not really having a counter argument for once. What was I going to do? Claim to have a rare sleep disorder which prevented me from getting out of bed before noon? I went for the daughter angle, the only one I had left in my arsenal.

"I'm sorry."

"You think that would work in the real world, Jayden? I'm sorry? Come on."

I could still hear Shira's wine-infused protests that I was making a mistake as I tossed sundresses and tapestries from the beach into oversized suitcases. "What are you going home to, Jayden?" she asked, her wine glass loosely hung in her hand, slopping some of its contents onto the linoleum floor. "I shouldn't be here watching you pack, we should be at our favorite restaurant…Dizengoff 77 with the bartenders doing shots. You know, our version of Shabbat dinner."

"Shira," I began to explain to my dear friend who was 27 and still being supported by her surgeon father based in Toronto, "I haven't found a job yet. Just let me go back and find something and I'll be back."

"Jayden! I just have a bad feeling about this." Needless to say, the girl had premonitions.

And here I was, practically a year later, getting a lecture from the man who was supposed to be my number one fan. This was the man who let me run around the living room looking ridiculous in his loafers. Or the father I could always convince to take me for ice-cream on a Sunday in February on the way home from skiing, when it was barely 10 degrees. Where was this real-world "grow up" boss man coming from? Ew. I was so not picking up a pint of Ira's coveted Half Baked by Ben & Jerry's from the grocery store later as I usually did for him.

But what I did pick up was my Coach purse and hairline-fractured ego, and march out of the office, slamming his hollow door. I had no clue when the next door would open.

CHAPTER 2

And a few days later, one door did open in the form of a phone call. A very early one, unfortunately for my nocturnal sleep patterns.

At the crack of dawn of 10:00am, my phone rang and awoke me from a drunken slumber. I didn't recognize the number, but I hit the answer button and dry-mouthed some verbal form of "hello," into the receiver. A very friendly, professional sounding woman started explaining that she found my resume somewhere and the international company she worked for was looking for fresh talent, blahblah. The specifics were unabsorbed as they passed in one ear and out the other. All I heard were the words, "international," "managerial," and opportunity" followed by a question asking if I wanted to come in for an interview the next day. Shit, these people move fast!

Perhaps it was the hangover taking over, but something from the depths of my half-asleep state told me this could be my chance. Since the 48 hours that my dad had fired me, I was already turning into a townie alcoholic. You know shit's bad when your friends decide to start drinking in the shower while the parents are at some dinner event for their tennis club. Something drastic needed to happen, considering the most recent male to be blowing up my phone was a plumber. I know, I know, a plumber. By Grayton standards, he was pretty hot, and I didn't see his butt crack when he bent over. But really, this just couldn't be what twenty-five was supposed to be. Not in my life, anyway.

"Yes, tomorrow, 10:30 will work for me," I told the chipper woman.

"Great," the Very Chipper Secretary answered and made sure to tell me that I would be receiving a confirmation with the office's address.

Sure enough, the next morning, armed with loosely fitting professional looking attire from my college internship days - I'd knocked off some of the cheap beer pounds from my sorority days - I drove to the address listed in the email. As I approached a newly constructed office building which was clearly home to several businesses, I was surprised I'd never noticed it before, considering it had to be about ten stories high. Then again, the only things I noticed around the area were mostly any new bars that might have crept onto the townie boozing scene.

I pulled into a space labeled "Visitor" and did a quick once over in the rearview mirror to make sure my eyeliner wasn't smudged and that all my blemishes were well hidden. Satisfied, I decided it was time to get this show started.

A young office-manager led me into a large presentation room. There were about a dozen unknown faces, all dressed in suits and skirts facing the front of the room where a white board and a flat screen TV stared back at us. Curiosity hung in the air as people fiddled with their phones, crossed their legs half a dozen times, or tapped their pens on notebooks. Those must have been the really ambitious job seekers, because I sure as hell hadn't brought my leather bound notebook and pen with me.

"Good morning, ladies and gentlemen!" A guy with a politician's stage presence strutted into the front of the room with his arms wide, ready to take command of our attention. If you looked up "bright eyed and bushy-tailed" in the dictionary, this was the guy.

"How's everybody doing today?" *He's kind of hot*, I thought, in that business dude way.

Everyone grumbled their quiet versions of, "Good." This was unsatisfactory.

"Come on, come on! I said, 'how is everybody doing today?'" We got the picture and answered with some spirit.

"Now we're talking! Okay everyone, my name is Monte De Luca and I'm the director for D'Angelo Enterprises here in the Grayton office. You have all been selected specially to learn about our opportunity. Sit tight. I'm going to explain how being here can change your lives."

It was with this opening that those of us sitting with the clipboards and nervous smiles were cast under a spell. We gave in to Monte's inescapable charm as he vibrantly rolled into a spiel aided by a diagram. It was divided into four labeled quadrants with accompanying pictures of white-toothed professionals representing complex ideologies such as organizational structures or marketing mixes or financial plans. I wondered how old Monte was. He looked like the kind of guy who would be young for his age. He had to be, he was just so damn well spoken…

"… A little bit about me," Monte began to tell us. "I was born and raised here in Grayton and graduated from Penn State University. After working with D'Angelo Enterprises in Pittsburgh for a few years, I was offered the opportunity to come back home and run an office. Okay, enough about me. Let's get down to it. Who wants the opportunity to make some serious money? Who wants to stop living paycheck to paycheck? Who wants to make enough money to change your life? To change your family's life?" We all exclaimed our own versions of "Yes!" "Amen!" or "Hell yeah!" in response. We didn't know exactly what we were excited about, but we were fired up.

"Now, I know what you guys are probably thinking. Life insurance? Isn't that awfully boring?" he continued. *Wait, what? That's what I agreed to an interview for?*

Maybe it was the fact I hadn't been around anyone with crisp professionalism since my collegiate career, or the fact I had just discovered a new hottie in Grayton. After all, I hadn't been setting the bar too high lately by fucking a plumber. But it wasn't just me: I looked around and noticed everyone else's gaze was focused solely on him, not a pair of eyes on their phones. I was completely captivated by the "recipe for success" he wrote out enthusiastically on the whiteboard, an unartistic compilation of boxes and tree branches with dollar signs and motivational quotes. You know, the famous ones like, "You lose 100% of the shots you don't take," by his favorite hockey player, Wayne Gretsky. According to this Monte character, the way we were going to be swimming in gobs of money was by selling life insurance. Apparently the death industry is making a killing.

In reality, it was the greatest sales presentation I've ever heard. I was sold on the deal.

"But ladies, and gentlemen," Monte said with extra oomph as he began to wind down his magic show. Apparently at this time they only had limited spots available for "about two, *maybe* three of you here today. So as much as I have had the pleasure of speaking with you all, we will not be able to bring everyone here on board."

At this point, I was so close to the edge of my seat I was probably exhaling on the poor soul's neck in front of me. I wanted a branch of the money tree, damn it. I wanted to be one of those special people who got a phone call later that day. I wanted this as much as I wanted to be able to eat brownies endlessly and still lose weight. For a millisecond, a doubtful thought crossed my mind. If I wasn't good enough to work with this guy up here, maybe I could date him. I mean, Matt, Mike, whatever the guy's name was - he's an Italian. That was always my type, you know, before I stooped down to a plumber level. Flashy clothes, funny accents, usually well equipped - *I always was a sucker for them. No, stop,* I told myself, *you are so good enough to work here.*

As it turned out, later that day my awesomeness was verified by another phone call from the chipper office manager asking me to come in for a final interview tomorrow.

The next day, I ended up staring at a pen and a stack of papers in front of me.

"The possibilities are endless Jayden. If you want something here at D'Angelo Enterprises, you can make it happen. We give you the tools, and then go see what you can make with them." As Monte sat in front of me, I had the sense he had a genuine interest in knowing me as an individual, not just sizing me up against my resume which lay next to him.

I lifted the pen placed before me which was next to a contract that seemed to have as many pages as the Harry Potter manuscript. The top page of the stack had a highlighted "X" next to the signature line, which was what my eyes immediately focused on.

I looked up at Monte. "You said that D'Angelo Enterprises is an international company, right?" I asked as he sat calmly in his black leather swivel chair.

"Now, now, Jayden, did you pay attention to anything I said yesterday?" he chided, tapping his Montblanc on his notepad which was bound by a leather binder. "Well, your lack of stage presence kind of put me to sleep," I said in a tone of voice letting him know I was being utterly sarcastic. He laughed appreciatively and I continued.

"Monte, I just want to be clear as to why I'm asking you this. I want to take on this challenge and join your team. But this place," I emphasized by gesturing my hand to his wall length window which displayed the view of an ugly manufacturing company and the valley beyond it. "It's not home for me. I'm a city girl. I like subways and bright lights. Not old towns where corner bars are the main attraction. Will I have the opportunity to go elsewhere?"

"What's wrong with corner bars?" he asked as if I had questioned his Fantasy Football picks.

"Nothing, if your idea of a good time is skunked beer on tap." He laughed, which put me at ease knowing we could share a similar sense of unsophisticated humor. "Give me a year," he said. "Give me a year to get you trained as an agent and then put in management so you can run a team. Then, you can go wherever you want. Just give me one year to work with you, and then you can have a team anywhere."

"Anywhere?" I reiterated. "Anywhere," he repeated.

Long, drawn out hemming and hawing decision making processes were not my thing. I functioned on impulse and intuition. I took a deep breath. "I'm in," I answered as I picked up the pen and as neatly as I could, signed my name on that dotted line next to the X. Little did I know, the second it took for me to scribble my signature on that piece of paper was a seemingly small decision that would ignite a large impact, to say the least.

CHAPTER 3

For two weeks, I was convinced I was suffering a slow, painful death by boredom as I studied the most yawn-inducing material developed by mankind: the life insurance exam. After fourteen days of tutorial videos hosted by a man with a handle-bar mustache and endless online practice tests, I was ready to get this official state test over with. Somehow I flew through the multiple choice questions, and hit the Submit button. I twiddled my fingers and was graced with a passing grade from the Pennsylvania State Department from an overweight, overly unhappy employee at the front desk. I didn't care if she was a bitch who hadn't gotten laid since Moses parted the Red Sea. I had passed the test and was about to embark on my new career. Immediately I called Monte to tell him the thrilling news.

"Enjoy the weekend and get ready to rock and roll on Monday!"

Forty-eight hours of some celebratory debauchery later...

Monday came. At 9:00am, the conference room where the mass interview had been held was filled with over twenty fist bumping agents. My oversized tote bag and I tried to make our way to the back row where I spotted an empty seat without knocking over anyone's coffees or laptop cases. I was so not a front-row seat girl. I scanned the room. The fresh male college grads were dressed as though they were gallivanting down Wall Street in suits they had not grown into yet. There were ladies dressed very unladylike, their shirts plunging or unbuttoned so low I could tell how padded their Victoria's Secret bras were. Since the office was run by these visually stimulated twenty and thirty something men, I guess the boys weren't running to the Human Resources department to file a complaint. Was there even an HR department?

"Good afternoon everyone!" I heard coming from the speakers. I looked up and realized that our office was on camera in a video conference with eight other offices throughout Pennsylvania and a few other unimportant states.

"Okay, let's get down to business," a well-dressed man wearing stylish rimmed glasses began. In between trying to check out everyone else from the other offices on the screen, I forced myself to pay attention to what Mr. Fancy Glasses was saying, when all the sudden the room erupted with two thunderous hand claps from every person. And then Mr. Fancy Glasses announced a name, and it was followed by another set of CLAP! CLAP! Little did I know after just a couple weeks I wouldn't even be phased by the noise or the sting in my palms.

My eyes ran through the room trying to spot a sensible female whose chest was somewhat concealed. You know, someone I could peg as a friend.

And then, I saw her a few rows ahead of me, the only other person who seemed as though she also didn't know what the hell was going on with the clapping situation. She was wearing a respectable navy suit with her hair twisted in a bun. What really caught my inner JAP was her stunning camel colored Michael Kors bag. Upon seeing it, I decided I should introduce myself. I have always been astute in selecting friends.

As soon as the CLAP CLAP session adjourned, everyone scattered to take a coffee or cigarette break before our next task, whatever that might be. I just hoped it wasn't anything along the lines of banging on pots and pans as my eardrums were vibrating. I made a mental note to bring earwax for next week's meeting.

My luck, Michael Kors purse girl was at the elevator when I arrived at them. "God, that was some meeting, wasn't it? Are they always that long?"

"I don't know, that was my first one too!" she said smiling. "You headed down for a cig?" she asked as her eyes gave me the once over girls do when they non-sexually check each other out.

"I just need to get some air," I said as the elevator doors opened. I didn't smoke, but soaking up a few minutes of sunlight sounded perfect. Plus, there was something about this girl I just liked. I decided to be really nice to her and make her like me too.

"I love, love your bag," I remarked as we descended. She glanced down and then proudly smiled back at me. "Ohmigod, thanksss!"

"So, how long have you worked here?" I continued. "My license came through last week so today is technically my first day." Boom, my life insurance soul sister was born.

After stepping out of the elevator, we walked out of the building and into the Indian summer, falling into an easy conversation. The entrance to the building was littered with cigarette smoking cliques so we formed our own near the front doors. Scarlett, as I learned her name was, offered me a cigarette from her pack which I politely declined. I took note of how she positioned herself so that she purposely exhaled away from my face, which I appreciated. Nonsmokers like me don't enjoy a puff of tobacco in our faces.

As it turned out, Scarlett was a couple of years younger than me, had never left Grayton except for the typical Ocean City,

Maryland beach trip, and had just finished college. She spoke of her accomplishment with that "I just graduated from college" glow which pretty much fades as soon as a recent grad is smacked with the realization the real world doesn't give a shit that you have a Bachelor's degree. I had that same glow when I graduated. Or maybe it was just that my face was bloated from all the beer over the course of eight semesters?

"So, did you hear about the scripts?" Scarlett asked me as the ashed out her cigarette.

"Scripts?" I was completely unsure as to what she was referring.

"Yeah, we have to memorize a script for when we're presenting during appointments."

"Shut up. You're kidding me. What is this, drama club?" I was not about to start memorizing scripts unless a Hollywood producer was knocking at my door.

"No seriously, my friend used to work here and told me all about it. It's like twenty pages and we have to use it word for word."

"And what if we don't use the script?" I asked, in disbelief that people would actually memorize a script and then recite it to sell something. What talent did that take?

"Then we don't make sales I guess," Scarlett said, who probably was just as confused as I was. "But apparently it works. I mean, look how much money these guys make!" This was true, but I was still apprehensive.

Then it occurred to me.

"Scarlett...what happened to your friend?" She took a long last drag of her cigarette and aimed it into the sandy pit where the rest of the butts laid.

"She quit."

■ ■ ■

Later that afternoon, Scarlett and I had the privilege of locking ourselves in a small conference room in the back of the office where some dozen pages of scripted dribble stared us in the face. I guess she wasn't kidding.

"Here, memorize this," Monte told Scarlett and me. "You have to know it like you know your ABC's." Shit, I still got a little fuzzy around LMNOP... He left us in the conference room to our own devices. Scarlett immediately began recopying everything in a notebook, convinced the best way to memorize was by rewriting. I decided her method would result in way too much hand cramping, so I sat there, reading each line, closing my eyes and repeating it in my head, just like I had memorized lines from plays in high school. *Was this really the path to success? Memorizing an insurance script?* I wondered. Scarlett must have been reading my mind.

"Jayden, we better get some fat paychecks from doing all of this crap."

A few days later, we hadn't seen any fat paychecks, but we had seen more of Grayton than would have ever bargained for.

After a morning of sales training, we would head into the field with our respective managers to learn the ropes of the presentation by observing what they did, and eventually starting to take over the presentation until we could do the whole thing on our own.

"Dude, we met some serious psychos," Scarlett said to me, one night when we had arrived back at the office at the same time. Our managers had gone off to probably get stoned with each other, so we sat in her car where she could puff cancer sticks and we could rehash all the "crazies" we met throughout the day. I told her about how I was dumbfounded by one crazy in particular I encountered. How could a sixty-something man with wisps of hair and a serious lack of teeth, possibly manage to chew a sandwich? She recounted a story of how when her manager, Randy, began explaining the dental benefits of a supplemental insurance card, the mother smiled and exclaimed, "I can sure use those!" showing off her missing front teeth. Was this really how people lived? Was this really the town I came back to?

I ran my tongue across my upper row of teeth to make sure they were all there. After seeing the toothless wonders, I felt like it was necessary just in case one fell out or something.

"Trust me girl, I didn't see any of this nasty shit in Israel," I told Scarlett, suppressing a yawn. It was after 10:00pm, and we had been in the office since 9:00 am, only stopping at local gas stations to grab snacks in between appointments.

"I know, I can't believe you came back here," she said. "Scarlett... I can't either," I thought out loud, wishing I could smoke a hash joint and drink the $6 bottle of Israeli wine I always picked up at the corner store. But I didn't want to think about that right then. I wanted my bed.

"I'll see you tomorrow, girl," I said, getting out of the car. "My bed awaits- you know, the thing we don't see much of anymore."

"I feel ya," she said. I had the feeling that soon Scarlett might be one of the few people who really would be able to say that.

■ ■ ■

Veronica, one of my best friends, called as I was folding laundry and was probably regretting deciding to catch up with me as I carried on with my usual nonsense. "Why, just why can't I do laundry and have the same amount of socks that I put into the washer come out of the dryer? Now I have an odd number of fucking socks. Why, socks? Why must one of you always disappear?" I whined. She was used to my white girl problems and seemingly had a penchant for topping them like it was a competition. Whatever the problem was, it usually resulted in the major reassurances we continually needed: "He'll text me back, right?" "I'm so much prettier than the ex, right?"

"I don't know, maybe because the sock knows your fat feet are absolutely disgusting, so the poor piece of fabric wanted to get away before it would be encrusted with your nasty foot smell." "My feet are just fat, they don't smell," I countered.

"Oh my god, I'm one of those girls. One of those snobby first-world problem girls that they invent quizzes about on Huffington Post to see just how sheltered of a white bitch you grew up to be."

"Yeah, pretty much. But at least you recognize it," she said.

"Ugh, I hate this. Now I'm going to spend the rest of my day berating myself for obsessing over a fucking sock when there are starving children in Africa, who don't even have access to high grade vodka."

"Jay, relax. It's a sock." Veronica was one to tell me to relax. She was usually in a hissy fit white girl state herself.

"I have to learn about all these color brands and how to mix them so that my future customers don't stand up from the chair looking like a Katy Perry music video." After years of color dyeing and braiding her own mane, Veronica decided she could change the world, tackling botched ombre hair and – gasp - split ends, one custom color and scissor snip at a time and was now enrolled at a beautician academy (not a beauty school, she emphasized).

"Well, we can't have that now, can we?" I asked. Not one to keep a conversation too PG, Veronica brought up what was really on her mind.

"How do you feel about anal?" she continued casually.

"Nothing goes up the poop shoot, babe," I answered. I felt like my butthole had an EXIT ONLY sign. "First of all, that's something which is boyfriend limits only. But honestly Veronica,

I'm pretty scared I would just poop on the weiner. You think the guy would stick around after that mess?"

"No, no you don't shit, Jayden. You just feel like you're going to," she clarified.

"Oh, that sounds so much better."

"But then that goes away and it feels good," she continued.

"Veronica, where are you going with this? I have other things to do than talk about sticking that thing up my butt."

"Well, Jeremy wants to try it."

"Veronica, what about that guy you live with? You know, Craig? The boyfriend you've lived with for six years?" *Who the hell was Jeremy?*

"I know, but Jay, you don't understand. Things are so broken with Craig and me. We just don't communicate anymore, the spark is totally gone. Jeremy really gets me and we just have a lot in common. We talk for forever after class while we clean up. And then go to the bar around the corner obviously." *Straight guys go to beauty school? Maybe he's bi?*

"Yeah, how do you do that and still go out?" I asked. I mean, we weren't twenty-one anymore. Energy wasn't limitless and hangovers were real.

"Well, it's the guy."

"Another one?" Did she have a man gambling problem?

"No, no, same guy. Stay with me!"

"Why can't you just call him Jeremy?"

"No, Jayden, stop! We're calling him 'the guy,' okay? I hate talking about it on the phone. You know, in case anyone can listen in."

"Your love affair guy? That's how you have so much energy? Who cares, this isn't a 1950s spy movie? Veronica, newsflash, our lives are not that interesting."

"Stop, Jayden. I'm paranoid. Craig can't find out."

"So besides the anal, there's something else that you might benefit from."

"And what would that be?" I asked, perplexed.

"Well, 'the guy' hooks me up with..." and then she murmured the name of a drug I had heard passed around the library during finals week in my college days, but never paid attention to. It was a pill used to treat ADD but for those of us able to sit calmly at our desks, it was a miracle pill enabling you to focus for hundreds of hours and completely lose your interest in anything edible. Although, losing an appetite did seem fabulous to me as I was usually scarfing down baguette chunks from Panera Bread smothered in strawberry jelly. My apologizes to those I may have farted near. I just didn't believe the hype, especially not enough to go chasing down the frat boy who had a stash and was able to use the law of supply and demand to his advantage and charge obscene prices per pill. Then of course, there was the goodie-goodie political science major, Amy Baumberg who had a serious quantity but refused to sell it.

"I mean, first of all, they're not prescribed this medication. I am. And secondly, if they take it, and then, go to the bar? I mean they could have a heart attack. I can't have that on me." I'm sure Amy Baumberg couldn't have any cum stains on her shirt after giving a blow job to her International Economics professor to secure that A either. But hey, everyone has their own moral code to uphold. I suppose if it wasn't for Amy's pharmaceutical ethics, there may have been some premature cases of heart failure.

"So those work? That's how you get all this shit done?" I asked surprised. I thought most of this fuss was just an excuse for the sorority girls to get all excited about doing something illegal in the name of academia. But I was feeling a little jealous that Veronica had this secret weapon I didn't. Even though she wasn't my direct competition, I still like to think I have a leg up on the next person.

"Yeah. 'The guy' has a script he doesn't use that he gets every month. Gets a ridiculous amount. Let me know if you want in and then we get a discount." We got off the phone and I thought about it. As much as I loved getting drunk and sometimes smoking a joint, drugs just scared me. But this pill, Adderall, apparently gave you the high without a hangover.

My conversation with Veronica stayed on my mind for weeks. Meanwhile, the pain of crawling out of bed at an hour where real addicts were still doing lines of coke at an after-party was starting to convert into what we were all chasing: dollars. I was now my third month "into the business", and I was a rising star. Sale by sale, week by week, I was making a name for myself. Consequently, I was also wearing out. By the time I got home from the field on Saturday evenings, I collapsed into my bed, savoring my post-field nap until my phone rang and I was summoned to go drink. Although, eventually those weekly outings ended as well and I would just pass out completely. Fuck the whole work hard, play hard thing. Work hard, sleep hard. Sundays were the only day I allowed myself to disengage from work and park myself on the couch. Going out anywhere was completely out of the question. Even when my friends still invited me places, on Sundays, the thought of getting into my car and having to drive somewhere or even be out past 7pm brought as much enthusiasm as a drug dealer deciding to file taxes.

During the week, I would come into the office armed with my laptop, coffee, and breakfast sandwich from which I would only eat the egg part, because carbs are evil. I would relentlessly dial to schedule appointments or take notes in a workshop, starving for success more than I was for the processed food in my lap.

After twelve hour plus days, I was delirious, tired, and ravenous as soon as I walked into my parent's house way after they had finished dinner. And they generally ate European style (later than the average 6:00pm American family). I realized I would have to break off my once committed relationships with my coveted TV shows such as *Gossip Girl* and *Revenge* along with eating dinner at a legitimate hour when I missed an episode of Blaire Waldorf throwing her beloved French macaroons at Chuck Bass because I got home too late. Now at this point, most people, especially any twenty-something female with impeccable taste in television, would question their career choice. However, I was newly converted to the religion of "No Quitting. Ever." And I was a devout follower at that.

Pissed off that my mom rattled off the synopsis of the episode just as I was kicking off my nude patent leather pumps, I stormed off to the fridge. Obviously that would show everyone who was boss, me stuffing my face with leftover grilled chicken and broccoli florets. *Oh my god, leftover latkes and applesauce from Chanukah?* My eyes began to twinkle and my mouth salivated and I wanted to just sink my teeth into that sweet comfort of fried potato deliciousness. *Stop it, you want your pants to button tomorrow. Put some calorie-free Spray Butter on your vegetables and call it a night, Jayden.*

■ ■ ■

It happened the night after I missed out on an episode of *Gossip Girl* with Blair Waldorf hurling top of line artisan macaroons at her on-and-off boyfriend, Chuck Bass, and my almost Chanukah grub disaster. If there was something to suppress my appetite and get me through disgustingly long days, it only made sense for me to seize the opportunity. Lying in my bed bloated from broccoli and calorie-free chemical butter, I texted Veronica: *Okay, I'm in. When can we meet so I can snag the stuff?*

I could feel the fiber binding in my stomach. In the dark, I reached for my nightstand, knocking over what sounded like a picture frame in hopes of snagging my bottle of Tums. Those chalky antacids were like candy.

Let's meet tomorrow, she answered quickly.

How much? I asked her. When she answered me with a dollar amount, I practically spit out the Tums I was chomping. I almost backed out, but I had a quick conversation with myself. Applying logical business concepts, I concluded that this transaction was actually an investment in my career. If I could focus sharper for longer, then I could work better. If I could work better, I'd make more money. If I made more money, I'd cover my initial investment and still come out ahead. That's what they call a win-win. Oh, and these pills suppress your appetite, meaning I'd spend less money on food? Things couldn't get better.

The next night we met in the parking lot of my office, since I was there all evening making phone calls and it was on her way home from the beauty school.

"Look at you, all professional looking," she grinned, admiring my new black blazer I snagged at the Banana Republic outlet, clearly high end fashion for Grayton.

"Thanks, babe," I said, sliding her a wad of bills.

"Have you ever tried one before?" she asked me nonchalantly. I knew Veronica had an affinity for popping a Vicodin and slugging it down with a bottle of wine occasionally, and probably dabbled in some other street stuff a few years back. But the craziest things I had ever done drug wise were get really drunk and smoke blunt. Upon toking, I'd end up entering my own world where the only brain power I had was to converse with my own idiocy.

"No," I told her honestly.

"You. Are. Going. To Love." She handed me a pill bottle filled with little orange circles. "Don't take a whole one, you'll be like a jackrabbit. Just take a quarter."

"Am I going to have a heart attack and die?" I asked. Those pharmaceutical ads with disclaimers three pages long in the gossip magazines or commercials concluding with the serious dude talking a million miles a minute about all the serious side effects, which always included sudden cardiac arrest and death, scared me shitless.

"No, Jayden, you're not going to die," Veronica said, rolling her eyes. "Jeremy wouldn't give us street crap. These are the name brand ones."

"Ooh, designer drugs? I like," I said, breaking a pill in half, and then in half again. I figured I might as well give these things a test drive. I saw Veronica's eyes widen as she realized what I was doing.

"Jayen, no!" But it was too late. The piece of the pill was already crushed in between my teeth. "It's already after 7:00! You're going to be up all night."

"From that little thing? Nah." I looked at my phone and saw a text from Scarlett.

Where are you? Get on the phones before you get yelled at!

"I gotta go babe. Be careful with this Jeremy character," I added.

"Please, I'm sure you'll have a character coming. You always do."

"I don't really have time for new characters," I said, rolling my eyes. I grabbed my purse and headed back for the remainder of the "dialing for dollars time."

Within twenty minutes, I felt something kick in. The dialing didn't seem so repetitive, and each person was a fresh opportunity to chase the real result I was after: a check. I wasn't just focused, I was in the zone. Suddenly, I felt a rush of energy as I sat diligently, with my phone script in front of me and a pen in hand to jot down all the information I needed from the person I was speaking with. I could do this for hours! My teeth were chattering and I couldn't keep my feet still. I felt like if you dropped me from the top of a building I would just spread my wings and fly. I couldn't stop talking.

"Omg, Scarlett, you have to see this sick schedule I have," I said proudly. "I just got to talk to so many people tonight, I just feel so motivated!"

"What's gotten into you Jayden?" she asked. "Usually you're dead tired and want to die at this hour."

"Must have been that late afternoon coffee!" I rationalized.

As I drove home, my mind was going a million miles a minute. Presentation scripts, outfit options, *god that billboard with the ugly people is still there?* I thought as I sped down the highway, completely disregarding the speed limit. Cops? Who were they to pull me over?

When I walked into my parent's house, I went right to the fridge out of habit, but realized I wanted nothing it had to offer when I stared at the contents. I gave a quick hello to Ira and Renee (my mother), who were watching something on CNN, and raced off to strategize for tomorrow's wardrobe and go to bed. The problem was that after I laid out my outfit, washed my face, brushed my teeth, tweezed my eyebrows, hung up clothes from days earlier, I got into bed… but nothing happened. I closed my eyes and rolled onto my left side as I had for about two decades expecting to pass out in milliseconds. Just teeth chattering and euphoric thoughts that took me back to the happiest time in Israel… *Lights flashing in trendy nightclubs, sipping whatever men were buying for Shira and me, our hair puffy from the Mediterranean humidity, but what did we care in our barely there dresses? Lying on thin tapestries drinking white wine, our toes buried in the silky white sand, the sea in front of us stretching endlessly as we saw boys playing matkot.* Veronica was not kidding about not being able to sleep. I was awake, staring into the darkness, thoughts flashing at rapid fire pace through my mind playing like a commercial of my own life. This Adderall might suppress my appetite and heighten my focus, but perhaps it didn't completely block out suppressed emotions. Before I finally faded to black for the evening, I felt a tear fall down my cheek.

■ ■ ■

Where the fuck are you? Scarlett texted me. Shit. It was 8:45pm Saturday night, two days after my first Adderall popping. Scarlett was already on her way to black out drunk but I had barely sipped my shower drink. Yes, one can booze in the shower. It makes the process of shaving your legs, blow drying, and straightening your hair much less tedious. The only hazard in doing this is that sometimes you will leave your dwelling wearing something which says, "I fuck on the first date" because your judgment is slightly impaired. This is why having at least somewhat of a sober roommate or friend present is a proactive approach to avoiding to this situation. Lucky for me, I live with the parentals, so Renee has indirect control of the slut meter, and helps me keep it to a respectable range.

I straightened my hair and finished my make-up, and stood in my room wearing a bra and matching thong staring at my closet. Finally I decided on black skinny jeans with a leopard top which was see through and had two buttons securing the otherwise open back. *Leaving now, see you in 15,* I answered. I was so tired. I needed a pick me up for the evening. Thank God Veronica had met up with me the other day. I reached into my purse where I kept a small stash in an empty Mentos container, broke one in half and swallowed it with the bottle of water next to my bed. *This is just a little something fun on the side.* I told myself I deserved a little fun for working so hard each time I dropped a quarter or a half of one of those bright orange beauties.

Half an hour later I was standing with a vodka soda on the deck behind Grayton's pitiful version of a club listening to Scarlett gossip about all of the managers at work. My heart was racing and my senses were heightened. I was totally focused on how focused I felt. And on what Scarlett was saying. It seemed fascinating. "Randy," she stated as she took a deep drag of her cigarette, "is a complete pothead. Don't you dare tell anyone this but we smoke in his car after the field before we head home. When we were in training, we got offered to smoke up in a house, but Randy didn't want to. He said I could, but I felt too awkward being high with him sober, ya know?"

"You guys smoked together while you're working?" I was appalled.

"Yeah, don't say anything."

"No, I won't. Jesus, Mack wouldn't be caught dead with anything smelling like grass near me. He treats me like I'm fifteen, not twenty-five..." Mack was my field trainer, and only thought about his next meal. I sipped my drink but realized only the suction from the straw was coming up. "I'm going to get another drink," I told her, and walked over the bar. As I reached into my clutch to pay the bartender, my foot slipped from the bar stool I had it perched on and somehow I ended up stumbling backward bumping into something. Before I turned around, I felt a hand steady my back and someone whispered the words "easy killer," in my ear. By the time I turned around, whoever had whispered the words had walked away. It sent a chill down my spine.

"Did you see who just was behind me? I think someone whispered something to me?" I asked the bartender as I handed him a $20.

"Nah, didn't see anything," he said and gave me my change. I left a tip and went back to Scarlett.

I surveyed the room. My eyes landed on someone I hadn't seen before. "Who is that?" I asked Scarlett. "Alex Reyes. He went to college here and then moved back to his hometown. He came back here a couple of months ago. Apparently something fucked up happened but no one knows why. Sexy as hell. But not worth anyone's time. He fucks and chucks."

"Fucks and chucks?" I asked.

"Yeah. He bangs one girl and is on to the next girl so fast that girl number one hasn't even realized he's onto the next girl before she had the chance to go buy Plan B."

"I see," I said, unable to not glance in his direction. He was tall, but not to the point where you still had to crane your neck in a pair of heels. Wearing a pair of dark wash jeans, loafers, and a white button down, he had the appearance of being put together without trying. Although he was still quite a distance away, I could see his features were chiseled and his lips were the perfect size. Without having to show his ID, the bouncer let him through. It was obvious he knew people in the area. There wasn't one girl who didn't run up and give him a kiss on the cheek. Even men seemed tickled to run over for a bro-hug or fist bump. Scarlett was included in this throng of girls. As soon as he came within hearing distance, she turned away from me and bounced over to him. "Alexxxxx!" she cooed, giving the most sweet sound to his name. Flattered, but distant, he bent down to receive yet another kiss from an adoring fan. "I heard you moved back! I am so excited!" she exclaimed. Funny, she was just trashing him seconds ago.

"Yes, I did," he answered charmingly. Up close, I could see what the fuss was about. It was like an exotic creature stood in front of me. His features were dark, but impossible to pinpoint in terms of ethnicity. I noticed his shaggy, thick hair and decided I'd maybe want to run my fingers through it. His toned bi-ceps were visible in his white t-shirt. I decided at that moment I hated him.

"What are you up to now?" he asked her. "Oh, I just started a new job. So busy. I work like eighty hours a week," she answered, like this was something worth bragging about. Such an American thing to do, brag about how much you work. In Tel Aviv, everyone competed to see who could work the least and make the most cash.

"Sounds intense," he answered, unfazed. I noticed him glancing in my direction as they were making small talk, but I was leafing through my phone as to not stand there looking awkward. "And, look who it is," I heard him say. I looked up quizzically. "Sorry?" I asked.

"The girl with two left feet at the bar," he said with a wink.

"You know each other?" Scarlett asked. Neither of us broke eye contact. I waited for him to answer.

"Not quite. Looks like this girl can't handle her liquor. She almost face planted at the bar," he told Scarlett, still holding my gaze.

"Really?" I asked. "I didn't know having two drinks put me in the lush category."

Confused, Scarlett began introductions. "Umm, Alex, this is Jayden. We work together. And Jayden, this is Alex... we went to college together."

"So, Jayden, do you work eighty hours a week as well?" he asked me.

"No, just seventy-eight. I slack off," I retorted.

Clearly feeling uncomfortable, Scarlett discretely walked away towards another guy I didn't recognize and at this point, really didn't care.

"What a shame you have to work so hard," Alex continued, getting on my nerves.

"Oh really? I didn't know you could see my pay stubs to know what my income is?"

I had no idea why that snobbery flew out of my mouth. There was just something about this guy that made me snap and kind of unable to censor myself.

"And what is it exactly you two are spending eighty hours a week doing?" Alex asks.

"Well, it's technically life insurance, but I like to think of it as protecting families with the financial security in preparation for the worst day of their lives," I responded as I sipped from my drink.

"Okay, so pitch me," Alex requested.

"This isn't a baseball game, Derek Jeter."

"Oh, well I think it is. What's wrong, are you too afraid I'll say your sales game is weak? Can't handle it when someone passes you the ball?"

"Oh no, I'm not afraid of that. I just know that it's 11:53 on a Saturday night, and my game is so good that I don't need to pitch you. I have enough people lined up on roster for my phone night on Monday. If you need to speak insurance, you can call me and set an appointment." I prayed I delivered the bullshit convincingly. Even though I had my script perfectly memorized and was able to set a perfect schedule, I was still nervous I was sounding like nothing short of moronic. "Well, someone put a sass pill in that drink," Alex said, taken aback.

"Find someone else to go pitch you or whatever you're looking for," I replied.

"I'm not looking for someone else," he said with a confident tone that took me by surprise.

"What is it that you are looking for?" I asked. "Because you're doing an awfully good job of bothering me."

"Funny, women don't usually say I bother them. But then again, you must still be a little girl being sloshed on two drinks. A real woman handles her liquor."

"I think you should walk away. I don't need to spend my evening being taunted by a boy with some insecurity issues. I can give you the name of a good therapist in the area."

"That won't be necessary. If anything, I can have the bouncer over there escort you out of here."

"Excuse me?" I asked him. "On what grounds?"

"Well, Jayden, I'm one of the owners of Blue Moon."

"Oh, of course you are," I answered. And with that, I decided I had enough of this stupid conversation, did a 180, and marched away. How is it the assholes always sniffed me out and knew exactly what to say to take a bite out of my confidence? Better yet, what was wrong with this Alex that he felt the need to be such an asshole to me, yet shower every other woman with kisses? I ran into the bathroom to calm down. Hopefully Alex didn't have the balls to demand one of his security guys push into the ladies room to "escort me out of the bar."

Locking myself in a stall, I made a silent prayer that I could leave this place without a completely embarrassing exit. Where the hell had Scarlett gone? I waited a few minutes to let my anger come down from a boiling point and then opened the door and stood in front of the mirror. I ran my fingers through my hair and looked at my make-up. Satisfied, I squared my shoulders and stood straight. Who the hell was this Alex character to make me feel incompetent? *No one*, I told myself. Halfway to the door, I found

Scarlett grinding up against the guy who she had spotted while I was in my verbal flogging with Alex.

"Scarlett, I'm leaving," I said to her.

She barely broke away from her dance partner but replied, "Okay, byeeee."

"How are you getting home?" I asked her, praying she wasn't going to be driving.

"Dude, it's fine. Mikey and I, we're gonna go on a smoke ride and then he can take me home." Leaning into my ear she said, "And maybe I'll let him realllly take me home. Ha. Ha."

"Scarlett, wrap that shit up so I don't have to take you for Plan B tomorrow."

"Haaaa. Plan B. Good thinking!" Scarlett answered, as though I had suggested a revelation. I knew this girl wasn't on the pill. No way she had the discipline to take something every day. And no one had used condoms since freshman year of college. If that.

Unfortunately for me, Alex had snuck up at this point.

"Plan B, huh?" he asked us. "Jayden, who knew you also opened your legs that fast, too?"

"Not for you, anyway," I answered. Scarlett seemed too intoxicated to understand the hostility in my voice.

"Alex, this is my girl. Like seriously, this is my fucking girl," she said stepping away from her dance partner momentarily and hanging onto Alex.

"Oh yeah, Scar? She's your girl?" he teased back. At this point, Mikey sauntered over and gave us all the head-nod signaling he was not interested in making small talk, which was fine with me. He grabbed Scarlett who had somehow roped herself between Alex and me for physical balance and peeled her off. Before either of us could say bye, I could see her being carried into the Jeep Wrangler with the top down he had somehow parked right in front of the bar.

"What is your problem?" I asked Alex.

"My problem is that you seem to have quite an attitude."

"Not the first time I heard that one."

He stepped toward me and took my chin in between his thumb and forefinger. I wanted to smack his hand away, but my arms were frozen to my sides. It was as though his touch paralyzed my body, and yet, I didn't want him to remove his hand from my face.

"Doesn't surprise me," he answered, his eyes widening and staring right into me. Even though it was dark, I could feel them pierce right through me, as though he could read my thoughts.

I finally gathered the ability to move my limbs again and I raised my hand to remove his fingers, but he was too fast. He grabbed my hand and pulled me closer to him.

"You're too beautiful for your own good," he whispered in my ear. "Did anyone tell you that?" And as quickly as he pulled me to him, he released me, and walked away. I stood there, unable to catch my breath. Had I just met the devil? I needed to get out of there fast. The door was only a few yards away and I bolted for it, probably stepping on plenty of drunk people's toes, not caring.

The worst part of going out is having to go home alone. This is when I take my feelings out on the refrigerator and berate myself the whole next day for finishing off drinking empty calories with a 3,000 calorie pity party. That fridge needs a chastity belt. And after my encounter with Alex the Aggressor there was no telling what my paws would begin to shovel in my mouth, even with an appetite suppressant in my system. I called a taxi and walked a block away. I waited in the brisk cold and mentally planned what I was going to feast on back at home. For an appetizer, I would have a low-carb peanut butter and jelly feast. I would open a jar of "reduced-fat" peanut butter (because that really cut calories), and a jar of sugar-free jelly that I forced Renee to keep in stock in the pantry. Then I'd crack open the low-fat, sugar-free, chemically filled half gallon of chocolate ice-cream…

Once I was good and stuffed, I'd tromp up to my room, take all my clothes off, and grab the vibrator from its secret hiding space in a box underneath my bed. And then before I had a chance to let the damn thing rip, I'd pass out.

Yes, that's exactly what I was going to do.

CHAPTER 4

Monday came and promptly at 8am our office had a surprise visit from two of the corporate vice-presidents, Calvin Williams and Nicholas Kingsley. Cal was blacker than a shot of espresso, charismatic, and generated an income that is reserved for high powered attorneys. He wasn't even thirty. There were also rumors he generated action in some of the various offices he was responsible for overseeing, including one of our very own managers, Andrea. It didn't matter. He was a tip-top VP.

I had a feeling something had happened between them when I noticed he was lingering in her office for longer than what seemed necessary. Not one to be private about her personal affairs, Andrea was more than happy to brag when I asked what was up with Calvin.

"Yeah, last year he came into town and we all went out to the casino. I ended up staying in his hotel with him. I heard he just knocked up some manager in Pittsburgh. Lucky her. She'll be set for life." I wondered if I'd let someone knock me up to be set for life. No, no, I was set to make it on my own.

"And then the next day he was in my office and asked to see my glue stick."

"Why? He needed to start crafting or something?"

"Nah, he wanted to snort it to get high. Jayden, these guys will shove anything up their noses to get a rush. Cocaine is the tip of the iceberg."

I obviously was in the clear since I didn't put anything up my nose. I also obviously didn't know much about the drug world.

And Nicholas Kingsley? Everyone just knew he had been an insanely talented salesperson who just worked his way up the corporate ladder and always had some underlying competition with Monte. Whenever his office did better than ours, Monte threw a man's version of a hissy fit. It went something along the lines of him hurling nerf balls across his office and declaring to his junior managers, "I will NOT lose to Nicholas Kingsley again next week. Cannot happen, gang!" They usually were covering their heads to protect them from any flying objects. Monte acted this way in his private office, thinking no one noticed, and then he would step out into the main office smiling like nothing happened.

Cal and Nicholas were in a meeting with the managers and I was researching companies we viewed as competitors so I could be prepared to explain to potential policyholders why D'Angelo Enterprises was superior to any other company in the industry. Being as subtle as I could, I reached into the side pocket of my purse and felt for a pill that had already been broken into quarters. I grabbed one and nonchalantly slipped it into my mouth. I kept them in my purse and discretely slipped them into my mouth if I felt like I was dozing off. No one ever saw. Everyone was too busy worrying about themselves to see what's going in another person's mouth. They only cared about the bullshit coming out of their mouth.

"What are you doing?" Scarlett asked me, staring at my computer.

"Eating a Tic-tac, want one? It's the new flavor!" I answered guiltily. I reached into the same pocket, extracted a packet and gave it a desirable little shake.

"Yeah," she said as I poured her half a dozen.

Cal and Nicholas emerged from Monte's office and it was immediately obvious they were a big deal. They introduced themselves to the agents who either shook their hands with the gusto of a mobster, or flashed as much cleavage as they could get away with if they were female. Scarlett and I were way above that kind of behavior, since neither of us barely filled a B-cup.

"I've heard a lot about you from Monte," Cal said after I introduced myself. "You're doing some very impressive deals. Keep up the good work." I blushed at the praise. Since my desk was right by Joey's, I could hear his conversation with Nicholas. It sounded pretty similar to the one I was having.

"Well, thank you, Cal," I replied, noting his demeanor. Granted he was extremely professional, but with that bad boy charm, I could see how the women could be convinced of a little extra training outside the office. I glanced over at Nicholas Kingsley, who was right in my line of sight so I wasn't actually looking away from Cal. With hard features, his face was much more serious. No wonder why he had such an infamous sales record. Who would dare say no to him?

I focused my attention back to Cal. "Make sure you're writing quality business," he said cautiously. Quality business? I didn't see any reason why I wouldn't be. It's not like I ever did anything illegal or anything I hadn't been instructed to do.

"Of course I am." I basked in the undivided attention as Cal asked me a few more questions about how I did things in my presentation. The other agents walked by and saw him taking time to speak with me individually and I could see the jealousy etched into their faces. It was like having one on one time with a sales celebrity. In a mixture of guilt and pleasure, I ate it up. Before I left the office, I passed by Nicholas Kingsley, and I decided to introduce myself.

"Jayden Rosenberg. You were the top sales person in your office for January." With ten offices, how did this guy have time to remember who the number one person was in a particular month?

"I was?" I asked. I never kept track of this stuff since managing numbers wasn't my forte.

"Yes."

"How did you know?"

"Because I keep track of these things. And so should you." The guy had a point, so I made a mental note to learn how to track stuff. Then I cut to the chase.

"How do you sell such big policies?" He was companywide known for selling policies big enough to insure an entire village.

"It's very simple, Jayden." I looked at him expectantly. He remained stoic.

"Ask for a bigger check."

■ ■ ■

Later that afternoon, the sky was still clear as I pulled into the driveway of 67 Oxtail Rd. *Oxtail Road?* I thought to myself. Who creates with between street and such a street such a name? Hillbillies. In front of me was a run-down house with rickety wooden steps that as also begging for a paint job. The Samson residence, a referral from someone who worked at Dunkin Donuts who didn't have a bank account. This should be a real treat.

I hesitated as I stepped out of my car. I reached into the back seat to grab my snow boots since the ground was still a solid half foot deep in snow. There was no way I was going to make it up the steps in pointy high heels. It was 3:30pm and already I was exhausted. However, when your day begins at 5:00am, that is understandable.

After having time to digest how simple Nicholas Kingsley's answer was to what I thought was a complicated question, I felt stupid for asking it. However at that moment, stupidity was taking a backseat to my fatigue and my day was barely half over, which wasn't a good sign. I dug into my purse and reached for the orange piece of energy, put in my mouth, and savored at the thought of the rush I knew would come soon. I surveyed the ground again and realized I wouldn't make up the stairs so I changed into my snow boots I kept stashed in the backseats for winter days like this. I grabbed my bag and stumbled out of the car, feeling awkward in my snow boots, and walked up the worn steps. Banking that this house was a complete broke bust, I knocked on the door and prayed this would be over soon.

"I thought you weren't coming," a woman I presumed to be Jennifer said as she opened the door.

"It's 3:30. Remember I said I would be over sometime between three and four? I apologize. My last appointment was running a little late," I lied.

"That's okay, come in," she said, ushering me through the door. I walked through the living room where three kids were camped out in front of the TV in a sea of toys, not bothering to look up as I walked through. The trouble started when I walked into the kitchen.

"You're the one here to try to make me buy something?" My interrogator was a blatantly out-of-shape man who clearly didn't-give-a-shit. He was leaning on the countertop opening up a can of Budweiser and staring right at me as I stepped onto the linoleum floor. I was immediately convinced I had stepped into the epitome of white trash.

"I'm sorry?" I asked, trying to not seem caught off guard.

"The insurance lady?" he said a little louder. That insurance lady phrase got me every time. I'd envision myself about forty years older and wearing my hair in a bun tight enough to pull back my wrinkles.

"I'm Jayden." I extended my hand, ignoring his comments. I was above feeding into the bullshit. He continued to sip his Budweiser.

"Don't mind John," Jennifer said, nodding her head towards her husband, as she cleared off the table. "He's never in a good mood." At least she was woman enough to recognize her man sucked. As we sat down, John immediately began setting his parameters.

"Now listen, what's this all about?" he demanded.

"Well, John, I'll get to all that, I just wanted to take a couple minutes to get to know you guys. Relax, you have a beer in your hand. I'm not going to bite," I coaxed, trying to bring some semblance of humor to the table.

"Yeah, well don't try to sell me nuthin' because I ain't buyin' nuthin'," he reiterated.

"That's fine by me, you'll just save me some paper work." Fast forward sixty minutes and I was filling out applications for the whole family while John and Jennifer deliberated over which policy they wanted to sign up for. *Go for the big one*, I thought to myself. For the unwelcoming greeting, I deserved to get the gold.

"We need this," John said. "We can't not have it," he repeated to Jennifer. I had to bite my tongue so that I didn't mouth off with a "told ya so," attitude and blow the whole deal.

"You're right," Jennifer said. Come on, come on, I thought as she dangled her pen around the three policy options I outlined.

I could see her mind reviewing each one with my explanations playing like a recording. If I spoke a word at this point, I would have killed the deal. But I had learned when to shut up and let the customer convince themselves instead of me doing the work. I held my breath as Jennifer tapped the paper.

"We can afford this one, right John?" Her pen was pointed on the big one.

"Oh yeah, that's fine," he agreed.

"Well guys, I just need you to grab a voided check. I'm going to ask you a few questions for the application and I'll be on my way out."

"Wanna beer?" John asked. If only it was vodka.

After I collected everything I needed, I walked out with a commission large enough to fly my ass to the Mediterranean beach. John even walked me to the door and smiled at me. "Be careful out there," he said nodding to the snow that was now coming down like big white pebbles. Good-bye clear skies. I decided I liked John, even if he had initially greeted me with obvious disdain and drank beer out of a can. On my way home, I sent the policy amount into the office's group message on my phone. The texts started coming in.

Random phone number: *How do you do it, Jayden?*
Joey: *How much dick are you sucking in the house?*
Scarlett: *Good job girl!*

And then of course, Monte: *JayJay I'm so proud of you. Keep the momentum, girl!*

While everyone always calculated their exact commission after a sale, I just forgot about it. I felt like it was bad luck to keep track of my sales. So, the next week, when I stared at my bank account balance, my jaw dropped when I saw the dollar amount that had been deposited. Monte walked by desk and paused once he saw what I was staring at on my computer, probably having a de ja vu moment from his early days. He pointed to the top item, which showed the recent deposit.

"Now, that, Jayden, is what we call a money boner."

"A money boner?"

"Yeah, the amount is so big it makes your dick hard."

"But I don't have a dick, Monte."

"Well, if you had one, than you would. Keep going girl, stay hungry for success!"

At this point, I was starving.

I closed the online banking tab and decided to get to work as I pulled a cashmere sweater from The Limited over my slimming frame. I let my mind wander for a moment and realized I was actually making it on my own. Being the best had never been my initial goal. On day one, all I wanted was to avoid failure since it was a shade I simply couldn't wear. And now that the dollars started rolling in, I decided I wanted more. I picked up the phone and dialed the number for the first person on my referral list. It was grind time.

Meet me now, bitch, Veronica's text read. After a few cookie runs, she and I had quit the niceties of anything resembling, *Hey babe, you busy? Let's chat quick and do a swap!* to *Where the fuck are you? I need the cash and you need the pills.* But then of course face-to-face it was all "Woman, you look like, so skinny, miss you!" Hugs, exchange of how Jeremy could throw down harder than a Roman warrior, me whining that I didn't have time for sex, and I would have loved a good railing. So I just rattled off how with my seriously impressive paychecks I was going to open up a Roth IRA, tax deferred obviously. But maybe that was a bit over Veronica's head?

She was probably taking a cut for acting as a middle man. I didn't even care at this point. These babies were my investment -

some chemicals in, lots of energy and focus out. Let's not mention this appetite disappearing thing.

Much to my ego's chagrin, I swallowed the urge to type back something nasty and met Veronica at our usual spot about a mile from her duplex, because god forbid her highness be inconvenienced. I spotted her Lexus coupe in the deserted shopping center where a K-Mart had yet to be torn down and replaced with yet another bank. It was all Grayton seemed to have, banks and gas stations. I parked my car next to hers and knocked on the passenger door.

"Hi babe," she said, staring at herself in the overhead mirror, coating her thick lips with enough gloss for a full meal.

"New shade?" I asked her.

"You like?" She turned to me and smacked her barbie-pink lips, ready for approval.

"You look fucking exhausted, Jayden." It wasn't even lunch time and my body already felt like it had put in a full day. But my mind was running and ready for the next challenge: whoever was on the schedule.

"Yeah, thank God for our cookies!"

Veronica was holding her cigarette, puffing with a pensive expression on her face. Originally from D.C., she ended up in Pennsylvania because of her boyfriend's family. Therefore, she immediately took to me since I had not only used a passport before, but actually resided somewhere outside Grayton's town lines - past the fucking Atlantic Ocean. She was one of the few people at home who actually took an active interest in hearing my Israeli shenanigans.

"You're getting out of this shithole once you have enough in the bank, right?"

Her question caught me off guard, being that I had been so obsessed with obsessing over my sales goals, I forgot about the future.

"Well, Monte said I have to wait a year until I can go anywhere and they don't exactly have an office in Tel Aviv, so it's pretty pointless to think about that right now."

"So now you don't want to go back?" she asked, clearly confused. I closed my eyes, trying to picture my skin baking under the Mediterranean rays at the beach, a bottle of wine next to me. But that was then and this was now. And right now all I knew was I needed to make this errand quick so I could get to my first appointment of the day. But of course I couldn't say that out loud.

"Of course I want to go back," I said defensively. "Just because I'm not able to go back tomorrow doesn't mean I'm not ever going to."

"Well when I first met you when you came home all you did was talk about the beaches there, how drunk you were all the time, and how hot the guys were."

"None of that changed."

"What about boys?" she asked. You never even talk about them anymore. Please, like when did I have time. "Don't you ever meet anyone?"

"Ew, you mean like clients?" I asked, trying to hold back the vomit as I thought of chain-smoking middle aged men with beer guts.

"I mean, some of mine are pretty hot."

"Yours are getting a haircut or highlights. Mine don't always have hair necessarily." I thought back to the night I met Alex and shuddered. I certainly was not about to bring him up. Ew, why did his name even register?

I reached into my purse and pulled out an inappropriate amount of bills for an equally inappropriate amount of pills and put them in her eager hands.

"Careful," she said, not wanting the exchange to be visible.

"Veronica, no one is here," I said, nodding to the vacant parking lot.

"Jayden, you never know who's around."

Veronica was getting paranoid and annoying. She grabbed my empty pill bottle, put it in her lap and poured the pills in.

"Did they have this shit in Israel?"

"Of course, Veronica, except I didn't know it at the time. Now I know why everyone's teeth were chattering constantly when we were drinking."

"God that sounds amazing."

■ ■ ■

"And the top producer for the week is… out of the Grayton office: Jayden Rosenberg."

Boom. I was the Insurance It Girl.

Everyone in the room stared at me. Our office never had one of the top three producers for the week out of the entire agency. A knot formed in my stomach confirming that I was nervous as shit. I was expected to make a quick speech. I hadn't given an impromptu speech since class in high school, where half of the class was napping. Monte looked at me and pointed to the phone which was next to the TV screen where we tuned into the meetings. I needed to cover my bases before I went public. "Monte, does my hair look okay?" I asked.

I may have been slightly shaking with nerves, but I can't deny a part of me wasn't I starting to love the dazzle within the bullshit.

"Get up there," he said, shaking his head. "You look fine."

"Come on, girl!" Scarlett whispered in my ear and gave my arm and encouraging squeeze. Part of me almost felt guilty that it was me and not her. Or was I just nervous she would resent me? I didn't have time to analyze this at the moment. I knew everyone was anticipating the weekly delivery of brilliance, or betting to listen to some obscure bullshit they could rip apart later amongst each other. That was one of our favorite things to do after meetings, mimic the top producers' speeches and make fun of their arrogance and fake humbleness. There was no way I was going to speak and then be the butt of some jealous person's jokes from another office. The thought made me shudder as I stood up from my seat and walked over to the front of the room, trying not to stare directly at the eight camera screens. Two hundred fifty pairs of eyes were staring back at me, sitting like little corporate soldiers. The knot in my stomach tightened and my mind went blank. Come on, get your shit together Jayden. I turned one last time back at Monte, who was sitting next to the TV out of view. "You got this, Jay Jay." It was do or die. And I didn't wanna die.

"Hi, everybody. I'm Jayden Rosenberg and to be perfectly honest - I'm pretty surprised by this announcement - and especially by the fact someone just put a microphone in my hands.

The thing is - there's nothing different I did this week than I did from any other week - which is listen to what my managers tell me what to do and then go do it. I haven't been in this game very long, but I've been in it long enough to realize if you want something bad enough and someone give you the tools to get it... don't leave them in the shed, use them."

I knew I nailed it as soon as the clapping started. For all my bitching about the clapclap meetings, I was really appreciating those claps right now. After some high fives, I sat down, the adrenaline rush making me shake. What was this feeling called? I think it's what those women's magazines refer to as empowered. Monte looked up me and pounded my fist. "Proud of you girly." *I want to do that again*, I thought.

"I'm so proud of you!" Scarlett was on me as hard as she hits the bowl when I sat down. I looked at her and knew everything was okay when I saw her smile. I knew her fake smile, and this wasn't it. I felt hands tapping my shoulder, I heard the clapping, Monte screaming "Let's fucking go, Grayton!" like he yells at the 49ers, but none of it amounted to how I felt that moment. I had seen paychecks bigger than I ever dreamed clearing my bank account and savored every check I collected in a house. But being the top among a group of five hundred equals - it was a sound of success ringing. I can't deny the fact I liked being in the center of attention. After all, I am an only child. However, I never fought for the spotlight at work. But now that it was delivered on a silver platter, I wanted to eat off that china any to every second I could.

When I mentally climbed down from Everest, I reached for my phone as I sat back in my seat, the thrill of success still at my fingertips. A text message appeared on my phone from an unfamiliar number. All it said was, *Great job.*

I didn't care about the clapclapping at that point, my eyes were glued to iPhone screen.

Thank you... who is this? I responded. I could see the three dots on the message screen indicating they were typing, and again I tensed.

Nicholas Kingsley.

Nicholas Kingsley? My heart beat picked up and I think my hands got a little sweaty. What was Nicholas Kingsley texting me for? The same Nicholas Kingsley who had shown up at our office just weeks earlier who drove a black BMW 7-Series and made more money in a year than most college grads make their first decade of working? How was it that he cared to take the seven seconds to shoot me a text message to tell me good job? How did he even have my phone number? Where I would normally pull out the wit and sarcasm, something told me to leave them belted securely in the backseat. Instead I acted like a professional, which was most difficult.

Thanks, Mr. Kingsley. There, simple.

"Shut up," I heard Scarlett say, who I forgot was sitting next to me.

"I'm not talking," I answered.

"Nick Kingsley?" she asked, pointing my phone. "Why is he texting you to say good job?" If my curiosity was piqued, I could see her brain trying to read in between the lines of a simple two word text. Women, we're just ridiculous creatures at times. I tried to keep it cool, but instead my mouth verbalized the thoughts I was trying to suppress.

"I don't know Scarlett. I was wondering the same god damn thing."

■ ■ ■

I tried to bury the whole Nicholas Kingsley text message thing, but Scarlett couldn't miss out on an opportunity to gossip. Who could blame her? Seriously, selling people the concept of protection against death was only so interesting. The water cooler talk was a way for our brains to recharge.

"Well, ew, Marissa is such a bitch anyway. She lives on vodka and diet pills," Scarlett was telling me as I sat at my desk, rewriting my schedule so that it looked fresh. She was sitting on the edge, filing her nails. I'm telling you, multi-tasking was the only way we could stay on top of any sort of beauty regimen.

"Who's Marissa?" I asked. I was loving this Marissa girl's diet, but maybe I could tweak it with some lettuce or something and write a book.

"Nicholas Kingsley's girlfriend. She used to be an agent and then I guess she just became his assistant after she started dating him. She probably sucked as an agent." For a second I forgot about filling my 4-5pm time slot and let Scarlett's information sink into my head. What, like this should surprise me? Successful men always come with arm candy. I wasn't surprised Scarlett knew all about Nick's girlfriend either. Before she could sell a scrap of insurance, Scarlett knew who was who in the company, which toys they bought and which women they paraded around town. During office meetings, she thumbed through Facebook, drooling all over the girlfriends' skinny bodies or the fiance's massive rocks. With all of her journalistic skills, she should have a gossip column in *Us Weekly* instead.

But sadly, the thought that this Marissa sucked as an agent and was swept into a wallet of security made me feel better. I'm more independent than her. Before I could probe any further into Marissa's career and diet, we looked at each other the moment we heard a hyena laugh coming from Monte's office. With raised eyebrows, we redirected our focus to Monte's door. We could see Monte was sitting at his desk, leaning forward, a wide window behind him showcasing Gratyon's finest melting snowbanks which were now blanketed with layers of dirt. Sitting opposite of him, with the glorious view of the building's parking lot, was a dark haired man, who instead was leaning back, relaxed. Ugh, no, not him again...

CHAPTER 5

And then Scarlett confirmed what the knot forming in my stomach was expressing.

"Ooh, Alex is in there with Monte!"

"God, what is that asshole doing here?" I asked.

"I don't know. They have been friends since their college frat days. He probably just came in to say hi and bring him some bud, whatever."

"Ew, when did he come in here? I feel like he doesn't do anything quietly."

"Not sure, but it looks like he's coming out," Scarlett observed as they stood up and walked towards the door. I didn't mean to look. I really meant to look back at my schedule and get back re-organizing it. But my eyes were focused on him stepping into the main part of the office like he owned the place. Prick. Two of the managers walked up to Alex, giving the customary fist bump and "What's up man?" greeting.

Why was everyone so eager to say hi to him? I'm sure he ate and shit just like the rest of us. I must have had a less than pleasant expression on my face because his eyes found mine and turned cold. He didn't acknowledge me outright, he just stared intently at me just long enough for my heart to skip a beat. He stared and somehow managed to continue to hold a conversation with Randy, Scarlett's manager.

"He's so arrogant, I don't see what all the fuss is about," I said.

"You're nuts! He's the nicest guy ever. I was good friends with his girlfriend in college." Of course Scarlett was good friends with Alex's leading lady, she was good friends with everyone.

I looked down and started recopying Tuesday's schedule. The original was too messy. Scarlett insisted on continuing to distract me by switching subjects and talking about how Mikey, the stoned guy she went home with after our night at Blue Moon, was dodging the "R" word.

"The 'R' word?" I asked Scarlett cluelessly.

"The R word, Jayden, Hello!"

"The "R" word...I'm talking about relationship. Seriously girl where is your head at?" Scarlett asked me playfully.

"Oh, sorry," I said sheepishly. "Well, we don't have time for relationships anyway," I reminded her. "Where do you fit in cooking dinner for the man or weekend getaways with our schedules?"

"I don't know, I'll figure something out. I don't want him banging other girls."

"Just YouTube how to deep throat. He won't go anywhere."

"Yes, Scarlett, learn how to deep throat," a voice said from behind me. I swiveled around in my chair and found myself eye level with Alex's Prada belt.

Whatever, it was probably Frada, I thought. I hated this dark haired designer clad guy.

"Alexxx," Scarlett beamed, dialing up her charm as she twirled her hair and giggled. I knew she didn't want to get in his pants, she just liked being associated with him. Apparently he was considered the man around here.

"I beg to differ," I muttered under my breath. He didn't hear me, but Alex knew something smart was coming out of my mouth.

"What are you doing here?" I asked, looking up at him, feeling completely inferior in a sitting position. "This is my office," clearly pushing the envelope considering it wasn't my office.

"Actually, this isn't your office, it's Giovanni's," Alex replied smartly. "He pays the rent for it." I was surprised he knew who Giovanni was, never mind who was paying the rent.

"Whatever. Why are you here anyway?" I pressed again.

"Don't worry about it, Jayden."

"I'm not losing any sleep over it."

"Always one with a comment, aren't you?"

"That's one thing I can't argue with you about, I guess."

"I'd watch your mouth if I were you, your boss is my best friend."

"Alex, Jayden was the top sales person for the week," Scarlett said, trying to squash our elementary banter.

"Oh were you?" he asked me. "Congratulations," he said, as he took his right hand and bobbed it up and down in front of his mouth, insinuating I hadn't earned my accomplishment based on sales skills. "I knew that mouth would get you places," he added, laughing at his own joke.

"You're hilarious," I said. "I actually have been working very hard."

"Well, Jayden, keep slaving away. Doesn't seem like there's much else going on in your life anyway. Scarlett, babe, I'm out of here," Alex said and leaned to give her a kiss on the cheek.

"Jayden, I know it's phone night, so you get dialing now, Sweetie," he said looking me up and down. "Damn, that's a tight dress for talking on the phone all night. What are you doing, FaceTiming the husbands?" he added as he started to move towards the door. "Don't come back any time soon, please," I said, rolling my eyes and turning back to my laptop, clicking on the list of people I needed to call. And pulled my dress down as far as the fabric would stretch.

"Yo, Monte, I'll catch you later," I heard him say. I knew he had walked away because his voice sounded more distant. The sting of his words was crawling close under my skin.

"Oh, Jayden, I saw you met Alex!" Monte said as he walked passed my desk.

"Yes, I have," I answered curtly.

"Don't get any ideas girly, I know you," he added with a smile slapped on his face.

"What do you mean?"

"He has a bigger panties collection than Victoria's Secret. Stay away, I need you focused."

"Um, Monte, he is not my type at all."

"Oh, Jayden, he's every girl's type. He turned and sauntered back to his office, greeting some of the newest agents on his way. "How's it going today guys?" I heard him say enthusiastically.

Every girl's type of guy? Well I'm not every girl, I thought.

Hours later, the office was getting antsy. "Joey, I'm going to murder you!" I yelled as a flying nerf ball bounced off my head. "It wasn't me!" he yelled back, like the gassy third grader who tries to blame everyone for his abominable farts.

"Jayden, quit your bitchin and get back on the phone!" Monte yelled from his office. My phone started vibrating and I look at the caller I.D. to see an unfamiliar number. Luckily, I'm super-fast and was able to match the number with a name of someone I had been trying to track down for days. I was smelling victory.

"Hi, Jackson?" I began energetically. "Yeh, who dis?" I didn't let the working class vernacular throw me off.

"Oh, Jackson, we spoke last week. Does the name Jayden ring a bell?"

"Eh, I was upta mall when yas called, but yeh, I remember. What ya got for me?" And with that, I shmoozed and negotiated until I got the appointment I thought I wanted, just as the clocks were signaling the end of our work night at 8:59pm. Joey was hanging over me when I got off the phone. "You dirty little whore, you."

"What now?"

"You set a single dad last call? Definite sale. You're going to get railed."

"Joey, I'm not trying to bang one out at the house."

"Hey, do what you need to do to close a sale."

"You're an asshole," I said laughing, as I shut my laptop for the evening.

I came home, thankfully to an empty house. Apparently my parents were more socially active than me. After making phone calls for five solid hours the last thing I wanted to do was talk to anyone. Which is saying a lot coming from the girl who probably deserved to have a sock shoved in her mouth at one point or another. Before my head hit the pillow, I scanned through my phone once more before putting it on the charger - probably the same routine every girl does. Just as I decided I had read enough Facebook status updates filled with selfies, I went to turn my phone to the Do Not Disturb mode, I was interrupted with an incoming text message.

You're welcome. Keep up the good work. ;)

The winking face from Nicholas Kingsley made my stomach muscles tighten and the corners of mouth curl into a slight grin. Suddenly, I wasn't missing my old life so much.

CHAPTER 6

You know time is an issue when you're constantly behind, no matter how many minutes ahead you set your clock. I was running around the gym's locker room in a towel as rough as sandpaper. My rubber flip flops made a smacking noise under my feet as I ran in between the mirror and the changing room. I knew my getting ready routine was completely inefficient, but no matter how many times I realized I showed up to work with my thong inside out or my tank top on backwards, I never made a change. I just kept banking on the notion that the 'rushed' look would become chic.

Speaking of chic, I don't think that's how I looked almost wiping out on frozen rain as I threw my gym bag into the trunk of my car. Pointy heels look killer but they're god awful in inclement weather. My phone started vibrating and I knew it was crucial if Scarlett was calling me before 9am. And then I remembered. "Oh, my god, fuck! I'm sorry!" I said into the phone as I started the ignition. I was supposed to call her to wake her up so she could start working out early too.

"It's okay, I went out last night. Are you going to Dunkin, boo?" she asked sweetly. I put her on speakerphone and grabbed my go-to shade of OPI Cha-Ching-Cherry nail polish from my glove compartment.

"You're still in bed, aren't you?" I asked her, as I carefully balanced the bottle next to the shifter and spread my fingers open on the arm rest in between the front seats.

"No, I'm up. Thank God I live like five minutes from the office," she said yawning. "Yeah, you're so lucky," I said, thinking how great this shade looked on me even though I was so pale.

"If you're swinging by on the way to the office, can you grab-"

"plain bagel with strawberry cream cheese and an that stupid large crappuccino with 800 calories in itself?" I finished for her.

"Yeah, but get me a small one, and no whipped cream. And a water. I'm on a diet now. Is cream cheese really fattening?"

When I pulled into the parking lot which wrapped around the entire building, I made a loop until I found a spot I deemed close enough to the main entrance. For someone who kills herself during cardio, I loathe parking my car far away when I am wearing heels and have a ton of shit to carry. Finding one that was sufficient, I swerved in before anyone else could swipe it. I put the car in park and leaned back in my seat and looked at the clock. It was 8:54am. I had six minutes to get my shit together. The clock read AM, but my body felt like it was 8:54pm.

I really didn't like to take one this early but I knew the caffeine wouldn't help... so I reached into my magenta Michael Kors tote which Renee Dearest gave me for Chanukah, and grabbed my lipstick holder. I opened the satin case and looked at all the perfectly round pills staring at me. I carefully picked one that just looked particularly appetizing and broke it in half. I swallowed it with my iced coffee, because obviously you should always take a stimulant with a caffeinated beverage for a turbo-charged effect. I noticed the clock mark the passage of time and grabbed my work stuff along with the Dunkin' Donuts grub and coffee carrier. *It will be okay soon, you'll feel awake*, I thought as I rode the elevator up to the office.

"Alright, it's 9:31, I'm shutting the door," Monte announced before making a grand push on the metal handle. I was sitting in my designated seat - second row back in the center aisle, saving a spot for Scarlett with her high-calorie "diet" food on the seat next to me. The devil herself managed to squeeze right by Monte before the door slammed in her face. "Sorry, Monte, I had to ask Randy something about a policy I wrote," she started to explain, standing at the doorway. There was a good chance she would be banished from the grand world of an insurance workshop and be exiled to the main office with a sentencing of time management skills. Monte rubbed a marker between his hands, weighing if he should let her stay or let her go.

"Can't happen again, Scarlett," he answered. "Okay gang, let's get going."

Scarlett booked it to what she recognized as her saved seat. I held her breakfast for her so she could get situated because I'm such a good friend. She began pulling down her pencil skirt which kept bunching up. I looked down and noticed a run in her stockings and pointed it out. "Fuck," she muttered under her breath. This wasn't Scarlett's A-game day.

That's what I was here for as her D'Angelo Enterprises bestie. Breakfast runs, and TicTacs. She took a bite of her bagel and then looked at me sincerely. "Are bagels high in fat?" I looked away from the caloric catastrophe Scarlett was about to chow down on. It was time to focus on what really mattered at this hour of the day: how to make more money.

■ ■ ■

It was 9:02pm, twelve hours later in my day. Crossing my fingers, I was praying Jackson, the single dad who had I spoken with, who seemed to only know townie English, wouldn't hold my two minute tardiness against me. With no porch light on, I used the flashlight app on my phone to make it up the uneven, wobbly steps to the front porch. My three inch suede pumps were not pleased with this situation. I surveyed my surroundings before knocking on the wooden door. Two folding chairs sat on the porch on either side of a table that barely looked sturdy enough to hold the glass ashtray which had remnants of cigarettes from whenever it was still warm enough to smoke outside. Although, maybe the family living here smoked out here during blizzards and negative temperatures. That wouldn't surprise me. People seemed to do anything to get their nicotine fix. To suggest that allocating their welfare money to something more substantial than endless packs of Camels such as a life insurance policy was probably just as ludicrous as suggesting toothpaste to brush any enamel that might be left in their mouths.

The hillbillies insisted "fuck it, they can throw my body in the backyard." Or the self-pitying single mothers excuse was "I don't ask for much, just my Pepsi, *Days of Our Lives*, and my Virginia Slims. I don't got no money for nothing else. I'm on disability for my asthma." I wanted to take two cigarettes, stick them up their noses and light the ends and see how that upset their asthma. Instead, I would simply pack up my laptop, leave my business card, slap a smile on my face and declare I had somewhere else to be.

But then there were the families where the wives would look at their husbands as if a light switch finally turned on and would say, "Honey, she's right. You want to quit smoking anyway." What she really meant was 'Honey, your teeth are yellow and your skin has turned a shade of gray over the years. You're probably gonna kick the bucket soon and I will need that insurance money.'

Being that I was in a less than desirable neighborhood, I braced myself for Grayton's finest and knocked on the door. At that point, I was past worrying about a fat commission like I had when I set the appointment. I was just hoping by the grace of God I wouldn't come back to find my car keyed, broken into, or stolen. From inside I could hear an older man screaming, "Get the damn door!" and footsteps pounding. *This was going to be so fun*, I thought as a guy around my age with a horrible haircut and a physique that needed some remodeling opened the door.

And boy, was it fun. For three hours I got to hear about a farting three year old who was gonna love them Eagles just like his daddy.

"Of course you're in great shape!" I had to feign as Jackson was about to show off his 'muscles' aka enlarged fat deposits in his what would be bicep area.

The cream on the cake was when Cathy, his sixty-something year old, chain-smoking mother who was probably using the cigarette to cover up spaces where missing teeth were, entered the house. At the end of my presentation, which did result in a sale, Jackson closed the deal by deciding it would be a great idea if he and I went on a date sometime. I looked at his eager, beady-eyed face and gave that close-mouthed, "no thank you," smile, but his mother wouldn't hear of it.

"Jackson is such a gentleman," she exclaimed, huffing on the ashing American Spirit hanging from her mouth. This was clearly not the future in-laws I had envisioned for myself, so I bolted.

As I got back to my vehicle safely and punched in my policy revenue, my phone immediately beeped.

Monte: *Big day tomorrow, Jay. Call me when you're out of the field.*

"Is it solid?" he asked right away when I briefed him on the sale.

"Yeah, the mom and stepdad were encouraging him to get a policy."

"Good stuff. So I got news for you, girly."

"Why what's going on?" I asked, almost hitting the car behind me as I pulled out of my pathetic parallel parking job.

"Need you in at 8:30 - can't be late tomorrow." Usually we were allowed to come in at 9am. My heart began to thump. How the fuck could I possibly wake up any earlier?

"Giovanni and Nicholas Kingsley are going to be in the office tomorrow. They're holding a special workshop and I need you and Joey in there early- they want the top agents there."

I gulped.

My first reaction was excitement and then I realized Scarlett wasn't going to be in that meeting with me. I felt a twinge of guilt, and then silently thanked the marijuana gods for not making Scarlett a jealous, backstabbing pothead. Just a pothead who liked to shop and gossip.

As soon as I got home, I was in front of my closet, half asleep with four different tops, three blazers, two pairs of pants, and five pairs of shoes laid out on the carpet to choose from. I was finally beginning to visualize a finished outfit when my phone beeped again.

Nicholas: *Giovanni and I will be in the office tomorrow. Make sure you're on your A game.*

(No emoticon inserted.)

My initial reaction was to call Scarlett for a full text message dissection, analysis and response strategy, but I would never get to bed or worse, end up picking out an outfit. And I didn't feel like explaining the whole conference situation and seem like a bragging bitch. So instead, I did something crazy and answered Nick's text without any outside input.

I wouldn't think of bringing anything else…

CHAPTER 7

A familiar piercing noise jolted me awake, one that I have grown to loathe. It was the sound of my alarm, displaying that the time was 4:47am, for that matter. *Hadn't I just put my head down on the pillow?* I stared at those piercing red digits intently for a few moments, hoping in my half-conscious state that I could magically turn back time to give me another hour of sleep. Instead, that sensation of having to pee ejected me from my bed and sent me running with my eyes still shut to the bathroom. Well bladder, you win. I think pee was already dripping by the time I sat on the toilet. Gross, right?

I threw on the sweatpants, my old chocolate stained hoodie and my coat. I grabbed my gym bag which had the final outfit selection. That had to be done before I went to sleep, because god knows I wasn't going to have the brain power to do it at this hour.

I walked towards garage door and braced myself for temperatures that seemed comparable to Siberia's. Holding my breath, as though that would keep me warmer or something, I opened the door and cried out an unattractive "UGGGGGHHH!" sound as I dashed to my car, a whole ten feet away. As I put the key in the ignition, I cursed myself for making the decision to suffer through another Grayton winter. *Well, Jayden, this is what you get for leaving the fucking Mediterranean.*

When I walked into the office after my work-out, I heard Giovanni's voice booming from one of the conference rooms in the back of the office, alternating between praise and demands for more action. "I gotta give it to team Fanelli rockin' the deal down South. Lookin' at these numbers here, they want to win the baddest out of all of you. Hustle, let's go!" He was on a conference call with the managers from every office and I guess whatever he had to say didn't need to be censored.

I was sitting at my desk trying to make sure I had everything I needed for the meeting, including my brain, when the door opened to the conference room. Monte, Nicholas Kingsley, and Giovanni strolled out, three mafia men. I shied away from accidentally making direct eye contact with Kingsley.

Is he looking at me?

God he's so fucking mammoth.

Don't even go there, Jayden. He's a fucking regional manager.

Once Giovanni was within earshot, I grabbed my balls and walked up to him.

"Hi Giovanni, I'm Jayden Rosenberg. It's such a pleasure to meet you." I extended my hand which he shook firmly. Finally, a real man. I knew not to get excited, he was engaged to a stunning brunette, plus even I understood he was out of my league. A CEO and Grayton agent affair would be too solicitous.

"Why thank you Jayden. You definitely have a lot of studs in the making around this office." He started to step away and I noticed him glanced down. He beamed at me and said two words which sang through my mind for days, "Nice shoes!"

"Oh god, we won't hear the end of this," Olivia, Monte's personal assistant, said when I sprang over to her desk and recounted two of the favorite words anyone ever spoke.

"No, probably not until something more monumental happens to me like getting railed. And that's not guaranteed to top this. Come pee with me." As soon as we walked in the ladies' room,

I whipped out my makeup and began scrutinizing my face for any visible open pore or smudged eyeliner.

"Jayden!" I looked up at Olivia with the same reaction a student in middle school has when their teacher has caught them trying to pass a note. "What?!" I whipped back at her.

"What can you possibly be looking for? You just got here not even an hour ago and you probably were touching up your makeup in your car before you walked into the office. Just get into that meeting. You look fine!"

"Thanks, I said," ducking into the stall with my clutch for a last minute pee. I opened the zipper and took out my trusted lipstick case, pulling out my normal half of a pill. I bit an extra quarter off because I knew today would be an intense day and I needed to be alert. That was just being responsible, after all, I rationalized. After another coat of mascara, just because I couldn't help myself, I double checked that I wasn't wearing my coffee on my clothes. Satisfied that for now they were stain free, I walked back to the office.

I caught Scarlett on her way into the workshop Nick was running for the rest of the office. "Good luck babe!" she said to me energetically. When we had arrived at the office earlier, I gave her the abbreviated version of the conversation Monte and I had on the phone and she wasn't phased in the least. And if she was hiding it, she was a damn good actress.

She pulled me aside quickly adding, "How does my bun look? Can you see the sock? I am trying to make it like how Kourtney Kardashian does." Since she has a good six inches on me, not to mention a pair of killer legs even with all the bagels she ate, she squatted down to my height so I could inspect her style job.

"I don't see any nylon sprouting from the hair," I told her.

"Jayden, let's go." I looked up to see Monte pointing towards the room he had been in earlier. I walked into to the conference room and sat next to Joey who was tapping his pen furiously on his notepad. A trickle of sweat may have been visible on his forehead.

"Jayden, I'm so fucking nervous," he whispered to me. I wanted to tell him I was equally shitting my pants, but was cut off.

"Is everyone in?" Giovanni asked Monte walking into the room, who nodded quickly in response. "Alright then," he said as he shut the door. "You all better have something to take notes with because we got a lotta stuff to go over today, gang." Thankfully, none of us were stupid enough to walk into a meeting with the CEO without something to write on or type with. I knew that college degree would come in handy.

"Alright Grayton… you all want to know a little secret as to why I'm standing here in front of you versus working some dead end $12 an hour job? When opportunity knocked, I answered. I didn't have a rich daddy to put me through college. My mom raised me by herself and half the time we were on welfare. So gang, I know what it's like to be poor. And I know what it's like to be rich. Let me tell ya, it's a lot better to be rich. Money can't buy happiness but you sure as hell can buy a lotta nice stuff." He paused so we could laugh a little.

"That being said, the secret to making it in this business isn't that complicated. When I was an agent starting off here, I wasn't any smarter than the next guy. The only thing I did different was get up earlier and stay out later. I got rid of distractions and I focused. Day in and day out, no excuses. You gotta go all in to be successful gang, there's no other way around it. That means you all better be gettin' off your damn Twitter and Pinterest feeds and cut your nasty smoking habits."

I noted he might not have supported nicotine and social media- but he didn't say anything about prescription stimulants. So I was in the clear, of course.

"You want to be out on a Saturday at 2pm in the middle of the summer sweating in some client's house closing a deal, or do you want to be by the pool, with a margarita in your hand and your current girlfriend next to you?" The guys laughed.

Giovanni mockingly picked up his cell phone, acting like the guy lounging by the pool. "Hi, Monte." He turns to us, collectively his girlfriend, and covers the receiver, "sorry, this is my agent, I'll be one second." "Oh those assholes stood you up? Yeah, that sucks, man...now, stay focused. Utilize your time efficiently. Start going through your leads and make some phone calls..." He covers the phone piece again, and turns to us, "Hi, yeah, can you put another ice cube in that, the margarita and top it off? Okay great." Back to his make-shift phone conversation he continues, "Okay, Monte... yeah hit me up at the end of the day with your numbers. Remember, you have sales quotas!" Dropping his hand he asks us, "Wouldn't you want your summer to look like that instead?" We took a moment from furiously writing and typing to pause and look up, visualizing ourselves on lounge chairs in front of an infinity pool, maybe a beach, most definitely with a beverage in hand. The guys probably fantasized having multiple desirable females drooling all over them. I fantasized about being tan, drinking vodka, and a bikini clad Victoria's Secret model's body. The bikini could be from Target, I didn't give a shit. I was ready to make this fantasy a reality.

"But the only way to get that summer," Giovanni continued, putting some more emphasis into his words to regain our attention, "is to follow my instructions exactly." He wrote out an entire plan on the whiteboard organized with goals, tasks, and of course script changes. He was going so fast through his ninety day plan to success that I started to wonder if I should have just taken three pills instead. And if my hand was going to fall off at any point from writing so furiously.

I looked at Joey, who was chomping on his pen furiously, looking like he might pee his pants any second. Mack was dripping beads of sweat from his forehead. Randy, who had probably gotten high before the meeting, looked confused. Monte looked up from his iPad keyboard and spoke for us. "We got you, Giovanni."

"You guys are all talented," Giovanni said, looking us all individually. "But talent doesn't bring you success. Hard work does. And hard work beats talent when talent doesn't work, don't forget that guys. Alright, go hit the field, let's see some magic out of this office." I felt like a rocket had been lit under my ass by someone wearing very expensive suits and really good cologne. Nothing could stop me now. I was getting to the summer of cocktails and bikinis, out of the field. I was racing to greatness.

"I'm scared," Joey said as we got out of there. "That was the most intense three hours of my life."

"I'm obsessed," I said, ready to click my heels three times; positive I could teleport myself to wherever I needed to be next. I had an appointment in half an hour so I packed my stuff up quickly. I zippered my coat, grabbed my bag with my laptop and headed towards the main doors. Giovanni was in the waiting room with his fiancé, who was absolutely stunning with long, layered dark lots and matching deep brown eyes.

"Giovanni, thank you so much for your time today. It was really a pleasure to sit in on the meeting with the managers," I said sincerely.

"I look forward to seeing good things from you, Jayden," he said and gave me a wink as he stepped onto the elevator. *A wink?!*

I saw Scarlett having a cigarette when I walked out of the lobby.

"How was the workshop?" I asked.

"It was really good, he went over a lot of stuff," she said casually. I got the feeling she was a little envious that I was invited into the managers meeting, but I knew she would never voice it.

"I wish I could have sat in on it…" I said half thinking out loud.

"Who cares? You were in the managers meeting. That's way better," she said with an edge to her voice that confirmed my suspicions.

"Maybe I can ask Nick what he went over in the workshop tomorrow if he has any time."

Scarlett's eyes widened. "You totally want him."

"No, I don't Scarlett, that's ridiculous. He's our boss's boss!"

"So what? Besides, he broke up with Marissa. Free game."

"I don't think that's such a good idea."

"Jayden he's hot. You're in complete denial. You're just making excuses to talk to him."

"Ew, he's definitely not hot," I said pulling out my phone and clicking on my Messages icon. I typed and read to her simultaneously:

Hey Nick… heard your workshop was really good today. Do you have a few minutes tomorrow? I just have a couple questions.

I hit send before I lost my courage. My stomach started to do acrobatics.

"Scarlett, I'm nervous!" I squealed.

My phone alerted me I had a new message immediately.

We read the text message together: *Yes, I'm meeting with the managers in the morning and then I have some time before my flight to Florida. I can meet with you then.*

"See, I told you it would be fine!" Scarlett said. I took a huge breath. Why was I getting so worked up over this? Cal gave me a few minutes of his time and I didn't have an anxiety attack. *He is just doing his job and trying to help you become a better agent. Nothing more. Nothing less*, I drilled into my head.

But that didn't stop me from taking extra time to pick out *another* stellar outfit for the following morning.

CHAPTER 8

Sitting in the parking lot at 8:22am, I had 8 minutes until my butt had to be in the office for my "meeting." Running on five hours of sleep and a two hour work out, I was already physically exhausted but mentally nervous. I reached into the lipstick holder and took a full pill. I needed to be focused like a razor for this meeting. The butterflies started in my stomach as I walked into the office building and up the elevator building. But why? This wasn't a big deal. I was just getting some needed one on one attention. I braced myself as I walked into the conference room. Showtime.

"Sit down, Jayden," Nicholas directed. Thank God I lowered myself into a seat before my knees buckled and I really made a mess of myself. And Thank God I was wearing a pencil skirt so that the back didn't bunch up and reveal my inappropriate underwear. Then again, who even wears *appropriate* underwear?

"I really appreciate you taking time to help me out, Nick," I said, finally letting myself take a breath and trying to ignore the scent of his masculine cologne. He cut me off before I could continue any further brown nosing. "I have a conference call with Giovanni in half an hour, so your questions need to be very specific, Jayden." I knew Nick did not usually meet with agents individually, so I had to make use of my time and keep it quick. This also meant I couldn't fall into any word vomiting or stumbling. Nick was sitting at the head of our conference table dressed in a gray suit with a purple paisley tie and expensive looking cufflinks. He drummed his fingers on the table, his left hand sporting a gold ring. I wondered what the significance was.

Most of the men who rose to fame and fortune with Giovanni came from modest backgrounds like he did. Maybe it was why Nick subconsciously fingered his tie during conversational pauses or how he rolled his ring around his finger with his thumb. Everyone in the company knew he grew up as one of four siblings with a truck driver for a father and his mom stayed at home. Nick's father had died at some point from a heart attack when he was a teenager and luckily had a significantly sized life insurance policy that allowed his mom to care for the kids. Most families we knew that had no insurance and lost their breadwinner were forced out of their homes into the projects, put on programs like welfare and used food stamps to buy generic soda and pop tarts.

Curious to be sitting next to someone who had accumulated so much in such a short time, not to mention being a physical wonder at 6'6" and practically 250 pounds of solid muscle, I could feel myself being disarmed as his confident eyes stared right at me, waiting for me to ask whatever question I had.

"I want to learn how to get a big check, how to sell a big, fat policy like you can."

He didn't answer me right away instead he looked at me intently. I noticed his lips were slightly parted and this created a problem. The problem, was that I wondered what they would feel like on mine. *No, Jayden, stop, stop, stop.* He's probably a horrendous kisser. He sells life insurance for God's sake.

"The key is confidence. You can tell people that the sky is green and the grass is blue but if you say it with enough emphasis and conviction, people will believe you."

Instead of responding with something appropriate, a thought that had been hindering at the front of my head spilled out into a question. "Why are you overseeing our office now?" I don't know what happened, but it just fell out of my mouth.

The expression on his face conveyed that he was definitely taken aback by my forwardness as his eyes widened. "Now, being that that does not concern your paycheck directly, why don't you use your time asking questions that will help you grow in this business and not worry about something that you can't control?"

"Sorry, I was just curious. Bad habit," I answered. He rolled his eyes at me. "Where were you working before D'Angelo Enterprises, Jayden?"

"I thought we're only discussing topics that will increase our paychecks. That question has no correlation to your bank account."

"No, I said your paycheck. Not our paychecks." Perhaps his question was going to lead somewhere.

"I was working with my dad. He has a wholesale company. But long story short apparently in our household business and family don't mix very well. Needless to say, he fired me."

"Your own father fired you?"

"In a manner of speaking yes. He brought me into his office and told me I was to start looking for a new opportunity effective immediately."

"How interesting. And now here you are, killing it in insurance."

"I wouldn't say killing it."

"You were the number three producing agent out of over 200 sales agents last week, Jayden."

"Yeah, but that was just a lucky week."

"There is no such thing as luck, Jayden. Only effort and preparation being converted into results."

What he said made sense. But that still didn't answer my original question.

"I suppose you're right. So back to the question at hand, how do you sell these big policies?"

"Okay, Jayden. Usually I take over an hour to explain this in a high level workshop, so listen carefully..."

I found myself hanging on to each word that came out of his mouth. Was it because in the back of my head I was intrigued by the fact that without a college degree he still put himself in the top 2% of America's income earners? I'm not really a *gold digger* per se, but I wouldn't turn it away. Was it thinking about his position of power that automatically made me bite my lower lip?

■ ■ ■

Climbing into my Mazda, I had to be careful not to spill the coffee I had just bought inside the gas station. I glanced up at the gas pump which read $47.61. "All these mother fuckers on my schedule better be home," I thought to myself as I snatched the receipt. At least it was a tax write-off.

I took a gulp of my coffee and drove towards the exit, and of course I saw the familiar black BMW 7-series pulling in. As the car slowed next to mine I felt my chest tighten. I put my coffee down before I did something stupid and spilled it. The tinted window rolled down to reveal Nicholas Kingsley in a pair of some sort of designer gold-rimmed Ray-Bans. I don't own expensive sunglasses. If I did, they would end up in a toilet or cracked in half from my ass sitting on them on accident within four days of me purchasing them.

"What time is your first appointment?" Nick asked me. Business as usual. "It's at noon, about twenty minutes away."

"You're late then."

"No I'm not. I'll be there at 12:30. We always give the clients an hour time frame."

"If you are on time for your first appointment, then you are actually running late. You should know better."

"Better late than never, I guess." He shook his head.

"Jewish Jayden, what are we going to do with you?"

"Jewish Jayden?" I ask.

"Yeah, Jewish Jayden. Everyone else in your office is Italian, so you need something to stand out."

"I'm pretty sure I don't go unnoticed."

"I have to get to Florida and you have some appointments to run."

"Yes, I do. So stop holding me up."

"Behave yourself, Jayden."

I rolled up my window and carefully turned out of the gas station, taking extra care not to hit any curbs or run any red lights like I am very prone to doing. Last thing I needed to do was hit something in front of his highness. I couldn't help but quickly look in my rearview mirror and see that 7-series parking, wondering when the next time I would see the man inside it. And there was a small part of me hoping that he was wondering the same.

The rest of the day passed in a blur, a series of four appointments where I sold policies to three out of four houses.

I typed into the group my sales amount for the day and a few words of praise followed from other agents of *Nice job, Jayden*. Of course, the reading, the texting, it was all while I was driving. This business of me texting and driving was extremely absurd, but it was the only way I knew how to run my life. Multi-task. Focusing solely on one task at a time was practically a waste of time for me in itself. I even painted my nails in my car after I left the gym and let them dry as I drove to the office.

Just as I hit the interstate that put me only twenty minutes from my house, my phone dinged. Excitement pulsed through me rapidly like an electric current. The iPhone was an iExtension of myself and placed strategically so I could glance down and see who was calling or texting me as I was driving. A text message icon with Nick Kingsley's name appeared. I tried to suppress the butterfly feeling fluttering around me.

Nicholas Kingsley: *Nicely done, Jayden.* My brain was too exhausted to start up the wittiness so I replied casually, *Thanks! I know the drill - get in as many appointments as you can :)*

Nicholas: *That's the golden rule, girl.*

Jayden: *It's late! Shouldn't you be sleeping or with Marisa?*

Twenty minutes later, as I pulled into my driveway, still nothing. Perhaps I was too inappropriate mentioning his girlfriend? I should have probably just stuck to business. Of course, once I was finally in bed and curled up in my down comforter, I heard that familiar ding sound.

Nicholas: *I'm not with Marisa.* The psychoanalysis started as soon as the words registered in my mind. Was he with someone else? Was Marisa just not there this very minute? Or, did he mean that he's not dating Marisa? *Stop jumping to conclusions,* I told myself. He's probably at the bar with his friends or waiting for her to get home. I had no clue how to get the answer I wanted from such a vague jumble of words.

Jayden: *Oh, why?* I figured if I could close a sale in a house, might as well apply it to a text message as well. What was the worst he could do? Fire me? Wasn't exactly like we had a pressuring HR department enforcing some anti-snooping policy.

Nick: *That's irrelevant.* What did he mean by irrelevant? As in they were broken up and the reason why was irrelevant?

Jayden: *I'm sorry, I didn't realize. I didn't mean to upset you.*

Nick: *I'm not upset. Just not worth talking about.*

Jayden: *What is worth talking about?*

Nick: *You're being extremely annoying.* Crap. What am I doing bantering with my boss's boss? This is completely insane. Unprofessional. Completely out of my league. Nick could be texting or sexting or whatevering practically any girl in the state. Make that states - if I was in Pennsylvania and he was in Florida then who was to say he didn't have a whole thread of texts from gold diggers.

I started to type something and then stopped. I was being annoying so I probably couldn't dig myself out of any hole now. I decided it was time for bed and time to put this Nicholas Kingsley thing to a stop.

■ ■ ■

With an industry turnover probably higher than the servers working at The Cheesecake Factory, our office was essentially something of a revolving door. New agents would come out of training all bright eyed and spirited, determined that they were going to be the next sales superstar. And then, they were rejected in houses without managers to rescue them. They got flat tires in the middle of the snow. They couldn't be at happy hour with their friends because they were stuck in an office until after 9pm on a Thursday. They had a few bad weeks and were trying to figure out how they were going to pay off their credit card bill. It happened more often than not. They crashed, burned, and decided failure wasn't such a bad road and left silently, for the better pastures of a steady-eddy job with bi-monthly paychecks and their two week's vacation. They got their lives back.

There was never a send-off party with cake and office good-byes. When they walked away, they immediately were referred to in the past tense. Suddenly a Monday would roll around and we would wonder in the team meeting, "Where is Frank? Where did he go?" Sometimes we whispered to each other, sometimes it was a fleeting thought. At first, Scarlett and I were stunned by the rapid drop off of agents. After a couple months, we didn't even bat an eye. We would brush the dirt off our shoulders. We weren't one of *them*.

Eventually, if you're not one who falls off the radar, the only other place you go is right on the map.

"Ladies and gentlemen," I heard Monte tell the room, "Let's welcome Jayden up here to sign her level 1 management contract!" *Me? A promotion?*

I stood and walked to the front of the room where Monte was holding my contract with a pen, and Mack was next to him. Mack was the manager who trained me. For the three weeks I was in his car learning the presentation, I drove him utterly insane.

"Is this a joke?" I asked. "Like an April's fool's joke?" They laughed and assured me this was a real deal. "This is a really long contract," I half-joked, leafing through the eighteen page document with ridiculously small print.

"It's pretty standard, you're all good," Mack said casually. Something told me I wasn't the first and probably wouldn't be the last to make the same comment. Again, there was another X highlighted where my signature was supposed to go, another written commitment into the D'Angelo Enterprises circle.

I looked at Monte and gave a mischievous smile. "Are you sure you want to do this, add me to the gang?"

"Yes, I am, you earned it," he said with a genuine smile. I placed the contract on the table and signed my name on the highlighted X... just like I had all those months ago for my agent contract.

"Alright, congratulations JayJay!" Monte yelled out, as I sat back down to my seat. Scarlett and Joey gave me a hug and high five, but I knew they trying to swallow a bitter taste in their mouths.

"I'm proud of you babe!" Scarlett half-whispered, putting her hand on me knee as I sat down.

"You're fucking next, I can't be the only girl in management with those wild animals."

A part of me felt guilty for getting to what I considered a finish line first, but then I pushed it away. *I worked fucking hard for this*, I thought. I didn't leave the office on phone nights to go smoke a blunt or drink at the dive bar by my house. I didn't sleep through my first appointment on Saturdays because I was too hungover from Friday. No, I was the first one in and the last one out. And now, it was time to focus on building a sales army and become a mini-Monte.

In a past life, I would have immediately texted one of my friends or my parents without thinking. Renee and Ira would be happy for me, but I could wait to tell them after work. My friends? If I had scrolled through my contacts, I knew I would feel jolts of guilt as I read the names in my "Favorites," some who would have helped me hide a dead body a year ago. Now, they probably would have answered, "Insurance is ugly and so is your face," or something. The thing was, it wasn't my parents or my friends who I initially thought to reach out to.

Well, looks like I'm no longer just an 'agent.'

Nicholas Kingsley answered me almost instantly: *I know. Who do you think approved the request for your promotion?*

Me: *You approved my promotion? You knew about this?*

Nicholas: *Yes, the regional director always signs off on any agent being promoted to management. I've known for a couple of weeks.*

Me: *A couple of weeks??? And you didn't tell me???*

Nicholas: *No, silly. It was supposed to be a surprise ;)*

Before I could answer, Monte switched from babbling about rehashing office memos to something which interested me more.

"Gang, get ready to pack your snappiest suits. We're headed back to Pittsburgh in two weeks for the quarterly recognition meeting."

Like most companies in the industry, D'Angelo Enterprises hosted quarterly meeting at a very upscale hotel in downtown Pittsburgh... you know, one which was frequented by corporate executives of Fortune 500 companies. Besides the glamour of being surrounded by the agency's richest and flashiest professionals along with their supremely dressed arm candy, there was something else. Nicholas Kingsley would be there. The same Nicholas Kingsley who had just called me silly and used a wink face emoticon.

"Okay, Jayden," Monte said as I walked into his office that evening during the phone session. He wanted to give me a quick run-down of what was expected from me as a manager versus being an agent.

"I wouldn't have promoted you if I didn't think you were 100% ready for this," he began. "But things are going to change a little in terms of your focus. So as an agent, you learned how to grind and make sales. Now, it's time to build a team so we can get you out of the field." He smiled as he said this, knowing this is the big motivational to make everyone hustle hard. "Every day, you're here at 8:00am to recruit. This is absolutely vital..." He continued to go through a list of additional responsibilities that were now being put on my plate. I nodded where appropriate and mentally started figuring out how the hell I was going to get up at the crack of dawn every day and be in the office at 8:00am. Not 8:02, 8:00am. He meant business. Maybe at 8:05 if my sales were stellar. Which was another thing- I needed to now recruit new agents, train them, and generate enough sales to hit my own quotas. The first person I needed to get ahold of was Veronica. I shot her a text as soon as I left Monte's office:

Hey girl, I got promoted today. Good-bye life and hello longer hours. When are you meeting your guy? I need you to bake extra cookies.

I now had to text in code to Veronica because she was paranoid of the cops intercepting the texts. She was bizarre.

Awesome job! Yeah I'm meeting him in a couple days, I'll let you know.

I looked in my purse and opened my container, which was now an empty mint case. I had enough to get through another week easily. Okay, I was safe. It was only 5:00pm, which meant I had another four hours until I could go home. Making phone calls for another four hours was the last thing I wanted to do. *If I had a little pick me up it won't be so bad*, I thought to myself. And so I did just that. I slipped half of an orange piece of euphoria and let the bitterness roll on my tongue. For the next four hours, I was the most chipper agent in the office. When everyone took a break from their phone calls for pizza, compliments of Monte? Pshh. Not that I'd ever eat pizza anyway, but I kept zooming along, setting one of the best schedules I'd had in weeks. *Salads set up schedules with sales, pizza just put on the pounds.* It was my mantra.

■ ■ ■

Over the next few days, I found myself reaching out to Nick more often for more than just professional purposes. In the car, it was just Pandora and me. Oh, and my cell phone. *Next year I'll give up texting and driving,* I told myself. Everyone else did it. The shit our brains tell ourselves to rationalize our less than stellar actions, habits, or beliefs. It's kind of disgusting. Our text messaging was pretty generic. I would make comments on how a presentation I had just sat through was in a house with a smelly dad and a wife with missing teeth or how I was jealous the weather was sunny and warm in Florida and we were stuck with unrelenting April snow flurries. At the end of the day once I was back in the comfort of my parent's kitchen, I would scan back through the text thread, standing at the island digging a fork through my massive container of the chemical filled, calorie-emptied chocolate ice-cream.

    Being that I had just been promoted, it was now my responsibility more than ever to absorb as much knowledge as possible at all times. And somehow, Nicholas's contact information was just extremely accessible in my list of text messages. Not that there were too many threads in the list anyway. I had long since given up on contacting my friends throughout the work day and usually ignored their calls unless I knew it was something dire. I was in the car alone with no one to monitor what I was doing but the voices in my head telling me I should be listening to sales books on audio, calling prospects, or listening to 'pump-up' music- anything to keep me focused at the twenty-five hour work day at hand. Listening to Friend A's boy troubles or letting her gossip about Friends B and C was not going to further my success. At this point not even friends D, E, or F wanted anything to do with me anyway. I was an insurance junkie, only caring about my next high of a sale. In fact, I was such a junkie, that I had even tried to persuade all of my friends to become users (become a part of my team, or at least buy a policy) which repulsed them about as much as fucking the guys who swiped their V-cards. Needless to say, they were over calling and texting me for a good chit chat. No one calls the insurance junkie.

One night, I was this close to falling asleep when my phone rang. I looked at the I.D. and answered, surprised.

"Hello?" I yawned into the phone.

"What's up, Miss Rosenberg?" Mr. Kingsley asked enthusiastically. I looked at my clock next to my bed. It was just after midnight.

"Well, Mr. Kingsley. What are you doing up at this hour?" I was caught off guard and witty banter just wasn't rolling off my tongue.

"I was out selling all day. Giovanni wanted higher numbers out of my office, so I had to play ball. Were you sleeping, Jayden? You sound tired."

"Because it's midnight. It's a school night. You're going to make me sleep through my alarm."

"I'm waking up at 5:00, when are you getting up?" he asked.

"I can do 5:00. Want to call me and make sure I'm up?" I asked. That wasn't something I would normally do, but it just felt natural to ask for that favor for some reason. Coworkers called each other to wake up, right? I was already Monte's human alarm clock calling him to get up and get to the gym as I was already mid push-up (which is extremely difficult to do, trust me).

"Yes, I can do that," he said. "Get some sleep eye, champ."

This was normal, right? Having my boss's boss wake me up at the crack of dawn? It's not like it was going to be a social call. Just a very direct reminder to get my ass out of bed.

My heart palpitated when the ringing scared me into consciousness at 5:00am on the dot with Nicholas Kingsley's name on the caller id.

"Hello," I croaked into the phone. I felt a rush of nervousness, as though he could see me in a vulnerable state with bed head and cotton mouth. I've never been one to wake up and claim to look like Beyoncé.

"Are you out of bed, Jayden?" This man was all business at all hours.

"How could I be out of bed already?" I whined. "I just opened my eyes. You said 5:00am as a wake-up call. Don't I get a couple minutes before the get up part?"

"No, the getting part is implied in the wake-up call part. Get out of bed, Jayden." Something about the way he said my name spurred me to actually sit up and swing my legs so my feet landed on the carpet.

"Fine, you win," I said, walking to the bathroom to brush my teeth. You know, in case he could smell my cottonmouth on the other end.

"I always do," Nick said.

■ ■ ■

Come to Center Bar, I'm buying you a drink to celebrate! Monte texted me the Saturday after I was promoted. Center Bar was creatively named for the fact that it was in the center of downtown. But being this was Grayton, our choices weren't exactly plentiful. So we rotated a selection of bars based on which boys were at which location. I had just gotten home from a long day of work. It was almost seven. There was no way I was going anywhere unless I got a good nap in. God, I loved my Saturday evening naps. Crawling into bed knowing that I wasn't going to be waking up for a work out at the crack of dawn, but rather that I was going to be refreshed with a vodka bottle dangling itself at my fingertips. I texted Monte back and told him I would be out later, that I needed to pass out for a minute. I could skip out on the pre-gaming. He texted me back reminding me that I was crazy and he would see me there. Of course I'm crazy. What sane person works these hours?

I texted my friend Lana and Veronica to come with me, but apparently they had taken a last minute road trip to New York to visit one of Veronica's friends who was trying to break into modeling.

Sorry we didn't invite you, we knew you would be working late! they texted me after explaining where they were. I got the feeling that somehow they weren't sorry and then passed right out, without even taking the time to feel hurt. I threw my phone on my nightstand and rolled over, knowing my bed would never disappoint me.

"Sweetness," I heard Renee's voice, "get your *ass* in gear if you want to meet your friends tonight." I looked at the clock, which read 9:30pm and groaned. My mom had taken on the responsibility of making sure I didn't sleep my entire Saturday night away, which I probably would have. Feeling completely disoriented, I grabbed half of an orange pill from the stash in my nightstand after she shut the door. Thank God I wasn't responsible for hyping myself up; I had these bad boys to do it for me. *Outsourcing,* I rationalized. Instead of focusing time and energy on trying to change my mental state or doing jumping jacks and shit, I was just paying for a pill to get that rush for me.

I stared at the clock which kept ticking away. Time seemed to slip away quicker each day, no matter how early I got out of bed. The familiar feeling of being rushed came over me and too tired to care, I walked up to my closet and stared at the familiar pieces of clothing, each staring at me and jogging back old memories of college and my early 20s. "*Remember that time you wore me, got really wasted and tripped over that crack in the cement and cut your hands on the way to a frat party?/ used me as a cover up on your international flight while you watched old movies?/ silhouetted your figure as you had drinks with that pony-tailed Israeli in that bar on Dizengoff Street?"* No, I told myself. *That was another time. Your life has taken a different turn. Plus, you started to get some cellulite from all that damn falafel.*

I went for what my high school best friend Mika refer to as sexy hit woman: black on black on black. Tonight, that meant skinny black jeans, a long blank tank top, peep-toe booties with gold zippers and a new present from my Mom, a black leather motorcycle jacket. I'd be cold, but whatever. To accessorize my look, I stacked on some obnoxious rings and slipped on big gold earrings. Mika would have been so proud of my outfit, if only she were here. But instead, she was in Manhattan having an affair with someone in her office who was engaged. My friends who had made it out of Grayton were doing such cool shit with their lives...*Stop. You are on a pathway to success, you will be in a different place one day too with a fat bank account. Focus, Jayden,* I thought, admiring my profile. Hmmm, my butt isn't quite as circular as it used to be. It was more streamlined. Too bad the disappearing ass didn't go to my boobs. Oh well, can't have it all.

I took one last look in the mirror. The nap did me well, except my eyes were still a little red. Trying to move quickly, I clambered down the stairs, the clanking of my pointy heels across the hardwood floors announcing my departure.

I yelled good-bye to my parents who were in the family room watching TV, but I wasn't getting out so easily.

"Come sit here just for a minute, Jayden," Ira said to me, not unkindly.

"Am I in trouble?" I asked, something I have done since I was about three.

"No, not at all," he said as I plopped on the grandfather chair across from him. I hoped this was going to be a quick minute because I was starting to itch for a drink and could start to feel that body buzz from the piece of the pill I had chomped on.

"Is it really worth it, honey? Working all these hours? I mean you barely see your friends and every night you come home so tired and we never know when you're coming in," he started. Well this was a buzz kill.

"Dad, I really don't have time for this right now. Look, I'm making a lot of money and this won't be forever. One day I won't have to be running appointments, I'll be like Monte where everyone else does the work and I kick back and just you know, run everything."

"Okay, and how long did that take Monte to do?" he asked sternly.

"A year, Dad. I'm learning from the best."

"Well, you have been doing this six months. How much longer can you sustain these crazy work weeks? Don't you want to just pack up your shit and get out of here already?" How do dads have the best timing ever?

"Dad, seriously, I have to go. I'll move when they open a new office in a few months. That's what they told me. It's my only night out. We'll talk later," and with that I got up as my mom sat back down.

"Fine, if this makes you happy, Jayden," he said as I opened the side door to step into the garage. *Don't start with the happy stuff...*

"I'm going to drink. That will make me happy," I answered, and shut the door. I couldn't win. Either I was a lazy, broke bum, or I was working too hard and needed to slow down. Slow down? I could hear Giovanni's past lectures in my head, "Don't slow down now. Don't lose that momentum. Push through the pain to get to greatness."

Whatever my father did to reach success worked in his day, but Giovanni's vigor was like an extra fire bolt in the batteries charging the ambition I had. The men I worked with enabled me to think bigger. I loved my father, but maybe he just didn't know what it took to make it in today's world of business. Apparently I knew what it took: sixty-five plus hours of grinding a week, and pills to grind through my teeth along with it.

∎ ∎ ∎

I relished the wide-eyed greeting I received from the table full of male managers as I walked into what Grayton could pull off as a swanky bar. They were dressed in faded jeans and ridiculous t-shirts that meatheads buy in bulk, chugging draft beers, which of course were washing down the protein shakes they downed after their late afternoon lift sessions at the gym. The exception was Monte, who wore dark wash jeans and although he kept on a dress shirt, he had ditched the tie, and sat energetically holding a high ball glass with what I was guessing to be a scotch on the rocks.

"Damn, girl," Joey said as I slid into the seat next to him.

"You were allowed off the leash tonight?" I asked jokingly. Joey's live-in-girlfriend, who was also the mother of his absolutely precious four year old daughter, was not a fan of Joey going out for escapades. Being only twenty-three, he was constantly torn between being a family man and just wanting to go out and living a night of sin.

"JayJay, what do you want to drink?" Monte asked, standing up to make his way to the bar.

"Kettel and club with a lime please." Obviously. Knowing that his previous paycheck could have paid for a handbag that celebrities are put on waiting lists for, I didn't feel so terrible ordering top shelf liquor.

"You got it girl," he said smiling and strolled over confidently to the bar, a simple head nod grabbing the waiter's attention.

"Where are your hot friends at Jayden?" Joey asked me. I knew he was on the visual prowl.

"Apparently they're in New York," I said.

"Lame," Joey said pouting at me. I pulled out my phone and held it up.

Leaning into Joey, I said, "Smile. Let's take a pic." One drink down and I was already snapping a stupid selfie. Lord knew how the rest of the evening would pan out. We examined what the iPhone lens captured.

"God I'm sexy," Joey declared. I had to agree. Not bad for an over-worked insurance guy. I copied the photo into a text with the caption *Do the Florida managers have any fun?* and hit Send.

Texting Nick is trouble, the voice of reason inside my head said. *Fuck you voice of reason,* my other voice said.

"Who are you sending that to?" Joey asked as I put my phone down.

"Don't worry about it," I said putting my phone back in my purse, knowing I would just stare at it waiting for a response.

"I was told to give you the Kettel and club with a *lime*," I heard in my ear as a tall glass was set right in front of me.

Without turning, I took the lime in between my thumb and middle finger and squeezed it around the stirrer it was speared through.

"I like the tart kick the lime adds," I said, staring straight into Alex Reyes's eyes.

"Matches your personality, I guess," he said sitting in the seat next to me. His red button down shirt made his features even more distinct than I had remembered them. Like Monte, he was also drinking the hard stuff straight.

"Johnnie Walker," he said, noticing that I was eyeing his glass. "Your street cred would go way up if you were drinking this."

"I'm not really worried about my street cred, Alex. Where's Monte?" I asked, wishing he had brought back my drink which had seemed to be the original plan.

"He had to take a phone call. So he asked me to bring over the drink he bought you. That was generous of him, wasn't it?"

"Yes, it was." I looked down at my glass suddenly feeling uncomfortable. His appearance threw me off guard, which translated to a knot formed in my stomach. "What are you doing here?" I asked him, trying to turn the table.

"Making my rounds, Jayden. And stopping by to see my friends." His friends happened to be the managers at the table of course, who were engrossed in a debate over whose trainee sucked the most that week. It was a toss-up between the college grad who thought he literally knew *everything* and the single mom who had permanent P.M.S.

"Yeah, I heard you're pretty good at making rounds," I said rolling my eyes. My comment completely rolled off his back.

"The perks of working in nightlife," he said as he took a swig of his Johnnie and winked at me.

"Hmm, sounds just like the perks of working the insurance industry," I said smirking. "Although, some of the girls in our office dress like they're ready to go bar hopping. Maybe they come to work straight from your place?" I asked.

"Aww, jealous?" he asked me, leaning in much closer. He was now in what I refer to as the box. *No, not that box-* the physical area around you which is a protective comfort zone. I don't like anyone being in the box unless it is someone I am very comfortable being around. Alex Reyes had completely crossed over the box's borderline. But I couldn't back away. His stare completely paralyzed me and I knew that could only mean trouble for me.

"Not. One. Bit." I said, praying my voice was confident because a part of me didn't believe the words and I had no idea why. Wasn't his bad boy charm reserved for impressionable naive college girls?

"What are you doing here tonight with all of *my* friends anyway?" he asked trying to get the upper hand back. Apparently, Joey had been half listening and turned away from the managers' conversation for a moment and answered Alex on my behalf.

"Dude, she just got promoted," he said, putting his arm around me.

"This broad's been closing some serious deals," Joey added.

"Joey you don't do so bad yourself," I said winking at him. I took a sip of my drink and could another surge of that rush coming from the half of a pill I took earlier. And now I wanted more.

"Climbing the corporate ladder, I see?" Alex asked. I looked up and saw Monte walking back towards our table with Scarlett. She wasn't exactly walking steadily, which meant she must have just come from another bar, several drinks past everyone else. I didn't care, I was just grateful there was someone to save me from this testosterone fest.

"Got your drink?" Monte asked as he sat down.

"Yes, your friend was nice enough to bring it over," I said looking right at Alex. Scarlett immediately rushed up and threw her arms around him, giving him a big "*Alexxxxxxx!!!?*" greeting. As she stumbled and teetered on her heels, I was guessing she was about four beers and three shots of fireball deep by now.

Alex smiled and gave her a kiss on the cheek. The attention he got didn't even faze him.

"Scarlett, let's go to the bathroom," I said, grabbing her arm so that she didn't have any time to disagree with me.

"Did you drive here?" I asked seriously as soon as we walked into the vast bathroom which surprisingly empty.

"It was only a couple of blocks," Scarlett muttered as she played with her hair in the mirror. "Scarlett, you have to stop being so stupid. It doesn't take much to get caught," I said, turning away from her to open my lipstick holder and slip another half of a pill into my mouth. Miss Wasted Face wasn't paying attention and was still playing with her hair.

"Jayden, stop being up tight. Relax, let's go have fun for once. Before you know it we will have wrinkles and we will wish we had taken advantage of being young."

"You'll never let getting old stop us from having fun. Plus, we'll be rich enough for Botox. Remember, we're going to be running an office? I won't have to worry about you drinking and getting behind the wheel because you will have a chauffeur."

"Stop worrying about me!" she said as we walked out the door and back to our table. Alex was walking straight towards us alone. Then again, guys don't go to the restroom in herds like ladies have the need to.

"I love what you've done with the place, Alex. I'm going to get a drink," Scarlett said and continued to walk back towards the bar.

"What did Scarlett mean when she said that?" I asked before he could walk away.

"I own the bar, Jayden," he said, his voice missing its usual cocky tone.

"And Blue Moon?" I asked.

"Don't forget about the Sandwich Shack," he added. I wanted to throw up. Here I was thinking I'm Joe-Cool for getting promoted to an entry level management position. Of course it was drilled into our heads that because we were 1099 workers, that made us "business owners," but really all I owned were some killer shoes.

"All of them?" I squeaked. I felt my knee buckle and I leaned against the wall. A drop of sweat started to run down my arm. It was a pretty common side effect from the pills. Thank God I was wearing black-on-black-on-black for pit stain protection.

"All of them. I'm everywhere, Jayden." *Yeah, apparently you are, Alex. And in every girl's skirts too.*

"How did you have the money to invest in all these places?" I asked boldly. My boldness didn't throw him off track one inch.

"I learned how to save when I was very young," he said as he stepped forward, closing in on my space, crossing over my personal comfort zone border. Why was he so close?

"Oh." Something changed in his face. His eyes became softer. I felt my heart racing and decided to throw a verbal wall up before he was close enough to hear the pounding in my chest.

"So, that's the kind of person you are, one who makes their dough by getting others wasted?" I might have been lower on the financial corporate ladder but at least I was making a real difference in peoples' lives. Right?

"Jayden, there's more ways to help people than just making sure there's money around when someone is dead."

"It's easy to give people alcohol to drown out their problems," I said. "What I actually do prevents the real problems when the worst day of their life comes," I counted.

"How about giving people a place to go to create memories with their friends. Isn't that what you're doing now?"

"Not if they get too drunk and forget their night, or do something regrettably irreversible." His eyes darkened when I mentioned the regrettably irreversible part, but he didn't act on whatever thoughts were in his head.

"Is it worth it, Jayden? The sleepless nights, long hours, the stress? Just to give yourself another title? And then another one?"

"How would you know? Not like you ever worked at D'Angelo Enterprises. You don't know what my weeks are like." But he was spot on.

"I'm friends with those guys you work with, don't forget. And I can see it in your eyes. They're bloodshot. When's the last time you really slept without worrying about how soon your alarm was going to go off? Or even ate a real meal at a restaurant?" He took his fingers and wrapped them around my arm. "Look how skinny you are." I swallowed hard. I didn't want to hear this crap. Sacrifice was necessary for success. And if you are a woman, so is being skinny. His words could not get in my head, I wouldn't let them.

"I doubt Sandwich Shack is about to close because of my lack of business. I'm fine," I said sternly, flinching my arm out of his grasp.

"You think you're cut out for this. Your skin isn't thick enough. Just wait. You'll break one day." I felt tear drops starting to water in my eye ducts but I forced them to retract before they could stream down my face. I couldn't let Alex have any satisfaction of getting to me. I bit my lip to keep it from quivering.

"You're beautiful, but you're still naive, Jayden."

"You seem to have plenty of less than desirable qualities, but I don't feel like wasting my time listing them." Without waiting for whatever he might have had the need to say, I walked straight to the bar where I ordered another vodka soda and two shots of Patron for Scarlett and me. Sobriety was no longer in the cards for me that evening.

I paid for the drinks and called Scarlett's name, holding up the shot of tequila. She smiled and held up a finger to signal she would be right over. I pulled my phone out of my purse and saw that I had a text back from Nick. I practically forgot I had even messaged him.

He sent a picture of one of the other managers and him holding fluorescent colored drinks with the caption : *More than you do.*

Hmmmm, not so fast I wrote back, taking a picture of the shot glasses and my drink.

We weren't flirting, just competing as to who was having the better Saturday night out. Sales people are always competing whether it's about their weekly numbers or who can do more push-ups. So this was no different, obviously.

"Who are you texting?" Scarlett asked seeing my face was nose to iPhone screen.

"Don't worry about it," I said, putting my phone back in my purse.

"It's Nicholas, isn't it?"

"No, why would you think that?" I am so bad at lying.

"Because you have that weird smile on your face that you always get when you text him."

"Umm, I always smile weirdly. Because I'm just weird."

I handed Scarlett her shot. "To getting paid and getting laid," we said at the same time before knocking back our tequila. She slung the shot back with the finesse of a true binge drinker.

"Ahhh I can't believe you made me do a tequila shot," she said contorting her face.

"Yeah, I'm so terrible for buying us top shelf tequila. I know you love me."

We spent the rest of the night glued to our bar stools, never letting our glasses sit empty. At one point Scarlett was telling a story to the bartenders and I extracted another half of a pill from my clutch to keep me from being overly sloppy. Scarlett and I envisioned our lives as masters of an office far away, somewhere with palm trees and a Whole Foods. Although I doubted Scarlett knew what Whole Foods was. We had decided we wanted our office to be like *Mad Men,* but with more modern couches. And if Jon Hamm could make an appearance, that would be even better.

Just as we were deciding to have mini fridges with celery sticks (me), imported bottled beer (Scarlett), and cans of club soda for the vodka filled decanters (both of us), I felt someone else's back press into mine suddenly. I turned around as that someone tossed a long mane of hair over her shoulders and a few strands brushed across my face. Although I could only see the back of her, I knew the chic was a wannabe Barbie judging by the hot pink bandage dress I caught a glimpse of. And then, she let out a cackle-giggle, that god awful laugh girls make when a guy is flirting with them.

"Alex, you're soooo bad," I heard her coo. I craned my neck further. Alex was standing in front of her, fingering some enormous and obviously fake diamond bracelet wrapped around her wrist.

She continued to babble on with some story, but Alex locked eyes with me, staring passed her. Barbie just didn't realize it, she was too into herself. *I bet Nick would never entertain himself with someone this cheap,* I thought to myself. "Let's get out of here," I said to Scarlett, deciding I didn't want front row seats to this show anymore. I faced away, flagging down the bartender to pay my tab. I was so drunk I didn't even flinch when I saw the amount. As I waited to get my card back, I looked at my phone hoping for a text back from Nick. Nothing. I could get as drunk as I wanted to, but going home alone at the end of the night inevitably resulted in loneliness. And unless I was drunk to the point of being unconscious, no amount of booze or pills could make that feeling go away. At least in the cab ride home, the loneliness feeling dissipated and was replaced with numbness.

...

My pounding head the next morning was a reminder as to why it's a plain stupid idea to drown your emotions with shots and strong drinks. The fireballs I was trying to throw at Alex Reyes only ended up burning me. I was angry I lost control of myself and gave him that much power, even if he didn't know it directly. Why did he get under my skin so much? He wasn't anything but a club and sandwich shop owner who got his kicks from the attention the dime a dozen wannabes. Clearly, his depth didn't reach anything past appreciating a good Brazilian wax. His words were nothing but background noise and I wouldn't let that turn down the sweet sound of success. No, Alex Reyes couldn't dial down the volume.

I reached over to grab my phone to see if there were any embarrassing texts I sent once I had passed tipsy and entered the black-out drunk phase. During college, the amount of times I sent morning messages of "Sorry, I was hammered," was not something I would want to count. Instead, I had a new message from Nick Kingsley. *I'm hurting pretty badly myself.*

I looked above his text and saw I had texted him at 2:37am saying, *Stupiddd drunkk. food time :)* Well, there were worse things one could say, I thought. Stumbling into the kitchen after getting out of the cab popped into my mind followed by lunging for the freezer to grab that crap ice-cream I eat along with a fork, of course.

You're an asshole, Alex, I had said to myself as I stabbed the frozen chemicals and popped a heaping forkful in my mouth. It was easier to focus on the satisfaction this industrialized chocolate flavor was giving me instead of the bitterness or whatever it was nagging in my chest, the same place my heart was.

At some point, when the satisfaction turned into fullness and guilt, I threw the fork in the sink as thought it was something dangerous needing to be destroyed. I wouldn't have dared to entertain the notion the only thing destructive in that kitchen was me.

No wonder I worked so hard. It was unsettling to deal with the thoughts in my head whenever I had a minute to myself.

No more hitting the bottle for this girl... I typed to Nick.

We'll see about that ;) he answered almost instantly.

Was Nicholas Kingsley flirting with me?

CHAPTER 9

On Monday I woke up about 85% hangover free and sweated out the remaining 15% at the gym. It was game time. No more dealing with bullshit but focusing in on the one thing I wanted: success. I was newly promoted and ready to kill it. Whatever I was supposed to kill I wasn't quite sure of, but I had my guns out. This was going through my head as I added an extra twenty minutes on the stair master. That little ice-cream mishap the other night was not going to show up as mush on my thighs. After my legs felt like Jell-O and it seemed as if my next breath might be my last, I decided it might be a good time to get in the shower. I did have that office to be at, anyway. *Dying, but I sweat it out at the gym. Go me,* I texted Nick. And then I wished there was an Unsend button. Why did I have to act impulsively and communicate the most pointless insights about my day? *You are cray cray*, I thought to myself.

Once I had popped my morning pill and washed it down with a giant iced coffee, I resumed my superstar mentality. It lasted a whole forty-three minutes until it was interrupted by a text message a text message.

I bet you sweat real hard. I was so taken aback, my phone slipped and landed with a smack on my desk. I began rummaging through my drawers, looking for something to distract me from this unexpected message.

"Jayyyyyden," I heard from the other side of the corkboard cubicle.

"What's going on over there?" Joey asked with drawn out words.

"Nothing, why?" I answered, clearly

"You're huffing, puffing, and throwing shit."

"So call me the big bad wolf, then."

Too bad I didn't realize I was dealing with a big bad wolf with razor-sharp teeth.

■ ■ ■

We should get dinner when we're in Pittsburgh was a text message I woke up to on the Sunday before I was going to leave for Pittsburgh. I hadn't gone out the night before because I didn't get home from work until after 9:00pm and my body was screaming for my bed, even though I had pumped in a total of three Adderall over the course of the day.

"Maaaa!!!!" I called from my bed, at a volume I was certain she could hear, like any traditionally raised JAP would do. I needed her to read this.

"Whaaaat?!!!" I heard Renee yell back from her bedroom.

"I need you!" *Please work. This used to when I was little.*

"Jesus Christ, Jayden, I gotta get in the shower, your father wants to go wine tasting today," I heard her say as her footsteps approached my room. She opened the door, wearing the lavender Ralph Lauren terry cloth robe and matching slippers I bought her for Chanukah. Even though she wasn't wearing a stitch of make-up, I always thought she was beautiful. Hands down, she aged the best of all the moms I knew. I prayed that I had inherited the same age defying genetics. Her hair was perfectly styled, a custom-colored blend of chestnut brown with honey highlights. My dad totally hit the jackpot with her.

"What is it?" she asked impatiently, but I knew she was loving the fact that I, her little girl, still needed her.

"I got a text from Nick." I had been keeping my mom up to date on this whole texting thing. Not a woman to follow the rules, she was totally for pursuing this whatever-this-texting-business was turning into.

"*Nu?*" She asked, raising her eyebrows and grinning. "Nu" was her favorite Yiddish expression and she used it more than was necessary. I showed her my phone and she immediately pinched my cheek. "Ooh, sweetness!" as she always called me when she got excited about something in my life. "What are you going to wear?"

"I don't know yet! But you gave me an idea of what to say back."

You just want an excuse to see me in a dress I replied back to his text.

"Jayden, you're so bad!" my mom said, overlooking my shoulder.

'Really? Who did I get it from?" I asked her. Nick answered my text right away.

Maybe ;) let's call it a celebration for your promotion. I knew there was no way in hell he was taking out every agent who got promoted.

He suggested going to Ruth's Chris but the thought of sitting through seventeen courses with an abundance of silverware where you need proper posture and manners was not what I had in mind. I went to college in Pittsburgh, so I still knew the city's scene to a degree. So I kindly made a suggestion to go to a hibachi place I loved in the South Side, which he completely went for, thankfully. *When the hell was the last time I went on a real date? Two years ago? By a guy who ended up dumping me on my birthday who now delivers pizza?*

Yes, this was definitely an upgrade. But how would they end the night? An awkward hug and hailing a cab for me? That didn't exactly rile me up, but anything else would just be ridiculously inappropriate, right?

As it turned out, a few days later, I got my answer, an inappropriate one. Wednesday morning, while I was working with the trainee on that god forsaken script, my phone rang. It was Nicholas Kingsley.

"I'll be right back, Amanda," I said, hugging the phone to my chest so she couldn't see who it was and ran into the hall, away from the masses of nosey people.

"Heyyy," I said, trying to sound completely casual, not crazy or anything.

"Hey," he said quickly. I had a feeling this phone call was one with a purpose. "So, about this weekend. Where are you staying Saturday?"

"Ummm," I had to think fast, being that I had absolutely no idea where my ass was ending up that night. "I'm planning on staying with one of my college friends, I just haven't picked the lucky one yet."

"I was going to stay with Cal but I decided to get a room in Southside near the restaurants and bars."

"Oh, really?" I asked, my voice climbing a few notes higher than I had intended. "That sounds like a good idea," I added, not really sure what to say.

"You can stay with me there." He was assuming the sale. God he was good.

"Okaaay," I stuttered. "Just as long as you sleep in the bathtub."

Scarlett was going to shit herself when I told her what I was getting into.

...

"Jayden, you guys are just mutually attracted to each other. There is no marriage proposal or even a condom being ripped open... if people still even use those." Scarlett rolled her eyes at me as she simultaneously continued to roll her beautifully crafted joint. She usually smokes out of her bowl, Bertha, which was named for its ugly color. She figured she would never meet someone with a name as ugly as Bertha, so it would never be offensive to anyone. But she was offensive all the time, so I don't know why that was a factor.

"Scar, I know, but you know how these assholes are. They think because they have big bank accounts that automatically their dicks are supersized and we're just supposed to drop our panties and spread our legs."

"Yeah, that's true. They're all fucking assholes."

She passed me the joint and I took a deep hit. I stared at the joint and wondered out loud, "Do you think Nick has a big dick?"

"I don't know. I mean he's so tall. That would just be so awful of G-d to make him that huge and that stick an acorn size dick on him. Just wouldn't be right you know?"

"Oh Scarlett listen to us! He's like our boss! This is ridiculous."

"Jayden who cares. Besides, they sit around wondering who's got a golden box underneath their dress."

"Scar, what is a golden box?"

"My god Jayden, you're twenty-five not fifty-two, come on!"

"What?!"

"If you have a golden box it just means you have a nice pussy."

"Well, I sure hope so! I mean I've never had any complaints anyway."

"Then you're fine. Just make sure you're wearing hot underwear."

"Ugh, this is stressing me out."

∎ ∎ ∎

No expectations, no expectations, I told myself as I meticulously blow dried and straightened my hair. The only person who knew what I was about to do from work was Scarlett and I knew she would keep her mouth shut on this. And my dad? When I told him what the figure from Nick's 1099 statement was from last year and the extent of his managerial control, I think he was ready to draft a dowry. Granted, had Nick been the manager of an Arby's, my parents would have been singing a much different tune.

Before I hit the road, I made my religious stop at Dunkin Donuts for some caffeine to go along with the pharmaceutical pick-me-up. As usual, my girl Shaniqua was waiting at the window to hand out the coffee and swipe my plastic. My trainee met her one afternoon and introduced me a few days later while I treated us to an evening caffeine boost on a phone night.

"Girl, I've never seen you in no sweatpants before, whatchu doing? Don't you work Saturdays?"

"I do, but Shaniqua. I'm doing something bad." She perked right up. I was always the goodie-goodie who worked too damn much but made enough Dunkin stops to run the place single handedly.

"What are you gonna do?"

"I'm going to Pittsburgh and going on a date with my boss's boss."

"Oh shit. Damn girl, you got yo' self a man!"

"Stop, I don't have anything yet. Shaniqua, I'm so fucking nervous."

"Get yo' ass goin' girl and tell me everything when you get back!"

This ass had to get some gas first, so I pulled into the Sheetz which was only about half of a mile down the road. Being quite the rebel, I didn't dare tell Monte I was skipping out of town early. This was the equivalent of a misdemeanor in my book and the guilt was making me feel wiped. My day hadn't even started and all I wanted to do was take a nap. Real criminals must have some serious stamina. I locked the gas pump in the tank and ran inside the gas station to grab a bottle of water for the road. As I was deliberating intently whether I should purchase Smart or Fiji bottled water. I felt a tap and my shoulder and jumped.

"Scare easily?" that damned voice. I looked up and Alex Reyes was apparently devilishly pleased to have scared the shit out of me.

"Maybe. What are you doing here?"

"Jayden, it's a gas station that sells food. Lots of people come here. Now, what are *you* doing here dressed in sweatpants? It's Saturday morning. Monte would kill you if he knew you weren't in an appointment right now." Fuck, I was caught red handed. I was never good at playing hooky and now ten years later I wasn't any better at skipping work.

"My day finished early!" I said trying to think on my toes.

"Bullshit. I know you go until at least 5:00 on a Saturday. It's only 11:00am. What are you up to?"

"Why do you care?"

"Whoa, killer.." He picked up two bottles of Smart water.

"Here. You're looking a little stupid," he said with a wink and putting one of them into my hand. "No, that would be your Friday night girl," I said, taking the bottle as I rolled my eyes.

"I didn't give her an IQ test, but she got the job done."

"Wow, you're such a romantic." *At least you're not stuck with him. You're going to dinner with Nicholas Kingsley*, I thought.

"Well, I have places to be Alex, which are more desirable than listening to who gets to shift around your joystick."

"Oh, so you're doing something you shouldn't be doing, then?" *How did he know?* I must have worn that question on my face because he answered it. "Don't worry, I'm not going to run to Monte. He has more important shit to worry about than having a GPS on you, Jayden." I let the GPS comment slide, but it stung a bit.

"No, I'm just going to Pittsburgh a day earlier than everyone else from the office."

"Why?"

"I went to college there. I figured I'd take an extra day and catch up with some friends who still live there. It's not like I have tons of time off." I said it resentfully, and I realized I felt that way as well. I hadn't taken any time for myself in over six months and here I was trying to keep my one half day away from work a secret.

"No, you guys definitely don't." He motioned me to follow him to the register, where he paid for both of the bottles of water. The fluctuations between his prickly comments and sudden acts of generosity were not easy to keep up with. What did he want from me?

"I don't know, Jayden. Something tells me you're not telling the truth," he said staring intently at my face as if he could read my thoughts. He was wearing a fitted short sleeve v-neck white t-shirt, which only emphasized his creamed-coffee skin tone and ridiculous biceps. I'm not a meathead chaser, but I do appreciate a man who keeps his body in check. It's something about the visible protectiveness they could provide. Call me primal, I guess.

"You're ridiculous, Alex." He didn't relent.

"I don't know about you, Jayden. I don't know about you." I stared at him for a moment, knowing if I said anything too fast, something too emotional might slip out.

"It's okay, I won't lose any sleep over what you do or don't know. Thanks for the water," I said holding up the bottle and started to walk towards the door. It was my weekend, some designer jean wearing male chauvinist didn't get to run the show. But he was faster than me. Alex grabbed my wrist and yanked on it just enough to force me from walking away.

"You're good, Jayden. In fact, you're probably the best they've seen in a while. Just enjoy it while it lasts. Someone better always comes along. And then you will just be a name on a plaque in the supplies closet."

I looked at him and was determined to give nothing but an icy, unemotional stare as flames of fury burned in my chest. I couldn't tell if he was being sinister or had some sick idea of conveying concern, but I didn't want to stick around to figure it out.

"I better go. You know, to make sure the plaque ends up on the wall and not next to the vacuum cleaner in the closet."

I walked with a pace bordering on a jog and jumped into my car, my hand already in my purse before I started the engine. I opened the lipstick tube holder and felt the immediate relief seeing those little circles smiling at me. With a burned ego and three hundred miles ahead of me, I decided a full pill was what I deserved. I put it in my mouth, hating the bitter taste but knowing the elated feeling would come faster than if I swallowed the pill with water. *Who did Alex think he was, getting all Nostradamus and predicting I would become some washed up has been?* I started the car and followed the signs for Interstate 80, my foot much harder on the gas pedal than it should been.

Forget about Alex, he's just trying to knock you off your game. You're smarter than to fall for that dumb shit.

As soon as I passed a car who was pulled over by an undercover cop, I decided to heed it as a warning sign and slowed down. It was going to be a long drive, no need to get in trouble this early into the journey.

Reciting your times tables is more inspiring than driving on 80 West and soon enough, no matter whichever old school rap song I had blasting, Alex's words played in my head on repeat. He even managed to creep in between the beats of the song that always got me to lift my head high. *Na-na-na Diva is a female version of a hustla… of a hustla… of a hustla...*

Even Beyonce, the queen herself, couldn't block that sucker out of my head.

What felt like thirteen hours later, I finally passed the Oakland exit for Pitt's campus. I began to veer off to the right before I realized that wasn't my exit anymore. Maybe if I took the Forbes Ave. exit and turned onto the Boulevard of the Allies, rounded the curve to my old apartment on Atwood Street, my roommates would be there waiting for me on the rickety porch with a plastic wine glass filled with Sutter Home White Zinfandel. But I kept heading East on 376, the downtown skyline distracting my pang of nostalgia. The rush of massive buildings popping into sight gave me that natural high just as it had the first time I saw it when I was still a senior in high school touring the city. I followed the highway onto the bridge which leads to the Ft. Pitt Tunnels, remembering to stay in the right lane because the Southside exit appeared without much warning, and the impatient traffic was never forgiving to a confused driver. Three years passed like nothing, but I could still navigate the city's utterly illogical streets like a local, not a passing tourist.

At this point, I was on my second Adderall and third coffee, praying both stimulants would keep me awake once that natural high wore off from doing something dumb like nodding off at a traffic light.

Nick had texted me telling me that his flight was delayed, and that he hadn't had a chance to book a room at the hotel. He texted me explicit instructions to get a room with a king sized bed and that they only needed my credit card to hold the room, but he would pay. *He is so sleeping in the bathtub*, I thought to myself, not wanting to be responsible for anything other than collapsing on a bed. The hotel was smack in the middle of the Southside, a neighborhood filled with nightclubs, bars, restaurants, and few and far between expensive parking lots. I pulled up and told the attendant I was checking in.

I walked into the lobby, took a deep breath, and pinched the skin on the back of my hand. Yes, I was about to get a hotel room for Nicholas Kingsley and myself.

"Hi, I need a room," I said to the plump, African American woman with a mane of braids standing behind the front desk. I felt as though she knew what I was up to when she glared at me intently and asked, "Do you have a reservation?"

"No, I'm sorry."

I had only ever stayed in a hotel with my parents or a couple girlfriends when we went out of town for a vacation or a wedding. I could feel myself sweating.

"Not a problem. Do you have a smoking preference?"

"Non. Please."

"Okay, and will that be two doubles or a king size bed?"

My heart pounded. I was really doing this. I was really getting a hotel room in Pittsburgh that I would be sharing with not just my boss, but my boss's boss. Maybe there was a pull out couch.

"A king size bed, please."

"Okay and can I see some ID? We'll also need to need a record of your credit card on copy."

"Sure." I felt like I was 19 trying to raid a liquor store. But then again, plenty of women my age were friggin' married with kids. So clearly I was old enough to just get a damn hotel room? Right? Maybe not mature enough, but that wasn't the issue.

The woman handed over two room keys. I made sure to tell her that when Mr. Nicholas Kingsley arrived to give him a key to the room as well.

I took the elevator up to the room and surveyed the obvious. There it was, one big bed in the center of the room. *I can do this*, I thought to myself - but only if I could nap first. I kicked off my shoes and climbed under the plush duvet and closed my eyes, signaling my body to fall asleep. But with the caffeine and Adderall running through my bloodstream, that nap was far out of reach.

Eventually I caught some shut eye, because I was jolted awake when the alarm went off on my phone. *If only I could sleep longer...just half a pill. Just half. Go, Jayden. Get up.* I had to get my shit together, Nick could walk through that door any minute and see my face as a naked canvas, and then he would probably make a run for it. Chomping on my third pill of the day, I pulled out my make-up and laid out the evening's clothes. *Just pretend like it's another night out with the girls*, I thought as I steadily applied my liquid black eyeliner, Cleopatra style. I learned the single swipe from the inner corner to the outer corner of my eye from watching my mom do it expertly when she went out with my Dad on Saturdays, mentally counting down how many years until I could stand in the same spot using the same effortless technique. *And here I am.*

As I used my finger to sweep a bronzed shadow across my eye crease, Maya and Vika Jigulina's "Stereo Love" began playing from my phone which I had left on shuffle. Instantly Pavlov's effect flashed an image of a Saturday rooftop party in Tel Aviv at a DJ's house, where Shira and I were drinking cheap cava and mango juice sitting leaning against the railing, our bloodshot eyes hidden behind aviator sunglasses. Dark, mysterious men were talking to us in broken English and heavy accents, but what did we care? They spoke to us with such intensity burning from their eyes, like we were the most beautiful creatures they ever had the pleasure of encountering...

Stop, that's not your life now, I snapped at myself and fished around my make-up bag until I found the new tube of mascara.

Moments later, I stared at the girl in the mirror. She looked back at me more confidently than she had in a long time, despite the exhaustion behind the artificially freshened up eyes. *I got this.* The power of pills doing the convincing.

I put on a fitted long-sleeved black dress which now had plenty of wiggle room and black heels. Maybe I looked good, but I was nervous as shit, taking forever to hook the clasp on my necklace because my hands wouldn't stop trembling. Just as I was about to put on my perfectly accessorized jewelry, there was a knock on the door. Before I had a chance to move or say anything, the door opened widely, with Nick standing even taller and more massive than I remembered, rolling a suitcase and a garment bag casually slung over his shoulder. My knees started shaking and I knew I lost the battle of trying to buckle my bracelet. Seeing messages on a phone, hearing a voice on the phone, or even seeing his face on a computer screen in a crowded room didn't prepare me at all for how I actually felt seeing him in the flesh. After all, it had been over a month since we had last seen each other.

"Well, hello there," Nick said as he put down his luggage.

I walked up to him for a hug. "Hi! How was your flight?"

"Not bad at all, easy flight." He looked me up and down, surveying what he was working with for the evening. "Very nice, Jayden." Mentally I patted myself on the back.

NAKAMA is not a hole-in-the-wall B.Y.O.B. sushi joint. It was the restaurant to see and be seen, whether it was the Steelers or any various corporate executives. Completely modern with Southeast Asian decor, you walked in and immediately felt like you were in the hot spot. That's how I always felt whenever I had the off chance to eat here as a broke college student, as in, when my parents came to town and I dined on Daddy's' dime. But all these years later, that feeling of being in a glamour spot was still there when we stepped inside the crowded entranceway. I shimmied as our bubbly hostess galloped towards our table to catch up and I felt Nick put a protective hand on the small of my back. My insides were fluttering by the time we got to our table and Nick *pulled out* my chair for me. *Finally, a man with some damn manners.*

I saw a whole new side to Nick once our food arrived. Before I could even dip my first piece Alaska roll into the soy sauce and wasabi concoction, he had devoured every piece of raw fish and rice on his plate like he had never seen food before. I guess that's what it took feed someone the size of a linebacker. In one of our previous text-a-thons, I had asked him if he ever cheated on his diet (which was rumored to include a dozen egg omelet for breakfast, a gross shake of whey protein, spinach, banana and water for lunch, followed by a grilled chicken dinner). His answer: "No." Maybe I was a special occasion, like how dieters cheat on a holiday?

A couple who looked a few years younger than me was sitting on the other side of the hibachi table from us. Although Nick was technically off the clock, the seasoned salesman struck up small talk. After we wished the girlfriend Happy Birthday - the big twenty-two, the boyfriend asked, "So, what are you guys celebrating?" I looked at Nick and tried to suppress and chuckle.

"Well, actually, I'm her boss. We're not supposed to be together right now."

"Nick!" I was not expecting that to come out of his mouth.

"Oh, wow," the girlfriend said practically choking on her miso soup.

Nick and I locked eyes and grinned, relishing in knowing what we were doing was bad, but we just didn't care. This game we were playing didn't come with painful push-ups or doors being slammed in our faces like our jobs did.

"Are you finished?" he asked me, ready to dive in with his own chopsticks. I looked at the eight untouched pieces of my sushi which at this moment had absolutely zero appeal to me.

"I thought you're supposed to save room for the main course," I said, tapping my chopsticks with his. "But you look like you need a lot of food to feed this machine," I added, gesturing at his Greek god physique. Hercules decided we could box it along with the sushi that was still there.

"Have you ever drunk eaten sushi? It's disgusting." While I was in college, my roommate and I had gone for a sushi dinner one night before the bar and put the uneaten pieces in our fridge to save as our "drunk snack." After inhaling leftover raw fish, it was awhile before either of us could even say the word sushi, never mind eat it.

He smiled at me. "I'm up for the challenge."

The main course consisted of a little bit of picking at chicken and N.Y. strip steak on my end as Nick wolfed down his entire Kobe steak, fried rice and butter drenched grilled veggies.

Our waitress came with a doggie bag and the bill, which Nick snatched instantly and whipped out his wallet. I believe in the extinct practice of chivalry, yet my head isn't so far up my ass that I assume that men immediately cover the bill. So nonchalantly, I grabbed my clutch and fished inside for my Visa. Glancing over, he saw me and stopped me immediately. "Put that away, Jayden," he said in the same tone he uses when he is talking to one of his agents. He was chivalrous alright and apparently liked to be in control. I would have pounced on him right there, but even I knew that would be inappropriate.

I obliged without a fight and tucked my debit card back into its zippered compartment and thanked him.

"You're welcome. It's nothing."

I glanced down at the bill's total which was $248.72. Nothing? Then again, the guy earned more money last week than most Americans make in a whole month. It wasn't like this dinner was going to leave him destitute.

"Let's grab another drink somewhere," he suggested with a tone that I knew was going to be the only option.

"Whatever you want to do," my drunk alter ego stammered. I decided maybe it was time to take charge. "Let's grab another drink at a bar across the street and then we can head back, sound good?" Minutes later we were staggering down East Carson Street, which was packed with every twenty-something, thirty-something, and desperate forty-somethings all on the prowl for their next prey. And if the prowl turned to shambles, there was always the comfort of cheap, cheesy pizza and questionable gyros, which still smelled appealing to me although I was no longer a blacked out college senior.

It was just cold enough where he put a protective arm around my shivering shoulders to block out the late night wind. *This is what I want*, I thought. *To be protected.* And somewhere far behind that voice, behind the cobwebs, another voice said, "But you're going about it the wrong way." But with an expensive dinner in my stomach and vodka flopping through my bloodstream, I didn't hear it.

By the time we got back to the hotel lobby, I was conscious of the fact that we were committing the cardinal corporate sin but at that moment I didn't care what the punishment would be one day. I wanted this. Every girl deserved a fairy tale, and I was convinced that I wasn't any different.

I shyly grabbed the clothes I carefully selected for bed time and went into the bathroom to change and brush my teeth. When I opened the door, he stood next to me wearing shorts and a t-shirt.

He fingered the edge of my satin camisole as he put his toothbrush back carefully into its travel carrier. "Bed time," he grinned, leading me to the king size bed which had only been slightly ruffled by my nap earlier. I felt like an actress in a 1950s movie, carefully pulling back the duvet and slipping onto the edge of the bed. I wasn't there long.

"Come here, you," he said, and scooped my body close to his in one swift movement. I never have, nor probably ever will, be with someone so massive who has the body fat percentage of probably 2%. You could bounce a quarter off any inch of the surface of his body. And I was getting to sleep next to it!

Apparently I was too busy oogling him to realize he was doing the same thing to me. "Look at this body on you, Jayden. Come here," he said, placing his hand over my protruding hipbone and sat down at the front of the bed.

"You're perfect," he said grabbing my arm and pulling me close to him. It didn't even register that this man, who was so in need to control every aspect of his life, would be one to control how thin his women were.

And then he was on top of me, my hair tangled in his fingers, completely in control of my body. I was just too drunk to pick up on how intent he was on maintaining control. He leaned over me and soon his lips met mine. I felt his carnal instincts taking over, like he wanted to consume me all in one bite. I was not having that.

"Stop. Make your first kiss perfect," I commanded.

He laughed. "Only you would say that, Jayden." But he acquiesced, kissing me slowly. Like a real prince charming, not one of those sloppy frat boys whose mouths would seemingly go to battle with mine. With Nick, it was all the excitement of kissing someone new for the first time and surprisingly feeling natural, like you should have kissed this person years earlier. How did it actually come to be that I was in a bed with someone who could have any girl he wanted?

And suddenly his head moved south. Thank God everything was smooth as silk or I would have died of non-grooming embarrassment. My insides melted and my body turned to Jell-O. I felt something ignite between my legs. A full calendar year was too long for any girl in her prime to be left untouched by anything other than a vibrator. His head was in between my legs, and I was ready to burst as he slid a finger inside me. His murmurs of approval only sent me even more wildly. There I was, my inner sex goddess in love with being desired. But there was still a sobering part of me simply desiring to be loved.

"I'll have the hangover special with the five egg Mexican omelet," Nick rattled off to the waitress. Keep in mind, this "omelet" was filled with salsa, black beans, ham, pico de gallo, pepperjack cheese, and onions (if I ordered that I might as well just wear a diaper for the rest of the day). He scanned the menu for sides and finished off with, "home-fries, toast, and bacon. Can I also get an order of the banana-chocolate chip pancakes. The super stack?"

"Okay, great," the waitress smiled and jotted this all down, unfazed by the size of his order, being that we were sitting in the city's premiere breakfast joint.

"Can I get the omelet made with egg whites by chance?"

"Of course." Now who orders their omelet to be made with egg whites next to a stack of butter-filled pancakes and bacon? Apparently, Nicholas Kingsley did.

"I'll have a veggie omelette, no mushrooms please, cheddar cheese, and wheat toast. No homefries. And lots of coffee." My head was throbbing with a hangover but I was equally elated with that post-orgasmic joy that I didn't even care that I felt like someone had taken a frying pan to my skull.

Nick devoured his entire first course of the hangover special before I had barely eaten a piece of my eggs. The pancakes? Inhaled faster than a frat boy bonging a beer. I stared in astonishment. Why could he eat so much and just stay so rock solid? If I ate those pancakes, my legs would be decorated with new cellulite by the following day. The saying of, "A minute on your lips, forever on your hips," unfortunately ran in my DNA. My mom had a metabolism of a track star, but I had inherited my dad's tendency to put on weight from just looking at food in a magazine. Nick offered for me to try the pancakes. This was after he offered a taste of his omelet, which was delicious, except for the fact I had to fork around the ham. My mom and grandmother would collectively have strokes if they knew I ingested any pork product. Bad enough I ate something on the same plate it shared. I stared at the pancakes, my mouth watering. God, I wanted to stuff my mouth with that fluffy griddled goodness filled with bananas and chocolate chips which was drenched in maple syrup just like I did at our favorite diner. In the 1990s, calories did not exist, and it was completely acceptable to eat pancakes for dinner. And even have ice-cream for dessert.

But it wasn't the '90s anymore. I was convinced if I even allowed myself to have a taste the sugar laden caloric fest on my tongue would just erupt into fat rolls on my body. And then surely, Nick would not like me. So I avoided that whole scenario with a simple, "No, thank you." When the bill came, he snatched it before I could even extend a finger towards it. I tried offering to go dutch, then to at least cover tip, but he was the dominant force here. Who was I kidding though? It wasn't exactly hurting to be taken care of.

"Let's go shopping," he said, signing the check.

"Do you like these?" We were browsing the racks of the men's section at Nordstrom's. He held up a pair of khaki shorts.

Instinctively, my fingers reached for the price tag just as every woman in any Jewish family would.

A hunk of material that doesn't even go past the knees costs $209.00. "Are you for real?" I asked. "What?" he said. *What the hell, we weren't shopping on my money.* I turned the charm back on. "Let's see what else we can pick out for Mr. Kingsley," I said, grabbing the shorts and putting them on top of his growing stack of clothes.

This was purely entertainment for me. After his arms held about $1,500 worth of clothing, he decided it was time to go to the dressing room. I walked awkwardly behind him, not really sure what to do at this point. Probably sensing my hesitation, he turned and told me to come in the room with him. I sat on the leather chair, watching the giant change into the first pair of beige khaki shorts.

"Did you ever think you would be in a dressing room with your Regional Sales Director?" he asked me. *Did he think I forgot his job title?*

"Actually, I don't think Monte went over that part in the company overview." I had to crane my neck up to see his face. He towered over me and put his hands on the wall above me, trapping me in a cell of muscle. "You're lucky we're in public, because if we weren't… god what I would do to you right now."

"I think you got a taste of that last night," I responded, biting my lip. He chuckled.

"How did you like it?" he asked bluntly, which suddenly made me feel uncomfortable. The thought of praising his performance out loud made me blush.

"Well, Mr. Kingsley," I began, crossing my legs and clasping my hands around my knee, "as your performance supervisor, I am giving you a five star rating for finger dexterity, tongue twisting, and of course, your customer service."

■ ■ ■

That night, we had to attend some welcome party for the agency and pretend we hadn't been together for the past twenty-four hours. Scarlett was itching to know details but we didn't have the opportunity to do a full dissection.

"Bye guys!" I called as I walked over to my car and sat inside. I turned it on and put the radio on until my real designated driver came to collect me. His car pulled up next to me. "Hey sexy," he called out the window. I grabbed my purse and locked the car. "Thank you," I said getting into the car. We drove back to the hotel blasting Jay-Z, or Diddy, or Kanye, or someone rapping about money, weed, and pussy. Oh, and getting head. Back in the hotel room, we resumed right where the previous night had left off. He pulled me on top of him and something inside me pulled back. Too bad that something didn't yank me off the bed and throw me into a cold shower to shut off my sex hormones.

Maneuvering my body in some contortionist position, he started working his way into my pants, but I crossed my legs as a preventative detour to the road his fingers were taking.

"What's wrong?" he asked me, sensing my stiffness. I rolled over to the other side of the bed and leaned on my side, facing him.

"Nick," I began. "Look, I'm not very good at casual sex. I haven't been with anyone in a year." I was referring to the guy who had dumped me on my birthday a year earlier, the now pizza delivery guy. Talk about an awesome birthday present. I also decided to not count the plumber. "It's really not in me to sleep with someone and then brush it off with no emotion. I wish I could, but I'm not able to."

"The thing is… I'm in a really good place in my life right now, probably the best I ever have been financially and mentally." I sat up and looked him in the eye, the honesty of my words sobering me.

"I know this is probably awkward to even bring up, but I'm laying all my cards out on the table now so that you know exactly where I stand. I just don't want to sleep with you and then regret it tomorrow." His expression softened and he didn't hesitate to smooth over any bumps of hesitation I was feeling. This was it, I had laid my heart on the table and now was left in a vulnerable position.

"I understand, Jayden. And no, I don't want to hurt you either. Obviously, I can't promise anything in terms of what the future holds. But what I do know is that I like you, and we are together now. I'm not with anyone else. I think we should just have fun while we are together for the time being and then just see where this goes." There was something about his words that I trusted - he had a point. I couldn't keep my guard up forever, and I deserved to have some fun. Who knows if I really believed him. But the part of me desiring nothing but only to be desired wanted to believe him. If my intuition was flexing its alarm bells, I ignored them as he leaned in and kissed me.

He reached over and climbed on top of me, where I had nowhere to go. He began to kiss my neck and that was it, I was done for. "Plus you look so sexy right now and I don't want anything else but you."

It didn't matter if my moral and my carnal compasses were congruent or running tracks in separate universes. In moments, Nicholas had my clothes off along with all of his. Once I looked down and saw exactly what I was working with, my whole speech of *are you sure we should be doing this* went completely out the window and into some other universe. Nicholas Kingsley could smell my anticipation as he slowly pushed his body on top of mine. By the time he pushed inside me, I wasn't mine to control anymore.

■ ■ ■

"And now, we are going to hear from the top Regional Director for the quarter. Good job, man! Mr. Nicholas Kingsley!" The entire room began clapping and Scarlett stared right at me. She leaned over and reminded me, "And, you fucked him last night!"

That morning Nicholas had to attend a very early gym session with Giovanni and a few other master managers. I convinced Scarlett if she picked me up from the hotel we stayed at, where I finished my own frantic work out, that I would treat her for coffee and a bagel. Naturally, she accepted. And naturally, I couldn't keep my mouth shut about what had happened in the wee hours of the morning.

Nicholas walked over to the podium, with a few papers containing key points he needed to hit under his hands discretely. His effortless strides showed no signs of nervousness. He could give an acceptance speech in his sleep. When had he even written the damn thing? Oh, right, he was mumbling about an acrostic poem at about 5am as we were getting ready for the gym. He had also asked me if I regretted what had happened just hours earlier.

Feeling like I was just struck by a thunderbolt, I told him I was too tired to contemplate any feelings of regret at that point. The only thing I was regretting was the vodka from the night before.

I stared right him, seeing if I could catch his eye before he began speaking. I had just slept with one of the most successful managers in the entire company. What did I do to get so lucky? I pinched myself believing he saw something in me that made me special. After all, he could have been fucking any of the women in the room. Sitting there with an invisible scarlet letter on my chest, I blushed as I envisioned his rock solid body on top of mine. And then I had to stop so I wouldn't act like a thirteen year old boy.

"Okay guys, I'm going to make this as quick as I can, because I'm sure you are all sick of hearing my name anyway," he begins with the room being won over as they respond in chuckles.

"This deal comes down to one basic fundamental. Making a commitment and sticking to it. Commitment is sticking with what you said you were going to do long after the mood has passed. Commitment is knocking on the last door even if you are running on three hours of sleep and are so hungry you could eat a twelve egg omelet. Which is what I eat for breakfast. If you stick with your commitments, you will find success at D'Angelo Enterprises...."

He went on about the top five factors to success and everyone in the room was either furiously typing into their phones each word he said or writing down bullet points in notebooks. "Lastly, I want to thank my team for all their hard work. This award isn't mine. It's yours and is a reflection of the hard work you do day in and day out. Let's keep rockin' it!"

"He kills it. Every quarter, he kills it," one of the managers on the other side of me commented as the rest of the room applauded his remarks. The others at the table agreed. Nick Kingsley was a warrior.

When the meeting ended, Miguel forced our office into a huddle. "Alright gang, let's get gassed up, grab a coffee, and hit the road. It's 1:45 right now. It only takes about 4 and a half hours to get back. There is no reason why anyone should be back later than 7:00, alright? Gives you plenty of time before you hit the road to get what you need. Drive safe, everyone!" Immediately, I scanned the dispersing room for Nick. He was wrapped up in conversations with practically a dozen people waiting to speak with him, and I knew I couldn't idle around. Way too suspicious. I distracted myself by grabbing my trainee and walking over to my car.

As we rearranged our bags in the trunk, I saw Nick approaching some of the cars close to where we were parked, which belonged to other managers and agents from our office. He fist-pumped a group of drooling groupies and surprisingly turned and walked towards my car. That flip-flop thing in my stomach happened and suddenly I became nervous. "It was good to see you, Jayden," he said as he stood at a respectably professional distance. "You too, Nick. This is my trainee, Amanda," I introduced. He turned to her and said, "Listen to your field trainer. You are in good hands. This girl knows her stuff." He turned back to me and said, "Drive back safely." I thanked him and got into my car, the reality that the weekend was over finally sinking in. I watched him walk, back to the Escalade he was driving for the weekend, wondering when I would see him again. My heart fell to my lap but I tried my best not to wear my emotion over the black blazer I was desperate to change out of before this journey back home. Amanda and I stopped to refuel, change out of our professional get up and get snacks. I was envious as she downed an entire bag of Cheetos and M&M's in a matter of ten minutes without the worry any of it would end up on her skinny figure. As I got back into the car, I looked at my phone. I had a message.

Nicholas Kingsley: *You have no idea how bad I wanted to kiss you before I left.* I prayed Amanda couldn't read my mind as I stared at the message for a little longer than necessary.

I texted him back: *I wish I didn't have my trainee, I would have met you at Sheetz for more than a kiss goodbye.* Being in management was literally like being a parent to agents in training - no way could I leave Amanda. He answered me right away.

Nick Kingsley: *I would have liked that ;)*

I took a minute and reflected on everything that had happened in just the past forty-eight hours. I spent two nights with someone who was in reality practically a stranger to me, and parted ways feeling closer than I would have ever imagined. But he is my boss's boss. How do I get myself into this shit? Feeling confident and on a high from the whole weekend I wrote back more emotionally.

Me: *Nick I just want to thank you... so much. You treated me like a princess and no one has ever done that for me before. I don't know what's going to happen from here, but I just want you to know that no matter what, this is always going to be one of the best weekends of my life.*

Nick: *You have no idea how happy that makes me.*

They say to ride the high when it comes. Who would have known this was my "high?" Money was oozing from my bank account. And now one of the most powerful men in an agency of 500 people wanted *me*. At twenty-five years young, this was living the good life. I suppose that I let the realities of fading childhood friendships, my roommates being my parents, and that my clientele roster included people missing teeth slip past me. All in the name of chasing the yellow brick road…and now, Nicholas Kingsley.

CHAPTER 10

The next few days my head was somewhere in a haze between being drunk on lust alternating with bursts of paranoia that everyone in the office knew what was going on. Each time in a manager's meeting when Nick addressed us, I stared down at my notes, covering an invisible scarlet letter I was praying no one else would see. And then my mood would immediately switch when my phone would vibrate in my lap as I checked to see who was contacting me.

You look so hot on camera with those glasses on. What I would do to you right now.

I was sitting in direct view of the camera, so every manager in every office could see me. Not that they were looking at me - we were all writing and typing furiously or checking our phones and tweeting whatever bullshit was on our minds. This afternoon a guest speaker from another agency was going over the importance of recruiting if we ever wanted a serious career. Normally I would make sure every syllable had been noted, however my thoughts were somewhere between Pittsburgh and hormones that seemed to be raging involuntarily. *Focus, Jayden. Focus.* The harder I tried to focus, the farther my mind wandered. I gave in and answered his text. *What I would let you do to me right now. With these glasses on.*

Obviously I wasn't being very discreet because Joey nudged me with his pen and said to me, "Who are you texting? You're smiling. You never smile."

"Yes, I do smile." I flashed him with my biggest grin. My phone vibrated again and I moved it to make sure Joey wouldn't be able to read the text, and more importantly, who it was from. Joey had been promoted earlier that morning so he had a fat ass grin on his own face.

"Did you get laid?" he whispered to me.

"What does it matter?" I couldn't come out and tell a bold faced lie.

"Come on, just tell me," he pressed on. He was speaking so low that no one else in the room could hear him.

"Don't worry about it!"

"And it wasn't me? So mad at you, Jayden."

Nick: *You're going to make me hard.*

Me: *Then stand up, so I can see for myself ;)*

Nick: *Haha. Okay, talk later, focus on what this agency owner is saying. He could buy a Bentley each month with his income.*

A middle aged man by the name of Charlie Fox was holding a glass of wine as he stared into the camera, showing off an infinity pool and a fiancé with a stomach you could bounce pennies off of and artificially-inflated chest surrounded by Florida palm trees. We laughed as he took deliberate sips and told us how hard his life was and that this meeting was cutting into his tanning time.

As Joey stated the obvious. "Yo, that chick is so hot," nodding to the fiancé who was wearing a bikini so skimpy I wouldn't dare to wear in public.

"You think she's hot? You should see his daughter." Monte was in the know of everything. "How old is his daughter?" I asked. "Definitely younger than you." What, like I'm some old woman?

■ ■ ■

For days it continued, this back and forth text-message bantering that piqued my interest past my now limited world of appointments, presentations, and sales. My heart skipped a beat every time my phone vibrated or dinged with a text message alert. Somehow with these welcomed distractions, my work performance was turbocharged. After all, how many others in the company could say they had the number one agent in company history in their back pocket (along with shirtless selfies to really rev my engine?)

All day, whether I was driving with a trainee or waiting for a client to grab their checkbook as I collected another sale, flashbacks of Nick thrusting on top of me would jump into my mind. It took every ounce of energy not to rock back and forth in whatever seat I was in to satisfy myself. The worst was when I would check my phone and see a text that with words that would literally make me want to rub one out.

Send me a pic of what's under your clothes, naughty girl.

Like an idiot, I snuck a peek at my phone while one of my trainee's was giving the presentation. "Something wrong, Jayden?" the thankfully sweet natured mother asked as I sat in her kitchen, praying I wasn't getting wet on her wooden seat.

"Oh, no! I'm just so pleased with how well Kasey's work is coming. Good job!" I high-fived the trainee, and let her continue. And as soon as I could, I excused myself to the bathroom and answered Nick's text message with a profile shot of the white satin thong which skimmed my protruding hip bone.

You are a bad, bad professional, Jayden, I thought to myself. *Sending bad, bad pics to your boss's boss. This is not what good girls do.* Then of course the other half of my brain chimed in. *But it feels good to get this dirty, Jayden. You work hard, girl. You need a little spice in your bland, boring existence of life insurance applications.*

Before the two voices could really start battling out, my phone vibrated on the sink.

Nick: *Your vice-president likes the goods. Go close that sale baby.*

You bet I walked out of the bathroom and said whatever was necessary to get a check from the weathered mother at the kitchen table.

■ ■ ■

The following Monday, I was giving Scarlett the privilege of scrolling through my dirty text messages before our office meeting started. "Oh. My. God. Jayden, you look so skinny here," she said, tapping at the pic I sent from the client's house days earlier.

"Meh, just sucking in," I said, hoping she would get distracted soon so I could sneak into my purse and grab half a pill. I seriously didn't see what the hype was about coffee anymore. I just drank it because I loved the taste.

But unfortunately, as I sipped, Scarlett continued to scroll, gasping every once in a while at how the regional vice-president could talk so dirty. I bit my lip thinking about fabulous I felt to know I could simultaneously make a guy's dick hard and sell some good old insurance. Before I could disappear into my own big head, I decided to be a good friend. "What's going on with the dude, Scar?" But Monte cut off what was sure to be a thorough play-by-play of eye contact at the bar, followed by sexting while in the same bar, followed by blunt-sharing in the car, followed by…

"Gang! Good morning!" Our boss started, everyone suddenly facing forward and temporarily putting down their iPhone. "Morning," we chanted back.

"Okay, let's get pumped up for the company meeting!" One of the managers was connecting the TV to the video conferencing software so we could all gawk at each other in neatly assembled rows from our office's respective meeting rooms. Monte was obviously excited because as most Italians do, he started using his hands very rapidly along with his verbal communication.

"Guys, Giovanni is in Pittsburgh to announce a very special competition that only a few have qualified for due to their outstanding performance." He was reaching his hands up and bringing them to his chest to emphasize the grandiosity of what was about go down.

"Let's see if any of my rockstars made the cut!" Joey and I immediately made eye contact but didn't say anything. We both were praying for a shot to stand out from the crowd. Monte was rambling on about this one and that one's recent achievements but my mind was focused only on what Giovanni could possibly have up his sleeve for the company. You never knew what was coming from the mouth of that bald firecracker head on his linebacker shoulders.

After Monte's grand M.C. introduction to the weekly *D'Angelo Enterprises* show featuring mass insurance news and entertainment (celebration of over achiever's awesomeness such as myself), the ten offices came onto the screen in neat little squares, including our office, so we could see ourselves as well. Technology never ceases to awe me. Scarlett nudged me. "Gimme a piece of gum, my breath smells like dead people." I bent into my purse and gave her a stick of Trident spearmint. While my hand was down there it gave me the ideal opportunity to fish out something a little stronger than a piece of gum for myself.

"Scarlett, it's a virtual meeting, no one can smell except me." Then I took a whiff and coughed in disgust. "Damn woman, what are you eating?"

"Girls, shut up, you're in the front row, set a damn example!" The wrath of Monte was fast and furious, and I obeyed. I turned away from Scarlett and slid the pill into my mouth, using my fingertips to create the illusion I was simply playing with my plump lips. As I swished that bitter circle under my eager tongue, it dawned on me. Shit, I was in the front row! That meant I was dead center. I looked at Scarlett and made sure I looked okay, which I obviously did, being that I put my face on just forty minutes earlier and hadn't eaten anything so my clothes were stain-free.

The Jacksonville office's screen popped up and Nick was staring straight into the camera, adjusting it so the jammed packed room was in full view. And being that he was that close to the screen, there was no way he could miss me. *Fucking breathe, Jayden. You look fine. Breathe.*

"Look at you all! All you rockstars sitting and smiling. I can feel the energy, I'm diggin' it!" Our stout, yet thunderous leader began his always inspiring welcome and I even almost gave him my full attention but of course I couldn't help but stare at the square where Nick's office was positioned on the screen. He sat off to the side, leaning forward with his elbows pressed against his knees, his phone swinging between his left thumb and forefinger. We were probably the only company that condoned cell phone use during meetings because it was a sign we were 'taking notes.'

I didn't have a need to transcribe anyone's words yet, I was busy taking mental notes. Specifically, how I wanted to transport through the screen and pounce on him like the underfed tiger I was. Just as I was flying through technology, space and time and landing spread eagle onto his lap, Giovanni's voice brought me back to the Grayton office.

"Ladies and gentlemen, who's ready for game time? I'm ready to see some up and coming all-stars come to play. Who's ready to prove they're ready to play with the big dogs?" I was no longer bouncing on Nick's lap. Instead, I was completely in tune with the words coming out of Giovanni's mouth. I might have sat on the bench during athletic games, but when it came to this sales stuff, I was always down. We have two hundred agents in their first year with D'Angelo Enterprises, the largest amount of fresh faces I've ever seen in my ten years as your leader. A round of applause communicated the agents and manager's enthusiasm for what we were now conditioned to believe as being part of the greatest company not just in the insurance industry, the country, but probably the whole damn world.

"What we did here is take the top ten percent of all your sales from the past six weeks and came up with a list of twenty people to compete for the first ever Smash Out Competition. I came up with the name myself," he added with a grin. "I want to see who's got it to smash everyone else and rock this deal. Now I'm going to turn this over to your vice-president Cal who's going to go over the rules and what you're really itchin' for: the players who are competing."

Cal stepped up to the podium and began rambling about greatness of the company, how he always took advantage of these opportunities to shine, but my eyes were glued to the paper I could see him holding which definitely had the list of names. It took all my self-control not to start kicking my feet to get Monte's attention. I knew he was privy to the names on that list.

"Dude, I want to know who's on that list," I said ventriloquist style to Scarlett to conceal the fact I was already yapping away about something on my mind.

"Not me, I've been shitting the bed," she said under her breath. In addition to a trophy and bragging rights, the company was sending the winner on a trip for two anywhere in the continental U.S.

A trip for two? No, don't even let your mind go there right now Jayden. If I let my mind run wild I'd already be at the Hard Rock Cafe pool party in Las Vegas with Nick slamming $30 vodka drinks in a cabana listening to beats from some international DJ.

Just like I had called, he grabbed the sheet of paper in front of him and began reading the list of names. After each name he called, the office where the agent was from would start clapping in support. I ticked off how many names he was calling, the knot in my stomach growing tighter the higher the number went.

"And we got two guys out of the Grayton office who are going to step up to the challenge. Joseph Capelli and Jayden Rosenberg!" It was game time.

Joey and I stood up just as all the other contestants were instructed to do and high-fived each other. Not one to remain unemotional during anything remotely exciting, Monte jumped up out of his chair and fist-pumped us with a very serious "Let's freaking go!" By the time we sat down, I was shaking. Scarlett grabbed my hand.

"Proud of you babe, you got this. Those clowns have nothing on you."

"Thanks, boo," I said, smiling back. I was lucky she was sincere and not a closeted conniving bitch.

When we got out of the meeting, I checked my phone and saw I had a text from Nick. *You're gonna dominate ;)*

Did you have anything to do with this? Some... secret agenda? ;) I typed back.

Well, let's say I have a vested interest in this competition. Just focus, Jayden and this is yours.

Hours later, I was jittery from caffeine overhaul and god knows how many milligrams of a controlled substance pumping through my bloodstream. I jumped over to Joey's desk, bopping my weight back and forth in my turquoise patent leather stilettos. They were a great pop of color for the fitted black dress. "Joey, one of us has to win this fucking thing. We DESERVE it. When is the last time we even had a day off?"

"I know," he said, scribbling notes on his schedule. "I know, right?" he repeated to me, like he was a robot now being controlled by this competition. Monte was taking a lap through the office and spotted us. He came over and put his arms around our shoulders. He knew what we were thinking.

"Game time, you two. Focus. I want you both to have a vacation, you're my top rockers." He pulled me aside and said, "Jayden, come into my office in ten. I'm jumping on a call quick." I scanned his face for some sort of expression to give me a clue as to what was going on, but I couldn't detect anything. Immediately, I assumed it was something bad.

"Oohhh, what did JayJay do?" Joey cooed as Monte walked back to his office.

"Shut it."

Just as I was asked to do, ten minutes later I tapped on Monte's office door and he waved me in as he finished up his phone call verifying what time his dry cleaning would be delivered to the office. "Yeah, after 7:00 will be great. My assistant Olivia will meet you downstairs. Thanks, brother." It was my turn.

"So, Jay, I got a phone call earlier today. Requesting that you be allowed to go to Florida for a work-vacation weekend." Play dumb, I thought. "Oh, really?" I responded.

"Mr. Kingsley told me about Pittsburgh." Shit, shit, shit. "Oh," I said, looking down, much too afraid to see whatever look of fury was surely to be on his face. "Are you mad at me?" I asked my chipping fingernails.

"No, silly, I'm not mad at you," he said. I looked up at his seemingly carefree facial expression and the knot in my stomach loosened. Okay, no job lost so far. He leaned a bit more forward and lowered his voice, which told me he knew this wasn't something we were going to go discussing as loosely as we did our weekly sales performances.

"Look, these things happen, I understand. As long as it does not interfere with your performance here, I don't care what you do or who you get involved with outside the office."

"I completely understand that," I said, utterly relieved.

"That being said, Nick and I came to the conclusion that we could work it out for you to take a couple days to go down to Florida, but you would be working from their office."

"You mean, I can go?!"

"Yes, you can go. You have worked so hard and haven't had a break since the day you started in October."

"Okay, when can I go?"

"Here's the deal. Nick and I are giving you a little side-incentive for this competition, okay? You're going to love this. You can go after the Smash Out Competition. Just got to be in the top three."

Oh my god, I had to chance to go to Florida! With this news, I had jumped from game-face time to bull-fighting mode. All I was hearing was an opportunity; the stipulations had yet to register: Nick was setting obstacles I had to beat in order to see him. I was so far into the glorified chess game I didn't realize I was turning into a pretty marble pawn that the managers - the ultimate players, were using as a strategic move to push themselves to greatness. But in that moment, I processed Monte's words as though I was scratching off the winning number to a lottery ticket.

"Oh my god, I can go to Florida? Holy shit, holy shit. Okay." As usual, I was jumping around in my seat and my mind was bouncing off my skull's confines. One thing was still gnawing at my thoughts which I couldn't help myself from digging into.

"So...what did Nick say exactly about Pittsburgh?" I asked Monte.

"Well, he told me you guys stayed together in the Southside and I said to him, 'did you fuck her?' And he said yes."

I rolled my eyes at his response. Being that they were men with teenage minds, I wasn't really surprised. Although it did sting a bit that Nick was so open about our rendezvous. Didn't the word *privacy* apply to any circumstance anymore?

"Whatever, I doubt he had any complaints in that department. Unless I've completely forgotten how to ride that bike." A sly smile crept across his face confirming that I was correct. "I think that's a good way to put it. Now, get back out there and knock this thing out of the park. Got me?"

"I can do this, right Monte?"

"I have no doubt in my mind, Jayden. No doubt in my mind."

I was so nervous about this competition that I did what any amateur sales person would do. I looked up to the big wigs for guidance. And this one happened to be Candice Carpezio. I contacted her on Facebook the next morning and explained how I was feeling and just wanted some guidance. Enthusiastically, she gave me her phone number and said to call her ASAP. What a woman.

"Canddddyyyyyy," I cooed, which was the nickname everyone had for her. I then immediately relayed the little side bet Monte had set up with Nicholas for me to have the opportunity to go to Florida.

"What the fuck is that Kingsley nut job doing with this competition? Let tell you something, Jayden, I don't know what these men think they can do but it's just bullshit. That man is bad news, I swear to Jesus. He's probably such a dickhead because he doesn't have one."

"Candy, I wish that was the case. I would have been over him in two seconds."

"Who the hell knows. Prince Nicholas calls his boy toys in Pittsburgh and whatever he wants, he gets, because of his title. I'm telling you, when I'm a managing director, I'm going to raise some fucking hell." The only reason Candy hadn't beaten out Giovanni and started her own agency by now was because she respected him too damn much to leave him, and she loved the field too damn much to pursue management seriously.

"I'm not taking any trainees out with me during this competition, no way. I can't have any distractions. My last trainee? I made her cry in a house when she tried to undermine my authority. The one before her? I left her at McDonald's after she was pissing me the fuck off saying I was dressed motherly." Candy did not dress motherly.

"I'm like, excuse me?! Let's see you at fifty-five with this ass! Get out of here."

"I'm so glad you weren't my trainer I would have cried. How am I going to place in this competition? I need to be you Candy."

"Jayden, stop trying to be everyone else. Just be you. You know what to do. Work the system. Use referrals. Outwork everyone! That's it! You can do it!"

"You're right. I just always forget that. I always seem to think there's some magic secret everyone is in on except me. Just how are you so good at this?"

"I outwork everyone! I need to, Jayden, or I would go nuts. I went through a nasty divorce and this is how I channel my energy." Everyone knew Candice was somewhat of a cougar, just the specifics hadn't been disclosed. Until now. I could feel Candice was on a roll so I let her keep talking, without having to pry everything out.

"My ex-husband cheated on me with my best friend. I came home after teaching an aerobics class and there she was fucking spread eagle on my imported Italian marble counter top. Right where I had eaten my god damned egg white omelette that morning. Fucking cottage cheese thighs and all."

"Holy shit, what did you do?"

"I took my water bottle out of my gym bag and hurled it at them. It hit the bitch in the arm and she's all, 'Candice, it's not what it looks like.' What do you think I am, fucking blind? I told her she was a two faced whore and to get the fuck out my kitchen."

"I am so sorry."

"It's fine, I regularly sleep with her husband now."

■ ■ ■

Twelve hours later, 10:30pm that night, my day of playing defense had turned into approximately 720 minutes of experiencing one of my least favorite phrases: strike-out. I had done four presentations and gotten a no at each kitchen table where my butt was sore after attempting to cajole any yes. When I heard the last emphatic no at 10:15pm, I resigned to the nasty fact that I was shit out of luck for the day. So when I got into my car, I didn't immediately *brush off the rejection and recognize every no is one step closer to a yes* as I had been carefully trained to do. Instead, I switched into low-blood sugar inducing Crazy Bitch Mode. No matter how *chill* of a girl you may think you are, every female has a threshold which, if met, induces Crazy Bitch Mode. Once in Crazy Bitch Mode, rational reasoning and considerate verbal sentiments cease into an abyss of manic chaos. See below:

"Are you kidding me?" I asked Nick, who immediately picked up when I dialed his number. For added measure, I slammed the accelerator to weave through the passing lane. The offending slow driver was a hundred year old woman who barely reached the steering wheel. *Didn't these people have a fucking bed time?*

"Hah, Jayden, what are you talking about?" he asked. I could hear the uneasiness in his voice, as though he smelled the lightning bolts I was about to start throwing over the cell phone carrier towers.

"You know damn well what I'm talking about, Nicholas."

"Jayden, calm down, what is going on?"

"How dare you think you can use the Smash Out Competition as the way for me to come to Florida. That in order for me to get on the plane, I need to finish at a certain place? What do you think you are, some sort of prize that I have to work extra hard for? It's unfuckingbelievable that you would put me in that situation, *Mr. Kingsley*." I dialed up the sarcasm as I spat out his name. "Jayden, calm down. I said that so you would be motivated to do well."

"MOTIVATED? Listen, Nick. I'm not motivated by how many policies I can sell to see your face. That is completely separate. If I win this competition, I'm doing it for me. No one else. Not you. Do you understand that?"

"Whoa, okay. It's just that, Jayden, you're already so motivated that it's hard to find other ways to motivate you. Monte and I just thought this would be a good way. That's all."

"Yeah, well find another way, okay. You guys are supposed to be my mentors here, not using me like a piece of meat."

"Jayden, come on. If I had known you would react like this, I would have never suggested it."

"Whatever."

"Just place in the top five, okay baby?"

"I'll fucking place whatever fucking place that I'm going to fucking place in. Okay?"

"Where are you now?" he asked.

"Driving the fuck home so I can do that really crazy thing called sleeping. Why?"

"Well, I don't want you driving all worked up. I'm going to let you concentrate on the road now. Let me know when you get home safely, okay Jayden?" Great, just great. Now he's being fucking reasonable, which makes me look even more so of a lunatic. I turned down Crazy Bitch Mode slightly.

"Fine. Thanks for your consideration of my safety." He ignored my shit instead of dishing it back. "Bye, Jayden. Drive safe." I hung up the phone and concentrated on my thoughts instead of the road ahead of me, as I usually did. Was I overreacting? Was I acting like some super-feminist nut who refuses to shave her legs and denounces lipstick? Or, was Nick for simplicity's sake, being a douche bag?

I pulled into the driveway and took inventory of the obvious. Nicholas Kingsley didn't just take control in a sales presentation. He took control over everything involved in his life. Maybe he thought he could control me in this Smash Out competition, but I was determined to focus on doing this for me. I win for me, and no one else. Sadly enough, even though I was somewhat infuriated by being what I saw as manipulation, the longing to see him outweighed the fury. Just like all the other stupid girls, I would do whatever I had to in order for me to get on that plane and see the bald headed powerhouse who made me feel like a princess. Wouldn't you do something crazy so you could feel like a princess?

■ ■ ■

For the next two weeks, I was feeling nothing like a princess. I was a pill-popping, blabber-mouthing, Selling Cinderella. The days blurred to the point that I had no care, clue, or concern if it was Wednesday or a Sunday. All I knew was that when the alarm went off at 5:00am, I would experience a mild heart palpitation, hit the snooze button and savor the extra fifteen minutes of a dream-like state before beginning the whole routine again: gym, pills, sell, crash. Each night when I got home, I threw away the remains of questionable take-out salads and protein bars thrown in there as well, food particles sticking to the schedule hanging from my clipboard. Yes, I was now a disgusting human living and eating out of her car, accessorized with bloodshot eyes. *Perhaps I could pass for a drug addict*, I would think to myself. *No, not at all*, I would argue back. *You are too classy for needles and snorting. These pills are only performance enhancers. Everyone uses them.* The only thing that kept me going was the initial buzz I would get from the first burst of my pill releasing its chemicals in my bloodstream. *I'll quit when I'm rich*, I would tell myself, sliding the lipstick holder back into my purse, where it was hidden from sight, so that I could hide my habit from the rest of the world. Aside from chomping my way to a false sense of euphoria, the sheer delight I felt when Nick texted or called after I closed a deal was what kept pushing me each hour, each day.

One step closer to Florida, Baby, his messages would say.

To which I usually responded:

Wish you were inside me right now. Gotta get to my next appointment!

The managers even had side bets on who was going to win this whole thing. It was how they got their kicks from sitting behind a desk and yelling at people or interviewing idiots all day. I only gathered this from the few minutes I would burst into the office to restock my car with the paperwork we gave to new policy holders. With a few waves and nods, I would fly back out the door, obviously too busy and important to deal with anyone else. On the final day, I paused to listen in on Monte's managerially intensive phone conversation, especially since I could tell it pertained to me.

"No, my girl cleaned up shop yesterday, check your stats!" I could hear him yelling into the blue-tooth headset. He paused a moment to let whomever was on the other line look up the competitors' stats, and his response clearly appeased Monte. "Yeah, what did I tell you brother? Total knockout." He saw me at my desk and got off the phone.

"How's my girl doing today?" he asked, placing a reassuring palm on my shoulder. Any day I came into the office after a winning streak, he treated me with the care of a new puppy.

"She's good," I answered nonchalantly, pretending like I didn't hear any of his conversation. This was me playing it cool. "Last day, Jay. This is big. Huge. You're coming to play," he said looking me in the eye and giving a customary fist-pump.

"Don't even tell me what place I'm in right now, Monte, I don't keep track of that shit, you know."

"I know, I know. You got this, just kill it. I know you can." As soon as he walked out of eyesight, I dug into my purse and eye-ball counted my pills. Yes, it looked like I had a couple days' worth of energy in stock.

∎ ∎ ∎

Thirteen hours later, at 10:37pm, I inched into my driveway refusing to succumb to defeat. I had just logged a disgusting amount of hours, with sales so meager they'd barely earn me a ride to the airport, never mind the whole damn vacation. *Where the hell was my game?* The dramatic part of me wanted to bang my head off the steering wheel like some lunatic in a movie would, but I settled for grabbing my bags and slamming the car door to really channel my energy effectively. I stormed into my house and dropped my gym bag, work bag, and purse in a heaping pile on the kitchen floor. Losing was not acceptable ever, but this time it was absolutely out of the question. I whipped out my phone and texted Monte a sad face. He answered me right away. "9am tomorrow. It ain't over til the buzzer." A giant ticking time bomb dictated our success as we literally had to transfer our business electronically in order for it to count. There needed to be more sales on my computer within the next ten hours - when this time zone was sleeping. Who the hell was going to talk to me at this hour?

I called Mimi, my work mom. At forty-eight years old, Mimi a newly widowed grandma who looked pretty damn good with her bright features and naturally curly hair that never frizzed. Mimi also had a penchant for younger men, and dating monogamously was not something that was part of her agenda. Between forty-five year old Frank in New Jersey or the ex-marine Charlie fifteen years her junior, and her slam piece Georgie for when she was drunk, I couldn't keep track. Once she showed the proof with a photo of Charlie's tanned, muscular build, I dubbed her a "GILF." She was a grandmother, after all. After explaining that it was an expression adopted from *American Pie's* "MILF"- mom I'd like to fuck - she proclaimed I was her new favorite person. Then when I told her I was single, she offered to hook me up with Charlie. As much as I appreciated the offer, taking Gilf's sloppy seconds was not exactly what I had in mind for any evening on my schedule.

My heart sank. I had to figure something out to get to Florida. *Bitch, think* I ordered my brain. I stared at the clock - it was just after 11:00. I knew if I took a Xanax at this point, I would pass out and then there would be zero chance of salvaging this Florida trip. *These are the times when winners emerge. This is how champions are made. If you want something bad enough, you will find a way to get it.* Everything drilled into my head throughout the countless meetings played on the flashing billboard inside my head. Facing the possibility of failure when I so badly wanted to succeed was not something I was prepared for. I texted Nick: *I'm not throwing the towel in yet.*

Nick: *That's my girl ;)*

For every problem, there is a solution. How was I going to pull off going from a loser to a dominator in ten hours, with a serious constraint being that general population was asleep and not making financial decisions? I called Mimi back to commiserate.

She picked up the phone, just like a good mom does for her work baby. "Mimi, I am fucked," I started. "I need to go to Florida. I have to."

"Why do you care about Florida? Didn't you live over there in that damned beach Gaza Strip place?"

"No, Mimi, I lived in *Tel Aviv*." I loved Mimi, but I did not have the patience to give her a proper Middle Eastern geography lesson. And yes, I had been to Florida more times than I could count growing up to see my mom's family, but now was not the time to address that fact. "Whatever." Clearly she didn't want a lesson anyway.

"I don't know about you, girl, but I need a drink." *A drink. People get drinks at bars. What bars have anyone still drinking on a*

Wednesday at this hour? And then it dawned on me. "Mimi, where are you?" I asked. "Almost back at the office, it took us forever to get home from the last appointment."

"Stay there. I'm coming to get you. We have something to do."

"Okay, but will it involve alcohol? What about Georgie? I told him I would meet him."

"Tell Georgie you're running a little late." I was not going to lose any arguments to a man whose name made me picture a monkey chomping on a banana. I looked in the mirror and was taken aback by my reflection. My eyes were red from a lack of sleep, the make-up I had carefully applied that morning now looked like I had spent the day at a hot concert, and my outfit was all wrong for what I was about to attempt. I needed something simple, sleek, yet professional. Trying too hard was not going to win me any points. I grabbed my black cigarette pants, a white long sleeved button down shirt with the cuffs rolled back, nude patent leather pumps, and a nude skinny belt to pull it together. I kept my watch on and grabbed a strand of pearls for a touch of class. A little foundation, bronzer, blush and mascara later, I looked more recognizable. My mom walked into my room just as I was finishing my make-up.

"What are you doing?" she asked me, probably surprised that I was going somewhere in the middle of the week.

"Going to sell life insurance."

"Jayden, it's almost 11:00. Nu?"

"Mom, I want to win this Florida trip."

"Honey, it's not worth killing yourself over. Plus, it's just Florida. It's not like you haven't been there before." *Yeah, but Nick Kingsley is there now*, I thought to myself.

"Yeah, but this is important to me, Mom. I'll be home later." I grabbed my purse and trotted down the stairs before she had a chance to continue any argument.

■ ■ ■

"Well, here we are," I said to Mimi as we walked into Grayton's claim to fame: the casino.

"Where do you want to check out first?" she asked me as we stood in the lobby. Ahead of us was a circular labyrinth of slot machines, tables, and cocktail waitresses, all flanked by a track edging the row of restaurants and shops. Yes, on a Wednesday evening, teetering on midnight, the casino was the only place in town with signs of life.

"The Red Bar?" I suggested the bar in the middle of the whole establishment, dubbed "Red Bar" creatively for the carpeting and matching colored leather couch and bar stool cushions. We walked past the slot machines, where I had to grab Mimi by the hand as she began salivating. I promised her we could come back and waste money by pulling levers after I had sold the policies that I needed to. I wasn't even really sure what my plan was, I was just shooting blanks at this point. When we actually reached the bar, we surveyed our surroundings and noticed that the only other people in that bar were two men in their late 60s who were missing teeth and had not had a haircut since the recession had hit. "Let's go," I whispered and again ushered Mimi back through the slot machines.

"I need a cigarette," she announced. "I used to spend a lot of time at this casino after Michael died," Mimi told me as she took a deep drag. Mimi talked about her husband often, but not in a way that made anyone uncomfortable. It was therapeutic for her to relive their happy times, to remember that sometimes the world we lived in did bring love into our lives.

"We came every weekend. It was our date. We would pretend we didn't know each other and then meet up at the blackjack table and gamble against each other all night. There usually would end up being a crowd of people rooting either for him or me. We had everyone fooled into thinking we were strangers who ended up in these intensely competitive blackjack games. After one of us finally folded, we would shake hands and part ways without even a smirk. Then we went took separate exits and met up in one of the hotel rooms here. It was so freakin hot. God that made for some hot sex later." I was never grossed out by hearing about the GILF's marital or extracurricular sexcapades. I just hoped that I had that active of a sex life when I was almost fifty. You know, to make up for the current lost time.

"After Michael died," Mimi continued, "I would come here night after night. I couldn't look at the blackjack table. But I would play the slot machine. Just sit here and drink and feed the slot machine dollar after dollar. As if feeding these damn things would give me the answers as to why he was taken away from me. And to feel closer to Michael. Because this was our happy place away from home." I didn't know what to say, fearing whatever came out of my mouth would either make Mimi cry or even worse, angry, so I just tried to appease her.

"We'll come back and play the slot machines. I'll stay with you as long as you like. I promise." With that, Mimi put out her cigarette, and we walked our way over to the casino's version of a pub, McDraught's, and ordered drinks. We spotted a group of about half a dozen people on the other side of the bar. While normally they all looked to be potential clients, they were laughing so hard it was clear none of them were in any condition to make any financial decisions. Mimi and I looked at each other and knew this was the perfect opportunity. We positioned ourselves closer to our targets and decided a plan of attack.

I looked over at the men, sitting at the bar stools surrounded by two women who had guzzled enough beer and shots that they now exuded the confidence that only comes from alcohol - which means one of two things. You are either extremely friendly to anyone you meet, or you are a bitch at the drop of a hat if another woman enters the territory. Judging from the cackles and consistent shots being tossed back, Mimi figured they were the second type. And for once, I listened.

My phone went off with a text from Nick. "Who the hell is hitting you up this late on a Wednesday? Sighing, I realized nothing got past Mimi. I bit my lower lip, debating how to proceed with the conversation, but she pressed on, not giving me an option to take control. "Who are you texting?" she asked.

"Can you keep a secret?" I asked. After making her pinky promise that she would keep this conversation top secret, I spilled everything. "So, how big is he?" she asked as I concluded the Kingsley saga, where perhaps the liquor made me spill more details than usual. "Jesus Mimi, who are you, Scarlett?"

"Oh no, I don't smoke weed. And I definitely have a lot more sex than she does."

"Well, let's say he's proportional to his height."

"Oh shit, girl." Her eyes grew wide. Clearly she could imagine what size junk we were discussing.

"Yeah. I walked like a duck for a few days."

"No wonder you want to go to Florida so badly."

"I mean, I just feel ridiculous."

"Don't. Look, Nick is a successful, driven, and sexy guy. But you are also ambitious and on the road to success. And when two people like that connect and can do so on a personal and a professional level… that can be something very powerful. If this really turns into something, you two could complement each other and take your careers to places you never imagined. What if the two of you did work together? When you combine two people who can achieve his level of success and the level that you are about to embark on… girl, as long as you can separate your personal and professional lives… now that's something special. Just embrace what comes your way, Jay." I so badly wanted to internalize and believe what Mimi was saying, but unfortunately, she had a lot of booze doing the talking.

"Relax, Jayden. It was a two week slip. You're still the one everyone has their eye on as the top girl. You'll get to Florida one way or another."

■■■

The next morning I was running late, dressed like a slob, and feeling defeated. There was no way I could have won at this point. Right? My late night plan to sell insurance at the casino was a total bomb and it was precious sleep time I could have had.

All five hundred of us sat conferenced in, channeling into Giovanni's right-hand men delivering the competition's results. First Candice Carpezio, obviously. Then the second, third, and fourth names were called. I stared out the window, my dreams of a Florida trip clearly over. And then something crazy happened. I heard my name being called.

When the clapping and congratulating ceased, I looked at my phone and sure enough:

Monte: *I found out this morning but had to keep a secret. Congrats, Jay!* That fucker.

And then, from his Highness Mr. Kingsley: *That's my girl. Pack your bags ;)*

CHAPTER 11

Because you are worth it. I reread the text over and over, letting those five words sink into my head. When had I ever been worth $639.24 for a plane ticket? Who had ever taken the consideration as to fly me from the dinky Grayton airport so I didn't have to spend extra gas and parking money to fly from Philadelphia? I was totally a Jewish Mother Theresa in my past life and this was G-d saying "you're welcome" after dishing out years of assholes. Nicholas had really done it. He emailed me the flight itinerary and it wasn't until I glanced at the bottom that I saw the ticket price. And when I asked him what planet he was on to spend that kind of money on a flight from Pennsylvania to Florida, "because you're worth it," was his answer. This was so much better than being a freshman in high school getting asked to prom by the senior quarterback. Because the quarterback in high school didn't rake in half a mil last year and wasn't the damn managing director of a zillion offices. I showed Renee the text message, glowing, and she smiled. "See, sweetie. Good things do come to those who wait." And with that, she scratched my back with her perfectly manicured nails just as she did when I was little.

The next week stretched on forever. It was harder and harder to wake up in the morning. Most mornings I would have Nicholas call me to make sure I would get to the gym before work. Per usual, I started packing about three days in advance out of excitement. While sitting in a sea of tank tops and rompers, Nicholas called.

"Jay, I have some news. I have good and bad. Which do you want first?"

"Fuck. The bad I guess. Wait, is it really bad? I'm nervous."

"Calm down. I can't pick you up from the airport, I have to do interviews, but I'm going to send my friend to pick you up from the airport."

"Are you serious? You won't even get me from the airport?" Great, there went my visions of jumping into his arms, spilling the bouquet of red roses he surely would have for me, and pulling over on the side of the highway as we drove to the office so he could fuck my brains out. Just great. All of this, gone.

"I can't. It cannot be re-arranged." Apparently, the other manager in the office had a doctor's appointment that couldn't be rescheduled, which meant Nicholas had to be there to oversee everything. I was not happy.

"Well, then what's the good news?" I asked, probably sounding like a bitch.

"I thought I would go over the itinerary with you." Itinerary? Man he was type A.

"Okay."

"Well. The day you come in, I'm going to take you home after the office and fuck you senseless. So that you can't walk the next day. But then the next day I'll take you for an expensive dinner and make sweet love to you after. But the first night I just want to fuck you stupid." This was music to my ears and my vagina.

"Well, Mr. Kingsley..." I said, dragging his name out, "I suppose those arrangements can be made."

■ ■ ■

Of course, that during that week of anticipation, Monte threw a quota on me to hit, just to really make sure I earned that trip I suppose. The night before my flight when everyone else in America would have been getting their toiletries organized and maybe sleeping, I was out in the middle of God's country trying to close a deal with two uneducated twenty-seven year olds who had two children under the age of five. After midnight, it was clear I was on the losing end of the deal and I slumped to my car, berating myself for pushing a big sale, and also not having my shit together when it was asked to be.

I texted Monte with an apology and he answered me telling me he wasn't mad at me, just get some sleep and enjoy my trip. His words made me feel better, but I couldn't shake that pang of guilt. Or the anxiety. Everything was starting to weigh on that drive home. My parents called wanting to know where the hell I was at this hour. Who could blame them? It had been months of all in, no break, giving 115%, no questions asked.

When I got home, I peeled off the button down and creased pants held together with a black belt and glanced at my reflection. The once curvy body that had a butt you could spot from a city block away had waifed into something that looked malnourished. I touched the space between my shrinking boobs where a bone was starting to protrude. I didn't mind. I was sure Nicholas would think it was sexy. Thank God my mother was sleeping because if she had seen me she would have run down to the kitchen to whip up something Jewish and fattening. I looked at the clock. Four hours until I needed to leave for the airport. Going to sleep was going to be a waste. I changed into my gym clothes, popped a full pill, and snuck out of the house. The only thing to clear my head would be some cardio.

■ ■ ■

At 5:00am, I woke up Ira. "Daddy, we have to go," I told him. I hadn't even bothered going to bed. After I worked out, I finished packing, took a shower, and realized it was time to wake up my dad. "Okay," he answered. This was probably the only time he was excited to take me to the airport. I was going to visit a successful guy who was *paying* for the ticket? Too bad Nicholas wasn't Jewish. But hey, life's not perfect. The butterflies churned in my stomach. I hadn't been on a plane in over a year... who was I? We pulled up to the curb and just like a good father, my dad pulled my bags out of the trunk.

"Do you have enough cash on you?" he asked me. I had plenty of money.

"I do," I lied. I never carried cash.

"Have a safe trip sweetheart. Put this somewhere safe," he told me as he hugged me tight and put a couple bills in my palm.

"I'm proud of you, sweetheart," he said to me. "You have been working so hard, you deserve some vacation." I hadn't mentioned to my parents it was actually a working vacation...

"Thanks, Daddy," I said. "I'll let you know when I get there." As I was checking my bags, I looked to see what he gave me. Three crisp $100 bills. Going up the escalator, I heard my phone ding. It was a text from my Dad. *Just because I know you never carry cash. Have a safe trip... Love Dad.*

I smiled and breathed for the first time in what felt like weeks. It was time to do something for me. All the late nights, hard work, it was piecing together. The sun was coming up as the plane jetted down the runway. I was going to Florida. To see Mr. Nicholas Fucking Kingsley, who wanted *me*.

As I fastened my seatbelt, I had the vivid memory of fastening my seatbelt as I sat on an airplane on the tarmac in Tel Aviv's airport. Although I was in an air-conditioned cabin, the sun's rays were so strong I could feel them pouring in through the picture-frame sized window. I had buckled up not realizing I was leaving a whole life behind me. What was only supposed to be a month or two long stint in the States turned into two years. Two years of living in Pennsyltucky and that's what happened. I was now sitting in an eighteen passenger pathetic excuse of a plane recycled from 1975 ecstatic to get away to Jacksonville, Florida for a few days. Two years ago, I would have cackled at the thought of jetting off in pursuit of a man who sells life insurance. How things change.

■ ■ ■

"No TV?" I asked as I walked into the master suite of the condo. Nicholas lived with two other salespeople from his team he had dragged from his previous office in a remote part of West Virginia. Sandra was only a few months into the business and still struggling on closing consistently, whereas her brother, Brandon, had trained for an Ironman Competition and managed to pull off Agent of the Quarter. *These people work together and live together?* God, I thought living in a sorority house was a bit much.

Nicholas's master suite and access to the private garage were just two very unsubtle clues as to who ran the show. I had to bite my tongue when I saw a prominently displayed D'Angelo Enterprises weekly schedule on the refrigerator. Something told me Nicholas had put it there. At least when I went home, I didn't have to be reminded about work when I went digging for carrots and celery sticks in my parents' fridge.

"Bedroom T.V.'s are for poor people," Nicholas reminded me as he dragged my oversized duffle bag next to what I presumed to be my side of the bed, which was an *oversized* king. After all, at 6'5" and two hundred and something pounds of muscle, he was oversized himself.

"I guess my parents are broke," I answered, thinking about the countless evenings before I started selling life insurance being curled up in my parent's bed watching movies with my Mom, on the television, which was obviously in the bedroom as well.

"I'm tired," Nicholas said unenthusiastically as he went into the bathroom. I could hear the shower running. I had an unsettling feeling. From the moment I arrived at the office just after noon, it was nine hours of professionalism. I assumed it was so no one would think that my visit was anything other than work-related, which I was totally digging. This whole secretive affair business was just so much of a turn on. The rush was giving my Adderall a run for its money, which I had been popping all day since I hadn't even slept before my flight. I flopped on my back, aware that the probability was that I would pass out cold as soon as my body hit the duvet. Even with the dull sound of the water running from the shower, my heart pounded through my corpse-like state. *You have got to ween off these pills*, I told myself. *As soon as you get home, you're going to start cutting down.*

When Nicholas came out of the bathroom, I jumped up and began fishing through my suitcase(s) to find clothes for bed. Piles of clothes spilled onto the carpet and a wave of heels and flip flops flew about for me to find what I was looking for. I looked up and saw a look of disapproval across Nicholas's face.

"Really, Jayden, how much stuff did you need to bring for three days?"

"A lot, I like options," I answered unapologetically. I set aside the bathroom supplies and heaped the clothes and shoes into a giant pile on top of the suitcase. It still looked like a mini bomb went off in his room, but whatever.

I stepped into the bathroom and was impressed with the open space showcasing a walk-in marble shower, a jacuzzi big enough for three Nicholas Kingsleys, and a double vanity which ran the length of the opposite wall. I washed the sixteen hour make up off my face and then re-applied some tinted moisturizer so I wasn't completely hideous.

"You're going in the field with Sandra tomorrow," he said as I opened the door to the bedroom.

"Oh, okay," I said, surprised. "I thought I was going to run appointments with you in the afternoon. Wasn't that the point of me coming here, to see your presentation?"

"Change of plans. I have to give interviews until evening."

"Um, okay."

"It will be good for Sandra. You can coach her up," he told me. I knew what his angle was - to stroke my ego in order to get what he wanted.

"Okay."

"I'll pick you up after I finish for the day."

"Sounds good," I said putting an end to this conversation.

"I'm glad I'm here," I told him as we climbed into bed and I inched my way towards him, hoping this unease was just something I was imagining.

"I'm glad you're here too," he told me, pulling me towards him and instantly I felt as though I was with my Nicholas again.

Without any words, he peeled off whatever clothes were on my body and climbed on top of me. What happened next completely made my vagina shrivel. Without warning, as in any form of foreplay to rev my tired body up for the sex, Nicholas fiddled around with his ginormous penis and pushed it inside me. I have no idea how he maneuvered his way in there as my poor vag had no time to even get wet.

I felt a fast series of abrupt thrusts and a climactic groaning noise. Nicholas jumped up and headed to the bathroom, leaving my vagina and me completely frustrated. *What was that shit?*

Brush it off. Play it cool. You're the cool girl. Don't complain. Brush off the premature ejaculation. Just because you're in Florida doesn't mean you're entitled to cunnilungus…but wouldn't a little finger action have at least been too much to ask?

I didn't say anything. I kept Crazy Bitch Mode at bay. It was day one after all, I needed to start off on the right foot. Maybe he was stressed out from work. Maybe he was just so turned on by my protruding hipbone that he couldn't help but blow his load early.

I woke up to his roommate Sandra knocking on the door from a sleep that was bordering on a coma. "Hey girl!" I jumped up, startled, and dying to brush my teeth. Drool was all over the pillow. I'm so gross sometimes. I looked at the clock. It was 10:17am. *WTF?* Nicholas and I had planned to go to the gym for 5:30am. Before Sandra could answer, I stared back at the clock.

"What the hell? I haven't slept this late since before I started this job!"

"It's okay, you needed to sleep. So Nicholas said you're coming in the field with me today. My first one is at noon."

"Okay, no problem. I'll get ready, I just need to swing by the office to grab my bag. I left it there last night."

I jumped out of bed and began running between the bedroom and the bathroom, trying to organize my disheveled self.

"How are you so fucking skinny? I swear working at D'Angelo Enterprises *makes* me fat! All I do is drink and eat fast food on the road!" Sandra was eyeing me as I slid my legs into a pair of cranberry colored cropped cotton pants from Banana Republic and a short sleeved cream top. The thought of fast food made me queasy.

"Hah, I don't know, I eat a lot of salad," I answered. I wasn't lying. I just wasn't telling the entire truth.

I don't know how people dress in Northern Florida for work but I was not about to adjust my look. Sandra was wearing a boat neck black top with a one of those flowing skirts that does nothing for your figure and only accentuates wide hips. When we stepped outside, beads of sweat were forming along my forehead. It wasn't even 11am. I addressed the most critical factor of any in-home sales environment.

"Everyone has central air here, right?"

We stopped by the office so I could grab my computer bag. When I got to the door, it was shut. Shit. I knocked gently, knowing I was interrupting an interview. But I needed my bag, damnit.

"Come in," I heard. "Hi, excuse me," I began, smiling as widely as I could, "I just needed to grab my laptop and bag."

"It's in Brandon's office next door," Nicholas answered flatly, glancing at me long enough that I could smell his annoyance that I dared to interrupt his precious interview. The same interview he gives every day to potential new hires. Always searching for new talent. The next big star. I shut the door, retreating like a disobedient servant and grabbed my belongings from the office I had been directed to.

"Your boss is so moody," I said to Sandra as I climbed into her Ford Escape where she was waiting for me. My iced coffee was now coffee with melted ice and tasted disgusting. The thirty second walk from the office building to her car was already activating my sweat glands.

"Nicholas is that way when he gets stressed out," she answered. *Lovely,* I thought.

"Who are we off to see?" I asked, in attempt to channel to my attention elsewhere.

"Rayleene, who is a stay at home mom with three kids."

"Wow, sounds like a big check," I murmured as I rolled down the window and poured the watered-coffee liquid onto the concrete.

"At least we can get referrals," she added hopefully as I fished around the lipstick holder for my second half of a pill of the day. Sandra's focus was on the road so she wasn't paying attention to what I was fishing around for in my purse. The heat was probably burning whatever chemicals I already had in my system, so obviously I needed more.

■ ■ ■

My sales instincts were right. Rayleene was a chainsmoking asthmatic who was on disability due to her illness. I'm sure her doctor instructed her to smoke her three packs of Camels a day. The rest of the day's appointments all panned out the same. Two grandparents in their mid-50s raising a granddaughter because the mother was in jail and the father was unknown, so who knew. The grandparents were adamant they did not have an extra $17.00 a month to take out a policy on their granddaughter.

When Sandra broke out her calculator and explained that it would only be a fifty-cent per day investment, I appreciated her strategic approach, but I felt my dignity being stripped as fast as the sweat was dripping from my forehead. Clearly these people were broke being that the only sign of ventilation was a rotating ceiling fan which happened to be shaking directly over my head. I wanted to get out of that house before it dropped on my head.

If Nicholas had been with us at this appointment, he would have gotten the check, and probably a much bigger one, I knew it. And why we couldn't seem to accomplish what he was able to was getting under my skin.

"Well, that was fun," I said as we got in the car, a river practically trickling from my armpits. Finally Nicholas called me to tell me he would pick me up to grab dinner. "Can't I go back to your place and change first? It's 90 degrees out, I feel sweaty in these clothes," I asked.

"No, I'm starving," he told me and asked for the address of where we were so he could pick me up. I had Sandra blast the air conditioner as I fanned my shirt to the vents hoping to clear this nasty mess up in ten minutes. My make-up had completely disintegrated. I was repulsed by my own reflection. I reached for my purse to grab my make up for an emergency redoing of the face and found my trusty orange babies. If I was going to be able to carry on any form of a conversation and not have my head drop during dinner, I needed a pick-me-up.

Nicholas met Sandra and I at a gas station around the corner. As I climbed into his cool BMW, I was greeted with an icy "Hello." We met another manager, Andre, and his girl-toy-situation at a casual restaurant near the beach. Everyone was in t-shirts and I was still in my sweat-dripped sales clothes. I felt ridiculous. Nicholas barely looked at me during dinner. When Andre and Nicholas weren't making fun of people or bragging about their stellar sales teams, their faces were buried in their phones.

"Wow, you guys make such great dates," Natasha, the girl toy commented. I smiled at her. "Well, this is how we make our money to pay for *your* dinners and drinks," Andre reminded her and Nicholas laughed. I was ready to throw up. After dinner Natasha and Andre galavanted down the sidewalk laughing and holding hands. Nicholas walked and texted, barely acknowledging me, except to ask what flavor frozen yogurt I wanted when Andre and Natasha decided to wander into a shop five minutes before closing. The kids behind the counter, who were trying to clean up the place, passed each other looks of "I hate when assholes do this to us." I empathized with them. In high school I had worked at a pizza shop which closed at 10:00. At 9:58pm when someone came in wanting to sit down and order dinner I'd want to cry. But Nicholas and Andre didn't seem to care.

"They're about to close, guys. Why don't we go somewhere else?" I suggested.

"Whatever," Nicholas said. "We'll leave a tip." They left a $5 tip. Which meant $2.50 for each of the guys serving our frozen yogurt. How generous.

We said good-bye to Andre and Natasha and got into the BMW. Nicholas opened and closed the door for me but didn't say a word. What had I done? Did he have a bad day?

"Do you want to grab a drink or anything?" I asked him, hoping he would say yes. What was the point of a vacation with no bar hopping? "No, I'm tired. I gave interviews all day," he said. I tried making conversation the rest of our fifteen minute drive but I came up against a wall of short, disinterested answers. When we got back to his house, he got changed and climbed right into bed, facing away from me. I slipped into bed, feeling about six inches tall and clueless. I stretched my legs out and tried to loop them through his, craving any sort of connection. But why? Why did

I want attention and affection from someone who was being so distant? Where was the attentive fun loving guy who doted on me in Pittsburgh?

A few minutes later he rolled over and I thought my luck was turning. He reached and pulled my shorts down and pressed his mouth on mine. But I didn't feel any emotion from him. I touched him and felt him pressing into my leg, hard as a rock. At least I still had *that* going for me. He climbed on top of me and without a word, pushed himself inside me with one thrust sending a tearing pain through my body. "Ouch, Nicholas," I said, which fell on deaf ears. He grabbed the headboard above me and pounded. The physical pain of him moving around inside me was so acute I had to suppress a cry out. I couldn't move, not with this giant on top of me pinning my legs and blocking me from going anywhere with his arms over the top of my body.

"Nicholas, you're really hurting me," I said again, praying he would slow down, or kiss me, or hold me, or something tender so that I didn't feel so naked and alone. I just wanted this to end. It wasn't sex. It was something horrible I knew I'd never want to experience again in my life.

He finally finished, grunting, and rolled over. I went to the bathroom and sat on the toilet. I touched myself and his cum came dripping out. Fucking asshole. *What man has the audacity to have sex with a girl and come without warning?* I peed and looked in the mirror, hating what I looked at. The face of someone who was fucked and chucked on a vacation. I started to cry. A tear from each eye dripped down my cheek but I didn't wipe them. Maybe I deserved this. Maybe I deserved getting treated like shit, stupid for thinking I was lovable, especially from someone like Nicholas. Who did I think I was, galavanting to Florida to capture a manager's heart? I was a foolish girl with tears streaming down my cheeks on a Friday night and no one to call. I crawled back into his bed and faced away from the already fast-asleep giant, with only the cool dampness of my tears trailing down my cheeks to keep me company.

■■■

The next morning Nicholas didn't acknowledge what had transpired the previous evening. Instead, he declared that the "guys," meaning him and Andre, needed a "gym session." And therefore, he was going to link me up with Natasha so she and I could go to the beach. That was it. He didn't just hate fuck me. He really seemed to hate me.

When the boys took off in Nicholas's car, Andre tossed Natasha the keys to his Porsche Cayenne. "Time for the bar?" she asked me. I felt relieved as she drove straight to a beachside restaurant with an extensive drink menu. Maybe it was the vodka I decided to down at 2:00pm. But I told her everything. How we started talking, the Pittsburgh weekend, even what he had done in bed the night before.

"What a fucking asshole!" she said as I told her how Nicholas didn't stop when I said it hurt. Well, at least it wasn't in my head. I had verbal confirmation.

"I just don't understand," I said. "What the hell am I doing here?"

"Guys are weird," she said, sipping her beer. "You literally just have to pretend you don't give a shit. Just tell yourself always he doesn't like you. Keep that in your head and then no matter what happens, you won't be disappointed." Well, this was a fun realization.

"I mean, I didn't come down here with the intention of making him my boyfriend. But I just don't understand how he is being so cold," I reiterated, shocked and hurt by how this whole weekend was panning out. How was I supposed to act like I didn't care? Anyone with eyeballs could see how much I did care. I flagged down the waiter for another drink, hoping alcohol would work its magic and make these problems go away. Maybe a good work out would make Nicholas get out of his ridiculous mood.

■ ■ ■

"Which dress should I wear?" I asked Nicholas, with my hair blow dried, straightened, and my make-up finished. I stood wearing a black satin robe with three dresses, all colored versions of very fitted on the bed in front of me.

"Hmmm, that one," he said pointing to my favorite cap sleeved leopard print dress that is so tight but doesn't reveal an ounce of fat. Not that I had any to reveal at that point. He walked out of the room so I could get dressed. I threw on the dress and some jewelry, hoping maybe this was when the turnaround would happen. Maybe this distant stranger I'd grown to be intimidated by would pull his guard down and act like I was a woman he wanted around, and not a child he was being forced to babysit without being compensated.

I walked downstairs to him scrolling on his phone looking for a restaurant he wanted to go to. He didn't acknowledge my outfit or any effort I had put in attempting to look half pretty. I looked down and noticed just how short the dress was. A feeling of being overly exposed swept over me. I wanted a drink, now.

"How about a seafood place?" he asked me, eyes glued to the monstrosity of a mobile device in his ape sized palm.

"Sounds good," I said, doing anything seem in an agreeable mood.

"Okay, let's go." We drove the twenty minutes in complete silence except for some generic bullshit conversation about sales and how my office had done for the day. We walked into a restaurant with beautiful tables, beautiful servers, beautiful decor, beautiful everything. The only thing that wasn't beautiful was the obvious lack of chemistry between Nicholas and me at this point. It was so tense, the knife they use to cut a well done rump roast wasn't sharp enough to slice through it. I ordered a glass of wine and Nicholas decided he wasn't drinking.

"No, I'll drink later," he commented. My fate was sealed. What man takes a woman out to dinner and doesn't want to order a drink? I barely touched my food. Between my ridiculous dress where I looked like a Las Vegas club rat and sitting next to someone who clearly would have rather been doing their taxes than being in my presence, I wanted to crawl under the table like a toddler and just cry. After picking at some salmon that could have tasted like Filet-o-Fish from McDonald's for all I knew, the waiter came and offered coffee and dessert, which we declined of course. At this point, it was late and most of the diners had cleared out. As Nicholas fished his wallet out for one of his stupid plastic money cards, I took in the tablecloths, expensive china and bay windows in this downtown area. I sat shivering from the ridiculously high air conditioning, wishing I was at a fucking Chipotle eating a burrito bowl with someone who could look me in the eye instead of looking anywhere but at me. Being with someone who wants to be anywhere else than in your company when you are 1,000 miles from home made me feel numb and cheap. I was flown a thousand miles to be treated like a peasant in a sea of luxury. That's what I was to Nicholas, clearly. A cheap toy to be thrown around. My blood was boiling and I was at my breaking point.

We walked to the car and climbed in. As he shifted the car into drive, I started asking questions. "Nicholas, why did you break up with Marisa?" I had never brought her up. The question fell out of my mouth before I had a chance to censor myself. He looked down at the keyless entry key in the console and began to fiddle with it. I was sitting in an $80,000 car next to someone on the other side of the world wishing I was in an $8,000 car with someone who wanted to be there.

"I'm really fucked up, Jayden," he said, still looking down.

"What do you mean?" I asked. He looked up, staring straight through the windshield, unable to look me in the eye.

"I met someone else." I must have been starring in someone else's movie, with an awful script. This needed to be rewound and done over. The screenwriter got this all wrong.

"What?" I asked, calmly. At least, that's how I remember it.

"I'm sorry," he said, facing forward, into a new movie set I clearly wasn't a part of. A thousand emotions seared through me but anger took control of my body. "I have to get out," I said as I opened the car door and stormed out. I couldn't be next to him. I'd punch him. Granted, it would hurt my fist a lot more than his arm or chest, but I needed to be away from his physical being. *This isn't happening*, I kept thinking. This isn't what fairy tales were made of. Prince Charming didn't knock Cinderella's heart out of her chest as her carriage turned back into a pumpkin. The BMW was feeling like a prison, except luckily I had the power to escape.

"You're fucking kidding me," I said as I opened the door and stomped my four inch black stiletto onto the pavement, trying to avoid a Britney Spears moment where my dress rides up to my crotch. Some shred of dignity needed to be maintained. I slammed the door and started walking. If I stayed in the car, I didn't trust myself to not break into a full out *Girl Interrupted* manic rage. I heard the car inching behind me and then it stopped beside me, about ten feet away. Nicholas rolled down the window and looked at me.

"You forgot this," he said, dangling my purse out the window.

You're fucking kidding me. You're fucking kidding me. Mother fucking asshole. Please let me wake up from this nightmare. Please. Please. Please let this be a nightmare.

My jaw dropped and I could feel my eyes widen as another wave of rage rushed over me. "Excuse me?" I asked.

"Your purse?" he repeated, as though I were slow. "That's what you have to say for yourself?" I asked, my blood pressure probably as high as a morbidly obese person who just left Old Country Buffet. "Well, look where you're walking." It was dark, I saw pavement below my feet. My surroundings as far the architectural structures were not something particularly at the forefront of my thoughts at the present moment.

"What?" I continued. "Jayden, that's a hotel over there. I thought you were walking there."

"No, I just needed to get the fuck away from you."

"Come on, Jayden, get back in the car." Realizing I had no other option, I opened the prison door and slid back onto the cool leather seat. Oh the irony of sitting in a luxury car that is meant to be pleasurable yet feeling nothing other than pain and anger. I fired questions at him the whole way home, needing to know and understand how some gold digger swooped her way into my Cinderella tale.

"When the hell did you meet her? We work all the time."

"I met her last Sunday."

"The day after you booked my fucking ticket?"

"Yes."

"Where?"

"The beach."

"Oh, isn't that just cute."

"We haven't hooked up. We haven't even kissed. We just have gone out to eat a few times. But it's different."

"Oh, it's different?"

"Yes. I want to take things slowly with her."

"Excuse me?"

"We slept together too soon in Pittsburgh."

"Nicholas, that was your idea and we talked about that as adults, we had a mature conversation beforehand, we didn't recklessly fuck after being wasted."

"I know, and that was my mistake. I'm turning over a new leaf. I don't want to hurt anyone anymore. I want to take things slowly with her."

"You have got to be kidding me. So I get to be the last one in your line of fire?"

"Yes."

"You're a horrible person, Nicholas. What does this girl even do for a living?"

"She's a dancer for the Jaguars."

"I'm going to be sick. I'm surprised she's not an agent."

"Well, I'm talking to her about working for D'Angelo Enterprises actually. I think she has great potential."

"Oh, so you can fuck another agent. Real mature." I saw him smirk at that comment.

We sat in silence for a minute, Nicholas looking relaxed now that this weight had been lifted off his massive shoulders, and me with my legs crossed and arms folded wondering if the death penalty was still used in Florida. Questions were popping into my head rapid fire, I couldn't keep up with my thoughts. I picked one that seemed to dominate over the others.

"Why did you have me come down here if you knew you wanted to be with someone else?"

"Well, your ticket was already booked and you still deserved your vacation."

"This isn't a vacation, this is torture. I would rather be in smelly houses with no bank accounts for a whole weekend than being humiliated like this."

"I haven't seen you in over a month, so I decided I wanted to see if there was something there still."

"Oh, really? And you decided to do this all without even telling me an inkling as to what was going on down here? So I show up down here blind and looking like an idiot? What kind of sick person are you? Do you even have a heart beating in your chest?"

"I didn't think you would still want to come if I told you what was going on. I didn't want to tell you over the phone."

"Oh, but dragging me through a weekend of treating me like a third class citizen and ignoring me was a much more mature way. You know, I *deserved* to know what was going on and make that decision for myself."

"Jayden, this isn't exactly third class treatment. I just spent $200 on a dinner for you."

"I'd rather eat at McDonald's with someone who wants to be with me than eat surf and turf with an asshole, Nicholas."

"Jayden, I didn't think you would react this way. You're being dramatic." Oh, now I'm being dramatic.

"What did you do think I was going to do Nicholas? Ask to see a picture of her on Facebook and hit the like button?"

And on it went like this the rest of the car ride home until we pulled into the garage and we walked into the condo. At this point I was tear streaked, ready to be dragged off to a psych ward, and desperate to be on another planet.

"Sandra will be home soon," Nicholas told me. "You can hang out with her. I'm going out." He turned, and walked out the door, leaving me alone in a house that wasn't mine and with feelings of an emotional stomach flu. Ten minutes later Sandra walked in to find me on the couch, crying tears of anger and denial.

"What's going on?" she asked, running over to me, genuinely concerned. I paused my sobbing to explain what happened in the car after dinner. When I finished, she was pissed. "I'm going to kill Nicholas! I thought you were his girlfriend!"

"Well, no, definitely not."

Sandra decided we should salvage what was left of the night. My third night in stupid Florida and I hadn't even been properly drunk. Eyes blood shot and mascara smeared, I needed to make myself moderately presentable. By the time I fixed my face and we drove aimlessly to the boardwalk, it was 1:35am. None of the bouncers would let us into any of the bars. I was contemplating buying a bottle of wine from a grocery store and drinking myself into stupidity at this point, but Sandra talked me out of *starting* a night of drinking at 2:00am. Whatever, I had done worse things. I grabbed a bottle of whatever was available from a corner store that was next to the last bar from we were rejected.

Back at the condo, we sat in the living room, me drinking a bottle of some shitty white, me ranting and raving, Sandra listening empathetically, however unable to say anything to alleviate my misery.

A while later, Nicholas's buzzed crew stumbled into the door, deep in conversation about... what else. Life insurance. It's 3:00am on a Saturday night, drunken grub in hand, and they are discussing life insurance sales tactics. Maybe I should have gone to the hotel I was strolling past after I stormed out of Nicholas's car. I stared, listening to their conversation, running Nicholas's words in my head over and over. "I met someone else." Where the hell was Nicholas? I think Sandra read my mind because she asked for me. They looked up from their burgers and fries, as though we had been invisible that whole time and had just appeared out of thin air. I understood. When I was drunk and eating, there was nothing else that was going to get in my line of focus. And for a bunch of life insurance agents who are drunk, eating, *and* talking about their beloved life insurance, not even a gaggle of free pussy would cut their focus. Nothing like chomping on half cooked meat and arguing the semantics of permanent life coverage in the middle of the night, of course.

Suddenly Nicholas burst through the door and looked right at me. "You are a crazy bitch," he said matter of factly. Normally, there would be some truth to a statement like this, even for an undramatic, soft spoken person like myself. However, being that Nicholas had just ripped my heart and ego to shreds, I had no clue what would have prompted this accusation.

"You egged our friend Megan's car. You got the wrong car." *What the hell?*

"Who the fuck is Megan?"

"Our friend who lives two doors down. Her car just got egged. Pretty ironic considering I picked her up before we went out and you could see that from the window. I know you egged it. Well, Megan's the wrong girl."

Sandra came right to my defense on this whole debacle. "Nicholas, I've been with Jayden the whole time. She didn't egg anything. We don't even have any eggs!"

"You guys could easily have gone to the grocery store and bought some."

"Nicholas, you're fucking ridiculous. If I was going to do anything, it would be to your shit. You're the asshole here, not the other girl. Go check your room. Everything's in order." He went upstairs, and stayed there. The burger-eating boys stared.

"What?" I asked.

"It's fucked up you egged her car," they said.

"I didn't egg her car!" Sandra and I said at the same time. I went back to my bottle of wine and took a slug. Sandra sat with me, watching me drink until both bottles were empty. Filled with alcohol, my feelings were dulled. Having a drunken haze wash over me was better than all the awful feelings weighing on me from the moment he told me there was someone else. How was I even sitting here, on this chair? This black leather chair that rocked back and forth…which I really couldn't do at the moment without a wave of nausea coming over me. How was I here, here at this very moment? I was here because I got on a plane, and I got on a plane because Nicholas decided to fly me here. Nicholas was because of work. All because I signed that damned agent contract all those months earlier. Where would I be if I had put down the pen and told Monte, "No, this isn't for me?" I wouldn't be in this leather chair, nursing a broken heart. Or maybe I would be nursing a broken heart, drunk somewhere else, crying over a different man. But all from signing that dotted line next to the X, I ended up here, crying in this black leather chair.

It was obviously time for bed. Too much thinking about planes and leather chairs. I walked into Nicholas's room to get changed. Forget knocking, he didn't deserve that respect. He was in his walk-in closet, carefully inspecting his precious designer clothes and acquired jewelry. Nice clothes and jewelry don't make you a man. They just encase whatever kind of body is underneath them. In boxers and a Led Zepplin t-shirt, he looked like anyone else in their late 20s. Not like someone whose previous yearly earnings totaled half a million dollars. Not like someone who had 500 pairs of eyes staring at him with admiration and respect as he commanded an agency with workshops that were guaranteed to generate thousands of dollars in revenue with only a few steps of implementation on the agents' ends. For that small second, he could have looked like any average guy his age.

He looked up when he heard the door open and stared at me. His glance was passive, as though he was staring right through me and my eyes were insignificant. At that moment I knew he was really done. His emotional wall was permanently erected, without any cranes to knock it back down. The Nicholas who warmed up to me turned cold. I wanted to scream and cry, but even more so, I wanted to be loved.

"You can sleep in here. I'll sleep downstairs," the hulk said emotionlessly.

"Wow, thanks," I answered.

"Maybe you didn't egg her car. All my stuff is in order, just like you said. I don't know though. It's still quite a coincidence."

"I don't have the energy to argue with you," I said as I lied down onto his bed. I heard the door shut and then darkness filled the room. Brushing my teeth never happened. Oh well, not like my bad breath was going to be a deal breaker for the evening, anyway.

■ ■ ■

I woke up to my head aching and my mouth tasting like cheap, stale wine. I looked at my phone, which told me it was 9:47am. Next to me, the bed was empty. Oh, that's right. *Nicholas is downstairs, because he is in love with someone else and I am last season's Barbie*, I thought to myself as I swung my legs over the bed and stumbled to the bathroom to brush my teeth and wash an oily layer from my face. I looked into the mirror. My hair was still straight from the night before but my eyes were bloodshot from crying and chugging wine. I should have looked tan and radiant, but I just looked hungover. Screw this, I was going back to sleep.

I woke up as Nicholas walked into the room an hour later. "I'm going to rebook your flight from you leaving tomorrow to tonight."

"Um, okay," I replied, feeling even more hurt. He immediately called the airline and charged a cool $250 to his credit card to get me out of his hair a good twelve hours early. Every time I thought there would be a moment of emotional reprieve, he managed to dig the knife in even deeper. If my emotional hurt was translated into physical damage, I would look like something out of a murder scene. I grabbed my phone and went downstairs to call my parents. My dad answered the house phone.

"Daddy!" I cried into the phone. I may have been twenty-five years old, but in times of angst, I was the epitome of a Daddy's girl. Normally I didn't run to him with heartbreak problems, those were reserved for my mom. But today, I needed the Dad who carried me on his shoulders through the park and taught me how to point my skis like a pizza on the bunny slope.

"What the hell?" my father asked when I explained Nicholas decided to fly me down without telling me he had met someone else.

"Daddy, I hate him!" I begged him to call the airline get me an even earlier flight than Nicholas had, because i just couldn't bear to be in this city for another minute. Being the father who could never say no to a crying daughter, he looked up flights but only found ones that left later than the one Nicholas booked me on. I was screwed. He told me he loved me and to hang tight, he and Mommy would be at the airport to pick me up later that night.

"Who were you just talking to?" Nicholas asked me from upstairs as I hung up the phone.

"My dad, not that it's any of your business," I replied icily.

"Did you tell him what happened?" he asked.

"Of course I did," I answered.

"Why did you tell him?"

"Because he's my *father* and I tell him everything."

"I wish you didn't tell him."

"And why is that?"

"Well, I don't want your parents to not like me."

You have got to be kidding me. "Well, what, were you planning on coming over for family dinner? What the fuck do you care if they like you or not?"

"Well you never know down the road if I have to meet them or something, I wouldn't want them to not like me."

"You should have thought about that before, Nicholas."

And with that, I did a dramatic about face and stomped downstairs and slumped into the black leather chair which seemed to lure me in moments of emotional fury. I turned on the TV. Sportscenter was on. Skip. I had settled on focusing on watching Joan Rivers on *Fashion Police* shred apart famous people who apparently hire children trapped in adult bodies who haven't let go of taffeta and hoop skirts to dress them for events. Just as I had started to amuse myself with Joan's unforgiving antics, Nicholas thundered down the stairs and I felt my muscles tighten. He grabbed the remote from the ottoman under my feet and turned off the TV. He was turning Crazy Bitch Mode simultaneously.

"Are you for real Nicholas?"

"Come on, we have a few hours to kill before your flight. I'll take you to the beach." The beach? Oh, now he wants to go to the beach with me.

"I'm surprised you can stand to be within fifty feet of me."

"Forty five. Come on, let's get breakfast."

"I'm not hungry. I don't want breakfast."

"Well I am."

"Actually, I changed my mind. I'm going to order every menu on the item and then not eat a bite of anything."

"Fine, sounds good."

I messed through the mountain of clothing to find the bikini I had originally packed as a seduction tool. That was clearly a waste of suitcase space given the circumstances, but I didn't want the Victoria's Secret getup to return home unworn. Nicholas was on the other side of the bed, fiddling on his phone. *He's probably texting her.* A pang of jealousy accompanied the thought and for a moment I wished I was packing an extra two hundred pounds of muscle on my frame so I had a fair shot at inflicting bodily damage on him. I lifted my shirt over my head and placed my bikini top over my bra. My body was no longer Nicholas's temple. Maybe it never was. Was that it? Was something wrong with my body? I pinched at the skin alongside my waist, trying to determine if there were was an excess fat patch that might have slipped past my line of sight.

"What is it Nicholas? Am I too fat?" No response, So I tried the reverse psychology.

"Too skinny?" I asked, staring at him, waiting for his dancing fingers to finish their little texting routine so his eyes could focus their attention on me. But they never did.

"No, you're fine," he answered without lifting his eyes from his cell phone. I faced the mirror, my clavicle jutting out between the two unfilled bra cups. Anyone else would have told me to eat a fucking cheeseburger, but I was still convinced this wasn't good enough. This wasn't even my real body. It was a body I was renting as a result of downing amphetamines like a pack of lifesavers. I knew once I quit nibbling on my orange cookies I'd have to return this body and take my other one back. You know, the one that sometimes revealed cellulite and a double chin in unflattering photos. A few years ago, I would have run to the nearest drug store for various pints of Ben and Jerry's to spoon my way through, but I wasn't ready to break the lease on this rented body. If it was "fine," then something else was wrong with me. I couldn't let go of what *was* my saving grace, even if it wasn't enough to keep Nicholas around.

Being rejected and then getting fat on top of it would have been a suicide attempt. So I reached for what felt like the only thing that loved me back at this point. In a side pocket of the suitcase where I found a spare stash, I quickly grabbed a pill while Nicholas was in his walk-in closet, debating which pair of Nautica or Ralph Lauren swim trunks to wear for the day. I slipped three halves under my tongue and savored the bitterness as solace from the heartbreak which felt all consuming. These orange babies wouldn't tell me I was second fiddle, unworthy or unlovable. They threw me into a world where I reigned supreme. At that moment, I needed to be queen of something. Obviously, my vision of being the leading lady to some insurance honcho in his condo was shattered.

Although an asshole, Nicholas was not stingy. Granted, it wasn't really an inherent trait of generosity, but a symbol of power. But today, I was fine with spending his money. I was not playing the whole Miss Independent card. I was entitled to a severance package for all this bullshit.

He had already ripped my heart out of my chest and taken a shredder to my dignity. What did I have to lose at this point? We piled into the Escalade with Sandra and Brandon for breakfast. I was already envisioning ordering the entire menu to the waitress who would look at me shockingly. "How could a skinny bitch eat all this food?" she would think. Except Nicholas pulled the Escalade up to a Chinese buffet where you could pile food on as many plates as humanly possible for $8.95. So much for racking up a fat breakfast bill.

While everyone chowed down on three plates of low mein, sesame chicken and spring rolls, I picked at pieces of bok choy swimming in soy sauce along with a shred of grilled chicken and broccoli. If everyone else wanted to get fat in a sea of MSG and fried rice, so be it. My appetite suppressant and I were perfectly content on picking at some salty greens, even if that meant I didn't get to waste all of Nicholas's money. When everyone had sufficiently stuffed themselves and tried to convince Sandra that eating ice cream actually burned calories since your body has to work extra hard to digest it, I had had enough.

"Can we just beach it, already?" I asked, conscious of the fact I was losing out on tanning time the more the boys bullshitted. They looked at me with high-maintenance disgust. "Are you sure you're done eating your choy bok or whatever that is?" Brandon asked followed by Nicholas not doing much to suppress a chuckle. I grabbed my sunglasses from inside my purse and put them on my determined face. "Yes, the bok choy and I are finished. Shall we?" I asked, getting up from the table.

"Do you have to marry someone who's Jewish?" Nicholas asked me about an hour later as we were lying on our towels. The clouds had rolled in, which blocked the sun and an unrelenting breeze was making me shiver. Of course the day it was hot and sunny was when I was running around in un-air conditioned houses and the cool day was saved for the beach, but such is my luck.

"Why do you care?" I asked him in response.

"Don't get all excited Jayden, this isn't my way of proposing to you if that's what you are thinking," he said to me, as if that's what I'm really begging for. I turned to face him to see the mammoth propped up on his forearms, absorbed with his mammoth cell phone. Probably texting the new whore face. He answered me, but his eyes were still glued to the screen.

"So, do they have to be Jewish?"

I laid on my back but dug my right hand into the sand, making a fist around a clump of the grainy sand. I missed the

Mediterranean's silkiness beneath my fingertips, the sun above me and lying next to people who didn't question my family's religious requirements. Sure, men came and went but we were all Jews. It wasn't usually a topic of conversation.

"At this point, even if he was a convicted felon with tattoos on his face, that would be okay as long as he wasn't an asshole like you."

We laid in icy silence. He was probably counting down the hours until he could see his new *girlfriend*. Maybe he would take her for a lavish dinner of blackened salmon and steamed spinach and a stroll on the beach. They would go back to the yogurt shop where he took me but he would hold her hand and then order the low calorie frozen yogurt and spoon it into her eager mouth. Not too much of course, he wouldn't want to fatten her up. Maybe she was one of those lucky ones with a naturally waif frame who could slug down endless amounts of sugar and still wake up looking like a toothpick.

Yes, she was probably one of those bitches.

"Let's go in the water," he said out loud to the sky, not bothering to look over at me.

"Fine. I hope when you get in the water that the biggest shark in the ocean swims up to you and eats you, or at least takes a chunk out of your arm."

Without waiting for him, I sprinted from my towel and headed straight for the water and decided no matter how cold the Atlantic was, I was going to dive right in. Frigid waters had to feel better than this emotional hell.

Of course Nicholas ran passed me and dove right into an oncoming wave. Figures he would have to win this little race I created in my head he didn't even know he was in. Or maybe he did. He seemed to know everything anyway. Part of me was still praying for a sliver of a fin to cut through the water, next to him of course. But no, apparently only the seaweed was murking through the Atlantic today.

And then, it was time to pack up and leave Hades.

"What are you doing?" I asked Nicholas as he turned off the highway. We were on the way to the airport and I didn't realize there was time for a diversion.

"I wanted to look at this car," he said as he swung into a closed, small dealership with the Ferrari and Maserati emblems painted across the doors. How fitting.

"Seriously? Now?" I asked, irritated. Why did he have to stop and prance around a ridiculously expensive establishment when I had a plane to catch? "I like this one," he said pointing to an obnoxious lime green Ferrari. "Let's go, you don't want me to miss my plane and be stuck here longer, do you?"

"No, I guess not," he agreed. We hopped back in the stupid BMW and drove back towards the interstate, where the airport was imminently waiting. "Which car do you think I should get?" He asked casually. "Nicholas, no one with real money talks about it nearly as much as you do. All you do is completely flash your pathetic cash around, and honestly, you pretentious attitude is a complete embarrassment." Of course he ignored me. A few minutes later he asked me if I had any song requests. "I hate everything about you," I told him. I guess that was a good choice because Three Day's Grace's angry and sexy lyrics blared through the speakers.

"I hate everything about you…

WHYYYY do I love you…"

I looked over at Nicholas and with feelings of bitter anger tainted with some twisted desire to have him once more, a final send off. A sick part of me wanted to steer his car to the side of the road and tell him to park the car. I wanted to push his seat back as far as it would go and yank his shorts down and slam my body on top of him. He would be hard and ready to go, the filthy animal he was. I wouldn't even kiss him, just thrust as hard and deep as I could until he felt like his dick was going to fall off. But part of that was just the Adderall. You turn into a sexual prowess, feeling like Cleopatra but end up looking like Courtney Love. So I refrained from making an ass of myself. The odds weren't in my favor as I glanced at Nicholas's emotionless face. He looked at the road eagerly, I could feel this drive to the airport was just a means to disposing me so he could move on to his next female meal. While I would be crammed in an airplane seat, my luck next to an overweight travel consultant or some crap, he would be falling in love with the girl who should have been me.

We pulled off the exit for the airport and I really knew the end had come. He followed the signs for U.S. Airways and pulled up to the curb. "I'll grab your bags," he said and got out. I climbed out of the car slowly, a chapter closing I wasn't ready to end. I stood next to my bags and began to pick one up.

"Come here," he said, with a speck of sympathy glossing his eyes. I looked up and he opened his arms for a hug. I couldn't bear to look at him, but I couldn't bear to not feel his body against mine for what could be forever. He wasn't mine anymore, but for a while, those three hundred pounds of muscle desired me and it was my last chance to breathe in that fantasy. I ran into them and held the tears which were going to flood from eyeballs any second if I didn't get away. I took a deep breath and tried to muster the courage to verbalize a good bye, but the words wouldn't come up. I broke away after a final squeeze and craned my neck to look at his face. The only thing I could do was shake my head as I grabbed my bags and turn away before he could even say good bye himself.

Maybe he wasn't even going to. I'll never know. I walked towards the automatic doors and once I was in the security line, I let the tears flow. Everyone around me stared, probably wondering what the hell was wrong. I didn't care that I looked like a freak. My honeymoon turned honeyhell weekend was over and there I was in an airport, broken and alone.

Two airplanes later, I landed on the tiny runway after a flight so bumpy I had asked the flight attendant to toss me a precautionary barf bag. The only comfort were the lights from the landing strip guiding the pilot to a safe landing, and not into a field or into someone's yard. I was back in Grayton, where there was no telling what could happen in their air traffic centers. It wasn't exactly a jam packed job.

After the pilot landed the aircraft (I think the model the Wright brothers was more technologically advanced) with a thud that shot me forward (I hate tightening my seatbelt), I had a flashback of how many times had I landed in this very spot, usually melancholy from the realization an international adventure had come to a conclusion, with hope of a new one not being far away. This trip had scared away my desire for adventure for a while.

I had managed to keep the crying under control with a few Xanax throughout the flights, except for when I made my phone calls to Scarlett, Mimi, and Olivia detailing the first world equivalent of hell I'd just gone through. But once I reached baggage claim, plodding along with the rest of the half asleep passengers and saw my parents, standing there with mixed looks of relief I was alive and concern for my emotional well-being, I lost it. I ran to Renee and sobbed all over again. "I am so sorry, Sweetness," she said hugging me tightly and running her long nails through my hair. It was the first moment I felt comforted and put me back to two decades earlier when I would fall at the park and run to her crying with a scraped knee. I would totally trade a smashed heart for a scraped knee at this point. Ira doesn't handle tears well so he grabbed my bags and lead us to the car. I passed out during the twenty minute ride back to their house and by the time I crawled into my bed, I made a silent prayer that I would wake up in the morning and this all would have been a shitty dream.

CHAPTER 12

It turns out I didn't dream anything. When my alarm blared at its usual ungodly hour, I smacked the snooze button and then registered that I had been banished back to Pennsylvania with only souvenirs of a broken heart and a suitcase of shame. I was in my bed in Grayton, not the lavish oversized tempurpedic one in Florida. Then again, I hated the person who owned that stupid luxury bed. My heart hung so heavy. How the hell could I feel such intense emotions this early in the morning? I texted Olivia. *I am not coming in today. Too heartbroken. Seriously want to crawl out of my skin.* She answered back, *Maybe you should just take a personal day. Take a few days to regroup.*

Lying in bed in the comfort of my misery, the air conditioning on full blast and being under the safety of my goose feather comforter sounded divine. How could I possibly show my face in that office? After prancing around explaining that I wouldn't be in for a couple days because I was going to be in Jacksonville, compliments of Mr. Kingsley.

The clock said 8:15am. *Fuck you, clock.* I was officially late, and Monte knew where to find me since Nicholas texted him and explained that he had switched my flights. The moments passed as

I continued to lay on my back with my eyes shut, mentally weighing my options of telling the world to go fuck itself or to drag my ass back to reality.

The universe made its decision for me a few moments later when my phone beeped with a text message. Immediately my heart pounded and I fantasized it was a message from Nick saying what a mistake he had made and how much he missed me, how stupid he was for letting someone go who wasn't anything less than a goddess…

Where you at? It was from Monte. So much for my fantasy coming to fruition. My pity-party was now concluding. *I just woke up. Got in late from the flight. Sorry.* I actually wasn't sorry, that was a lie.

Monte: *Okay, get here ASAP.*

Already feeling defeated, I decided to screw putting in any effort into my appearance for the day. Since I hadn't unpacked, I threw on whatever wrinkled mess was on the top of my suitcase that was office appropriate. After I dabbed on the minimal amount of make-up possible to prevent complete social suicide, I stared at the person in the full length mirror who had my facial features, my hair cut, but other than that, she was a curve-less ghost whose face was absent of any trace of life. No wonder why Nick had tossed her aside. She didn't even look like she had a pulse.

"The usual, gurrrrl?" Shaniqua asked after I rolled down my window and said, "Hi," into the drive-thru microphone like I was on the way to a torture chamber. The crew at Dunkin Donuts knew my order by heart and knew it was me as soon as my window was rolled down. Whether it was because of my super-cheery voice or my car, I'm not sure. "No, Shaniqua, no breakfast sandwich today. Just the coffee." My sadness had completely taken up all the room in my stomach where an appetite would exist and on top of it, I hadn't worked out since before I left for Florida. Food just wasn't in the cards at the moment.

"Okay, bitch, pull around, your girl got you."

"How was your trip?" she asked me as I handed her my credit card, forgetting there was still the neat wad of bills my dad had given me tucked into my wallet. I hadn't even used them. I didn't even care I still had them.

"The mother fucking asshole had another girl before I even got there and I didn't find out until it was my third day there. I fucking hate him. Shaniqua, I want his balls chopped off and served to him on a cheap burger bun in a mess of ketchup with a side of fries."

"You motha fuckin' kiddin' me, Boo?"

"Nah, Boo isn't kidding." Fine, sometimes I forget I'm a white girl when I get on a roll with Shaniqua.

"Damn, girl, I'm so sorry. We'll find you another hot man."

I highly doubted I would enlist Shaniqua as my matchmaker, but I appreciated her offer. Being that Shaniqua was a convicted felon who had done jail time a decade earlier for tax evasion and wasn't exactly regretful of her actions, our values didn't parallel extensively. But, being that she was one of my policy holders (somehow I finagled her past through the underwriting team), I needed to appease.

When I pulled into the parking lot, it was 9:24am. Not too bad considering I had just rolled out of bed. I began replaying the words that stabbed me in the heart and changed any future I may have had with him.

I met someone else.

Being blindsided was what stung the most. Why me? Hadn't I looked him right in the eye in Pittsburgh and said, "please don't hurt me. I'm really happy right now." What possesses someone to take that happiness away from another human? I contemplated this as my worn heels clacked through the lobby and up the elevator.

"Jayyyyyy," Joey greeted me with his eyes still on the computer as I sat down at my desk opposite him. Technically, these desks were first come first serve for the agents and lower-level managers like Joey and myself, but at this point in my tenure, everyone knew better than to fuck with my spot.

"Hi, Joey," I said, as casually as possible, sure the grapevine had already babbled my weekend's details to the office. I grabbed a stack of resumes and got ready to start making recruiting phone calls. Monte stepped out of his office and walked over towards me. "Glad to have you back with us, JayJay," he said, smiling at me as he fist-bumped me.

"Thank you," I replied, doing my best to hold back the tears that were already starting to form behind my eyes.

Weeks later, I wasn't in any better shape. Every morning when I woke up my heart sank when I realized there was no message telling me how beautiful I was from Nick. In fact, there were no messages at all. The only beautiful thing in my life was the lipstick holder and the little treasures filling the satin lining. I played a game every day slipping them under my tongue, feeling them dissolve in secrecy. My eyes would scan the office, everyone around me too preoccupied with their own phone calls or meetings to notice little me digging through my purse. *You all don't even know what I'm doing, I'm that good*, I applauded myself as I'd bite my way to baseline from the dog tired state I inevitably dragged myself through each morning. But baseline was never good enough. *Functional* is no fun, and I was going through a heartbreak. Not only did I need the extra pep to make the long hours bearable, it was a salve for the pain of rejection aching my heart.

One dreadful evening of phone sessions, I hung up from my last phone conversation at 9:03pm, seething to get out of the building as though I hadn't seen the outside world in months, not hours. Then again, time dragged on and passed rapidly all the same, so maybe I had been holed up in the offices of D'Angelo Enterprises for an infinite amount of time. Even though I was wearing shoes that probably weren't safe for anywhere other than flat ground, I barreled down the flights of stairs, ignoring the shooting pains from my cramped toes. When I opened the side exit door and stepped into the parking lot, I could finally exhale.

Although the sun had set, the sky was freshly dark and retained that purple glow it holds as the last bits of daylight cling to the sky. It was the first time I actually noticed anything other than how full my schedule was or the amount of money it took to fill my tank several times a week. In that moment there was only the gentle breeze on my skin and the darkening sky. The anxiety overwhelming me only minutes ago somehow dissipated in nature's presence and a different emotion filled me. I think they call it a sense of calm.

Which was crushed only seconds later as I clicked the unlock button to my car. Timing- so beautiful, or so ugly.

"How was your little getaway?" I heard the unmistakable voice as I went to throw my hundred pound bag in the backseat. Scarlett or Monte must have filled him on my rendezvous. I didn't care to know the details of how Alex knew.

I wasn't in the mood to deal with his cocky crap, but even more, I wasn't in the mood to fight back.

"Don't you ever say 'hello' like a normal person to their face instead of talking to the back of someone's head?" I yelled back.

Alex was standing right next to the backseat door, apparently not taking the hint I didn't feel like conversing.

"I thought we were past the pleasantries, Jayden."

Whatever." I gathered up a script that had become unstapled and was strewn across the backseat in attempt to avoid having to actually look at stupid Alex. The pages were probably out of order but that wasn't really my main concern at the moment.

"So how was the South?" he pushed on.

"Well, if you knew that I had a little getaway, then I'm sure you know how it went," I said without even looking up.

"What did I tell you about playing with fire?"

"I don't remember, I try not to pay attention to the dribble that comes out of your mouth."

"You might want to rethink that."

"Alex, I'm really not in the mood. I got played bad, okay?" I wanted to lock my feelings away tightly where they could one day be squeezed like water into a bucket to be tossed away, but instead, they came out like the dribble I was accusing him of spewing.

"And now I'm back here completely heartbroken having to see some asshole's face on a screen running meetings every day. He completely humiliated me and I was blindsided. I got played by the master toymaker and it sucks. It just fucking sucks. And I have to try to keep it together all day because God forbid I have anything less than a happy, let's take over the world attitude, when I am nothing but a toxic waste of space. And I have to deal with crazy horny housewives on the phone. Who I absolutely do not want to do deal with!" He rolled his eyes at the mention of the sexually unfulfilled housewives.

"Damn, girl. Relax. He isn't worth it." So simple, right? And why is it I was letting Alex into the most vulnerable space of my mind right now when I knew absolutely nothing about him other than the fact he had a penchant for Barbied-out blondes? This registered for a millisecond but my pity party took back over.

"I know he's not. Really, I do. I just don't get it. How he could just do what he did?"

"Come on, you're smarter than letting someone like him get to you."

"You're saying I'm smart?"

"Well, maybe I said that prematurely. Your track record isn't looking too good." He stepped forward and the only place I had to go was against my car. He was invading my personal space, again. I inhaled sharply and was practically undone by his just-showered-and-shaved smell. Not a teenager cheap cologne smell bullshit seasonal luxury men's fragrance. He smelled like a real man. For a second I wished he would step closer so I could smell it again.

"Why do you get off on pissing me off and pushing my buttons?" Before he could answer, his phone rang.

"Hold that thought," he said, without moving away from me and his hand brushed against mine as he withdrew his phone from his pocket. I retracted my hands quickly and slid them to safety between my back and my car window. Moving oxygen into my lungs and carbon dioxide out seemed too scary at this second so I held my breath. Something so slight as his hand brushing mine felt too intimate. I craved closeness yet there it was in front of me and I was scared shitless. All I knew was that I was sick of feeling feelings. I just wanted to go home, curl up in my bed, turn off my thoughts, and wake up a lesbian so I didn't have to deal with men anymore.

"Yo, man, I'm coming up," he said and hung up. It must have been Monte calling to rally him to get in the car with the other managers so they could smoke weed and talk about bitches.

"Don't worry, I don't have time to push your buttons right now. Get some sleep, you look like you could use it." He tapped my nose and gave me one last look in the eye. And with that he walked away, leaving me feeling even more torn up about life than I had been ten minutes earlier. It wasn't until I started the engine and put my car in reverse that I realized my heart was racing.

CHAPTER 13

Several weeks later, on the eve of Fourth of July, Monte made me stay late for our monthly review. Actually, I was twitching at that point to leave the office for what was going to be twenty-four hours of *no work*. Meaning no phone calls, appointments, workshops.

"Be safe, and enjoy the day with your family and friends," Cal told us enthusiastically over our damn video conference. And then of course he paused before adding, "*But*, Friday morning, you are at an appointment at 8:00am or straight on the phones. Do not let one day break you from your momentum…"

While the rest of the office trooped off to get a head start on celebrations, Monte called me into his office.

"Jayden, you've done amazing so far this year. I want to make sure we get you to conference." Conference was an event to celebrate the year's most celebrated agents and managers. Apparently it was *the* event, as in Oscaresque, and was only attended by those who qualified. It was enterprise wide, so it was out of thousands of insurance freaks around the world. And I wanted to go more than anything. But in between my heartbreak and training new agents, my sales numbers hadn't exactly reflected that of a sales superstar.

"I just need you to focus, JayJay. We need you at conference and I know how much you want it."

The fact Monte wanted me there for some reason always lit a fire under my ass to hustle. I promised him I would do my best. But for the next twenty-four hours, I was officially off the clock.

The next day, my friends' turned up noses and obvious whispers were louder than the celebratory fireworks that fourth of July as I threw a bottle of Kettel One Citroen and various club sodas down on the table with a merry, "Happy fourth of July!"

One of our friends from high school picked me up so we could celebrate at Lola's Lakehouse. Her dad was loaded so we had access to a huge house and dock complete with jet skis. It wasn't so terrible, even for Grayton.

"Wow, look who decided to show face," the Queen Bee Lola sang, twisting a strand of her weave. My "friends," the ones whose incoming calls and texts were as frequent as my menstrual cycles (when you're really skinny, you don't bleed and it's awesome) all turned to look at me.

I had decided to wear a floppy hat to detract attention from my newly thin frame, which I was sure they would notice. "Jayden, since when do you wear hats?" Anastasia, our very proud MBA graduate, Manhattan inhabiting friend asked without a hello. She had no trouble reaching for the unopened vodka bottle I set down. Alcohol bottles were never sealed for long amongst our friends. We got down to business, I guess you could say.

Self-consciously, I reached for the top of my head, to make sure the hat hadn't flown away or anything.

Anastasia knew our wardrobe personalities down to the ripped sweatpants from college we still coveted. Looks like she still never skipped a beat.

"What? I love hats!" I said in a tone of voice inferring Anastasia was absolutely crazy.

"Must be since you started your life insurance career," she sneered, emphasizing the words life insurance. One day I wanted to relax and not think about life insurance and retention, or at least pretend like I was going to do that. I just wanted one day of it. And the universe delivered, but now it handed me the equally joyful obstacle of women who got off on looking to push buttons. No wonder why I don't call anymore. But today was a national holiday. Obviously I couldn't be doing nothing. So when I was thrown into the group text to be at Lola's dock, I figured I would show face and avoid social suicide. Then again, their words were daggers pointed at my forehead. They must have all been bitching and PMSing and nominated me as a targeted recipient for their attitudes for the day.

I grabbed the now opened vodka bottle which was calling my name and poured myself a generous amount into a plastic cup and topped it off with some club soda. Well, if it wasn't going to be my hat, then obviously it was going to be my career. Sure, no one gave Anastasia any shit about her career. But then again, even with Anastasia's *MBA* and her very important job as a *Marketing Director*, she still had time to constantly stick her nose and two cents into everyone's lives. Anastasia would hit the corporate glass ceiling and then marry rich. I may have turned into a money grubbing bitch, but at least I would be self-made.

The vodka burned the back of my throat, but I relished its distraction from the bitterness hanging in the air from the girls' snarky comments. I decided to ignore Anastasia's insurance comment. I decided to switch topics.

"Who wants to jump in the lake with me?" I asked the gaggle of six in front of me. I felt as though I was turning invisible when no one answered. So it was going to be one of those days, I suppose. *Whatever, I can go swimming by myself*, I decided and carefully placed my movie star hat on an empty lounge chair. My back was to them, but I felt their laser beam eyes glaring at me, watching and analyzing every motion I made, especially as I lifted my swimsuit cover up over my head leaving only my bikini clad body exposed. Their $1 happy hour draft beers and penchant for wings and cheesy nachos had turned their once taught teenage bodies softer and not quite the size four they were at prom. Neither was I, of course. My size fours were getting roomy. In any other city - Los Angeles, Las Vegas, my body would be a dime a dozen, minus the fact the other women all had silicone in their chests. But here in Grayton, in a sea of decade old grudges and judgments, my body was simply a work of disgust.

"Gross!" I could hear them screaming telepathically to each other. I couldn't look any of them in the eye. I looked at my 12 ounce Solo cup and slugged down its content and then headed straight for the dock, walking the plank to escape the sideways stares. What was I going to do? Look at everyone and declare that my Adderall penchant was speeding my metabolism and that's why my clavicle was visible? No, that wasn't going to happen. I dove head first into the water, but the stabbing pain of the cold attacking my skin like bullets was ecstasy compared to the social out casting frigidness. What if I just stayed down here, underneath the surface, with the murky seaweed and God knows what creatures that lurked in this lake? Fuck it all, I could just stay here past the point where my skin would turn pruney, past the point when the leaves would fall off the trees and the whole body of water would become a solid block of ice. That's how I could go, the lady in the lake who wouldn't get out of the water on the fourth of July because her friends were being little high school bitches and she didn't want to be around them. After a few seconds I realized I couldn't hold my breath much longer and I really didn't feel like drowning, so I popped up to the surface and floated. At least this way I was submerged, and couldn't hear anything except the various boat engines roaring in the not so far distance.

I didn't realize I was starting to feel the vodka until I struggled my way up the ladder and had slight trouble walking up the dock. I saw another gaggle of girlfriends had arrived with a tray of Rice Krispy treats that were topped with blue and red M&Ms spelling out Happy 4th of July!!!

"Oh my god, love!" Lola declared in between exhales of her oatmeal raisin flavored vape pen which I could smell as I grabbed an open chair next to her. I wanted to eat that fucking vape pen it smelled so good.

"Jayden, eat one of these, you skinny bitch," Lola pointed to the tray. Everyone glared at me, the elephant in the room had now reared its trunk.

"She won't, she doesn't ever eat carbs," Mika chimed in with the same disdain she reserved for people who voted Republican.

"Umm, yeah I do," I said and lunged over the table to cut a piece topped with a blue candied J. My hands trembled as I picked up the square, counting the grams of sugar with the terror a credit card abuser has when they see their monthly bill. Just like they need to make the minimum payment, I had to do the minimum and eat this square of popped rice and marshmallow. Oh, and the additional six M&Ms stuck to it had to go down my throat as well. *Fuck you all*, I thought as I took the square and shoved it in my mouth. The sweetness of *real* sugar, not Stevia or Splenda floored my taste buds with equal parts familiarity of a memory and foreignness of something strange. Immediately my thighs trembled, as if whatever fat cells that remained on them could smell their new neighbors. I looked up as I ground the sugary mess in my mouth, certain everyone's eyes were glued on me and probably ready to capture this rare moment for an Instagram post. With half of the bar in my hand and the other half in my mouth, I did a quick peripheral sweep and realized no one was looking at me. I was back to being the invisible girl no one cared to take notice in, now that I was a self-absorbed workaholic. I walked away from the group and headed towards my purse, where I pulled out a plastic bag I had brought in case I wanted to change out of my bikini. I wasn't going to use that bag for that purpose now. I spit the caloric mass out of my mouth and threw the remaining unchewed bar in the bag and swallowed a gulp of water from a bottle I found at the bottom of the bag. There, I could have my cake and throw it out too. Fucking bitches, I thought, grabbing my lipstick container, where all the pleasures of my life were wrapped into neat pharmaceutical circles. I grabbed a full one and bit into it, the familiar thrust of bitterness a comfort to the sweetness that had just molested my poor taste buds. I'll stick with the real candy in my life, these orange orbs of love dancing on my tongue. The day continued with an array sarcastic remarks. I drowned them out with as many vodka and diet tonics as my little body could consume. Why hadn't I just gone out with Scarlett and her townie friends?

■ ■ ■

The throbbing in my head and mouth which tasted like a funeral home woke me out of my drunken stupor. I was laying in my bed naked, alone, and remnants of low-calorie ice-cream on the floor next to me. I looked at the clock and since it was 7:20am. I definitely had no time for any sort of work out. "Get in the car, Jayden, you're drunk," was the last thing I remembered as I stumbled into the backseat of one of the second-tier posse girls who had been nominated to drive my inebriated ass home. Avoiding food all day and slamming solo cups filled mostly with vodka and a splash of carbonated water probably did the trick to land me in that state. Serves me right to wake up with a hangover the size of Uranus. I turned and laid flat on my back, forcing my eyelids to stay open. A few seconds later I remembered what I had to tackle. After being *blessed* with a day of relaxation, I was being punished with returning to my reality of fighting for my success. It seemed impossible. Instinctively, I reached to my nightstand and fiddled through the years of mounting crap in the drawer until I found the secret stash and grabbed a pill. The only way I could get out of bed, never mind get through the day, was going to be this baby as breakfast. I chewed it and then forced myself to stand up, which was an awful idea as the room began to sway. *Here I am*, I thought. D'Angelo Enterprise's finest insurance lady in all her glory. Unfortunately, glory wasn't exactly in store for me.

CHAPTER 14

A few days later, I was still reeling in the after effects from my Independence Day bender. But on a random Tuesday, I thought I had finally gotten it together when I magically woke up early to work out. Maybe this was the start of getting everything back on track. Yes, being a slave to the alarm clock was how I was going to hit my sales numbers and slap some policies back on the books.

Except, I should have fucking known. God forbid the day I wake up early, work out, my clothes aren't wrinkled, my make-up goes on the way I like it, my hair is cooperating, they don't fuck up my order at Dunkin… that shit will hit the fan. I arrived at my first appointment right on time, with a box of I'm-sucking-up-to-you-donuts and of course, the husband, who was laid off, was out for his morning run. I tried to hide my frustration, but the wife read it on my face quicker than you read an obnoxious tabloid cover.

"So, does he always run on Tuesdays at 10:00am?" I asked, tapping my foot and staring out the window.

"Well, every day, actually," she answered, as if I were asking if he brushed his teeth when he woke up. What? I was trying to make conversation. I felt a yawn coming on so I discreetly dug into my purse and grabbed half of a pill while Wife put the Keurig on. Could this dude just come back so I could get started already?

Wife read my mind. "Why don't we just get started and Mitch can join us when he gets back?" Man, this shit was pissing me off. I told this woman, Melanie, I think her name was, that I needed them both together.

"Well, Melanie," I began, "I would love to do that, but then unfortunately I'll have to repeat everything so that Mitch understands as well."

"Well, what's so hard to understand? He dies, and I get money?" I was saved from involuntarily shooting my mouth off when Mitch darted into the kitchen, sweat dripping from every pore of his body, and conveniently grabbed the cup of coffee from the Keurig I had my eyes set on.

"Hi, Jayden, sorry to keep you waiting," he said after Melinda explained who I was.

"It's okay, I enjoy my morning workouts, as well," I said, trying to be friendly.

"Yeah, you look like you're in great shape," Mitch commented. If I ate carbs, I would have wolfed down half of that box out of the discomfort I felt. Instead I gave a nervous laugh and asked Melinda if she liked to run as well as they sat down.

"No, I use the Stairmaster," she said, dismissing my inquiry. Unfortunately, Mitch grabbed the seat to my left and then Melinda sat on the other side of him, with the untouched box of donuts weighing in front of all of us. Of course, today, I encounter the house in a town full of junk food inhaling citizens the family who is watching their fat intake, which I learned during my few minutes of bullshitting with them.

"I stopped buying all of that junk. I mean it literally is just killing us, all of that sugar. No regular soda in this house, oh no.

Just fruit juice," she said proudly. I don't think Melinda knew how to read nutrition facts labels to realize that most juices have more sugar than soda, but I wasn't about to start that debate.

"That's great," I said flatly. And we sat, staring at the box of donuts. For the first time I felt like I brought a rectangle of poison into someone's home. Whoops.

Mindful that my two later appointments were a good hour drive away, I kept glancing at my watch, the ticking time bomb. With time as an enemy, I fell into two sales catastrophes: I rushed through the presentation, which meant Mitch and Melinda did not understand a thing, nor were they exactly interested in attempting to understand anything. In my defense, the scent of Mitch's sweat made it a little difficult to focus in a room without ventilation from at least a ceiling fan.

With the itch to move onto the next appointment, I turned into a used car salesman and pushed them out of any buying zone.

"Guys, I told you earlier you had to make this decision today. I mean, neither of you have any insurance. Which plan do you want to start with today?"

"Mitch, I mean, you haven't even showered yet, how are you going to pick something?" Melinda hounded as he looked intently at the paper where I had written out three options. He could have yelled out a choice from the shower at this point, I wouldn't have cared.

"Melinda, what does showering have to do with this? The insurance lady said we have to pick something today, what's the big deal?" Again, the insurance lady thing. What was it with this town?

"Yeah, I mean, I really can't come all the way back out here. I mean I did this as a favor for Nikki and Tony." Nikki and Tony were the couple who had referred me to these people.

"Well, then we will save you a trip. The answer is no," Melinda said.

"Wait, what?" I asked, surprised by her suddenly adamant attitude.

"Look, we have a lot to do today, Mitch is laid off, so this isn't a good time."

"Well, that's the thing, Melinda. There will always be something. This is the perfect opportunity."

"Look, Jayden, these options aren't going to work right now."

"That's okay, I can lower the numbers if that would work for you." I looked to Mitch to see if he could help me out but he looked scared of his wife. I would be too, her skin was so pasty she could have easily passed for a Twilight vampire. No wonder why she didn't eat any donuts, she probably fed on humans. It didn't matter, she didn't give me anytime to become lunch.

"You know what, I have had enough of this pushiness. I really don't appreciate you coming into my home and dictating what decisions I need to be making on the spot. I think this meeting is over," she concluded, standing up from her chair and walking towards the door. Well, I could take a hint. Mitch was still staring at the paper in front of him, looking quite embarrassed at this point. I closed my laptop in defeat and lowered my head as I slipped it into my bag. In one last attempt to salvage my dignity, I reached for a business card and left it on the table. "In case you have any questions for me." I walked to the door, where Melinda was standing with it open. She couldn't have made her message any clearer.

Half of me wanted to crawl into a hole and die and the other half wanted to pull out a verbal lashing, tell her that speaking to her stoic face for two hours was worse than dealing a hall monitor from high school, that she was putting me way behind schedule, she wasted my gas money, was ungrateful that I brought over a box of fried sugar, yes, but it was still a nice gesture, and that she really needed a spray tan. But I kept my composure.

"Enjoy the rest of your day," I said, stepping outside into what had turned into a muggy, hot day.

∙ ∙ ∙

I called Scarlett as soon as I got in the car and pulled out of the driveway. "Scarlett, this woman was such a fucking bitch! I can't believe I got kicked out of a house!"

"Jayden, everyone gets kicked out of a house, it's like a rite of passage. Brush it off girl, you're good. On to the next." Grrrr, she was right.

"I have no clue where I am, my GPS is taking me through Guadalajara. These back roads are ridiculous and haven't been paved in years!" I tried to simultaneously follow the GPS and dodge the potholes which had never been filled from the winter four months earlier.

"You have to go run more appointments later, right?"

"Yeah, if I ever get out of wherever I am and back to civilization."

"Okay, get off the phone then and focus on driving. I've been in the car with you before."

"Fuck you."

"Love you."

"Love-" And as I was about to say you, I heard an awful smash sound which blew my ear drum. As the world's luckiest driver, this was a sound I had heard before.

"Fuck, Scar, I got a flat."

"Are you sure? Stop the car and go check!" I pulled over to the side of the road and checked the rear passenger tire. I was right. I hung up with Scarlett and got back in my car, running the gas so the air conditioning would blow on my face. The next phone call was not one I wanted to make.

"Dad," I said in the slightly whiny, scared voice he dreaded hearing anytime I used it.

"What is it, Jayden?"

"I got a flat tire."

"Jesus what the hell did you do?"

"I hit a pothole. I couldn't see it!"

"Did you call AAA?

"Not yet, I didn't know where to tell them to tow it to."

"Take it to Kost by my office. Where are you?"

"Somewhere above 115 past Grayton. I don't know Dad I just follow the GPS."

"God damn it, Jayden, you're driving a car that's registered under my business, and you're not even employed here. Let me guess, you were yackin' away on the phone, weren't paying attention, and the pothole just jumped out at you."

"No, Dad, I was just staring at the road ahead of me, not that ground on the side of the car. Who does that?" White lie. White lie.

"Well how are you the only one who manages to hit as many potholes as you do?" He had a point, I really didn't have a good track record of anything vehicular related.

"Dad, I'm sorry!" What else was I supposed to say?

"Alright, I gotta go, I got ten other lines ringing here. I got work to do. Let me know if you need anything. Bye."

■ ■ ■

"So, do you have the tire in stock? I need to drive this car today," I said to the mechanic at the auto body shop where I had AAA tow my car. Thank God for that little card. Can you picture this girl changing a flat tire in heels in ninety degree weather? I don't think so.

"Yes, but, ma'am, there was something else we noticed as well."

"Yes, I know there is a scratch on the back passenger door, long story." I may have scratched something backing into or out of a driveway after an appointment, but I really can't keep track of every little mishap.

"No, that's not-" I stopped paying attention as I heard the bell jingle from the auto body's shop door opening. Without thinking, I turned to see who was walking in the door. My insides started churning and I felt my face turn redder than any of the brake lights on display.

"Jayden, what are you doing here?" Alex asked, like the Ghost of Christmas Past walking towards me. I hadn't seen him since that stupid night after work when he was practically pressed against me on my car in May. And here I was, sweating from sitting in a tow truck, my mascara was probably running and my foundation probably looked like a birthday cake on my face. Whatever, who cares if I look like garbage. I hated Alex anyway.

"I was getting new rims, what's your excuse?" I said sarcastically.

"Ma'am, excuse me" the mechanic tapped the desk bringing my attention back to him. "We have the tire in stock today-" My phone started ringing.

"One second, I'm so sorry," I said and began digging frantically through my mammoth bag, but of course, by the time I reached the damn thing it had gone to voicemail. Not caring I was letting the auto dude hanging, I clicked the play button. As I listened, my heart started racing. Shit, shit, shit.

"Jayden, it's Karen Jones. You were supposed to be here a while ago and I haven't heard from you. We have a lot to do today, so we will have to reschedule. I don't have time to be waiting around. Okay, talk soon." Shit. Shit. Shit. I had forgotten to reschedule my next two appointments.

"I'm sorry," I said as I hung up to the mechanic. Apparently Alex and the mechanic were speaking about my car while I was preoccupied.

"Jayden, did you understand what this man was trying to explain?" Alex asked me.

"Yeah, yeah, I can get the tire today," I said, my eyes still glued to my phone. Why hadn't I remembered to call them? After I had gotten off the phone with AAA, I was more focused on the tow truck showing up. Of course when it did, its conductor was a hillbilly driver who put more chew in his mouth than I complained- which I had to bite my tongue from as we listened to country the whole way to the auto body shop. Calling my appointments to let them know I was running late had just slipped my mind. Everything slipped my mind. I didn't even have a mind. I wanted a pill. A pill would help me focus. But my pills were in the car, which was in the garage. Why today? Of all the days to have a fucked up day, why today? Suddenly the heat of the shop became overbearing and I needed to get out of there.

The mechanic look irritated and rightfully so. I was overwhelmed and starting to feel a pit of guilt in my stomach for being a self-centered bitch in an auto body shop.

"I have to step outside. I'm sorry," I mumbled to the mechanic and walked out with my head down, right to a bench I spotted around the corner of the building. And just like every woman needs to sometimes, I put my head down in between my knees, and let the tears start to fall. *You can't close a deal, drive a car, or keep a policy open. You are a fucking failure.* The tears kept flowing as I accepted these thoughts as truth.

"Jayden," I heard Alex's voice not far from me, but I kept my head down. This was utterly humiliating and I could only imagine what the smear situation was with my eye make-up.

"Whatever shit you have to say, just keep it to yourself, Alex," I said to my knees, so it was slightly muffled.

The asshole started chuckling. I didn't pick my head up, hoping he would take a hint and leave a diva to cry for a bit. But that didn't happen. Instead, he sat down next to me and gently put his hand on my back.

"I'm sorry, I didn't realize you were crying," he said sympathetically. It was a tone I had never heard from him. "It's going to be okay, they'll fix your tire." I looked up and wiped my nose.

"You think I'm crying over a fucking flat tire?"

"Well, you do seem like the dramatic type, no offense."

"None taken." I took my fingers and quickly wiped under my eyes, in a pitiful attempt to clean up what I assumed to be smudged eyeliner. "But no, a flat tire isn't the isolated reason for me to be sitting on a dirty bench crying."

"Come on, let's go across the street to the diner and get something to eat while they look at your car. You can tell me why you're having a bad day."

"Why, so you can torment me and say 'told you so' for forty-five minutes?"

"Come on, Grouchy."

"No, I really should stay in the shop and make phone calls in the waiting area, at least do something productive. This is such a waste of time, this whole flat tire shit."

"Jayden, come on. You could probably use a break. Plus you look like you could use a meal."

I relented and got up from the bench. We walked to the other side of the parking lot and opened the passenger door to a black Range Rover parked in the sea of Hondas and Toyotas. Manners?

"Thank you," I said, stepping as gracefully as I could into the panty dropping car.

"Put your seatbelt on," he said, which seemed a bit strict considering we were only driving a half a mile away. I rolled my eyes and obliged. Monte would not be happy if he knew I was sitting in the Range Rover going to lunch instead of getting my shit together. And I never go out for lunch during a work day, unless it's a treat from Monte for the top performers during an office day. But I was enjoying sitting in this Range Rover. It was spotless, you know, just like my vehicle.

"Monte is going to be so pissed when he finds out how my day went today," I said under my breath.

"Don't worry about Monte. He'll live." Even though Nick drove a status car himself as it appealed to his ego and was practically a company requirement, the car always seemed to own him, as though he was just renting it for show. Alex spun the steering wheel and shifted through traffic nonchalantly, as if he had grown up doing this. But at the same time, I got the sense he would be just as comfortable driving one of the hoopties from a junkyard.

We pulled up to the family owned diner where I used to eat when I worked for my Dad. All of those afternoons where we would sit in a booth in the middle of the restaurant, in an uncomfortable silence as my Dad talked on his phone half of the time and I checked my Twitter feed. Half of the restaurant knew him and would drop by to say hello to the Copier King. Inevitably, I was introduced as his daughter who was "working hard so he could retire already and enjoy his three martini lunches." I don't think I have ever seen my father drink a proper martini. Of course, whoever we were speaking with would just laugh, because wasn't Ira such a jokester?

"I used to eat here all the time," I thought out loud.

"The owners are my cousins." I knew my Dad was acquainted with the owners from eating there so often, but I didn't feel the need to get into all of that.

"Is your family involved in anything that's not food or drink related?" He winked and opened the restaurant door for me. The hostess, who looked like she was his aunt, immediately walked over to Alex and gave him a warm hello with two kisses, European style. We were lead to a booth in the back, which I was grateful for. I was not in the mood to be sitting in the middle of a crowded restaurant feeling as vulnerable as I did.

"So what are ya buggin out about?" Alex asked after the waitress handed us our menus and took our drink orders.

"I'm not buggin'," I said looking at the menu. Breakfast selection? No, skip, definitely not on the Jayden approved food list. Salads, salads, where are you? Oh, okay, perfect. Greek salad no olives, dressing on the side, substitute chicken for that weird pepperoncini meat thing I don't eat. Oh my gosh, wraps with sweet potato fries? That looks delectable. *No fucking way, Jayden. No fucking way.*

"You look awfully uncomfortable. Your panties in a twist?"

"What?" I looked up from my menu. I hadn't realized that I was biting my thumb and tapping my foot on the floor.

"I've been trying to ask what happened to you earlier today but you're staring at that menu like you have never been in a restaurant before."

"You have been asking about my panties."

"Well the traditional methods didn't seem to be working with you. Your skinny ass body is here and it's like your mind is god knows where."

"I guess I'm just not a traditional girl then." He rolled his eyes at me as though that wasn't the first time he heard that line.

"No, Jayden, you are anything but traditional as I've started to learn. But you're stuck here with me now, so you might as well tell me what's going on."

I watched him leaning forward, his elbows propped on the edge of the table, his shaggy hair hanging casually. I pulled my hair into a side ponytail casually. I figured it was a better idea to play with my hair than to start fantasizing about touching his.

"Okay, sorry. Well, let's see. I got kicked out of my appointment this morning, missed another three appointments, I got a flat tire, so that fucked up those plans. And I probably can't go to the company conference unless I hit that stupid sales quota." I looked at his face to gauge his reaction, guessing when he's going to come in for the verbal kill. So I tried to beat him to it.

"I know, you warned me months ago that this would happen. I would overwork myself. Well, you were right Alex. Happy?" I shut my menu and threw it down on the table and crossed my arms tightly across my chest. Laying everything out on the table, literally, didn't make me feel any better. In fact, verbalizing it just made me more anxious and angry with myself. I was admitting to self-defeat and the fact that I couldn't figure out shit. I couldn't even figure out how to order a fucking salad.

"Oh, my god, you got thrown out of a house!" Alex was leaning back, laughing at my expense and I wanted to kill him.

"I knew I shouldn't have told you anything. You are such an asshole."

"What can I get you two lovebirds?" The waitress had obviously misinterpreted our interaction. She winked at Alex and I had a feeling I wasn't the first female that sat across from him at the table.

"We are not that by any means," I said, my eyebrows raised. "But, I'll have…" and I gave her my so complicated order, which she reassured me was completely uncomplicated. What a nice woman.

"I'll have the triple stacked club sandwich, extra bacon with the sweet potato fries," Alex said handing her the menu. That fucker probably read my mind... but ew, bacon.

"Jayden, I didn't bring you here to make you feel like shit. We're lovebirds after all," he said as she walked away.

"Shut up before I vomit. And, do you have to laugh at the fact I was humiliated?"

"Come on, do you know how many houses Monte has been thrown out of?" I rolled my eyes but he continued to prove his point.

"Jayden, everyone has been thrown out of houses. I'm sure even Giovanni did back in his day."

"I doubt the Life Insurance Prophet was thrown out of a house. Whatever, and the stupid husband was hitting on me too, it was so creepy."

"Aww, the life of a pretty white girl. So tragic." I rolled my eyes at him. I was not feeling any better.

"It is tragic when you have wives looking at you thinking you wanna jump on their fat husbands who don't even make enough money to buy name brand Coca-Cola and smoke American Spirits."

"You have to slow down a little. You're putting too much on your plate and look what's happening. You are running around like a mad woman and now a flat tire has you trippin'."

"Alex, I can't slow down. That's what a lazy person would do right now. I have so much to do by the end of the year. I am going to that conference. I deserve it, okay? I deserve Vegas."

"I mean I've been to the conference before, as Miguel's guest, and it was fucking awesome, but whatever. It's just a trip. Not like you couldn't book one yourself on your own terms. Like a real business owner."

I thought about what he was saying and immediately I thought about my own father who rewarded himself with trips on his own terms, but dismissed the comparison just as quickly. No, this conference was my gold medal and I was not going to let everyone else's bullshit opinions cloud my vision.

"What do you care, Alex? You were the one who made fun of me months ago and here I am, sitting in the exact spot which you predicted. Except add a flat tire to the sundae."

The waitress brought our food over and the smell made me realize just how hungry I was. Instead of pouring the dressing all over my salad, I carefully took a forkful of lettuce and a piece of chicken and dipped it slightly in the oily dressing in the tin container at the edge of my plate. Alex looked at me curiously and I felt uncomfortable. But he didn't make a comment, thankfully.

"Jayden, speaking of your flat tire, you heard what the mechanic was saying right?" I put my fork in my mouth and bit the food off, nodding my head. My phone beeped and I grabbed it, scanning the email Miguel had sent us about hitting our recruitment goals.

"Yeah, I did," I answered, assuming Alex was still just talking about the tire. If there was something else wrong, it would just have to wait another day.

"You do need to get your brakes looked at, remember? They're fine now but by the time winter comes, you really might be in trouble?" I was scrolling to the bottom of the email to see if anything had been forwarded from other offices, mainly if Nick had contributed to it. Nope, Nicholas Kingsley free.

"Yeah, I know, Alex," I said, putting my phone down and sipping my water, not processing anything he was saying at the moment.

"Jayden, when are you going to think about something other than work?"

"Until I accomplish everything I want to, that's not going to happen. Especially now that I need to qualify for fucking the damn conference."

"And what's that exactly? What are you trying to accomplish?"

"Greatness."

Alex started laughing and almost coughed up a bite of his sandwich. "That's ridiculous."

"No, it's not, Alex. If those boys I work with can end up driving the cars they do by working at D'Angelo Enterprises, so can I. I'm not quitting. I'm going to quit being a quitter. No one thinks I can do this. You don't even think I can do this. I'm not stopping. I'm going to prove every one of you fuckers wrong."

"I'm not saying you should quit, I'm just saying you should take a step back and look at your life."

"My life is fine, okay?"

"Then why don't you ever smile?"

Because I'm sitting through this useless, insane conversation, I thought to myself. This time I took my fork and speared a piece of chicken, sliver of cucumber, and a piece of tomato and dunked it into the dressing, swirling it around the little pool of fatty liquid and flecks of seasoning. Then, I stared at Alex and put the forkful of food into my mouth and chomped down dramatically, chewing for much longer than necessary. I swallowed and gave him the biggest smile I could.

"You have something in your teeth," he said, tapping his nail between his two front teeth to demonstrate where it was that I visibly had food sitting in my mouth. Could this lunch just be over already? I dug in between my teeth until I found whatever it was that was caught.

"Do you want a fry?" he asked, inching the plate towards me.

"No thank you."

"You have been staring at them ever since the plate was put in front of me." Yeah, because I wanted one in the worst way. I wanted them smothered in cinnamon and sugar and mashing in my mouth.

"No, I haven't. I'm full, actually."

"Jayden, you have had like five bites of food."

Fact: Food makes you fat. People like Alex who can obviously handle a few grams of fat on a plate. His bicep muscles were practically bulging through his black shirt. My mouth was watering at the food and my eyes were watering from my emotional confusion.

"It's hard for me to eat a lot when I'm really stressed," I said, not realizing that I was admitting exactly what Alex was trying to drag out of me.

"So, when you aren't stressed, you actually smile and eat?"

"Yes," I said grinning widely and eating another bite of my half eaten salad.

"I guess you would be more bearable then."

"Why do you enjoy taking the time out of your day to torment me? Don't you have your blond bitches making you bacon and eggs?"

"Nah, they usually leave before any of that noise."

"You would be that asshole. You don't even know me, Alex. All you know is that I sell life insurance, had my heart broken in Florida, and that I have a flat tire."

"I know you drink too many vodka sodas on a random Saturday." Okay, he had a point.

"Yeah, that's the same for every other girl in this town who counts alcohol calories. But that doesn't mean you actually know anything about me as a person."

"Then tell me something." This is always the hardest question for me, the imperative general inquiry. I wish he would have added something like "about 1994," or "that you want to do before you die."

"Well, I used to work a few blocks from here."

"Really? Where at?" And so I launched into my spiel of how I came to work for my dad after college, ended up escaping to Tel Aviv, only to end up back here in a moment of stupidity, and back to working for my dad. I explained I had a tremendous amount of respect for someone who started something from nothing, even if it's doing something I'm not able to identify with. "I've always loved the entrepreneurial way of life," I said, pouring cream and Splenda into the coffee the waitress brought me after she cleared our food. As I talked about working for my dad, thoughts poured into my mind of how I thought my life would turn out to be. But just because I've traveled down a different path doesn't mean it's the wrong one, right?

"So then why are you at D'Angelo Enterprises? Why aren't you taking over the business?"

Alex was taking a genuine interest in everything I was saying, and after a while, it wasn't so hard to speak even with his unrelenting intense stare. I had the feeling he was trying to read past the words coming out of my mouth, that the harder he stared, the more he would be able to read my thoughts. Why did he seem to want to dig so much? But instead of throwing a wall up, I kept talking. Something told me I could talk to him.

"So that I can run an office someday," I said automatically. It was like I didn't even know what I wanted, I was regurgitating what everyone around me told me I wanted, should want, or will want. "Scarlett and I plan to run an office together."

"How is that entrepreneurial if you have to listen to everyone else's rules?" he challenged.

"They're in place for a reason. They work."

"You seem like too much of a free spirit to work in such an environment that puts such an emphasis on the process."

"How am I such a free spirit?"

"You just are. Plus, who just jets off to Tel Aviv?"

I did not want to be backed into a corner. I refused to let that happen. So I decided to turn it around.

"Well then, what would you do if you were me, Alex?"

"Jayden, I'm not you and it's not my job to decide how to live your life. You need to decide what is best for you. I was just pointing out a few things that might have slipped past your mind. Look, I think you forget that I know a lot about the company you work for and how your brain starts to work after being there for a while. It's just that you have this extra intensity. No matter what everyone else is doing, you have to take it to another level. You take it so much more seriously."

"If I don't take it seriously, I won't get anywhere, Alex. You know what that wash out rate is. Every day when that alarm goes off, I don't think about choices or what everyone else is doing. I just know about what I need to be doing."

"You just look so stressed. I mean come on, you can barely eat."

"It's just temporary, Alex. It's just temporary. Everyone has to overcome obstacles to achieve what they want. Success requires sacrifice. I mean, I'm sure there are sacrifices you have had to make to get where you are."

"I did. But here's the thing, Jayden. I was in control of which sacrifices I wanted to make. The sacrifices never took control of my life."

Everything he said began to sink in and permeate through all of the ideals I had living, breathing, and sleeping for a year. And then, I began to wonder what Alex Reyes was doing in my life.

CHAPTER 15

They say positive and negative events come in "threes," so when in one day I got a flat tire, lost a sale, and then missed the remaining appointments for the day, I figured I was in the clear for a while as far as shit hitting the fan. But I was incorrect.

Every time the managers or the entire agency had a meeting, I could see Nicholas Kingsley on the screen, and I immediately was filled with an uncontrollable rage.

"Fucking asshole. He's not even good looking," I would begin to rant and rave at the screen. If I could have gotten away with it, I would have made paper airplanes out of the paperwork we kept in the supply closet and bombarded the screen with them. Maybe it could become part of the new agent training program? I brought this idea up to Scarlett and she just rolled her eyes. At this point, she was over my shit.

"Jayden, stop worrying about him. He's done. Focus on what you need to do. Work on getting more sales and building a sales team so you can go to conference." Since when did she become the sensible one? Her reactions were so unpredictable. When I told her I had lunch with Alex, she just smiled and said, "I told you he was a nice guy! Just don't hook up with him." She didn't have to worry about that. Man diet. No asshole was getting near me and I knew someone like Alex would just be there to hit it and quit it. After lunch when Alex dropped me back to my car, he grabbed my phone, put his number in it and made me promise to call him if anything else happened.

"Don't let any more potholes jump out at you," he reminded me.

"I'll do my best," I said checking my reflection in the mirror overhead for any romaine lettuce Alex might have "accidentally" forgotten to mention in my teeth.

"Yeah, you got something right here," he mocked as I picked in between my teeth.

"Bye, Alex," I said as I rolled my eyes and jumped out of the Range Rover.

Back at the office, I was summoned to Monte's office, for our usual monthly review. Ever since I came back from Florida, I entered these meetings with more feelings of trepidation than confidence, as opposed to the months preceding my trip to Florida. If only I could get past the obvious hurt Mr. Kingsley had caused me and get to the core of why I couldn't bounce back from the heartbreak. It wasn't like Nick was the first guy to love and leave. Not that there was ever actual love, but it wasn't the first heartbreak. Doesn't the heart become more resilient over time? Each arrow thrown at it wounds a little less? Perhaps my heart was the exception.

"Okay, Jayden. I want you to focus on getting these sales for conference, Jayden. And you can totally do it girly, I know you can. And I want to make this easier on you. Instead of you having to worry about recruiting new agents, training them, and being in all the manager's meetings, let's re-sign an agent contract. This way, you'll have a lot less on your plate and can tackle exactly what's important right now. There will always be a team to build down the road."

This was actually Monte demoting me, but I knew his twist on words was meant merely to soothe what he knew would be a deeply bruised ego. Sales: It's not what you say, it is always how you say it. I knew exactly what he was doing.

My hand shook as I signed the papers which made my demotion official. "Failure, failure, failure," the voice said in my head as I signed the papers. A year earlier, I signed those papers with a brewing confidence as a new sales agent. My head spun for the next few minutes as he mapped out what an ideal week would look like to optimize my time so I would be able to still generate the new sales I needed along with reactivating policies I had sold from earlier in the year that had somehow cancelled, therefore decreasing my total sales revenue for the year. Whoops.

Where had all the time and money I had invested in gone? This must be what the bottom of the pit was. It had to be. How much lower could I possibly go?

"I'm sorry babe," Scarlett said after I told her I was no longer a manager. "It's not permanent. Just get your numbers back to where they need to be and you'll be back to management in no time." In theory she was correct, but in reality I knew the chances of fixing everything and getting back into management quickly was slim. When most people get demoted, they just up and quit permanently. But I wasn't going to do that.

"Duh, we have an office to run one day, remember?" I said, trying to believe my own words.

"I'd still fuck ya. I'd still fuck ya," Joey reassured me even though I wasn't a manager anymore.

"Thanks, I'll sleep better knowing that," really not caring if Joey wanted to throw me a round of his Italian dick.

I didn't tell most of my friends. Are you kidding me, give them the perfect opportunity to say, "Told you so?" No, my ego could not take that. I hoped Alex wouldn't hear about it through the grapevine. Ethically speaking, Monte couldn't tell him. But I didn't know who else would talk or keep their trap shut. Alex was friends with all the bros in the office.

Without the pressure of being in the office at the crack of dawn with the task of building an empire on top of churning out a weekly quota, I began to shift my focus back to what made me a superstar in the old days. I refused to give myself a day off, working seven days a week, including running appointments on Sundays. I was running around ragged, but it began to pay off again. I didn't bring as much stress into the houses and so I began closing deals. A lot of them. It didn't go unnoticed.

"I'm proud of you girly," Monte said after my second week in a row of good numbers. In agency meetings, they began to announce my name again. I was starting to feel a little like my old self. The one that loved the dazzle within all the bullshit.

One Thursday, a phone night, in between gossiping and setting a schedule, I checked my mint box and realized I only had a couple of pills left. Shit. I needed a full supply ASAP if I wanted any chance of getting this thing in the bag. Wasn't Veronica getting a bunch soon? I couldn't remember anything. I texted her to come up to the office and meet me at the end of the night. Surprisingly, she agreed.

On the dot at 9:02pm (I needed two minutes to get my shit together), I dashed out to the elevators and scanned the parking lot for Veronica's car. She was parked in a side spot, so as not to be too obvious, with the window cracked open, smoking a cigarette. Why did all my friends smoke? I thought that shit all ended after high school.

"Hey," she greeted me, exhaling into the cool air. "Get in." I walked around to the other side and climbed into the front. Her car was black on beige leather interior and I would be lying if I said I didn't absolutely love it.

"Dude, I am so stressed," she started. We had gone from being the town party girls to working twenty-four seven and not going out anymore. "I just don't want to do this shit anymore, Jayden. I don't care." Veronica was not cut out to be cutting people's hair all day. Her dream job was to be a Playboy bunny - the furthest thing from her current career trajectory. What the hell did we know? All she knew was use the scissors and hair dye to keep the clients coming back. All I knew was staying at D'Angelo Enterprises would eventually bring me to the path of riches, *as long as I didn't quit*.

"I know, babe, but you have already come this far," I reminded her. "Besides, Heff wouldn't want to see that you quit on your transcripts when you do get to the Playboy Mansion." I loved having a friend with such a controversial dream. I wanted her to succeed that much more. When I became rich, I would buy her ticket to California.

"Okay, so I actually got some extra this time if you want them," she said with a mischievous grin.

"Obviously," I said. I reached into my wallet and grabbed a wad of bills and handed them to her.

"Where's your bottle?" she asked me.

"Fuck, it's in my car. Can you drive me over to it?"

"Yeah," she says, slightly annoyed. We pulled up to my car and I saw Alex's car parked right next to mine. He was in it, on his phone. Without wanting to start a conversation, I grabbed my purse and jumped back in Veronica's car.

"Don't pull your bottle out. Keep it in your purse. I'm going to put these in your hand and then you are going to put these in the bottle. Got it?" I nodded.

"Who is that guy?" she asked as she passed the pills from her container to my hand beneath the dashboard. "He's hot."

"Oh, he's one of Monte's friends."

"Get on that!" Oh that was the last thing I needed.

"The only thing I need to get on are these," pointing to the pill bottle on the floor. "I've sworn off men."

"Oh, god, Jayden. Why?" Veronica was in love with loving men.

"It doesn't look like it's gotten me very far wasting my time on them. I'm just better off focusing on myself, you know?"

"Oh, yeah true. You do have shit luck with them. Maybe it's not a bad idea in your case." God how I would love to be the heartbreaker and not the heartbreakee, life would be a walk in the park.

"Alright, I'm gonna get home. Thanks for stopping over here, babe." I hopped out of the car and was about to get into mine when I saw Alex standing at the door.

"Hi," I said, trying to be casual. Why was he standing next to my car door? Fuck me, I just wanted to get home. Although he was wearing a gorgeous wool blend coat which looked like it was straight off the rack from Nordstrom's in New York. His expression was intimidating but something compelled me to stand near him.

"What were you doing in that car?" he asked, leaning on my car door with his arm reaching the roof. I forgot how tall he was.

"Oh, that's my friend Veronica. She just stopped by to say hi."

"Then why did you have to pop in and out of her car just to say hi?" He leaned forward, towering over me. I was so cold I wanted to wrap my arms under his open jacket space and cover myself in that beautiful fabric.

"I didn't want to leave my purse in my car, I think that's actually pretty responsible for me," I replied confidently, standing tall and crossing my arms. I was not going to be intimidated.

"You were holding your purse when you dipped into your car real quick." Shit. Okay, on the defense.

"Ew, Alex, why are you watching my every move?" I asked on the defense.

"Just be straight with me Jayden and then I won't have to get at anything."

"Like an arrow, Alex. What are you doing here anyway?" I had noticed Monte's car had left so I don't know why he would still be standing around.

"Well I knew you would come out of that car at some point."

"And?" I was so confused. My heart was beating so fast. I thought my chest was going to explode. Why did I always leave my Xanax at home?

"I wanted to say hi to you, is that so terrible?"

"As in interrogate me, apparently." This hot and cold business always threw me off.

"It's been a while since I've seen you, I just wanted to say what's up."

"Well, what's up?"

"Did you ever get your car checked out like the mechanic told you to?" His phone went off and he started reading a text message.

"Oh, crap, no not yet. I will soon. I've been so busy and now I have quotas to hit."

"Jayden, you gotta get them checked out."

It occurred to me that Alex knew so much about me and what my life was like, at least what I what I was willing to let him know, but I really didn't know anything about Alex Reyes in return. Part of me wanted to ask who he was texting but the smarter part of me knew I wouldn't want to know the answer. That guy was always surrounded by a swarm of female mosquitoes ready to bite. Not that it mattered, I was on a Y chromosome-free diet anyway.

I wanted to ask him something substantial. Anything that would give me insight as who he really was past a Range Rover driving nightclub and sandwich shop owner. Who always happened to smell really good and dress immaculately. I felt like he had my life story in the palm of his hand and I was clueless as to who he was. I knew he liked sweet potato fries. That was a start I suppose. But there is more to a person than the fried food they eat.

"Jay, I gotta bounce. You be good." I don't know why, but I didn't want him to go, I wanted him to stay. Just so I could touch the wool coat, that's it. Again, I didn't have time to get any words out of my mouth. He drove away, and there I was, standing alone in the cold. What was it with me, everyone was always just dashing away? I couldn't be surprised with Alex, though. He probably had his own evening appointment with whatever broad was latching on to him at the given moment. Whatever, not my problem. I was in man-diet mode and sticking to it whether my vagina liked it or not.

CHAPTER 16

"What?" I answered the phone half asleep. Who dare call me during my Saturday evening nap?

"Get up, JayJay, we're going out tonight."

"Nonsense, Monte, I have so much to do tomorrow. If I go out tonight, I won't get shit done tomorrow."

"Girl, you have to take a break. Look, just come out for a little, have a couple drinks, and then tomorrow you can still get a lot accomplished. Have a little self-control." 'Self-control' wasn't exactly in my vernacular, but it looked like I couldn't get away with staying in bed.

"Come on, I need my dynamic duo out tonight to celebrate their stellar few weeks," referring to Scarlett and me. Monte did have a point. Scarlett and I had been making an effort to pump each other up every day and remind each other we'd be reigning an office soon enough.

"Where are we going?"

"Blue Moon." Great. Alex's bar. "Go get ready. I know you take half a day to get all dolled up."

I rolled out of the comfort of my bed and texted Scarlett to coordinate driving... meaning getting her to drive me.

I'll pick you up girl, I'm out your way anyway, Scarlett texted me when I told her we were demanded to go out. God, this was the last thing I wanted to do. I needed a pill so I could survive a night out or else I would face plant on top of the bar. Crushing the pill in between my teeth, as I powdered on foundation, I had a thought. Something was going to happen, I could feel it as I was putting my face on. *Stop it,* I told myself. I had a habit of being extremely superstitious.

"Do you think maybe Alex is working at Blue Moon tonight?" I asked Scarlett in the car. "Things were a little tense the last time I saw him outside the office."

"Yeah, what's going on with you guys?" she asked, hitting her bowl. She passed it over towards me, but I brushed it off. "I mean, nothing at all. He just always seems to be around when he's pretty much the last person I want to see. He's just so hot and cold, I don't get it.

"Jayden, he's not the type of guy to just take someone to lunch in the middle of the day. He's a really busy guy."

"Please, he probably just had a break in his schedule between his morning blow job and afternoon sixty-nine. Plus, it's not like he tried anything with me. I'd shut him right down and if Monte knew, he'd kill him. Dealing with my emotional shit after Nicholas was enough."

My mom always said the better looking the guy, the badder they were. Nick Kingsley might have used his twisted charm to get me under his spell, but Alex... he had eyes that could simply paralyze.

"Well, hello ladies," Monte greeted us as we strutted over to the bar where the managers and some of their non D'Angelo Enterprises friends were. "You two look great. What are you drinking? This round's on me." I welcomed the Kettel and club soda with a lime instantly. Thank God I passed on the weed because I was feeling anxious enough, a puff-puff-pass would have shot my nerves through the roof. Luckily for me, Monte got me a tall double, and about half way down I started to calm down and enjoy myself. For selling something as exciting as life insurance, you would think everyone who worked at D'Angelo Enterprises were the weirdos who couldn't make the cut for any of the college fraternities. At least that was what I had anticipated when I started working there. Instead, they were guys just trying to make a buck. Like most other twenty-somethings, we all just saw the cars and the cash, so we followed the trail.

And then I heard a cackling laugh that I recognized as what could only be a former sorority girl's. I was guessing she was going to be a tanorexic with blond hair from a box. As the noise got closer I turned around and realized my predictions were correct. The wannabe Malibu beach Barbie looked familiar but I couldn't quite place her. On each side of her were two girls who also looked like they abused their unlimited tanning packages. And all three of them were wearing obnoxiously high, sparkly stilettos to offset their Herve Leger inspired bandage dresses with cut outs which left as much to the imagination as wearing tissue paper would. Suddenly, I felt very underdressed in skinny jeans and a long silk top. The leading tanorexic was staring at something straight ahead. She tossed her hair, flashed a smile and before I even followed to where she was staring, I remembered exactly how I knew her. Same bitch who was tossing her hair in my face the last time I was here. And it seemed she was here for the same purpose…

"Jayden, stop staring, you're being ridiculous. Just have fun and enjoy being with us, okay?" Scarlett was trying to bring me back down to Earth. Right at the moment when I realized who the Barbie was, Alex had walked in from the other side of the bar and strolled up right to her with a charismatic smile so infectious…and it wasn't for me. After he bought the Three Tantastics a round of drinks, he came over to say hey to Monte and shoot the shit with the rest of the managers. Scarlett of course ran over to give her usual hello but I stood frozen. Before he left the guys' conversation, he gave me a little wink before headed back to the blondes, where the one I strongly disliked immediately draped her arm around him, marking her territory.

"Sorry, I'm just thinking," I said, confused.

"You totally want him. I knew it would happen. Everyone always does."

"Scarlett, stop. I don't go for guys who like girls like that." I took a sip of my drink and looked around. It was a sea of the same faces... the college students who had only a handful of bars to rotate through on their nights out, the twenty-somethings like us who were living back in the area, and then the mid-life crisis crowd of cougars and men who thought they 'still had it.' Giovanni better be opening another office soon so I could get out of this garbage town, again.

"I'm going to the bathroom, I'll be back in a minute."

I grabbed my purse and my drink and started walking towards the other end of the bar where the restrooms were, near the entrance. I walked into the bathroom, completely unprepared for what I walked into. Mika, Anastasia and Lola, were standing at the sink, touching up their lipstick and playing with each other's extensions. I hadn't communicated with any of them since that 4th of July day when I was hammered. Loyal to the grave they were, but cross them, and they would dig your grave. After endless months of missed birthdays, outings, and the general life bullshit girlfriends are there for, they had pretty much dug my grave and picked out the tombstone to say RIP: Life Insurance Bitch. I just kept telling myself one day they would understand when I finally reached the level of success I had been striving for and they got to ride in the fancy cars and come on expensive vacations with me. You would forgive your absentee friend if that was to come in return down the road... right?

Since their eyes were glued to their reflections, they couldn't help but see me in the mirror as I walked in the door. Tension mounted in the room like two crowds coming face to face in the high school cafeteria. Except we had no audience to keep us from holding back any true feelings. I could feel them itching for a fight.

"Oh, hi Jay-den," Anastasia started, speaking in a voice so high it could have shattered a window. This wasn't going to be fun.

"Hey guys!" I said, trying to be friendly and casual.

"Wow, I thought you don't have time to go out anymore, because you're always... you know, working," Mika said, turning to me and rolling her eyes as she sized me up. I was starting to think the whole forgiveness thing wasn't exactly beginning yet.

"Monte wanted to take us out, it was kind of a last minute thing."

"Oh, was it?" Lola asked in a nasty sarcastic voice. Memories flashed back of when the four of us would end up fighting. Somehow one of us was the bad friend and got the brunt of all the verbal abuse. We hadn't grown up at all.

"Ummm, yeah. Look, I'm sorry I haven't really been around much. I just have been trying really hard at work. Things will probably slow down after New Year's."

"Hah, that's nice. Look, you're not the only one with a job. Oops, I mean, a career." Mika was dropping some sarcasm bombs. She got the bitch gene rolling when she drank a lot.

"Yeah, it's not like there was even a point of inviting you here tonight. You wouldn't have even come with us. You came with your insurance friends. Of course," Anastasia remarked with the tone of voice so nasty I almost had to choke back the tears welling up. I couldn't let their pettiness get to me. "Well, I guess this conversation isn't going to be ending with flowers and candy," I said, sick of the passive aggressive shit. "This is just kind of sad," I said quietly looking down.

"No, Jayden. We were sad for a while. Now, we're just sorry for you. Speaking of candy, please eat some. You're skinnier than a drug addict. And those heels are so three seasons ago. You have worn those a million times. If you make so much money, at least order a new pair online." And with that, Lola took the spade and threw dirt on my grave.

"Bye!" Mika said with a big smile as the three of them trooped out of the bathroom.

As the door shut behind them, I felt a piece of me shut closed as well. I looked in the mirror. A year ago I would have been standing in front of the mirror with them, posing in pictures and sharing complaints of whichever douche bag we wanted to magically text us. This whole interaction made me feel like shit. Suddenly, I had a distinct craving for a euphoric feeling between the Mean Girls brigade and the tanorexic getting under my skin, whatever reason that might have been for. Why would I care about a fake blond anyway? Ducking into a stall in case anyone came in, I opened my purse and popped a pill. This was strange, being in a bar bathroom alone, without a posse clambering next to me as we would take turns peeing, all of us in a drunken stupor. Was this peace or loneliness? Fuck it, I didn't want to sit on the toilet contemplating.

When I headed back towards the bar, I crossed my fingers in hopes of avoiding the Alex and Barbie brigade along with my now ex-friends. Everyone was scattered luckily, so I went back to where Scarlett and the managers were.

"Can I get another Kettle and club with a lime, please?" I asked the bartender as soon as I reached the bar.

"Let's do a shot!" Scarlett chimed in.

"Two Patrons, as well, please."

"Damn, girl."

"You have no idea what just happened in the bathroom."

"Yeah, you were gone for a while." I told her about my verbal confrontation and she gave me the usual, "Fuck those bitches, they're not real friends," speech. Easy for her to say, they hadn't been Scarlett's friends for the past decade plus.

"JayJay, what's going on?" Monte asked as he stumbled passed us. I repeated the same story, thinking he would probably regard the incident as just silly female bullshit. But instead, he was sympathetic.

"Look, the same thing happened to me. You know, I lost a lot of my friends when I got into the business because they just didn't get what I was trying to accomplish, except these guys here that have stuck with me, obviously. The thing is, when people are truly your friend, the rift is temporary. You know, that's why we talk about balance a lot. Make sure you make an effort to invest time and keep these friendships. The people who just don't understand and don't want to - they weren't the real deal to begin with. It's going to be okay, Jayden. I'm actually going to bounce. Is Scarlett taking you home?"

"Yeah, I'm good. Thanks, Monte" I said, noticing Scarlett talking to one of the managers' random friends. I wanted to believe Monte, but he did not understand the grudge holding factor I was facing from these girls. I turned around to grab my purse on the bar behind me and immediately a knot formed in my stomach. Just a few feet away Alex was standing facing the Barbie, with his head tilted forward because he was still taller than her even in her cheap stilettos. It seemed as though they were having an intense conversation. I couldn't help but notice how their bodies were practically interlaced. They sat down on two bar stools, and Barbie immediately extended her legs onto the lower rungs of his bar stool, her hand toying with his watch. But what the hell did I care?

"Last call!" the bartender yelled out. I looked at Scarlett, who nodded. A shot for each of us, a beer for her, and my usual vodka soda. I downed the shot but my gaze kept going over to stupid Alex and the blonde. This was ridiculous. I just needed to get my head on straight. With another happy pill, of course.

"Scarlett, I'm running to pee, I'll be back out in a minute," and walked off, not realizing there was a pair of eyes watching me.

The bar was pretty much empty, so I didn't worry about anyone coming into the bathroom. A pill count was necessary considering I had definitely taken a larger than normal amount since I met up with Veronica and I wasn't sure when her next supply was coming. In my drunken haze thinking I was alone, I took the mint case out and carefully laid the orange circles next to the sink. I began to count the pills meticulously, losing myself to the sinking feeling I wouldn't have enough before Veronica got me another supply.

I heard the door open and my name being called. "Jayden?" It was Alex's voice. Embarrassment and rage filled my stomach, so the only logical thing to do was lash out in a pitiful attempt to hide what I was doing at the counter.

"What are you doing?" This is the girls' bathroom!" I said, turning away from the pills like an idiot.

His eyes began to fill with rage as soon as he saw the pills behind me. Before I could grab them, he had me pinned against the wall with one hand and swooped the pills up with his free hand. My kicking and screaming was powerless against his strength and tolerance for high pitch female rantings.

"Alex, what the fuck are you doing?" I screamed as he walked over towards the stall, grabbing his arm with all the strength I had in attempts of saving the one thing in my life that never failed me, my little orange circles.

He flung my arm away like tissue paper and I screamed as I watched him pour them all into the toilet and flush them away.

"What is fucking wrong with you Alex? I am prescribed those! How dare you just take someone's medication and just throw it down the toilet! Are you fucking mad?" I was burning with rage and crippled with fear. My temper got the better of me and I kicked the stall door next to him so hard my shoe dented the door.

"Look what you did now, Jayden. Man you are one self-centered, dramatic little bitch."

This fucker literally just threw hundreds of dollars of my prized possession down the toilet and now he was calling me names. I knew as soon as I laid eyes on this asshole that I hated him. Even more than Nicholas Kingsley.

He walked towards me and kept on his tirade. "You aren't prescribed those pills, Jayden. Don't think I'm stupid." I looked at him blankly, unprepared to be called out like that.

"Yes, I am, Alex, I've had a script for years. I have trouble concentrating."

"People who are prescribed medication don't carry it all at once with them in a mint container and then count their pills like my grandma counts her quarters alone in a bathroom."

"Whatever I do, is none of your fucking business, Alex. What do you give a fuck anyway? You barely even say hi and can barely keep your eyes of Barbie all night, so what gives you the right to storm in here and get all up in my business? You might own this bar, but you have no right to control my life."

"No, I can't control your life, but I can control what goes on in this bar. And you're not bringing in your street drugs in here, Jayden. Do you have any idea what kind of fire you're playing with here? First of all, if you get caught with these, you're dealing with the cops. And secondly, what are you taking this shit for? You're a smart girl, you're better than this," he said, shaking my empty mint container.

"Oh, really, I thought I was a self-centered bitch! You know what, fuck you, and fuck your bars!"

In my head I knew I was being unreasonable to say the least but I couldn't control what was coming out of my mouth at this point. I leaned against the wall and started to cry.

"Jayden, you have a problem. That shit can ruin your life. I don't know how long this has been going on or how much you take-"

"A problem? Please, I'm not some little drug bag. You don't know anything, Alex, okay? I know you think because you are Monte's best friend you know everything about this business and every aspect of my job and that I'm such a fucking idiot." I didn't have a problem. What was he implying, that I was some sort of addict? I brushed off the very thought with disgust. Drug addicts were criminals who stole from their friends and families for nasty illegal shit they snorted and shot up.

"Is this what you want? You want a life where you have to spend your paychecks on pills just so you can keep up and hustle?... You want to walk around looking so skinny when you turn sideways you disappear?" Actually, that part sounded appealing…

"You want to spend your free time tracking down more and more pills because you can't stop at the amount you had a few days ago? Which means more money out of your pocket? That could be money for a new car or a trip."

"Oh fuck you and your Range Rover!" I screamed back. The door swung open and Scarlett walked in. She looked back and forth between Alex and me, unable to surmise the situation.

"What's going on in here?" she asked, still standing in the doorway, as if she could feel the heated words still lingering in the air.

"Nothing important. Let's get out of here." I paused at the entrance to the bathroom where Scarlett was holding the door open. My eyes met Alex's, but all I could see in his dark eyes was emptiness. Even the fiery disgust from moments earlier was extinguished. At that moment I knew I was once again, alone.

"What was that about?" Scarlett asked once we were out of earshot. "Oh, I was telling him about my run-in with my high school friends and started to get emotional. Drunk tears, you know? So embarrassing," I played it, rolling my eyes for effect.

"Then why did you two look like you were about to kill each other when I walked in?"

"I'm a bitch, I always look like I want to kill someone. I can't speak for Alex."

"Dude, I was scared. I have never seen him look so intense like that before. He's usually all smiles or flirting."

"I don't know. Maybe he was mad about something with the blonde. Ew."

"Oh, you mean Staci with an I?" What?

"Who has a name like Staci with an I?"

"Well, I mean, obviously her name is Staci, but she's very adamant that it is spelled with an 'i,' so everyone just calls her Staci with an 'i'."

"Well who is this Staci who spells her name wrong?"

"You don't know who she is?"

"Um, am I supposed to?"

"Oh, she was on America's Next Top Model a few seasons ago. She lived in New York for a while working and now she's back home apparently because her Grandma's really sick or something."

"Wait, why am I supposed to know who she is? America's Next Top Model has a 'new cycle' every seventeen weeks with twenty girls. I can't keep track. And a few seasons ago my ass was parked in the sand on the Mediterranean. I wasn't keeping track of Tyra Banks's wannabes."

"Well, Staci with an I is somewhat of a local celebrity. I just assumed you knew who she was."

"So, is she like his girlfriend or something?"

"No, they dated a long time ago before she was on the show. Then she moved, dropped him because she thought she was hot shit. When she moved home, she found out he was rich and decided she wanted to un-drop him I guess."

"What a gold digging ho. So then what's their deal now?"

"Who knows. I think she really broke his heart the first time around and he is probably afraid of getting hurt a second time."

"What, like if she gets a second round of fame? Come on, you know the grandma story is bullshit. She didn't win the season, did she?"

"No, but still, Jayden. How many people from here end up on a national TV show?"

"I should with my fucked up life," I said, imagining a reality show based on the crazy antics of life insurance agents.

"We could call it "Slutts Who Sell," or "Oops! I Fucked My Manager," or-

"I'm taking your drunk ass home."

CHAPTER 17

That fucking asshole, I thought to myself as I woke up to a level 8 hangover. What was I going to do? I began bicycle kicking under the covers in frustration, furious with myself for being so stupid as to count pills in an open area. Why had I let drunken invincibility take over? That stupid mistake cost me mega bucks, robbed me of the energy and focus I absolutely needed to get through the end of the year, and of course, the fight with Alex. At least I knew what his true colors looked like. Manipulative, more nosy than myself, and completely ridiculous in his accusations of me being a drug addict. I could just turn around and call him a money hungry sex addict.

My brain recounted the previous night's events. The girls I had once deemed as 'friends' had blatantly, unapologetically disowned me, with good reason. Alex was a man whore and a pill stealer. Not wanting to face reality, I closed my eyes. But not for long. Like a thunderstorm, my thoughts turned manic and screamed at me to get more sales by the end of the year. "Time is not a luxury you own, bitch." That voice was so mean. It cared about winning, and winning only, no matter what got hurt in the way. Even if it was myself.

Somehow the thoughts of my friends and Alex melted from my mind and once again all that mattered to me was insurance. I clambered out of bed and searched for my bag to see what sort of schedule I had compiled for that afternoon. In a side pocket, I found a pill bottle. Trying to keep myself from getting all excited, I took a deep breath and anxiously fiddled with the damn child safety cap. The lid popped off and I looked inside only to find several perfectly shaped orange circular pills. I nearly cried with joy as I fished one out of the bottle eagerly and popped it in my mouth, a whole wave of excitement energizing me. *Screw you, Alex. I always have a back-up plan... even if I forget it.* I vaguely remembered putting a stash together for an emergency, but damn was I smart. I absolutely deserved a pat on the back for my slick planning.

Hangover and all, I threw on my gym clothes and packed a bag with Sunday work clothes. It was time to go make shit happen.

■ ■ ■

"Okay, we have to get down to business, Jayden. The updated report came out and… you have an opportunity to really change it around. We have three weeks and…" Monte told me how much I still needed to sell..

"Shit, Monte. I'm screwed. Screwed."

"Calm down, Jay," Monte said, trying to prevent a rant and rave from yours truly. "Look, we are going to break everything down that you need to do, and I promise, it's not that bad. You got this.

Now girly, remember to keep everything clean. No silly business. You can incentivize policyholders with a gas card or whatever in exchange for referrals, but do not ever give them cold hard cash in exchange for a sale. You can kiss your license goodbye, never mind the conference."

"Got it," I said and walked out of the office with a sick sense of confidence. There were whispers of agents and managers pulling a few fast ones to fulfill a last minute agenda, but nothing that was explicitly stated. Just little comments made by agents who did really know what went on.

■ ■ ■

The wife took me to the kitchen table and immediately offered me a drink. So far, so good. Where was her husband? - ah, the back door opened and the knot in my stomach loosened. This was not something I could swing with one spouse around. So, after shooting the shit and explaining why a policy was necessary, I went in for the kill.

"Here, I already have all of the paperwork filled out, I just need your signatures here."

"So, this isn't going to cost me anything?" the wife asked me, her voice filled to the brim with doubt. I couldn't necessarily blame her.

I knew if anymore dribble drabble nonsense explanations, I would completely lose these people's attention. *What were their names again?*

Sweat beads were starting to trickle down the side of my forehead and I didn't even want to think about how much liquid was coming from under my arms.

"I'm confused, how is this not costing us anything?" Amy asked me.

And in desperation, trying to fight a rapidly ticking clock, I was willing to push the envelope. I wanted that trip more than anything I had ever wanted. It was something all the agents dreamed of as soon as they started. Paid vacation? Free booze for three whole days? Opportunity to rub shoulders with the company's most revered? So, in order to convince them to write out the check, I would purchase a Visa gift card which they could use anywhere for an amount slightly higher than their monthly premium as an incentive. That was kosher, right?

That was my first and only easy house. And then I had a list of the families who may have kicked-me-out-of-the-house, the broke families, and then one last group: "I closed my bank account," aka, "I sell drugs."

"Okay, so I'll just need you to grab that check for your monthly premium to activate the policy, and we'll get you all squared away with the paperwork!"

"But I don't have zeh check book, Zayden, zeh bank eh cancel my eh account, because no money in it," Svedka, my little Russian mother downtown explained to me eloquently.

Ahh, since her bank account was closed, the company would be unable to do the auto withdrawal every month.

"Oh, well what about your brother's bank account?" I asked hopefully.

"Ehhh, Alexei no have bank account. He get paid on zeh debit card. You know of this debit card? No have in Russia."

Great, this meant I was going to have to drag along Svedka to the corner store so she could purchase a money order, which I explained to her. Svedka looked at me and appeared to be confused. Oh, she didn't understand the money order. I didn't blame her. I never planned on using one during my lifetime, either. So I explained to Svedka how a money order worked. To which she told me, "Oh, but me not have that much cash."

"Where is your brother's card? Maybe we can get cash from it at an ATM?"

"Eh, no. Brother has the card with him. I do not have zeh money, Zayden."

Well wasn't this splendid. I had a thought of what I could do. And it wasn't exactly what you would call kosher. I turned off that little voice in my head which tells you right from wrong and got in the car, in the direction of the nearest gas station.

"Hi, I need to purchase a money order," I said to the man behind the cash register. He took the money out of my hand and printed up an order for the designated amount.

"And where is the money going to?" he asked, bored out of his mind.

"D'Angelo Enterprises, please," I answered, in the zone. Svekda promised me she would pay me back when her brother was paid on Friday, so technically in my mind, I wasn't really paying for anything. Just loaning kind of sort of, but in the end she was the one paying.

"Friday, right?" I asked, verifying.

"Yah, yah, Zayden, I call you, yah?" she said as I was walking out the door.

CHAPTER 18

Veronica: *Where are you? I need that now.*

Veronica was not one to ever beat around the bush. We were friends and now only maintained contact because we liked our calorie free orange cookies which came in the form of pills. Veronica is very much the life of the party, the girl everyone wants to be friends with. However, Veronica also has no patience or concern for anyone else's time. When she needs something, she needs it five minutes ago and not a minute later. I could have been having open heart surgery, but she would demand I answer my cell phone, text her back, and get off the operating table instantly to contend with whatever request she was presenting.

Me: *I'm downtown working. I can't meet until later.*

Veronica: *Dude, I can't meet later. It needs to be now.*

Me: *Well can we meet half way? I had no idea you needed the money today, you didn't tell me. You always spot me a couple if it's last minute.*

Veronica: *You know it's always this time of month. OMG how fucking stupid are you?!*

Before I threw my phone in anger, I looked in my purse and in my little bottle. I had four left. This was not good. It meant my supply was shit and I was at this bitch's mercy. Now. The little orange buggers needed to be in my possession now.

Me: *Okay fine. But when can you get the addy?*

Veronica: *How fucking stupid are you? Stop using that word in a text. I won't answer.*

Me: *Okay, fine sorry. Can you meet me off River Street? I'm really far away.*

Veronica: *Oh my god, I am not leaving my house. Just drive here Jayden what are you not understanding here, I'm BUSY!*

Me: *Veronica, come on, I'm trying to work. Quit being a bitch and compromise with me.*

Veronica: *You aren't the only one doing shit. I'm fucking doing shit oh my god I'm really stressed right now I have a slew of clients soon, okay?*

I swerved to dodge a car as I stupidly text and drive being that the roads are covered with pockets of black ice and that little fact it is against the law. So is buying and consuming prescription drugs that aren't for you, but whatever.

Yeah, I'll meet you now, I texted her back. I was going to head back in that direction anyway, so I could just take the back roads, I figured. I looked at the clock and saw it was only 5:45. It had already been pitch black for about an hour. December was so depressing. This was a ridiculous way to be spending a December Sunday, driving around multiple counties chasing people down who just needed some life insurance. I should have been curled up on the couch with a mug of spiked (diet) hot cocoa watching the movie *Elf* instead. But no, I spent my day and gas chasing people who did not want to be bothered by me under any circumstance, much less be bothered by selling a damn life insurance policy as I was learning. The doors being slammed in my face followed by an icy gust of wind wasn't exactly putting me in the mood for Christmas cheer. Full of self-doubt and self-loathing, I reached into my purse and dug out half of a pill to calm my nerves and maybe redirect my mood. I didn't want to use a full one just in case Veronica was pulling a fast one and somehow wouldn't be home when I got to her apartment. She wasn't the most reliable.

I approached a green traffic light and couldn't remember which way I had to turn to get to Veronica's house. The downtown area could be so confusing as everything seemed to look the same in the dark. Blue Moon was in this neighborhood, but I was engulfed in confusion and couldn't get my bearings. In the rearview mirror I saw a line of cars stretch behind me. Left or right? Shit. For whatever reason, I decided to turn right. As I did so, I hit the gas pedal out of nervousness as the cars behind me began to honk. Flying down the road, I barely registered the orange sign reading: ROAD CLOSED IN 1,000 FEET. Shit, shit. What? My eyes spun left and right looking for a place to turn around, but no driveways were in sight. I didn't see the sign for: ROAD CLOSED IN 500 FEET as the ding of a text message went off and reflexively I grabbed my phone to see who it was.

Veronica: *Where in the fucking world are you?*

And that's how accidents happen. Hitting the brakes a millisecond too late, my car smashed into the concrete barrier where the sign screamed: ROAD CLOSED. As my body lurched forward twenty-six years flashed before my eyes. This had to be the end. Except it wasn't: some guardian angel whacked away the Angel of Death as I was stopped by the opposing force of the airbag popping, ringing in my ears like a gunshot.

Once I realized I actually wasn't dead, panic set in. *Ira is going to kill you. How fucking stupid are you? How are you going to get your pills now?* Before I could even think about attempting to drive the vehicle away, clouds of smoke began to emit from the hood of the car. *Fuck, fuck, fuck,* I thought afraid I was going to be a victim of a car explosion. I grabbed my stupid cell phone, jumped out of the car and ran back, petrified my stupid car was about to blow up.

"Jayden!" I heard someone yell. That voice. Oh, no, not now. I closed my eyes. Maybe when I opened them this would all go away and I would just get back into my non-crashed car and get on with my life. Meaning get to Veronica's now and got on with some life insurance policies.

"We heard the crash from inside the bar and called 911. An ambulance is on its way. Come over here, Jayden. Stay in my car until it gets here, it's freezing out." I looked at the smoke rising from the hood, and back over to Alex. Why, why did I do that? I couldn't do anything right, I couldn't even follow street signs anymore. I couldn't take it. I tried to fight them back, but the tears began pouring down my face.

I heard footsteps and was soon enveloped in a strong embrace that smelled like leather and safety. But I couldn't open my eyes and face him, to see any more look of disappointment. At the same time I couldn't let go, his arms were the only thing keeping me from falling to the ground.

"Alex, my car's now a piece of smashed metal with smoke coming out of it. The smashed piece of metal I needed for my job. Why did I have to smash the car now? Why was I so stupid?" I sobbed.

"Where's your coat, Jayden? Are you hurt?"

"I don't like driving with it on," I choked out. In my panic, it hadn't even occurred to me that it was December and I would be freezing without it. My body was in shock and I didn't even notice a pool of blood coming from my right knee.

"We're going to wait in my car until the cops come, do you understand?" He opened the door to the Range Rover and lifted me into the passenger seat, throwing his coat over my shoulders. At this point, I was hyperventilating. *Cops?*

"Alex, you're being ridiculous!" I screamed. "Just call AAA and have the car towed! Don't fucking call the cops! Let me just call my Dad and go home, okay?"

"Jayden, calm down. I'm handling this okay."

"Who the fuck do you think you are to try and control everything?" My words came out broken as I sobbed in hysterics.

"Jayden, you just crashed into a concrete barrier, you didn't get a flat tire. This isn't for AAA!"

"Alex, I can't get in trouble."

"You didn't do anything illegal Jayden." He looked down and noticed there was blood trickling down the car seat.

"Jayden, your knee is bleeding really badly."

"What?" I touched the pant leg and felt that it indeed was starting to soak in the blood seeping from my knee.

"Fuck," I thought as a police car pulled up and an officer walked over to us.

"Can you tell me your name, Miss?"

"Jayden Rosenberg."

"And your address?" I choked out my information and then was asked if I needed anything out of the car.

"Everything," I said. I really wasn't kidding. The cop rolled his eyes and I relented, compromising to only have my purse. The idiot grabbed the gym bag instead, which only contained sweaty clothes.

"What exactly happened here, Jayden?" I started to tell the officer my very skewed version of events when an ambulance pulled up.

"What THE FUCK IS THAT DOING HERE?" A medic stepped out and approached me, but Alex pulled him aside and apparently had a few words for him. Then he turned to me.

"Jayden, who do you want me to call to meet you at the hospital?" Alex asked

I still hadn't stopped hyperventilating and now this exasperated it.

"HOSPITAL?"

"Ma'am, you need to go to the hospital. You have been in a very serious accident. This is standard procedure."

"Fuck procedure I am NOT going to any hospital." All I heard was a losing battle of bullshit about concussions, possible injuries. This was not happening.

"Jayden. Who do you want me to call?" Alex asked again.

Who could he call? Did anyone even care enough? My mind went blank. Renee had left for Boca Raton earlier in the afternoon to spend time with my grandparents. I didn't have a boyfriend. My friends all hated me. The only person who could help me would be my dad. He was going to be so angry with me. *Damn it, Renee, why did you have to be in Florida now of all times?*

"My dad," I said.

"What's his phone number?" Reluctantly, I gave it to him.

"Hi, Mr. Rosenberg?" I heard him say. "My name is Alex Reyes and I'm here with your daughter, she was just in an accident...yes she's fine, she's just shaken up a bit...yes an ambulance is here..."

The EMT took charge again, "Ma'am, you are going to have to come with us in the ambulance. We're going to put you on this stretcher here okay."

"Oh hell no you aren't. I am just fine. He's on the phone with my Dad," I said pointing to Alex. No way am I going to the hospital. No. No fucking way," I told him. I was taking control.

"Miss, you have been in an accident, this is standard procedure. Plus, we really need to have your knee looked at because of the contusion."

"The whatchamusion?" I asked.

"You're bleeding, Ma'am." Jesus, this was just a bloody knee. Why was everyone overreacting about this?

"Um yeah, and I think CVS sells band aids. Look, this really isn't necessary."

"Ma'am, please cooperate," he said, as two other EMTs grabbed me by the arms.

"This isn't happening. Alex, don't make me go!" I reached for him as the men hoisted me out of the car and onto the stretcher. I felt two hands put something hard around my neck and I panicked.

"What is this? What's going on?" I could no longer lift my head up or turn my head. This must have been what the Spanish Inquisition was like before the bludgeon came down to slice the prisoner to pieces.

"We need to secure your neck. If you suffered from a concussion or any neck and spinal injuries, we need to prevent from furthering them." I was getting really sick of all this medical babble. Couldn't they just be honest and tell me they were doing everything possible to make me as miserable as possible with their torture contraptions?

"No, really, my neck is fine. Just get this thing off me, please. I can't even lift my head up!"

"Yes, that's the point of it." For someone who has very serious control issues, this neck contraption was triggering a full on OCD war. I was losing every bit of strength I had left to fight off this impending hospital journey. I really fucked up this time.

I lifted my arm up and cried out Alex's name, praying he hadn't fled the scene and left me with these strange creatures to just add more contraptions around me. I saw his face above mine as he grabbed my hand and stared into my tear-filled eyes. For a moment, his own seemed to mirror mine.

"Alex, please don't leave me!"

"Listen to me," he said soothingly, his free hand now covering my hand which was grasping his other one. He was doing his best to reassure me. "Your dad will be at the hospital waiting for you, okay?"

"Is he mad at me?" It was all I wanted to know. My dad. I wanted my dad. But was Ira going to finish this Spanish Inquisition mission and chop off my head?

"No. You're dad isn't mad at you. He just wanted to know that you weren't hurt. He's going to be there for you at the hospital. He seems like the kind of dad who would do anything for his daughter." The floodgates started pouring again. My body was going to dry up at this rate.

"We're ready to lift her," the EMT announced. I knew I was on my own now.

"Jayden, you're a fighter. You got this girl," he said, giving my hand an extra squeeze before he was forced to let go as I was lifted and wheeled into the ambulance.

"Wait! Alex, please tell Monte about this."

"Of course I will." With that, I closed my eyes and cried quietly for a second until I was jolted back to the reality of being on a stretcher.

"Do you have any medical conditions?" the EMT asked me as he rolled my sleeve to attach an IV to me.

"What on earth are you doing?" I screamed.

"This is standard procedure, Miss. We're giving you an IV." Why the fuck was I being called ma'am, miss, sir, mademoiselle, whatever? My name was Jayden, fuckers.

"Why do I need an IV?"

"It's to keep you hydrated, Ma'am."

"I want water. Can you please bring me water and take out the needle?" I begged.

"No, ma'am, you can't have any water."

"What the fuck? What do you mean I can't have any water?!"

"Because if they have to do surgery on you at the hospital, it could cause you to throw up and catch pneumonia."

"I have to get surgery?!" This was insane.

"No, I am not saying you're going to have surgery, I am just saying that just in case.

This is all standard procedure, you have to remain calm and understand that. Now, do you have any medical conditions?"

"Well can't you see I have fucking anxiety! Can you please give me some Xanax in this IV thing? A tranquilizer? Please? I want to crawl out of my skin. You don't understand. I don't do hospitals. You are literally killing me right now."

"Ma'am, you are going to have to calm down. I am not authorized to dispense any medications at this time, but after you go through the trauma unit, a doctor may be able to give you something."

"The trauma unit? What the fuck do I need to be in a trauma unit for? I have a fucking scrape on my knee!"

It was too much to take. My fear of hospitals and anything medically related is so intense I have a nervous breakdown if I know I have to get a shot. There were several occasions growing up where my mother had to excuse my manic like behavior in a doctor's office. This was my worst fear come to reality. My head and neck were literally secured to the stretcher along with the rest of my body so that I couldn't move even if I wanted to. I was so thirsty and my lips were chapped from the cold and dehydration. I was still crying, just not as intensely as before. My body was wearing out. And then I heard a beep. I forgot that at some point I had my phone on my stomach. I lifted it above my head so I could read the text.

Where the fuck are you? It was Veronica. Oh, that bitch.

Just got in a fucking accident trying to get to your stupid apartment, so sorry, I won't be making it right now, okay? I answered.

OMG seriously?! Are you okay? she asked. I didn't answer her back. Figured I'd let her sweat it out a little bit considering her incessant texting and inconsideration did contribute to my car's demise and my being in the back of a fucking ambulance completely immobile in these fucking neck traps.

I breathed deeply to calm myself, just as the yogis preach. It did work a little, for a minute.

"I'm really sorry," I said to the EMT. "I know you're just doing your job, I'm just very scared of hospitals and needles and all this stuff, and I just wish my Dad was here. You're really nice, but you're not my Dad."

"I understand, it's okay," he said with a chuckle which made me feel a little better. "But I promise, your dad is going to meet us at the hospital and you will see him soon. This will all be over very soon hopefully and then you can go home." And with that, I closed my eyes and breathed. I wanted to get out of this entrapped horizontal position as soon as I could.

■■■

But the trauma unit workers had other plans for me. I have heard horror stories of people with limbs falling off and hearts not beating waiting four hours in the emergency waiting room to actually receive medical attention. Apparently if you are coming straight from the ambulance, they rush you right in. My stretcher was rolled right into a large room with curtains hanging as partitions. I can't even describe it as shabby chic or vintage, it was just downright ridiculously ugly and exposing.

"Get her prepped for vitals," I heard someone say. *Prep me for vitals?* I wondered. Suddenly a man appeared with a pair of very large scissors. This did not make me happy.

"What on earth do you think you are doing with those?" I asked.

"We are going to have to cut your clothes off in order to put a dressing gown on you," the nurse/doctor person with zero personality told me.

"The fuck you're going to cut my clothes off! This is fucking ridiculous!" I didn't care that I sounded like someone in a mental hospital. Cut my clothes off? This was all completely unnecessary activity for a bleeding knee. I needed an extra-large Band-Aid, a lot of Xanax, and to get the fuck out of there. These trauma people were acting so *Grey's Anatomy* and their performance really needed improvement.

"Ma'am, we can't have you removing your own clothing because we cannot clear you to move your head and neck. You have not received an MRI. You may have sustained injuries of which you are unaware. We need to take these precautions. This is all standard procedure."

Fuck standard procedure.

"Well you're fucking lucky this sweatshirt is from Wal-Mart or else I would demand that you reimburse me for the cost of my clothing." There were other attendees around me, prepping things behind my head I couldn't see. But the scissors had now sliced open all of the layers of clothing, and I was completely exposed, A-cup breasts and all.

"What the hell are you all looking at? Can't you have some decency here? I'm fucking naked!" I screamed, livid and certain that these were men staring at my body. Finally someone had the decency to cover me with a robe. This was not South Beach, people.

"What does everyone else who gets rolled in here have to say about these standard procedures?" I asked the guy above me, the only person I could make eye contact with.

"Well actually it's a lot easier, because usually they come in passed out, so they don't even know what's happened until they wake up," he said casually.

"Oh," I thought. The drunk drivers.

"Well maybe I'm a raging bitch, but at least I'm sober," I rationalized.

"You're not that bad." I appreciated his lie. Okay, it's time for your MRI." They rolled me over to an intimidating machine where three people stood around me switching things and adjusting settings. This felt like a science experiment.

"Is there a chance that you are pregnant?" someone asked me.

"Not unless the condom broke." The three of them froze and no one said anything.

"I'm just trying to make a joke," I said trying to break the silence.

"I actually was trying to hold back my laughter," the tech next to me said. I entered a dark tunnel which was much too scary for my liking, so I kept my eyes shut. Forever had passed and I was still in there, hearing the hum of the x-rays and a beep here and there. What if I got stuck in here? *What if it broke and I was permanently encased inside of an x-ray machine?* I wondered. *Did shit like that ever happen? I started to panic.* Claustrophobia was not a reality I was enjoying at the moment. I wanted to get out of here. I wanted to see my Dad. Now.

After the MRI, I was wheeled back over to my designated cubicle, thinking that the end had come. Again, the nurses starting murmuring to each other and I was really not appreciating it.

"What's going on?" I asked, wanting to threaten them with anything possible.

"We need to stitch up your knee."

"Stitches?"

"Don't worry, we're going to apply a local anesthetic so you won't feel anything." I had stitches before, so I had reason to believe this blond talking to me. But there was something sinister about her. I closed my eyes, refusing to see the sight of a needle being put in my knee when a searing pain burned as though someone was literally tearing a fiery knife through my knee. To say a scream roared from the depths of my vocal cords is an understatement. The walls were shaking with the decibel level of my rage.

"Well, I guess the anesthesia didn't kick in yet," the soon to be dead blond surmised from my wall shaking scream. And then, she continued to stab my knee with the threaded needle, not giving a shit that I could feel the sharpness slicing and burning through my skin as I screamed in agony. When it was finally over, I was a heaping mess all over again. When was it going to all stop?

"Miss, are you Jayden?" I looked up and saw a middle aged man with kind eyes.

"Yes?" I asked confused.

"I'm the hospital chaplain. Your dad is out front and he just wanted me to come back here and see if you're okay. I just wanted to talk to you for a minute." The hospital chaplain. Weren't they the people who read last rights?

"You're a what? Am I dying? What's going on?" I couldn't even think logically anymore, not that I ever actually had.

"No, you're not dying." He grabbed my hand and smiled reassuringly. "I just wanted to come see how you're doing and let your dad know." The poor guy probably regretted asking as I began spewing out a barrage of hateful sentiments regarding the blond Nazi nurse, but he was very patient and promised I could see my dad soon.

Once my MRI scan came back clear, I was given a pair of scrubs and told I could go out front and sign out. The only thing left I had were my underwear and sneakers, which hadn't been taken off. Someone went and grabbed me a pair of hospital scrubs so I had something to wear. When I finally sat up and went to stand and put the drawstring pants on, I discovered that I could not walk anymore. I felt a searing shooting pain if I even put my right toe on the floor.

"Can someone help me put my pants on?" I begged. How had I not felt this pain right after the accident?

"Your body was in shock," a nurse explained, wriggling the pants over my legs and hips. Since I couldn't walk, she sat me in a wheelchair and took me to the waiting room, where I finally saw my Dad. And not to break pattern, I began to sob.

He gave me his coat and helped me hobble to the car, muttering what idiots they were for not giving me crutches. I hadn't even thought to ask for them because they are for injured people and I could not grasp the concept that I went from being in a gym only hours earlier to now not being able to walk. My dad wasn't outright angry with words but his tone was stiff, talking to me with a disgruntled employer manner. I would have done anything to turn back time and un-fuck up everything.

"Dad, I'm sorry."

"Well, you have a good track record for damaging cars, so why should this be any different?"

"I didn't mean to."

"You were very lucky you had a friend who was right at the scene and was nice enough to help you and give me a call. Seemed a lot nicer than some of these knuckleheads you get caught up with." I wished Renee was there and not in stupid Florida. She would have told Ira to shut up.

CHAPTER 19

Sleeping in the recliner left me with a stiff neck in addition to an immobile knee. My dad and I decided it was useless to try to get me upstairs to my bedroom when inevitably, I would want to come back down at some point. So, sleep in the family room it was for me. Before dashing off to the office for some sort of equipment shipping catastrophe, my dad fed me a hearty breakfast of Tylenol and cranberry juice. "Call me if you need anything," he said on his way out the door. I knew he was thinking, "Please don't have any more disasters. Please don't call me." Who could blame the guy? He had only one child, and she was an accident-prone disappointment wasting a perfectly good college degree and crashing cars. This was probably not a daughter he was bragging about.

As soon as he walked out the door, Renee called.

"Jayden, your father called me this morning! Oh honey, I am so sorry!"

"It's okay Mom." I really didn't feel like talking to I nipped the conversation short.

"I'm really tired, I want to go back to sleep. I'll call you later."

"Okay honey. I love you. And if you need anything, call me. I'll give your love to the family and let them know you're okay."

"Thanks, Ma." I hung up the phone and sighed. Maybe being alone wasn't such a bad thing. It wasn't like I'd had much of that in eons.

I stared at the TV and grabbed the remote. After I clicked the power button, the weather channel appeared. *Really, Ira?* I thought to myself. What channel was Bravo?! I couldn't remember anything. Sitting in the recliner watching TV was not something I had done in months. Maybe some Sunday the previous winter when I gave myself permission to relax for a minute. And then it hit me. I had to pee. Yesterday I was running around like a monkey on crack and now today I couldn't walk. This should be a fun trip to the bathroom.

With my functioning leg I closed the part of the recliner that popped out and hobbled to grab the rolling chair my dad left next to the couch. I maneuvered myself to hold the back of it, with my gimped leg dragging behind me. Trying to raise the dead leg with my own strength hurt too much. Hopping on my left foot, I pushed the chair through the living room and across the kitchen floor, into the bathroom where I grabbed onto the vanity for balance. How long was this going to last?

Accidentally, I tapped my right leg on the floor and winced at the pain as soon as any pressure was applied to it. Well, clearly the gym wasn't happening today just as the nurses told me while I was signing my discharge papers. I thought they were just underestimating my determination. Apparently I was just underestimating their medical knowledge. I hobbled back over to the couch and scrolled through my phone. No text messages. No Facebook messages. Maybe no one saw the post I put up on Facebook about the accident. Didn't anyone care? The pit in my stomach started growing. I scrolled through all my contacts wondering if I should send out a group text? No, that was weird. Shouldn't people reach out to me? And then it dawned on me.

No, no one really cares. After ignoring birthdays, not returning phone calls, missing girls nights, ducking out of holiday celebrations, those words from Mika came back to haunt me. "Well, when you have all that money, we just might not be there for you anymore, Jayden." Here I sat without a ton of money and no friends. That was a double loss. A tear went down my face. I tried texting Lana. "*I got in a car accident last night.*" Maybe that would generate some conversation? I put the TV back on and listened as the *Real Housewives* of some city started cat fighting in ball gowns and huge diamond earrings. Thirty minutes after losing some brain cells, I checked my phone. Two people who I never talk to 'liked' my status about my accident. Who "likes" a car accident post?

The reality of months and months of breaking contact with the girls I had been friends with for practically a decade caught up to me. I started to feel angry that in the time of need, they weren't there. But what right did I have to feel so angry? Work always took precedence. Being the best always took precedence. But at what cost? Getting into a car crash because my mind was frantically racing worrying about life insurance policies? I looked at my leg propped up and pulled up my sweatpants so I could see the bandages. They hadn't been changed yet and I was too scared to undress them and see what the stitches had turned out to look like.

I did not feel like sitting with these lonely and worthless feelings so I chose to endure physical discomfort and hobbled over to the kitchen, opening the fridge like a puppy dog in search of a treat. Lactaid milk, left over chicken, yogurt, some veggies in the bin, apples, cheese… nothing had any appeal. I looked up and saw the cupboard where the cereal was and decided that was going to be my selection. And there were plenty of bananas in the fruit bowl on the island. Great, this was perfect. I couldn't walk and I was going to eat carbs and nothing can stop me. Grateful at least my arms were still in working order, I grabbed a box of Life cereal and some sort of all natural sugar-filled granola my mother mistook for being healthy. Maybe I just wanted to fart a lot later. Finding the biggest bowl, I mixed equal parts with an entire banana, and drowned it in milk. It took two trips to bring the bowl and two boxes back to the couch. Because, who just eats one bowl of cereal at a time?

Usually it was a calorie free, orange pill in between my teeth instead. Now I was out of pills, a knee, friends, and a car. I don't know the importance of those items, but they all rate pretty highly on a needs list. Being that the cereal was only going to occupy me for so long and that the housewives were causing my IQ to lower a few points, I was getting bored and craving communication. Not to mention a dose of sympathy, to be completely honest. So I texted the three friends I had run into that night at Alex's bar where they told me to get a new wardrobe. Surely a car accident would warm their frostiness towards me, right?

When my phone finally did ring I had switched over to *Love & HipHop* on VH1 to really stimulate my brain. I found it fascinating that record producers could say to the camera that they represented "really big names" like "LiL Big," "DJ JayDee," and "Jo Squizzles," yet I had no idea who any of these so called artists were. All I knew is that the producer, Master Emz, was dating Dixie Diamond but needed a slam piece on the side, because, ya know. "Dixie travels a lot when she does back-up in DJ JayDee's rap videos. Plus she ain't got no diamond rock yet so ain't nothin' offish."

"Hi, Mimi," I answered without turning down the volume too low or moving my eyes from the screen. I was dying to know if Dixie was going to find out about Freshette, the slam piece.

"Girlfriend, what the fuck happened?" I heard the exhale of a cigarette puff. I recounted to Mimi the entire episode's events, even how Alex, whom of course hadn't contacted me since sending my basket case self into an ambulance. What did he think it was, a limo with a full bar and a leather seated stretcher taking me to the spa? He could have called…

"So all that and you haven't heard anything?"

"No. But I don't care. That guy is way more trouble than he's worth. I mean, he just has to take control of every situation."

"Do you think maybe it's because you're a little out of control, girl?"

"You mean, because my sales track record sucks, I have disgraceful corporate love affairs and I crash cars, I'm out of control?"

"Well, not like that Lindsay Lohan or whatever. But, maybe it's a good thing you're stuck on your ass for a few days. It'll keep you out of trouble," she added thoughtfully. Well, I could always find ways to get into trouble.

"I can still lie on my back, if you know what I mean."

"Girl, if you can manage to get laid with a busted knee without throwing anything else out, let me know."

"I should be so lucky."

"You're lucky he was there, Jayden. Who knows how long you would have been stuck outside in the cold and not to mention alone?"

"I know, I know. I just hated him seeing me like that, so utterly hysterical. They should have taken me to a psych hospital instead."

"Well, thank God you're okay. Everyone here at the office wanted to know how you are. I yelled at everyone for not calling or texting you. I know you would have called anyone in that office if it had been them." I sighed, knowing that she was right. But it didn't really matter if they did check in. I was still stuck on this couch with all my hard work towards conference blown up because I blew up my car.

A few trips to the bathroom and more bowls of cereal later, I got a text message from Lola, whose feelings towards me had not defrosted at all even though I was now handicapped.

Jayden… that sucks you crashed your car, although you've never been the best driver anyway. But you know, you can't just crawl to us when something bad happens and expect a pity party. You probably should have thought of that before when you were too busy working to care if anything bad was happening in our lives.

I wiped a tear that fell onto my phone and set it aside so I wouldn't keep staring at the message or hoping for a new one to show up in my inbox with sympathetic words. Neither of my other friends ever texted me back. I guess Lola was the spokesperson for the three of them. They didn't receive a group text but knowing them, as soon as one of their phone's beeped, they immediately did a three way call to analyze the situation and come to a unanimous vote to further remind me of how unworthy I was of their friendship and that most importantly, I was not one of them anymore. I wasn't one of anything anymore.

My phone rang and it was Monte this time. "JayJay, girly, how are ya holding up?"

"This sucks, Monte. This just fucking sucks." I hadn't spoken to him yesterday, so judging by his greeting, I guess Alex had filled him in like I asked. I wonder what Alex told him? Not that I was going to ask or anything.

"I know, but you'll be up and running in no time. Look, my Mom made some chicken soup so this is what I'm gonna do for ya. I'm going to run it up to your house after I get out of the office. How does that sound? Chicken soup always fixes everything."

"Even a busted knee?" I smiled, appreciating his gesture. At least someone cared.

"Even a busted knee. Okay, I gotta jet, I got a call with Giovanni I gotta jump on but hang in there. I'll hit you up later."

"Thanks, Monte." I hung up the phone and surfed through the movies on OnDemand. None of these titles meant anything to me. I settled for some Bradley Cooper flick and called it a day. Since I had no pills, I decided it was the perfect time for a cocktail. Not like I was working or anything that required a level of sobriety. Thankfully, there was a full vodka bottle in the freezer and a liter of club soda in the fridge. I grabbed the biggest glass in the cabinet, a straw and put everything in a bag to drag back to the couch. Before long, the movie I selected became extremely fascinating, so much so, that I put my glass down and promptly passed out.

When I woke up, my party supplies had been cleared and it was after midnight. I'm sure Ira was ecstatic about finding these remnants. My phone started ringing and it was Veronica telling me she was on her way over to collect her money and deliver the pills. She must have really wanted the cash for her to actually go out of her way, especially at this hour. But I wasn't complaining since I needed them ASAP. This ravenous appetite was not going to do me any favors long term. My dad slept like a rock, so I didn't have to worry about him coming down and intervening on anything like Alex did in the bathroom.

"There is a shitload of stuff in your garage next to the door girl, and it looks like yours," Veronica said as she swung open the side door.

"I guess my dad went to the car today and got all my stuff out," I thought guiltily. He shouldn't have had to do that. He shouldn't have to do most of the shit he has to do for me at this point in my life.

"Would you mind bringing in anything that looks important in here, babe?" I asked hopefully.

"Fine!" she said, bringing in what looked like a portable version of my life.

"Dear god!" was the first thing out of her mouth when she walked into the family room and saw me in the flesh. "You look awful!"

"Thanks," I said. She opened up one of the bags and found my make-up bag. "Well, at least you can fix yourself up now. God, you really did a number, Jayden." Her words were just so overwhelmingly comforting to me.

"What?" Veronica asked when I told her everything about the accident scene. "Jayden, he must care about you to be there like that." I refused to accept any truth to her opinion. My heart was still in pieces from the Kingsley debacle and it didn't need any further ruin. Besides, Alex was still off flitting with that dumb blond who spelled her name wrong. Collapsing all over him when the car was smoking was just a moment of weakness.

"I don't think so, Jayden," she countered. "People's true emotions come out when they're vulnerable. Maybe you feel something you don't want to recognize." Lalalala I can't hear you. "Veronica, you sound like you have been watching way too many rom-com's lately."

"No, Jayden, seriously. Plus he is so hot. Who cares about that other girl." He was not hot. He was not hot. He was not hot.

"She's a manipulative slut. With a heinous laugh."

"Then don't worry about her. Just be you. She'll fade eventually."

"I'm not in competition with her, Veronica. I don't want him. What I want is to somehow fix this mess I've gotten myself into."

"Yeah, I mean this job has wrecked you, girl."

"No, it has not. I wrecked myself. But this job is everything. I've poured so much into it I could never just quit. Quitting is failing, Veronica. You don't want to cut hair but are you about stop?"

"No, but it doesn't ruin my life."

"No, I just have a few more levels to get through until I'm at a place where I have my life back again."

"You will always say that. And you're never happy. This just isn't you. Come on, you're a Gemini like me. We're crazy and we hate authority." Veronica might have been a selfish bitch, but she was an insightful bitch. We did our usual "I'm sorry I'm such a bitch" exchange and like a good pill-popping friend, reminded me to store my orange presents somewhere safe. I could keep them safe. If only I could keep my heart and body safe too.

∎ ∎ ∎

The next day I woke up feeling exactly the same as I had the morning before, and received my same Tylenol and juice breakfast from Ira.

"I see you got all of your bags. How did you manage to get them in the house?" he asked me surveying them on the floor.

"Veronica stopped over late last night to see how I was and brought them inside for me since I can't walk."

"Oh, that was nice of her. Well, yeah, I was going to tell you when I got home but you were sleeping. Anyway, I went to where your car crashed to get your stuff out. That car is finished. You really did a good job, Jayden. You really could have hurt yourself badly. You're very lucky." I didn't feel so lucky laying there like a gimp. If anything, I felt more guilty now that my dad had actually seen the damage.

"I'm sorry, Dad."

"It's just a hunk of metal. The important thing is that you're okay." Sounded like the speech every injured person got.

"We need to change the bandage on that knee."

"Do we have anything?" I asked, having no idea what was needed to do this. I wasn't watching when the Nazi nurse was ripping my skin apart or when she was wrapping up whatever she did with a needle and thread like I was the bride of Frankenstein. My dad went to the master bathroom and came back with some supplies.

"Will you do it?" I asked, scared of what lied beneath the bandages. Carefully, we both ended up unwrapping the endless layers of gauze until it came down the actual knee itself. It looked different to me, after being buried for two days. He removed the top piece of bandage and I screamed. I was expecting a thin line of stitching with thin thread, like what someone who has had knee surgery gets. But instead, what was in my knee was an abstract zig-zag of not even thread, but something that felt like plastic. And it was through my knee!

"I'm going to kill her, Dad." He knew exactly what I meant and I think he even felt bad.

"What the fuck did she do to me?" My knee was now completely ugly. I had an ugly knee. I never liked my legs, and now I had an ugly knee on top of it.

"This woman must have been a complete retard. These stitches are all over the place!" At least he was sympathetic to my cosmetic dilemma.

"Just cover it up, I can't bear to look at it anymore," I added, leaning back and putting my hands over my face in true dramatic fashion. But when he made the dressing too tight and then too loose I had to do it myself anyway.

"Alright, I'm going to work, do you need anything else?" I raised my eyebrows letting him know if I opened my mouth the list was going to be unattainable and endless. He kissed me on the forehead and left to do exactly what I had done the day before: nothing.

That afternoon, my new idol Master Emz was spittin' some new lines to Dixie. At this point I had decided to get the full effect of the show by pairing with with a glass of Sauvignon Blanc. When I say glass, I mean goblet which I topped off with club soda to satisfy my desire for a carbonated drink. "Who dat trick ho blowin' yo phone? Huh? What's this bitch doing?" Dixie's arm motions were almost as loud as her voice and manicure.

"She ain't no one, Boo. You need tah simma down nah. I don't know whatchu be doin' when you up shootin' them videos."

"Oh don't you be callin me Boo when you got some hooker textin' you out da ass!" God I couldn't get enough of this shit. As soon as my knee heeled I was gonna up myself out of this crib and shake my ass for some dough. I was planning a shopping spree at BabyPhat when the doorbell rang. Who rang doorbells? Who was at my house? I rolled over to the powder room and examined myself. Some deodorant, body spray and tinted moisturizer was just going to have to do for the unexpected guest. Thank god these items were in the powder room downstairs. The doorbell rang again and I was getting agitated. Can't people understand I'm not really moving at lightning speed right now?

"Coming!" I yelled, pushing along on the rolling chair. Who needs crutches anyway? This chair was turning out to be much more fun. Without thinking, I opened to see the door who it was. It was too much to be moving the curtains next to the door for a peek. Probably some asshole trying to sell me lawn services. Hell, maybe it was Ellen Degeneres telling me I had won $1 million like she always does on her show. I could dream now, right? But it was neither of those people when I opened the door.

Something happened that I didn't expect. Butterflies swarm through my stomach and I suddenly felt very self-conscious that my face wasn't tastefully covered in my most subtle, flattering make-up. *Please don't smell like...someone who hasn't showered in a long time*, I thought. I was wearing sweatpants that I had in college, a t-shirt I slept in and a Hanes sweatshirt from Wal-Mart that probably had dried cereal on it. If Staci with an I was sacked to the couch she probably would smell like french vanilla and her lip gloss would match her black La Perla ensemble. Whatever, she was not important.

I gave Alex a surprised look but motioned for him to come in so he wasn't standing out in the cold. "Hey. What are you doing here?" I asked, shutting the door, unsure of how else to start this, whatever this drop by was. It was then I noticed he was holding a paper bag.

"Soup. Monte wasn't able to make it up here, so he asked me to bring it over." That was weird. He could have just given it to Scarlett, who had texted me last night saying she would stop by later today after she ran appointments. Monte ended up being too busy to swing by the first night so I guess he passed the task to someone else.

"Oh, thanks." I felt very awkward wheeling and hobbling through my house with an audience other than Ira, but Alex didn't make any comments for once.

"Can I get you anything?" I asked him, remember my manners.

"What do you have?"

"Umm, look in the fridge."

"You guys have all really healthy stuff," he remarked as he surveyed each of the shelves. Which was ironic, I did the same thing in everyone's house as well. "Yeah, I know. The glasses are in that cupboard." I didn't feel like hobbling any more than I needed to. He grabbed the cranberry juice and poured himself a glass.

"You like cranberry juice?" I was surprised.

"Yeah, I love it. It was always in my house growing up."

"I put club soda in it. I love carbonated drinks."

"Explains your love for vodka sodas. Let's get you sitting back down," he said and I lead him back to the family room.

"*Love and Hip Hop?*" he asked me as the rappers and producers were pulling two hair pulling broads apart from each other, their manicures lashing out at each other like swords.

"Yeah, I get a little stupider each time I watch it," I admitted.

"So... how are you feeling?" he asked nervously. I don't think either of us really knew how to talk at this point. I was so embarrassed he was in my house seeing me like this, after seeing me completely undone.

"Well," I answered, pointing to my knee. I didn't really want to admit all the guilt, shame, and pain I was really feeling. He always had the upper hand, damn it.

"You're really lucky that's all that happened was a hurt knee, you know. I told you that you needed to go to a hospital." Sure Alex, remind me how you once again saved the day.

"They made it worse than it is." I mean, they did butcher my knee, at least the Nazi nurse bitch did. Maybe she was related to Staci with an "i".

"So, what happened?" He put his hand to his face and started stroking the stubble like he was getting into the inquisitive mode. Dressed down in faded jeans, boots and what could have been a Brooks Brothers sweater, he still looked like he was a walking, well sitting definition of swag.

"I dunno. I guess with the black ice and stuff and I looked down for a second... by the time I looked up it was too late. I tried braking but I wasn't fast enough. Or they weren't fast enough. Either way the barrier ate my car."

"You never got your brakes fixed, did you?" The brakes. Summer. Flat tire. Holy shit.

"No, I guess I've just had a lot on my mind." I starting ringing my hands as I realized I would have done anything to get into my secret compartment in my purse and pop two pills in my mouth to get me through this conversation. And if it wasn't for Alex's complete psycho toilet rage last week, I wouldn't have been furiously texting Veronica and gotten in that accident anyway. I let those connected pieces of information simmer in my mind for a minute, getting progressively more irritated as I realized how the chain of events had played out.

"Jayden, come on, the mechanic and I both drilled it into your head you needed to take care of it. Who drives around with bad brakes?"

"Alex, that day was pretty hectic. Plus, it's not like I walk around every day wondering about my brakes. I mean, I still have to get all my stuff done to get to conference. This stupid accident is changing that." I was not going to be defeated by this whole mess. Although I had retreated to the couch injured, the war wasn't over.

"Are you nuts, Jayden? You give a shit about going to some stupid company party after all this?" Well obviously. Plus, that would really show Nicholas Kingsley I was made of steel after the pile of putty I let him turn me to.

"Alex, of course I care about it. I worked way too hard to get to the finish line and let something like a car accident get in the way."

"Jayden, you can't walk. You totaled your car. Monte won't let you come to work. What is it going to take for you to slow down? You're obsessed. I even dumped pills down the toilet, god knows how long you've been popping those."

"Is that what you came here for, Alex? To just sit here and yell at me about how I don't live your version of a perfect life?"

"No, it's not. I'm sorry. But something happened to you. When I first met you, you were different. You had such a fire in your eyes. You weren't afraid to dish out whatever was thrown out at you."

"Well, I'm sorry I'm not much of a bonfire today considering I'm bound to the couch."

"I take back what I said about not dishing back what's thrown out to you," Alex said rolling his eyes. It was one thing to admit the things he was saying to myself but it was another thing to have them verbalized by... him. How was he so perceptive of me? No one had ever been able to read me like he did. It was like my eyes were his windows that he could see everything I wanted to be covered and tucked away, unable to be toyed with. I took a long sip of my wine to fill the silence which was crowding the room. At least DJ Emzy and Dixie were keeping us company with their tirades. He eyed the wine and I was ready for slice of Alex's piece of mind pie.

"It's 5:00 somewhere," I said as I took a gulp and smacked my lips in satisfaction. And then I realized it was actually starting to go to my head a little as I set the glass down shakily. I forgot it's hard to gauge how tipsy you can get sitting down until you stand. Except I can't stand, so oh well. When I looked up, I moved my hair out of my face, combing my fingers through it as I usually do. Alex was staring at me.

"What?" I asked, thinking there was probably something embarrassing happening, like snot hanging out of my nose. But I probably would have felt that. Instead he smiled and asked why I hadn't offered him the good stuff.

"I figured Mr. Perfect Pants wouldn't dare do something on a work day," I said, bending down the recliner footrest to get up and fill him a glass.

"I can get it, Jay, you don't have to get up." But my stubbornness got the best of me and I inched forward in a very ungraceful attempt to get up. Alex jumped to his feet and pulled me forward, which would have been fine if I didn't have a gimped leg.

"Ouch!" I yelled as my left leg, the hurt one went to the ground without any support. I grabbed onto his shoulder with both hands and gave him directions to lift my leg up which was shooting pain.

"Lift it?" He looked confused.

"Nooowwwwww! Come on!!" He bent down with my hands still on his shoulders and locked his hand under my calf and extended it forward so that my leg was in front of me, raised to my waist, parallel to the floor. Ah, much better.

"Wait a second, this um, position doesn't hurt you? But your foot on the floor does?"

"Yes," I answered definitively. I realized at that moment we looked like a tableau out of *Dirty Dancing* except Alex is much darker than Patrick Swayze and I, well, wasn't looking too Jennifer Grey at that point. He looked up and down my leg. "God you're flexible," he observed.

"Well, yeah, I danced for a long time growing up." I felt very exposed suddenly.

"Why don't I grab that glass of wine and we put you back down on your chair, you tiny dancer." The hairs on the back of my neck stood up as he spoke to me. He was staring right into my eyes and I realized it was the first time I had ever been face to face with him in daylight, and still relatively sober enough to drink in every feature. His eyes seemed to change with his mood and at this instant they were so bright they were practically gold. With him literally in my face, it was undeniable how incredible looking he was. In a town of Italians and light complected Polish, you knew Alex wasn't a local. What was he doing here? But before

I could even ask, he had picked me up and plopped me back on the recliner in one liquid motion, continuing to hold my leg as I kicked out the footrest.

"You weigh nothing, I should get you something to eat while I grab the wine," he called from the kitchen. Food was absolutely the last thing i could put in my mouth.

"I ate a box of cereal yesterday," I said, before I realized how stupid that sounded.

"That was yesterday. You need to eat today as well." That was so not part of my plan, but it looked like I wouldn't be winning that argument.

"What are you doing?" I called out as I heard Alex rummaging through the pantry. "Alex, I'm not hungry, my dad made me something to eat before he left for work," I lied quickly.

"Jayden, it's 1:00pm. This is when the rest of the East coast eats lunch. Remember that meal?" Here was another battle I was losing. I wanted to reach next to the chair and grab my purse and sneak a pill but I was afraid he would come back unexpectedly. There was no way I could make a fast recovery in my condition. His phone rang on the table which I could see point blank. I really didn't mean to, but my eyes shot over to the screen and immediately when I saw who was blowing his phone up, my stomach tightened. Sure enough, Staci with an I had to weasel her way into the afternoon. I didn't say anything as the phone buzzed, rather I just took it as a sign that no matter how charming Alex could be, he was still an opportunist. And anything I felt needed to be pushed far away because it would only end in hurt, just like everything else did. But surprisingly, he ignored the buzzing noise as if his phone wasn't even ringing.

"What's this?" I asked as Alex put a round plate in front of me with a sandwich that had been cut in fours, just like my mother had done for me growing up. "I haven't had this in years," I remarked, staring at the plate.

"My mom used to cut them like this for me," he said.

"Me too. What's in it?" I pressed my index finger into the bread, weary of this grainy consistency. I begged my brain to stop calculating the carbs that were sitting on this plate before I had another anxiety attack.

"Just eat it, Jay. Don't question the chef." He was now sitting next to me, watching expectantly as he took a sip from his glass. I picked up the little square and bit off half of it in one bite. If there was one thing I loved about childhood it was taking that first bite into a loaded peanut butter and jelly sandwich in the cafeteria after an excruciatingly boring math class. The sweet and salty combination always made the frustration of solving for x and y disappear. And washed down with a Capri Sun? Couldn't get any better in the world of a twelve year old.

"You put in banana in it too?" I said smiling. I hadn't let myself eat a sandwich in years. I set it down to take a sip of wine.

"Of course," he said winking. His eyes moved over to the coffee table where a photo album was laying. "What's in there?" he asked nodding to it.

"Well, bring it over here and let me embarrass myself," I said. I was already sitting here looking my worst, pictures of pigtails and neon biking shorts from the '90s was just the perfect complement to my PB&J sandwich.

I didn't remember which album it was until I opened it. My mom must have been rearranging stuff before she left and that's why it was randomly on the coffee table. I scooted over so he could share the album with me as it was stretched across both of our laps. When I opened the front page, I realized which album this was immediately. It was the one from all my dance recitals, from when I was four until I was seventeen.

"So, you really were a dancer?" he asked with a not so subtle innuendo as he poked my side.

"Yes, and I was pretty good too," I said flinching from his unexpected touch. No one ever believed how ticklish I was.

Alex oohed and aawed at all of the little girl pictures. "You look so happy in these pictures, so proud of yourself." "Well, I mean, how could I not Alex, check out these get ups I'm in."

Little Indian costumes, prima ballerinas, dolls, you name it. I wore it. He opened up to a page of me posing with my hands on my hips, giving the death stare to the camera, then the impatient face. I could still remember my mom taking the photo after the curtain call from a particularly long recital. Leaning back into the recliner, I looked up at the ceiling, laughing at the memory of how dramatic I was even at age seven.

"Looks like nothing's changed," he said, our eyes locking. He gazed at me with that intensity which immediately created the tightest knot possible in my stomach. For what seemed like an eternity, we stared at each other, not saying anything. I wanted to close my eyes out of fear, but at the same time I was scared to have my eyes shut and miss every detail of him in front of me. Our faces were so close our noses almost touched. I could feel him breaking down the walls I had so carefully tried to build to protect myself. *He would only hurt you, Jayden. Just like all the others do...* God, he is beautiful. My thoughts were spinning back and forth, sending mixed messages between my temples. But my body was feeling only one message. I felt myself being pulled towards him like a magnetic force. I didn't understand what was happening. My brain knew this was bad but my heart wanted to be right here next to him. It didn't want to think about hurt later. But my head intercepted.

"Alex…" I said breaking the silence and taking my first breath since his eyes had seemed to knock the wind out of me. Not knowing what he was thinking was killing me. Or, at least not knowing for certain. "Why are you here?"

"Where else should I be?" he asked with an even tone which I knew he was using to put off the real answer I wanted. Part of me wanted to press the hot button and say "with Staci with an i" but I swallowed that response.

"You know… doing stuff. That people do during the day." I was grateful to be somewhat lying down because I knew if I was standing my knees would have buckled and now I was starting to have words come out of my mouth all stupidly.

"Like work? The thing you can't live without?" he said back playfully, poking my stomach. Reflexively, I grabbed his hand to stop him from tickling me again. I looked up at our hands, which had somehow begun touching palm to palm, like they had minds of their own. He put the base of his palm against mine and his fingers towered above mine.

"No, I can live without work. For a minute, I guess," I said smiling.

"Yeah, I mean, look at you all on top of me, groping my hand. Probably getting all excited there, huh, Jayden?" Immediately I recoiled in embarrassment.

"Shut up, I am not on top of you! Get over yourself, Alex."

But before I could turn away from him he pulled a one-eighty and leaned over me. In one swoop he tucked his hands under me and pulled me back close to him, somehow careful of my gimped leg. "Now you are," he said quietly, brushing the hair that had fallen out of my face. I felt my breathing stop. There was no more oxygen to be had for my lungs.

"Alex," I said, gathering the courage to try this again. "Why are you here with me right now?" I searched his eyes for a sign of what he was feeling but I didn't want to make any guesses. I just knew every nerve ending in my body was craving whatever closeness was happening right now. To say I was terrified was an understatement. But I couldn't bear to break away and not have whatever it was we might have been sharing for these few moments.

"Because there is nowhere else I'd rather be," he said taking my face in both his hands. With him holding me, I had nowhere to go. Once again, he was in complete control.

■ ■ ■

I've had a lot of first kisses. It's just what happens when there are a lot of men over the course of the years. Usually they were vodka induced, lustful, and meaningless kisses which were just stepping stones for the main attraction of a hedonistic bump and grind. The morning after, they were forgotten, maybe kept somewhere tucked away in a drunken memory at most if the guy was exceptionally skilled.

Pinned down on top of him, encased by his strong legs and my face between his hands, I couldn't deny any longer the physical burning of attraction I felt for him. For endless moments I'll never forget, he searched my eyes with his. And then, he lowered my face right on top of his. I don't know who moved in first. But one second I could feel his nose pressed against mine, and then as if they had minds of their own, our lips found each other slowly. And when they did, I never wanted to break away from his mouth which somehow fit perfectly with mine. I didn't think about my knee, work, the fact I had just eaten fifty-seven grams of carbs, or that a Staci with an i existed. All there was in the moment was him and me locked in an embrace no one had ever put me in.

"Jayden, do you have any idea how beautiful you are?" he asked, breaking away slowly and running his fingers through my hair again. I hoped he wasn't able to figure out how many days it had been since I had washed it. I decided to keep this information to myself. There were so many things I wanted to say, to admit out loud that I had kept locked inside myself for so many months, but I couldn't find the words.

"I like when you play with my hair, Alex," I said, choosing to be honest but safe. God knew how burned I could get from the fire he started by kissing me, but I didn't have it in me to change anything about this moment. Besides being completely entrapped by his strong body with no physical strength or willpower to move, I was faced with the reality he was the leader in this dance I didn't know the steps to.

And then, our spell was broken as my phone rang. I reached over to the side table to see who it was. Scarlett. Shit! She told me she was stopping over in between appointments and of course, I had completely forgotten.

"Hey babe, I'm outside. Open the door!" she said, forgetting I couldn't walk.

"Um, it's open," I said, laying awkwardly across Alex, who was looking at me trying to figure out who I was talking to. "Scarlett," I mouthed. Understanding, he carefully lifted me back up and helped rearrange me back into my original sitting position. My knee started throbbing, yelling at me for making out with the hot trouble maker.

"Alex!" she said, walking into the room, clearly surprised. And carrying a bottle of Kettel One vodka along with the container of soup. God love that girl. "Hi!" she said giving him a hug, and forgetting about me. It's cool, the dick came first obviously.

"Hey Scar," he said standing up to give her a hug and kiss on the cheek. The charm was turned back on. "I, uh, just swung by to check in."

"Oh, well that was nice of you!" she said, glancing in my direction. He decided it was time to make his exit.

"Well, I'll leave you ladies for your girl talk. I gotta run down and make sure the liquor shipments came in order anyway. Enjoy your soup and vodka, Jayden, feel better," he said and walked out.

As soon as the door was shut, Scarlett demanded details. "Um, so?!" she asked. "He looked pretty guilty of something, Jayden. Spill!"

"Nothing, we were just looking at old photo albums. He was keeping my gimped ass company, that's all." I wasn't lying outright. Just, what do they call it? Lie of omission?

"Bullshit, Jay. I know you and him better than that. Spill."

"Well, we kind of kissed. It's not a big deal. He probably just feels bad that I'm all out of commission." Scarlett maybe have been a boozing stoner, but she wasn't stupid. She took one look at my face and knew he had gotten to me.

"Fuck, Jay," she said.

"What?" I asked, suddenly another knot formed in my stomach.

"He's damaged goods, girl. Plus Staci with an "i" isn't out of the picture. You saw that at the bar last week!"

"I know, I know, it just happened. It meant nothing." At that moment I really wished I had a cigarette for how uncomfortable I felt on so many levels, but I settled for my wine glass. I couldn't seem to keep myself out of trouble.

"You're not looking me in the eye, Jayden. Look, I know how sensitive you are. And I just don't want another Nicholas Kingsley episode to happen."

"He hasn't flown me to Florida to treat me like chopped liver yet, has he?" I asked defensively.

"No, but he always finds new girls and then goes back to Staci. No one knows why they broke up this time, but they'll get back together, they always do." Another knot in my stomach formed. She was probably right.

"Scarlett, I have to get to the office to send in my sales," I said, letting the switch to business take back over. If I couldn't control what happened to my heart, I could at least control my professional endeavors.

"Jayden, fuck conference, seriously. Look at you, you're all injured from running around like a maniac and now you want to run around to send in paperwork?"

"Yes."

■ ■ ■

I was sitting in Monte's office reviewing my latest sales numbers.

"Im proud of you, Jayden," he said. "I know it wasn't easy for you to come in today."

"But I look really pretty," I said, putting myself on display by running my hand down the length of my sides, skimming the fabric of my sweater dress and snow boots.

It had been a project that morning as I went up my stairs mountain climber style, holding the banister and hopping every step, praying I wouldn't break the other leg. I used my parents' walk in shower so I could leave my leg propped up on some built-in chair thing away from the water so the stitches didn't get wet. They were permanently covered, the black, ugly things looking like barbed wire protruding from my otherwise unblemished skin. But after taking a much needed shower, going through the blow drying and hair straightening process, and of course, putting on my face, I started to feel a little more human.

"You're insane, Jayden," Ira, as he opened the passenger seat door to his Infiniti SUV. When I explained to him why it was imperative that I go to the office, it did not go over well with him. But I huffed and puffed until he relented, which we both knew he would do anyway.

"Yes, you look very pretty," Monte agreed, fist bumping me.

"All clean, right Jay?"

"What?" I asked, missing his point.

"The business. All clean, right?" A lump formed in my throat. It was all fine, technically speaking.

"Of course," I said, lowering my head and opened his door. With a few hops I and shut the door behind me as gracefully as a gimp could. I hobbled back over to my desk, not oblivious to the stares from the agents around me. A few people came up to me and asked if I was okay. I hated that question. "Are you okay?" So condescending. Yeah, I totaled my car, smashed my knee, doing great.

The papers were no longer organized thanks to the smash-up, so I had piles of papers to leaf through and put into separate piles according to policyholder. In a smaller envelope which somehow stayed intact were the few checks and money orders I had gathered. My face felt hot as I started folding the appropriate papers into separate folders, each addressed with the company's home office address. My phone rang and I saw it was Mimi.

"Hey," I answered.

"Where are you?" she asked, cutting to the chase.

"The office," I answered.

"The office?! You nutcase, doing what?"

"I need to send in this paperwork so I can go to the conference, Mimi!"

"Jayyy." She didn't sound happy.

"You got all the business you needed to?" I didn't tell anyone, but I actually had gotten enough to qualify. I was just shooting for extra because... well isn't more better than less?

"Yeah," I said, as if this shouldn't be surprising.

"Jayden. Is that all clean?" I didn't answer immediately, thinking of the money I had 'spotted' the policy holders like Zvedka, the Russian lady downtown (who I realized had never called me back with the money she owed me), until their paychecks came through the end of the week or whatever nonsense they gave me.

"Well, Jayden, is it?" Her words twisted a little deeper than Monte's had. That hot feeling was encasing my body and suddenly I felt sweat drip down my side. My face was hot and my hands were clammy.

"Well, mostly," I said, shaking. I mean, was loaning people money to sell a policy the worst thing in the world? It's not like I was robbing a bank. I mean, it wasn't like *real* insurance fraud.

"Jayden." Her voice was even, completely unemotional. "Jayden, it's a trip. It's not worth your license. It's not worth jail." Jail?

"Jail?" I squeaked out.

"Yes, Jayden. If you got caught, jail. You want to end up like *Orange is the New Black*?" No, I didn't want to be a rug muncher... but what were the chances of getting caught? She could hear the scales in my head weighing up and down.

"Jayden, I love you. Very much. It's just not worth it. Do the right thing." I began to choke up and needed to get off the phone. "Okay," I said almost silently, and put the phone down. The sea of papers sat in front of me menacingly. Everything seemed to swirl and I couldn't hear the conversations around me. I texted Alex. *I need you get me from the office now, please.*

CHAPTER 20

When Alex pulled up he got out of the car but had an angry look on his face.

"Why did you storm out of the office?" he asked. I looked at him quizzically, not putting two and two together fast enough.

"I called Miguel when you texted me to see what was going on, Jayden. What are you doing?"

"I'm not doing anything!" I screamed.

"You're lying, I can see it right on your face." I could feel his anger rising and I was scared. Not that he would do anything to hurt me, but I was scared for the disgust he would have knowing what shit I almost pulled.

"Just please take me home, Alex. Please!" I hopped up and down on the leg that still bent. Giving a slight growl, he picked me up, cradling me like a child, and plopped me on the heated leather seat.

We drove in silence through the uneventful downtown until we reached the highway, where he headed north towards my parents'.

"You went to turn in your stuff for conference today, didn't you?" he asked in a low voice. God, how was this the person who was looking at me so tenderly on my couch yesterday now about to ream me out for my latest shenanigans?

"Yes," I answered. My lips start quivering and I took a deep breath in, praying tears wouldn't fall again. I figured after the accident the damn tear ducts would have dried up.

"So what happened?" We were at a red light and he looked at me hard. I couldn't break eye contact even if I wanted to with his magnetic hold over my gaze. "What did you do, girl?"

"I didn't do it, Alex," I said curling up to the window so I didn't have to face him.

"Didn't do what?" he pressed.

"I didn't do it. That's all that matters," I said into the window. I watched the bare trees along the side of the road blur into each other, empty of any sign of life. This whole town was void of life. It was filled with townies who wouldn't know a passport if they tripped over one with their own photo in it, and then there was me, a little Bernie Maedoff in training.

"I don't know what to do with you," he said, shaking his head.

"Just take me home," I pleaded. "I just want to be alone."

"What princess wants, princess gets," he said icily. I chose to ignore his tone. I had nothing left in me to fight. He continued to drive on and we didn't speak. When my thoughts finally began to wonder, I realized Alex passed the turn to the road which lead to my house.

"You missed the turn," I said, annoyed.

"The gas light just came on, I'm stopping to fill up." He easily could have waited until after he dropped me off. I knew he was doing it just to get under my skin.

"Do you need anything?" he asked before running into the convenient store next to the gas pumps.

"No, thanks." I wondered how crappy I looked. I flipped the visor above my seat down and a sheet of paper fell into my lap. Without thinking, I unfolded it and read its contents, unable to believe what I was seeing.

Name: Staci Anderson
Date of Birth: 1/21/88

Some mumjo bumjo insurance information and then the phrase:

Human Chorionic Gonadotropin

Result: Positive

What the hell was a Human Chorionic Gonadotropin?

Oh yes, google. A minute later after a quick search on my phone, I learned the "positive" was for a pregnancy test. Staci's pregnancy test result in Alex's car. Staci was carrying Alex's child. I didn't know whether to cry, throw up, or scream. So instead, I stared, imagining Staci in utter glory carrying Alex's baby. She'd probably be one of those bitches who only looked bloated at 9 months pregnant.

I closed my eyes and took a deep breath. I decided once Alex got back in the car that now was not the time to address this, and either way, I couldn't. It was none of my business whether I wanted to stick my nose in it or not. *He's not yours, Jayden… and you don't want him to be, anyway.* For reasons like this. It was as if I went searching for gut-wrenching pieces of information. Except this time, it literally fell into my lap.

Resisting the urge to tear the test results into a thousand pieces, I folded the paper and hastily and placed it in the visor just as Alex was stepping out of the door. I hadn't even looked at my reflection. It didn't matter anymore. I wasn't sure what really mattered anymore. No job, no man, and a gimped leg.

"So, what are you going to do the rest of the day?" the future daddy asked, obviously unaware of my discovery. I tried to swallow the lump in my throat along with the emotions that had broken free in my family room yesterday. Just as I had feared, it was time to tuck them deep back under a guarded layer where they belonged. I would not let Alex Reyes have a hold over me anymore. I wouldn't. I couldn't, not with what I had just read.

I turned to face him to answer his question and saw he was holding an iced coffee for me. I eyed it suspiciously but took a sip. It was exactly how I make it. I could even see the clumps of chocolate powder swirling around the lid. I looked at him in surprise as the liquid slid down my throat.

"How did you know how to make it as I like it?"

"From watching you do it at the Sheetz by the office so many times," he said, winking. It took every molecule in my body not to break down into a million pieces.

∎∎∎

We drove back in silence, listening to some DJ mix he picked up from his Miami jaunts. This time he didn't miss the turn to my parents' house.

"Are you going to be okay?" Alex asked as he helped me out of the Range Rover and then insisted on taking me into the house.

"Yeah," I said, remembering why I was home again in the middle of a work day.

"I'm glad you didn't end up doing anything stupid," he said. *Yeah, like leave a pregnancy test in the car, because that was brilliant*, I thought to myself.

I looked at him as expressionless as I could. I had to bite my tongue about what I had discovered. It wasn't my place.

I looked at my phone for the first time since I left the office. There were two missed calls from Scarlett, and Monte, and then a text message. *I'm disappointed in you, Jay. Talk later.*

Reading that was a stab to my conscience, reminding me what I had almost just done. I had almost just committed fraud. Me, the girl who wouldn't dare of cheating on a Spanish quiz in high school because it wasn't the right thing to do. Even though all of my friends sat with cheat sheets up their skirts, I was now so warped that I was willing to do something I could possibly end up in jail for just for a fucking vacation with some ballers. I grabbed my phone, a bottle of water, three one-hundred calorie Greek yogurts and hobbled up the stairs to my room. At least I was wearing a dress, which I flung off in one fluid motion and replaced with an I.D.F. t-shirt representing the Israeli army. Removing my boots was more of a challenge, as I had to sit on my bed with my legs stretched out to unzip them. Satisfied with my change of clothes, I maneuvered myself under the covers. The desire I had just felt for Alex was now replaced with guilt from Monte's text message, which alternated with thoughts of seeing that letter in Alex's car. I wanted a pill so badly but I had left my bag downstairs. There was no way I was getting up now to go get one… too lazy. I leaned over and grabbed a notebook and pen out of my nightstand and wrote "My Life" at the top of the page and the following bullet points:

- fucked and chucked by Nicholas Kingsley
- shitty business
- illegally tried try to sell shit policies
- disowned by friends
- crashed car
- pill popper
- can't walk
- Alex is going to be a daddy
- Dad hates me

I looked at the list top to bottom, bottom to top, and then in shuffle mode, digesting each line item. This is what I had accomplished. I turned my head and glanced at a photo I kept on my nightstand, of my college roommates and I on our front porch, smiling and clinking our plastic wine glasses together. A Republican exercise science major, Indian finance guru, blonde pre-med, and then me, whatever I was, the four of us were like glue. You could blindfold us and we could identify each other by fart smell. I looked at that picture and I began to tear up, thinking of the person I had become. The college Jayden would smash a vodka bottle over my head knowing what I had done to my life. "Grow a pair and get the fuck out of Mom and Dad's house"… that twenty-one year old would say to the five year older version. Well, at least I had dropped a couple pants sizes.

I looked back at the list and the disappointment cracked open another well of tears. *God dammit, get your shit together…* I thought to myself as a tear fell onto the Jewish star on my t-shirt.

Like a movie reel, I began to reflect on some of the things I learned at D'Angelo Enterprises. One quote kept spinning through the wheels in my mind…"If you don't live your own dreams, you'll be living someone else's dream…"

Maybe D'Angelo Enterprises wasn't my dream?

CHAPTER 21

"Tennnn!" I grunted out loud before I collapsed on the mat, my upper body completely spent from trying to do a push-up routine I could have done in my sleep before the smash up as I now called that whole car incident thing. When my body was ready to give out, I just pictured Nicholas Kingsley's face on the mat and suddenly I was able to keep going. Visualization really does wonders.

I went to the gym straight from the appointment at the doctor's where they took out the world's ugliest stitches from my knee. Unsurprisingly, a deep purple scar ran across the top of my knee. When I asked how bad it was going to be, the doctor said "beauty is in the eye of the beholder." It was ugly, but I decided it was not a scar, it was a battle mark displaying my toughness. And it wasn't on my face. *Now that would have been a travesty*, I thought as I stepped onto the elliptical machine, already feeling five pounds lighter. A text message from Scarlett popped up as I went to open my music app. *We're going out later to celebrate your new leg. Happy hour at Blue Moon. I'm picking your ass up.*

Well... this could be interesting. I hadn't really spoken to Alex since he left my house the day he dropped me off. He had flown down to Miami to meet with investors to franchise Blue Moon or Center Bar. And then of course to go party with some of his friends in South Beach. I had no desire to know what happened on or around the topless beach, just as long as it didn't involve Staci with an "I". I selected the Jay-Z station on Pandora and made a silent prayer that I could finally work out again, convinced that a mountain of cellulite had built up in my thighs.

■ ■ ■

For the two weeks that I was prohibited and unable to do physical activity, I refused to eat anything other than salads and Greek yogurt. Except for the cereal day and that bite of a peanut butter sandwich, but we'll try to forget about that now. I had spent the days since I dashed out of D'Angelo Enterprises hiding out under the covers or attached to the TV bingeing on Netflix and all the movies I hadn't seen while working. I now understood why the average American watched so much damned television. Monte and I ended up talking. He yelled, I cried, like the good Italian-Jewish partnership we had. In the end, he apologized, which made me cry again, so then I apologized for crying again. When we were done going around in circles, he decided that I take some time off to think about what is best for me- and not what everyone else thinks is best for me. He reminded me something that he had said from day one, "Just be you, Jay. Just be you." I guess that would be easy if I knew who the fuck I was.

Mimi and Scarlett would call me every day, telling me horror stories from appointments, office gossip, but it started to fall on deaf ears. I didn't give a shit who needed insurance. Somehow, I was even not giving a shit about Nicholas Kingsley. One sunny brisk day, I took the spare car, my dad's old Cadillac, for a spin. I drove down the highway, playing my insurance career in my head like a movie premiere, reliving the snapshots which had ultimately landed me in my current broken and confused position. How could I leave? If I quit, I was a failure.

I was in that dreamlike state where I was driving but not really conscious of where I was going, so I was surprised when I found myself pulling up to my Dad's warehouse. Unsure of what was going to happen, I opened my purse and took out a pill. I needed to stop. But not yet. When I figured out my life, I would stop.

"Jayden!" Deb, his secretary greeted me as I hopped in the door. Deb was the reason for Secretary's Day and holiday bonuses. That woman ran the office with razor sharp precision, bootcamp authority, and a loyalty to Ira that could match my mother's. And no, she was not sleeping with my Dad. She was very happily married.

"Hi, Deb," I said smiling. Deb had also taken care of my over drafted bank account when I was in college so my Dad wouldn't rip my head off. "Is my dad around?"

"Yeah, hun, he's in his office," she said, pointing to his closed door. I walked up and knocked.

"Come in," I heard.

"Well isn't this a surprise! It's the world famous car crasher!" My dad was famous himself for using humor to deflect any anger he had.

"Yup, that's me!" I said, swinging my arms into a dramatic pose.

"Well. I'm hungry. Want me to take you to lunch?" he asked. Even I couldn't turn that down.

We sat at the corner pizza place where my dad had made best friends with the owner. After we ordered - a turkey hoagie for him and a grilled chicken salad for me - I knew the interrogation would begin. But then again, I brought myself to this situation.

"So. What's going on?" he asked openly. We hadn't really talked much since he took me to the office the day I almost became a criminal.

"Monte told me to take some time off," I began, which piqued his interest. Maybe it was the perfectly seasoned and grilled balsamic glazed chicken, but I found myself really talking to my Dad about my fears.

"It's just that… if I quit, Dad I'm so scared of being a failure. I'm scared to fail. I can't handle it."

"Honey, you have far from failed. Look how much you learned working there. At the end of the day, you have a skill. You can sell. It doesn't matter if it was insurance or toilet paper. You can transfer that to anywhere. Not a lot of people have that ability, Jayden. That's something you need to be proud of."

"What am I going to do, Daddy?" I asked, again, my eyes watering. This was just ridiculous.

"I think you know staying at this job isn't right for you. I know how much you love everyone you work with, and that's hard to leave. I get that. But do the math. With all the hours you work, is it worth it?"

"Well, once I get to Monte's management level…" I mumbled.

"When's that going to be?" he asked adamantly. He had heard this a thousand times.

"Dad, I don't know…"

"Jayden. What do you really want?" he asked pointing to me for emphasis. "It doesn't matter what Monte wants, what Mommy wants, or even what I want. It matters what you want."

"I don't know what I want, Dad."

"Well, you need to figure that out, Jayden. Look, your mother and I love you very much. We only want you to be happy. That's all. Just do what makes you happy." I set my fork down and looked at my plate.

"Honey, I know you don't believe this, but that Italian Enterprises insurance place isn't the end all path to fame and fortune. Look at all the stinkin' rich CEOs of the world. They ain't workin' there. There are other ways to be successful."

This was a concept completely new to me. I was completely under the spell that D'Angelo Enterprises was the only path to success and that everyone else in the world was a fool for not working there. It didn't register in my mind anymore that if everyone in the world sold life insurance there would be nothing else in the world people needed like doctors or even software developers and Hollywood actors. I had spent so much time feeling sorry for bartenders because each time they sold a drink they weren't generating any residual income that my brain forgot about the rest of the globe's economic opportunities.

"You know," he continued, "there is a whole big world out there with opportunities for you… you just have to look for them. This isn't the end, Jayden. It's just the beginning."

"I miss Tel Aviv, Daddy," I said, playing with the remnants of spinach leaves from my salad.

"I know you do, Jayden." And here it was coming. "But Jayden, you were volunteering teaching English to young kids. You wanted six months of fun to fill this resume gap of yours, and I let you have it."

My dad was totally right. It's not like Tel Aviv had been a real life. There were cheap bottles of wine and endless nights on the beach because I wasn't tied down to a real life there. For all I knew at this point, my friends weren't there anymore. Not that I kept in touch with them anyway. Since when did I make time for anyone with an insurance policy or Veronica to supply me with pills?

When the bill came, my dad swooped into his wallet and pulled out his AmEx.

"Thank you, Daddy." Out of the countless lunches we'd had together, I really meant it this time.

"You're welcome, Favorite Daughter. You're going to be fine."

...

"So, what's the deal with Alex?" Scarlett asked me as I got into her Jeep. We were dressed in casual jeans, booties and long sleeve tops. Happy hour in Grayton wasn't really a time for stilettos.

"I don't know, dude," I said, taking a swig of my bottle of fun that I made for the road and offering it to the designated driver. She took a sip and then made me promise not to let her drink anymore from the bottle for the rest of the drive.

"Jayden, I really don't think Staci is out of the picture. And he hasn't talked to you since he took you home that day?"

"Well, he was in Florida and he was busy, I guess," I said, making excuses for him like an idiot.

"Jayden, that's stupid. Look, he's hot and all, and normally I'd say yeah, fuck him and have fun. But he's a loose cannon. He isn't always around and Staci isn't gone. She's always around the bar so who knows what's going on." She was right. Not to mention she was carrying his baby. But I wasn't going to go into that right now.

"You're right," I sighed.

"I'm just afraid you are going to get attached and get hurt. And you're my friend, I don't want to see that happen to you."

"Thanks." We spent the rest of the drive gossiping about the office and as we got out of the car she asked me, "So, what are you going to do?"

"Don't be surprised if it's something unconventional," I said, scratching my head like the answer was going to shake out of my scalp like some loose dandruff.

We were chatting with the bartenders who had brought us two shots after Scarlett paid for our first round of drinks. Scarlett, being a gifted babbler of bullshit, much more so than me, was entertaining the muscled men in black t-shirts feeding us vodka when I felt two hands on my waist. I gasped.

"Glad to see you walking," I heard in my ear. Carefully pivoting so that I didn't fall, I gave Alex a look up and down. His rugged look of jeans, boots and a fitted V-neck shirt left no mystery to his insanely defined biceps and chest. He was close enough that I could smell his after-shave. It was starting, that feeling between my legs. God, he was good. He reached behind me to grab a beer from the bartender.

"Me too," I said, taking a sip of my drink. I was already tipsy between killing my drink in the car, downing a shot, and barely eating anything all day.

"How was Florida?" I asked, flashing a fake-ass smile to signal that I was in cold hearted bitch mode. He picked right up on it.

"Really good, actually," he said in a cocky tone.

"Well, that's good then." We stared at each other and instead of backing away and forgetting him as Scarlett advised, I asked the question which would ignite a fire.

"Did Staci who can't spell go?"

"Oh, god, Jayden, don't start," his raised voice feeling like spreading flames.

"No, I am starting, Alex. Who do you think you are to walk into my house, practically finger bang me and then prance off for two weeks with no word?"

I realized the people around me had stopped talking. Alex grabbed my arm and dragged me away from the center of the bar and through a door labeled "Employees Only." It was his office, a small room with a desk against the wall and a leather couch on the opposite end.

"Alex, you can't push and pull me around like a fucking doll! You can't mind fuck me and then go fuck that blonde!"

"Sit down," he said.

"Fuck you," I answered coolly, and tried to walk out the door but he was too fast and strong for me. He grabbed my arms and pushed me down on the couch. Well, even when I can walk I'm no match for him.

He bent down so that he was at my eye level and came within an inch of my face, staring right into my eyes.

"I am not with her, and I will not ever be," he said seriously. It was the first time he ever verbalized an opinion on her.

"Why not?" I asked. "I know she's carrying your baby. I saw the paper in your car, Alex. It fell in my lap the day you took me home when I wanted to look in the mirror." His face went pale.

"Jayden, it's not what you think."

"You're lying. I know Staci took a pregnancy test!"

"I'm not lying, Jayden!"

"Why should I believe you? The test result was in your fucking car, Alex. Come on, don't spit some lines to me that would work on the other bimbos whose panties you jump into." He balled his hands into a fist and pounded the wall next to us so hard that I jumped.

"You know what, Jayden. You might not have a reason to believe me. But I swear, it's not what you think." I couldn't believe this. I read the paper with my own eyes in broad daylight in his car. He couldn't charm his way out of this.

"Well then, why don't you provide an explanation?" I folded my arms and tapped my foot just like parents do when they're awaiting their child's excuse for whatever bullshit children pull.

"Don't worry about it," he said, releasing my arms and standing back up to his full height. I didn't understand this. The hot, the cold, god I never knew which weather season Alex would materialize.

"What do you want from me, Alex?" I asked, standing up staring right into his eyes and putting it on the table. The dance needed to end so why not cut the music.

"I'm not a girl you can turn to when shit goes south with her, it won't fly with me."

"I want you, Jayden."

"No you don't. You're just saying that to get something from me."

"Don't we all just want something from someone?"

"You're getting something from Staci, Alex. Hell, in a few months you're going to have a *baby* with her. Why are you doing this to me? Why are you just pulling me around for some joyride? You're sick. Sick." I wanted to be that cool, calm girl, but especially being that I was fueled with booze, I definitely wasn't that girl.

"Jayden, you weren't supposed to see that. It's none of your business. It's Staci's life. It's not my place to divulge."

"Well, too bad Alex, I did see the fucking paper." Tears began to fall down my cheeks uncontrollably.

"Oh, Jayden, the conclusions you jump to," he said as though he was getting tired of fighting with me.

"Well what else could I possibly think, Alex?"

"I'm not the father of that unborn baby, Jayden."

"What?" Confusion swept over my drunken self.

"I can't tell you whose baby it is, that's not my place. But I promise it's not mine. Staci just needed someone to confide in and left the test in my car."

Maybe I should have run away from all this, but I couldn't move from where my feet were planted. In one swoop my face was cradled in his hands and his lips were on mine. He kissed me harder than he did the first time, with a carnal hunger that hadn't been there before. He yanked my hair and I bit his lip, wanting him just as much as he wanted me. I felt his hand slide down my shirt.

"I'm taking you home," he told me. I was already wet with anticipation.

"Okay," I said, not arguing. He rearranged my shirt for me and took me out a side door to his car. I texted Scarlett and let her know I was leaving and then turned my phone off. I would deal with her yelling at me tomorrow. We didn't speak on the way to his luxury apartment which, was only a few blocks away. He lead me to the elevator and pressed the button for the top floor. We rode up in anticipated silence. The doors opened and he lead me down the hall to his apartment. He opened the door to an open area full of hardwood floors, modern light fixtures and white walls.

"You can have a tour later," he said, pulling me into a room on the right and throwing me onto a king size bed which I literally melted into. He wasted no time in getting me naked.

"You are so…" he didn't even finish as he pressed my legs open and expertly worked his tongue. If I died at that moment, that would have been fine with me to go out in sheer ecstasy.

I closed my eyes and let myself feel what was happening to my body. There were no pills, no calories, no paychecks. It was just Alex.

"Look at me," he said, climbing on top of me.

"I can't," I said, closing my eyes. He put his mouth next to my ear. "Yes, you can," he whispered. He stretched his arms out and intertwined his hands with mine as he pressed his nose against mine.

"We have really big noses," I said, as I opened my eyes, staring straight into his. He could see my soul, I was certain of it. He kissed me tenderly and I reached my hand into his boxers where I found the biggest erection of my sexual career. He groaned and sat up. I took him in my mouth until I felt my gag reflex and coughed. He didn't care, clearly, as he gently pushed me back on the bed and climbed on top of me. As he pushed inside of me, I cried out.

"Oh my god," I said, covering my eyes.

"You're going to say that a lot," he said, taking my body on a roller coaster ride I never wanted to get off.

We woke up in the middle of the night, tangled under the duvet. "How are you doing down there?" he asked me, sliding a finger inside me.

"Hmmm still wet, I see."

"OMG, stop, I'm going to kill you," I said, as he wrapped me in his arms and kissed me. We laid there in the dark; the only light coming in through the windows from the streetlights, staring at each other's darkened faces. For once, I didn't need to talk. I looked in his eyes, thinking how beautiful of a man he was.

"What are you thinking?" he asked me shyly.

"That you might just be better looking than me," I said smiling.

"You're cute, Jay."

"Why are you cold, Alex?" I asked.

"I'm not cold, we're under like five blankets here," he said, rolling his eyes.

"No… I mean. Like, hard."

"Well, I work out every day."

"Stop!" I said, punching his arm. "Stop playing dumb with me."

"But, I like playing with you," he said with a grin. And before I could argue, I felt something very big find its way in between my legs, ending our conversation.

■ ■ ■

I woke up at dawn, sober, naked, and in a cold sweat next to a snoring Alex. He was so beautiful, like a sleeping mythological god. Was last night real? I let my guard down, why? This was *not* part of the man diet I had created. I got out bed and tip toed into his bathroom and closed the door. I put my head in my hands as I peed out Niagra Falls. What was I doing? It was Nicholas Kingsley all over again. The money, the cars, the damn body. But Alex was different... Okay, so he lasted longer in bed than a YouTube commercial, great. But he was a serial womanizer. I wasn't any different. I was just pussy he hadn't had yet. I was never going to be anything more. I was the same as every other girl to him probably. Something needed to change. I couldn't keep doing the same thing expecting different results.

I grabbed my clothes and meant to quietly open the door. Except god forbid I create a plan and execute it the way it plays out in my head. I didn't turn the hall light on as I didn't want to wake Alex and was only using the light from my phone to guide me to the front door. I was only steps from the door when I whacked my toe into a very large structure and couldn't help but yell out an "Ow!" I flashed my light on the object and realized I had just tripped into one of those very large plants people keep in those massive vases in their entry ways, foyers, whatever they're called. God dammit why was I always so clumsy? My hand reached for the door but I heard that voice.

"Jayden?" Alex had opened his door and was standing in the hallway. "What are you doing?"

"Oh, um, I couldn't sleep," I lied. "So I figured I'd just call a taxi and head home. That way I'm out of your hair and everything in the morning," I said, trying to play it cool.

He walked over to me and took my hand, combing it through his locks. "I don't want you out of my hair in the morning, Jayden. Come back to bed." And so I did.

EPILOGUE - ONE YEAR LATER

"Race me." He put his beer into the cup holder and jumped up from his chair, waiting for me to accept the challenge. Obviously, I wasn't going to turn that down. I put my own drink down as well and sprang up from my reclining position. The breeze accelerated us through the sand. Perhaps he let me win as I sprinted into the water, which was cold even though it was 80 degrees out on a January day. The sensation made me freeze and for a split second I forgot about our little race until I felt two strong arms envelop me. I yelled out loud in surprise for him to let me go, but that wasn't happening. Instantly, he tackled me and dragged us underneath an incoming wave.

"Alex!" I screamed once we both came back to the surface. Before I could dish out any threats, he sent me a forceful splash, which of course prevented me from speaking.

"Ug! I hate you!" I cried out.

"Oh, really? You didn't seem to hate me too much this morning after your work out when I came into the shower and tornadoed your vagina."

Fair, I thought, but of course I wouldn't give him that satisfaction, so all I could do was splash him back. Which of course sent him wild and he tackled me into another wave. We went back and forth like this for a while until we were far past most of the other swimmers, nothing around us except the endless stretch of the Atlantic.

"Come here," Alex coaxed.

"Why, so you can splash me for the fiftieth time?" I asked.

He grabbed my arm and pulled me into a surprising embrace, wrapping my legs around his body and ran his fingers through my hair.

"Jayden, I want to tell you something," he said.

My heart began to race and I held my breath as he paused, looking at me with disarmed eyes. I looked into his eyes as he had looked into mine so many times, but this felt different. I braced myself.

"Jayden… I love you."

Let me back up. After that first time of spending the night at Alex's, I officially left D'Angelo Enterprises. I came into the office to tell Monte in person. With all he had put up with from me, he at least deserved that much.

"You're all good, JayJay," he told me when I broke the news. "You're going to be fine. And I'm always here for you." I walked out the door and never looked back. I wasn't a failure. I had only closed a chapter in my life.

Everyone else's paths continued. Scarlett and Joey continued to kill it. They were promoted to run a new office that was opening in Philadelphia.

Veronica worked as a hair stylist for another sixteen days before realizing that standing and having to sweep the cut hair all over the floor or smelling like hair dye was just not for her. In fact, it repulsed her. In fact, it repulsed her. to clean up the cut hair all over the floor or smelling hair dye. With the pay she received for working those sixteen days, she booked a one way flight to Los Angeles. Full of conviction, Veronica believes her D-cup boobs, ghetto booty, and tiny waist can't be wasted anywhere other than the cover of Playboy Magazine. *I drove her to the airport and wished her luck. The last I heard from her, she had scored a modeling agent.*

For three weeks, I detoxed from the orange circles. With insanely low energy levels and an appetite that rivaled a teenage boy's, my body shifted from being waif-like to a much more feminine physique, complete with a butt that once again filled out my jeans. Let's just say Alex enjoyed smacking it at every chance he got. That was the upside. The downside was that I realized I was a complete pill popper who really needed to get her shit together. Once the withdrawal symptoms subsided (I told Renee and Ira that I had a lingering cold which forced me to stay in bed way too late every morning. They didn't seem to mind as I had spent so much time up at the crack of dawn and working like a maniac.), I decided to make amends with the girls who had once been my friends. We exchanged words of frustration, anger, and resentment, but at the end of the day, it all worked out. They let me back into the circle of bitches. I learned that an "I'm sorry for being a self-absorbed asshole for months on end" really does go a long way.

Even though Alex was busy traveling between Grayton and Miami to oversee the franchising of both Center Bar and Blue Moon, we began spending time regularly together. Staci with the damn "I" became a distant memory as she was now busy with her growing baby bump. Alex knew how much I wanted to leave Grayton, but I just didn't know where to go. I spent days googling "quarter life crisis moves," "what should I do with my life," and "what to do when you quit your job and have no fucking clue what to do." I wasted a lot of time reading those self-help articles that really don't get you anywhere, they just seem to send your brain into never-ending circles of brain chatter.

And then one day Alex called me and disrupted my seemingly endless brain chatter.

"Jayden, what do you think of Miami?"

"Can't be any worse than this Grayton place, why?"

"Well, it's better than Grayton."

"Everything is better than Grayton. Why?"

"When I was in Miami, my business partner was telling me how his wife is starting a business selling reduced-calorie flavored vodka. Kind of how that Real Housewives *chic does with the Skinny stuff, but this has a social entrepreneurship model where for each bottle of vodka sold, a percentage of revenue goes to a charity that helps underprivileged women start a business."*

"And?"

"They need a business development person to expand their online presence and to network with retailers for shelf space."

"And?"

"Well, how about it?"

"Me?"

"Yes. I told him about you. Get your skinny butt on a plane to Miami."

"Miami?"

"Yes, Miami."

Well, one interview in Miami and very two supportive parents later, I moved to Miami for the next chapter of my life.

Over the next couple months, as I got into the groove of my new job, which afforded me crazy luxuries such free time to explore the city and make girlfriends, Alex was spending more time in Miami focusing on building the luxury hotel he was investing in with some other "business associates.". He had formed partnerships with local Grayton "serialpreneurs" (aka, they owned a bunch of Burger Kings in town). They basically partially bought him out, so he was able to keep a chunk of the profits without having to do the dirty work.

No, maybe selling life insurance wasn't the only way to fame and fortune.

■ ■ ■

I stared back at Alex's face, processing that little sentence he had just uttered with that little four letter word which held such a large meaning.

"I love you too, Alex." Immediately his lips found mine and he kissed me with the same intensity as he had all those distant months ago on my couch after my accident. Neither of us would admit it, but we had probably fallen in love that day.

"Come on, Jayden. Let's go back to my place and maybe if you're lucky I'll feed you vodka soda with some dick."

"Gosh, Alex, you're so romantic," I answered as he lead me out of the water and back to the sand.

I packed my stuff quickly. "Race you to the car!" I said with a wicked grin.

"You're on!" We trudged through the sand and headed for the parking lot, probably looking like maniacs.

But then again, if the love of your life was offering alcohol and some sex, wouldn't you run after it?

ABOUT THE AUTHOR

Jillian Rose

Although she has a professional marketing and sales background, Jillian's greatest passion has always been creative writing. Aided by glasses of boxed wine, she started writing short stories in between studying for business courses at the University of Pittsburgh. Jillian's writing continued after she jetted off to work in Tel Aviv after college where she kept her dreams of being a novelist alive.

After two years of a high-pressure sales job once she returned stateside, she knew this was the premise to a worthwhile story. *Don't Kiss and Sell* is Jillian's debut novel.

Originally from Pennsylvania, Jillian has since relocated to Los Angeles. When she isn't working on her second novel, you can find her running along the Santa Monica and Venice bike paths or enjoying a Sunday Bloody Mary.

CPSIA information can be obtained
at www.ICGtesting.com
Printed in the USA
BVHW041706020519
547216BV00016B/229/P